The Museum of Failures

ALSO BY THRITY UMRIGAR

Honor

The Secrets Between Us

Everybody's Son

The Story Hour

The World We Found

The Weight of Heaven

If Today Be Sweet

The Space Between Us

First Darling of the Morning:
Selected Memories of an Indian Childhood

Bombay Time

PICTURE BOOKS

Sugar in Milk

Binny's Diwali

When I Carried You in My Belly

The Museum of Failures

a novel

THRITY UMRIGAR

ALGONQUIN BOOKS OF CHAPEL HILL 2023

Published by
ALGONQUIN BOOKS OF CHAPEL HILL
Post Office Box 2225
Chapel Hill, North Carolina 27515-2225

an imprint of Workman Publishing Co., Inc., a subsidiary of
Hachette Book Group, Inc.
1290 Avenue of the Americas
New York, New York 10104

Printed in the United States of America.
Design by Steve Godwin.

The publisher is not responsible for websites (or their content)
that are not owned by the publisher.

This is a work of fiction. While, as in all fiction, the literary perceptions and
insights are based on experience, all names, characters, places, and incidents
either are products of the author's imagination or are used fictitiously.

Library of Congress Cataloging-in-Publication Data

Names: Umrigar, Thrity N., author.
Title: The museum of failures : a novel / Thrity Umrigar.
Description: First edition. | Chapel Hill, North Carolina :
Algonquin Books of Chapel Hill, [2023] |
Summary: "Remy Wadia left India for the United States long ago, carrying his
resentment of his mother with him. He has now returned to Bombay to adopt a baby—
and to see his elderly mother for the first time in several years. Discovering that she
is in the hospital, has stopped talking, and seems to have given up on life, he is
struck with guilt for not realizing just how sick she has become. His unexpected
appearance and assiduous attention revives her and enables her to return to
her home. But when Remy finds an old photograph from his adoring late father,
shocking long-held family secrets surface"—Provided by publisher.
Identifiers: LCCN 2023015385 | ISBN 9781643753553 (hardcover) |
ISBN 9781643755441 (e-book)
Subjects: LCGFT: Novels. Classification: LCC PS3621.M75 M87 2023 |
DDC 813/.6—dc23/eng/20230407
LC record available at https://lccn.loc.gov/2023015385

10 9 8 7 6 5 4 3 2 1
First Edition

For
Judy Griffin,
who loves this world

After the first death, there is no other.

—DYLAN THOMAS

The Museum of Failure in Helsingborg, Sweden,
was a collection of failed products and services.
It now operates as a traveling exhibition
throughout the world.

The Museum
of Failures

BOOK ONE

CHAPTER ONE

ALL NIGHT LONG, the crows fought as a jet-lagged Remy Wadia struggled to sleep in an unfamiliar bed. Occasionally, a dog howled, the sound hair-raisingly melancholy, and Remy had to cover his ears with a pillow. He heard the roar of a motorcycle and glanced at the alarm clock: 2 a.m. A few minutes later, he was on the threshold of a dream when loud voices from the street below jolted him awake. He swore under his breath, flinging the sheet off. Finally, at 6 a.m., even though he was afraid of awakening Jango and Shenaz in the next room, he got up to use the attached bathroom. Then he made his way to the small balcony off his bedroom.

A light breeze from the nearby sea made his thin muslin sadra flutter against his skin as he leaned against the railing. He looked down at the treetops. What had made the damn crows squawk all night long? There had been something spooky and unnerving about their nocturnal shrieking, but then this, too, was Bombay—the birds as defiant and absurd as the rest of the city. He looked toward the main road and wondered if his mother was awake, too. Her apartment building was only a few streets away from Jango's, where he had spent the night after his friend had picked him up from the airport.

Remy yawned; it had been a long flight from Columbus, Ohio, and he was exhausted. Then he reminded himself of the reason for his visit to India and felt a throb of excitement. Shenaz's niece, Monaz, was to arrive at 10 a.m. He thought about taking a quick shower but worried that the sound of running water would disturb his hosts. Still, he wanted to look his best when Monaz came, wanted no trace of his fatigue to show. "First impressions are often the last impression," Dad used to say.

Dad. The thought of his boisterous, warmhearted father made Remy smile. It was his first time back since Cyrus had died three years ago. He had not visited his mother since then, and he felt the usual pang of guilt at the thought. Well, he would see her in a few hours, would surprise her by showing up at her door. Maybe things would be softer between them now that Daddy was gone and Remy no longer had to protect him from his mother's grievances and sharp barbs.

A solitary crow rose from the tree and fluttered past the balcony. He'd hated them since his childhood, when one of them had swooped down and stolen the sandwich right out of his hand, its sharp beak slicing his finger. Remy rubbed his thumb against his index finger, tracing the path of the injury, which had faded to a faint scar. How old had he been on that Sunday at the zoo with his father? It had been a happy day but bookended by disaster.

His parents had planned a different excursion, but something had gone wrong. They had fought—Remy closed his eyes against the memory of the rumble of voices, as steady and incessant as rain, coming from his parents' bedroom. When at last his mother had emerged, her eyes were red. A wave of outrage had risen in the young Remy and he'd run up to hug and console her. Which was why he had been stunned when she'd gruffly pushed him away.

Cyrus had come out of their bedroom in time to see Remy stumble, had noticed the tears that sprang into the boy's eyes. His face flamed.

"Shame on you, Shirin," he said to Remy's mother. "You're taking out your khunnas against me on an innocent boy?"

It was too late to stop the tumble of memories: His mother's grief turning into anger. Her accusing Remy of putting on a show for his father's benefit. Cyrus roaring with indignation. The look his mother threw at Remy before she locked herself in her room.

Remy had crept away into his own bedroom, but a few minutes later, a grim-faced Cyrus stood in the doorway.

"I'll be damned if I waste this beautiful day waiting for Shirin to come to her senses," he'd said. "Where would you like to go?"

Remy didn't have to think. "The zoo," he said. A baby elephant had been born there a few weeks earlier. Jango had gone last week and was still gushing about it.

"Done," Cyrus said. "Go put on your shoes and socks."

They had stopped at the market and bought three coconuts and a rock-hard orb of jaggery to feed to the elephants. Remy squealed with excitement when the adult animals stomped on the coconuts with one foot, splitting them into two halves and expertly scooping out the meat; he shrieked with delight at the baby elephant's hapless attempts to imitate his parents.

As they left the enclosure, Cyrus put his arm around Remy's shoulder. "Happy?" he asked, and Remy nodded. "Good," Cyrus said. "Because, son, you have only two jobs in life—to be happy and to make others happy. You understand?"

Remy wondered what kind of jobs he'd have to get to keep that promise, but for now, he was content to nod. "Yes, Daddy."

They were walking toward the tiger enclosure when Remy's stomach growled. He looked up at his father, embarrassed, but Daddy didn't seem to mind. Cyrus reached into his bag and handed his son the chicken sandwich he'd packed. Remy took a bite. It was delicious. He'd opened his mouth to take a second bite when there was a flutter of wings, a blur, and bright blood on his finger. It took him a minute to realize the sandwich was no longer in his hands. Then he began to scream at the sight of blood.

"Hush, sonny, hush," Cyrus muttered. "Here, let me see." He removed his handkerchief and tied it around the boy's index finger. "Damn. Come on, let's get out of here."

By the time they reached Dr. Surati's apartment, Remy's screams had subsided into occasional hiccups of pain and outrage over the stolen sandwich. He resolved to pack small stones in his pocket to fling at the sinister, bold birds who were seemingly everywhere in Bombay. "I hate them," he said, and Cyrus made a consoling sound. The doctor, an old family friend, chuckled.

Remy had gotten three stitches, and his reward for being a brave boy was a promise from his father to take him to the movies the following week. When they'd reached home, Shirin took one look at the bandaged finger and covered Remy in kisses.

How mercurial she was, his mother! Still, his complicated relationship with her, the haste with which he'd fled back to Kathy in America after his father's death, feeling as if he were escaping from under the waves of some twilight ocean—all of this was, hopefully, behind him. For the first time, what had brought him to the city of his birth was not the undertow of the past but the tug of the future.

BY THE TIME Remy emerged from his shower, the rest of the household had awakened. As he dressed, he heard the clanging of pots in the kitchen and smelled tea being prepared the Parsi way, with fresh mint and lemongrass. There was a knock at his door. Jango stood at the entrance, still in his sadra and pajama bottoms.

"Saala, you've already showered?" he said. He sniffed in Remy's direction and grinned. "I can smell that aftershave from across the room. What're you trying to do, seduce my wife with your fancy American airs and all?"

Remy grinned back. Any awkwardness that he had felt at inconveniencing his friends the night before fell away at Jango's trademark irreverence. Superimposed over the well-built man with the thickening waistline was the wisecracking boy who had befriended moody Remy on the first day of second grade.

"Come," Jango said. "Tea is ready. What would you like for breakfast?"

"Anything is fine. Maybe some toast?"

Jango looked at Remy balefully. "Maybe some toast?" he mimicked, thumping Remy on the back as they walked down the short hallway into the dining room. "Has Kathy turned you into an anemic rabbit or something? Arre, saala, you're in a Parsi home, not at some fucking monastery. If I feed you breakfast without the requisite eggs and cream and butter, I will have to renounce my religion."

Remy laughed, shaking his head. "Okay, okay," he said.

Shenaz came to the dining table, carrying a tray with three cups of tea. As Remy took the tray from her, she gave him a peck on the cheek. "You slept okay, darling?" she said. "Bed was comfy?"

"Like a baby," he lied. "Everything was great."

"Are you sure you have to leave for your mother's today? Can't you just stay with us the rest of your trip?"

"I wish." He wondered how much the couple knew about his distant relationship with his mom. Despite their closeness, he had never discussed his family life with Jango. But Jango had spent many a day at Remy's home during their childhood and adolescence. Surely, he had noticed how much closer Remy had been to his dad. *Did* children notice these things? In some ways, they had led such innocent and oblivious lives, all their talk revolving around sports and music and girls.

"Well, you're always welcome here," Shenaz said. "You know that."

He smiled vaguely.

After a beat, she said briskly, "Okay, chalo. I want to be done with breakfast before Monaz comes. How do akuri and French toast sound?"

Remy moaned. "Oh my God. Akuri alone sounds divine." His mother used to make the dish, spiced scrambled eggs tossed in fried onion and cilantro and garnished with nuts and raisins. It had been their usual Sunday breakfast, but sometimes Remy used to ask for it for dinner and his mother unfailingly obliged.

"So what's she like?" Remy asked with his mouth full. "Your niece."

Jango and Shenaz exchanged a bemused look. "Slow down, yaar," Jango drawled. "A half hour ago you wanted to eat dry toast, remember?"

Shenaz smacked her husband's hand. "Okay, enough with the teasing," she said. She turned to Remy. "Monaz is . . . What to say? I mean, she's a typical college student, you know? Good in her studies and all, but the girl has no street smarts. She grew up in a very sheltered home. That's what makes this whole thing so tragic." She exhaled. "I mean, Remy, can you imagine? She didn't know she was pregnant for five months? How clueless can a person be?"

Remy felt a pang of sympathy for a young woman he'd never met. "Actually, Kathy said it's more common than you'd think. It's called a 'cryptic pregnancy,' where the woman doesn't know until much later."

"That sounds crazy to me." Shenaz shrugged. "But I guess we weren't so bright at nineteen either. And Monaz said she plays so many sports she was used to not getting her period for months at a time." She paused. "Thank God her best friend at college finally dragged her to see a doctor. That's when she found out she was pregnant with a boy. When she broke the news to us, I couldn't believe it."

Remy reddened and stared at his plate. *TMI*, he thought. They had emailed him Monaz's picture, and he had immediately seen the family resemblance between Shenaz and her niece—the straight dark hair, the sharp, clear eyes, the full lips. Unless Monaz's boyfriend looked like Shrek, her baby would be beautiful.

Jango cleared his throat. "To think I spent a whole year trying to help you guys adopt from here. Believe me, I was no further ahead than the day I started the process. You can't believe the red tape, Remy. Everything in this country moves at a snail's pace, man. I finally told the social worker, 'Arre, madam, at this rate, my friend will be an old man with a gray beard and dentures before he becomes a father.' So when Monaz confided in us, I immediately thought of you and Kathy." He gave his wife a sideways look. "This one though. She was in such a shock she couldn't function for a few days."

"You don't know my brother Phiroz," Shenaz said, addressing Remy. "He and his wife—well, they're not like us. They're small-town folks, very conservative. They live in Navsari. I don't know what Phiroz would do if he found out." She lowered her voice. "Jango is right. The timing of this was a godsend. If you were not willing to take the baby, I don't know what we would've done."

Remy bit down on the most obvious question: Why hadn't Jango and Shenaz offered to adopt Monaz's baby themselves? Sure, Jango had always claimed that they enjoyed being childless, bragged about how much they valued their freedom, their ability to be footloose and fancy-free. But faced with an unwanted child in the family, surely they would've changed their minds. He and Kathy had gone through their twenties certain that they didn't want kids. But when Kathy had turned thirty-one, she had abruptly changed her mind and he had agreed. It hadn't occurred to them then that they'd be unable to get pregnant. Remy recalled the small fortune they'd spent on fertility treatments that didn't take. After Kathy proposed that they adopt a child from India, he had called Jango and requested his help.

"I know what you're thinking," Shenaz said, misreading his expression. "You're wondering why Monaz didn't have an abortion, right?" Her eyes searched his face. "How could she? She was so far along when she came to us. Stupid girl."

"It's all going to work out," Remy said, putting an arm around Shenaz. "This—this is so much better than us adopting an unknown child. This way, it all remains in the family, you know? You and Jango can visit us anytime and get to know the boy."

"And also, yaar, we know that the child is half-Parsi and comes from a good family," Jango said. "If you'd pursued the other route, who knows what we would've gotten? Most likely an orphan from the slums, right? With God knows what family history and all. And almost certainly a Hindu or a Muslim child. Not too many Parsis give up their children for adoption, correct?"

Even though Remy had had the same thought when Jango had called him in Columbus, he winced at hearing it said out loud. He thought of himself as a progressive, secular man. Neither he nor Kathy was religious. But it was undeniable: adopting a Parsi child was hitting the jackpot. Their small, insular community had a higher death rate than birth rate, and so they were a dying breed, less than a hundred thousand of them left worldwide. To find a child from within this affluent and educated community was miraculous. He didn't know his mother's views on adoption, but at some point, he'd have to tell her about the reason for this trip, and getting a child whose provenance would be known to them would surely make the whole business more palatable to Shirin.

Embarrassed by his thoughts, Remy changed the topic. "Kathy and I . . . You know. We'll make sure that Monaz's baby—*our* baby—lacks for nothing. We'll be good parents, I promise."

"As if we have any concerns about that!" Jango said. "This will be the luckiest baby in the world. Arre, if I were a few years younger, I'd have begged you and Kathy to adopt *me*."

Shenaz struck her forehead in faux exasperation. "Thirty-six years old, and he still cracks his ridiculous jokes," she said. "God help me."

She looked at Remy. "Will you return to Bombay for the baby's birth? It might be best if Monaz doesn't get a chance to bond with her son."

There was a sudden silence at the table as if the enormity of Monaz's loss had hit each of them.

Remy sighed. "I'd like to," he said. "But let's talk to her about what she'd prefer when she gets here." He rose from the table. "I think I'll rest for a few minutes."

"Yes, go take a nap," Shenaz said. "You must be so jet-lagged."

HE WOKE UP with a jolt a few minutes before ten, brushed his hair, and went into the living room to await the mother of his future child. A pulse beat at the side of his neck and he put his index finger on it to quiet it. He could hear Shenaz in the kitchen, giving instructions to the cook.

Monaz was late but hadn't called to say so, and for some reason this disappointed Remy. *Relax*, he said to himself. *You're not adopting her, just her baby.* He imagined a small boy tottering around their yard in Columbus, an alert, curious child in cargo shorts and red sneakers, and his heart did a strange little flip at the thought. He fidgeted in his chair, unable to control his nervousness.

Remy rose when the doorbell rang, and remained standing while Shenaz opened the door and let in a slender young woman. Monaz was wearing a white T-shirt, blue jeans, and tennis shoes. A leather bag was slung across her right shoulder. She looked as if she'd be at home on an American campus, and Remy was pleased at the realization.

He smiled as he watched the teenager give her aunt a hug and then cross the long, rectangular room to where he stood.

"Hi, Monaz," he said, sticking his hand out to shake hers. "I'm Remy. I'm so happy to meet you."

It was only now that he looked her fully in the face and took in the red eyes, the strawberry nose, the trembling lower lip. "Hi, Remy Uncle," the girl replied. "I'm so very, very sorry."

"Oh, that's fine," Remy said, waving a hand to dismiss her apology. "You're not *that* late."

The girl stared at him and then scrunched up her face. "I'm sorry I made you come all the way from America. But I'm keeping my baby."

CHAPTER TWO

REMY FELT NUMB as he listened to Jango and Shenaz berating the girl, who had folded upon herself. Of all the scenarios he had imagined, he had not entertained the possibility of the girl changing her mind. *I've never seen Jango lose his temper like this,* he thought with an odd detachment. Shenaz was crying, accusing her niece of embarrassing her in front of her husband's oldest friend.

"Do you think Remy just strolled in here from Juhu Beach or something?" Shenaz said. "This poor man left his wife and his business in America to fly here to meet you."

"I had said all along that I would have to meet him first before I agreed," Monaz replied sullenly.

"What?" For a second, Shenaz faltered. "Yes, that's true. But we—we thought it was as good as done." She looked angry again. "Do you think you can ever find a better home for your son than what Remy and Kathy can provide? You remember what I told you about them? They are model people. A model couple."

"Shenaz, please," Remy said, emerging from his fog. "Let's all take a deep breath." They all turned to him, looking to him for guidance, but he fell silent. His head felt woolly, as if fatigue and disappointment had formed cobwebs in his brain.

"Shame on you for cutting my nose like this," Shenaz resumed. "Who are we going to find that's better than Remy?"

"There's no need to find anyone else." Monaz's voice had grown louder, more strident. "I'm trying to tell you that, only. I am going to keep my baby. Gaurav and I are getting married."

There was a stunned silence. Three pairs of eyes stared at the girl, who sat there shaking but defiant.

"Chokri," Shenaz said at last, "have you gone mad? Do you think your father will allow you to marry a non-Parsi?"

"I'm nineteen. I don't need his permission."

"Last week, you told us this Gaurav person didn't want anything to do with you," Jango said. "And now you're going to marry him?"

Monaz opened her mouth to explain, but Remy had heard enough. He didn't need to know any more of her personal business. His best chance to adopt a child from India had evaporated, and he felt foolish for having rushed here, for having put all his eggs in one basket. A private adoption had seemed like such an elegant solution.

"Excuse me," he said, standing up. "I—I need to call Kathy." His stomach heaved at the thought of his wife's disappointment. Adopting an Indian child had been her idea. "The child should look like at least one of us, honey," Kathy had said. "And getting a . . . a white kid is going to be hard." He had tensed at the thought of yet another link tying him to a country he had been determined to leave behind. But Kathy had seemed so convinced that he'd acquiesced.

"Remy, wait," Shenaz cried. "I'm sure I can knock some sense into this girl."

He shook his head. "It's okay," he said. He forced himself to meet Monaz's eye and smile. "Good luck with everything."

"I'm so sorry, uncle," she said, wiping tears away. "I didn't do this on purpose, I swear."

"I know," he said, feeling a trickle of sympathy. "It's okay. Congratulations to you."

"SHE *WHAT*?" Kathy said.

"She changed her mind. She's keeping the baby," Remy repeated.

"What?"

He fell silent, knowing that Kathy needed a few minutes to absorb the news. "I'm sorry, honey," he said at last.

"I don't believe it. I mean, how could she? What gives her the right?"

He didn't state the obvious: that they had no signed agreement with Monaz, and even if they had, they were not the kind of people who would force a mother to give up a child against her wishes.

"I knew I should've come with you. Maybe if she'd met me also."

His heart twisted at how crushed Kathy sounded. "How could you have? You have that big conference coming up."

"I know," she said miserably. "But this was more important."

"Listen," he said, forcing a lightness into his voice. "We're in our midthirties. We'll . . . As soon as I come home, we'll start the process in the US, okay? I'd much rather adopt in America anyway."

Kathy sighed. "This was my stupid idea. I just . . . I thought it would mean something to you. To have a child who came from the same part of the world as you."

He felt a gust of love for Kathy. But he couldn't explain to her that the last thing he wanted was to continue an attachment with the country of his birth. Once Mummy was gone, even his periodic visits to India would end. His wife knew about his fraught history with his mother, but she had grown up in a close-knit Irish Catholic family less than ten miles from where they now lived, and couldn't understand the complexity of his feelings—the fact that he had come to America precisely to get away from home, his childhood memories colored by the strange dynamic between him and his mother and tarnished by the gloom of his parents' marriage.

"Remy?" Kathy said. "You still there?"

"I'm here," he said. Although at that moment, he'd have given anything to be lying next to her in their bed.

"What're you gonna do now?"

"I guess I'll stick to the rest of the plan. I'll go over to my mom's flat this afternoon. Surprise her." He felt his body tense at the prospect.

"Will you still stay the full ten days then?"

"I'm not sure. I'll play it by ear. Would you mind if I did?"

"You do what you need to." Kathy paused. "You don't think she—Monaz—will change her mind?"

He hated the tenuous hope in her voice, blamed himself for it. "I don't think so, honey," he said. "Apparently, she and the baby's father are thinking of getting married."

There was a sudden silence, Monaz's reversal a brick wall they couldn't scale.

"Well," Kathy said at long last, "I'd better go. It's late."

He knew she'd lie awake in bed, flooded with disappointment, and the fact that he was more than eight thousand miles away, unable to hold her in his arms, made him furious at the thoughtless girl in the next room, who had dashed their hopes so cavalierly. He shouldn't have called Kathy at this hour, should've allowed her a peaceful sleep.

"I'm sorry, baby," Remy said.

"It's not your fault."

"Yes, it is. I don't know . . . I should have known better."

"Remy," Kathy said. "Don't be silly. There's no way you could've predicted this."

Except there was, he thought after they'd hung up. This is why he had flinched inwardly when Kathy had first proposed adopting from India. Why hadn't he spoken up then? Why hadn't he told her the truth? India always disappointed. He had often thought of Bombay as the museum of failures, an exhibit hall filled with thwarted dreams and broken promises. The reels of red tape themselves were worthy of their own display room. What on earth had made him imagine that adopting a child here would go smoothly?

Remy remembered a summer's afternoon lying on the hammock in their backyard in Columbus. He and Kathy had been married five years by then. "What was the happiest day of your life?" Kathy had asked.

He knew that she expected him to pick their wedding day. Or perhaps the day he'd met her at the party at Ralph Addington's house during Remy's second month in America. But he'd told her the truth: it was the day he'd received the letter admitting him to the MFA program at Ohio State. That letter had been his ticket out of the museum of failures and into a new world of possibility. And it had all paid off beyond his wildest dreams.

I'll cut short my trip, Remy now thought. *I'll spend a few days with Mummy and then return home.* After his father's death, he'd entrusted his mother's care to his cousin Pervez and his wife, Roshan, who now lived two floors below his mother's apartment. He would meet with them and with the family lawyer, tweak the arrangements for Shirin's care, and then he'd leave. There was really nothing else in Bombay to hold him.

He paced around the bedroom, debating whether to join the other three in the living room. As if in answer to his question, Monaz herself appeared at his door.

"Hi?" he said.

Without asking for permission, she walked into the room. "I wanted to see you for a minute," the girl said. "Privately." Her face crumpled. "To tell you I'm not a bad person. To explain what—"

"It's okay," Remy said. "It's none of my business."

"But I *want* to. Remy Uncle, when I found out I was pregnant, Gaurav was the first person I told. I was petrified. I mean, you know what the attitudes are like in India towards unwed mothers. And of course, Gaurav knows all this, but he—he was really mean to me. He said there was no way he could be a father, that he was planning to go to law school after he graduated from college. In any case, he had another girlfriend, he said. He wouldn't even talk to me after that. That's when I came to Shenazfui for help."

And that's the guy you're going to marry? Remy thought.

His incredulity must've shown on his face, because Monaz said, "I know what you're thinking. But Remy Uncle, Gaurav has changed. He came to me yesterday and apologized. He is going to tell his parents about us next week, only. He's promised me that we'll marry before our son is born."

The girl was looking at him with her large, liquid eyes, and despite himself, Remy felt a stir of avuncular concern. "And your parents will be okay with this? Gaurav is Hindu, yes?"

A look of uncertainty crossed Monaz's face before it hardened into determination. "I don't care. If they want to see their grandson, they'll have to accept our mixed marriage."

She is the oddest combo of trepidation and courage, Remy thought. He liked her. "Well," he said, "I wish you all the luck in the world."

"Thanks for your blessings, uncle," she said politely. "But I also need your forgiveness. Otherwise, I will not have a good marriage. I don't want to build my happiness out of your sadness."

Remy looked closely at the girl. *No American teen would act like this*, he thought, bemused by her earnest superstition. "There's nothing to forgive, Monaz," he said. "You have to do what's best for you."

She rushed to him and put her arms around him. "Thank you, uncle. You're so nice. Just as Shenazfui said you were. Good luck to you and your wife. I will pray for you."

CHAPTER THREE

———————

REMY STOOD AT the entrance of his childhood apartment, took a deep breath, and rang the doorbell. He plastered a smile on his face and rehearsed the "Surprise!" with which he would greet his mother, hoping it would appease her anger at not being informed that he was coming.

But a young dark-skinned woman answered the door, and his smile faltered. "Yes?" the woman said. "Aap kon?"

"I'm Remy. Shirinbai's son." He picked up his suitcase and made to enter, but the woman blocked his way.

"Can I come in?" he said, more sharply than he'd intended, and the woman moved out of his way. "Ah, Remy sahib," she said. "I recognize you now from your photos. Please, welcome. Sorry, no one told me you were coming. My name is Hema. I come every morning to do the sweeping-cleaning."

He nodded in reply and looked around the living room, taken aback at its deterioration since he'd last been home. The room badly needed a coat of paint, and there was a long crack in the ceiling. The crystal vases had a layer of dust on them, and the sliding glass windows were dirty and had not been professionally cleaned in a long time. "Is my mother in her room?" he asked.

The woman frowned. "No, sir," she said. "She's in the hospital, sir. I thought that's why you came, only."

His stomach dipped. "In the hospital? Why? Did she fall?"

"No, no, sir. No fall. She was having a bad cough and fever. Doctor sahib say to shift her to the hospital. And even before that, getting her to eat—oof. Big problem."

"She didn't eat?"

"How could she, sir, when all day long she cough, cough, cough?"

Why the hell had Pervez not informed him? "I don't understand. Didn't Pervez and Roshan help?" They were living rent-free in the third-floor apartment in exchange for looking after his mother, and Remy had promised to transfer ownership of the place to them after Shirin's death. When was the last time he'd spoken to them? Hell, when was the last time he'd talked to Mummy? Was it on Christmas Day? Had he really not called her since then?

"They never come up to check on her, sir," the woman said, looking around the room furtively, as if she half expected the couple to materialize. "The poor woman was so sick. I wanted to bring a God man here to do an exorcism, but Roshanbai say no."

"A God man?"

"Yes, sir. People in my basti go to him, only, instead of the doctor-foctor. But Roshanbai say she doesn't believe in such jadoo. Witchery, she call it."

Remy felt grateful to Roshan for at least having spared his mother such claptrap. But he kept his face impassive. "And now she's in the hospital?"

"Yes," Hema said. "Now she's in Parsee General."

"I see." Remy rubbed his face with his hand, trying to erase the sudden weariness he felt. He dropped onto the couch, trying to recalibrate.

"How long has my mom been in the hospital, Hema?"

"Since a few days, sir."

"And how long have you been working here?"

"Just for a few months, sir. Roshanbai had given me the warning about her temper. But with me, no problem. She say four or five words." She lowered her voice. "She hardly speaks, sir."

Remy felt a rush of panic. Shirin was notoriously voluble and critical when it came to the help. Even when Daddy had been alive, she had run through a veritable army of servants with her constant criticism. "She hardly speaks?" he repeated.

Hema nodded, twisting her hands in front of her. "You will take a cup of tea, sir?" she asked.

He looked at her blankly before deciding. "No, it's okay. I—I'll just drop off my suitcase in my bedroom, and then I'll leave you to your cleaning. I want to go see Pervez."

"As you wish, sir. But you please return your mummy's key to them, sir, if you're going downstairs. I'll just pull the door shut when I leave. Roshanbai hands me the house key every morning, and I let myself in. I come daily at about ten o'clock. Will that be suitable for you?"

"Sure. I don't wish to change your routine."

Hema made to lift his suitcase, but he waved her away. *I can damn well pick up my own baggage*, he thought. He smiled grimly to himself at the inadvertent metaphor as he headed into his boyhood room.

REMY TOOK THE two flights of stairs down and rang Pervez's doorbell.

Pervez looked stunned when he opened the door. "Arre, Remy," he said. "What are you doing in Bombay? Welcome, yaar. Come in."

The move to the apartment in the affluent Nepean Sea Road building had obviously been good for Pervez. He appeared to have gained about twenty pounds, and the old, sad-sack nervousness was gone, replaced by a new assurance. Pervez had quit his old job at the bank and was now a partner in a successful toy company. His cousin was only a few years older than Remy, but they had never been particularly close. Daddy's brother, Faroukh, had died young, and Pervez had been sent away to boarding school. Apart from the monthly check that Daddy had sent to Pervez's mother, the two families had seldom been in touch while Remy was growing up.

Remy looked around the apartment, which he still owned. He noticed the new coat of paint, the expensive furniture, the chandelier in the living room. What a contrast this airy, spacious flat was to the one-room apartment Pervez and Roshan had been living in three years ago. Remy could still recall the small double bed in a corner, the armoire that took up a third of the room, the metal filing cabinet, the tiny table with two folding chairs on the small balcony. Above all, he remembered the clothes folded and stacked on the floor.

"So how did you find out about Shirin?" Pervez was saying. "News really spreads through our small Parsi community, doesn't it? And when did you get in? You should have let me know, yaar. I would've picked you up at the airport."

No way was he going to reveal the real reason for his visit. Remy was thinking of an evasive answer when Roshan came into the room and greeted him with a warm hug and kiss. "This is an unexpected surprise," she said. "Come, have a seat. What will you take? Some juice? Pineapple? Mango? Guava?"

There was a friendly, proprietary ease in the way Roshan spoke to him, which belied the fact that he hardly knew her, that he'd met her for the first time when he'd visited their old apartment. Maybe the familiarity was born out of phone calls over the last three years—calls about his mother or the apartment. Roshan's manner telegraphed that she considered their debt to Remy already repaid.

Except it didn't sound like they'd provided much care in recent months.

"Why is Mummy in the hospital? And why didn't you inform me?"

"She has typhoid and pneumonia," Pervez said. "Apparently, she had been getting these high fevers every evening that she didn't tell us about. The doctor advised we transfer her, as she was too weak to be at home by herself."

Typhoid? Was that still a thing? Remy had thought the disease had been eradicated. "You know, pneumonia can be dangerous at her age . . ." he began.

Pervez sucked his teeth. "Listen, boss, taking care of Shirin isn't my full-time job. I'm also a businessman, you know? Same as you. Shirin knew she could call on us if she needed something. It's not my fault that she didn't."

"But Pervez—" Remy stopped, waited until he could control his temper. "Didn't you visit her regularly enough to know she wasn't well? I mean . . . that was the whole point of having you in the same building."

He said it as gently as he could, but Remy saw Roshan flinch. "I think you've forgotten how difficult your mother can be," she said. "This past year, she actually stopped answering the door when we knocked. And if we let ourselves in, she would refuse to speak. I tell you, that woman is impossible to manage."

"The thing is, boss," Pervez said, "even when she was healthy, Shirin was quite rude to my wife—to the extent that a year ago, I forbade Roshan from visiting her. 'Bas. Send her lunch and dinner and let her manage,' I said. And if she fires another servant, let her fend for herself."

Remy swallowed. "Why didn't you tell me?" he said, while thinking, *But this was part of our bargain—that you would deal with her moods. I was honest with you about the fact that Mummy could be difficult.*

Roshan threw her husband a quick glance. "Arre, how much to trouble you from eight thousand miles away? Besides, you didn't come to see your mother once after your daddy died." Her tone had changed. "What, you were going to rush here because she was being nasty to your cousin's wife?"

Touché, Remy thought, although he hated Roshan for saying this. "I'm sorry," he murmured. "What with the ad agency and everything . . ."

"No, no, no, we understand," Pervez said hastily. "You have your business to worry about, Remy. Anyway, we handled the problem."

"How?"

"After a few days, Shirin came to her senses, yaar. Chup-chap, she came to our apartment and acted as if nothing were wrong. Was nice and all to Roshan."

Pervez smiled triumphantly, and Remy had no choice but to smile back. But he felt a cold anger at his cousin for putting his mother in such a humiliating situation. Mummy was what, seventy? She was dependent on them. Surely, they didn't need to go around teaching her a lesson. Then again, he had outsourced his filial obligations, so he couldn't really blame them, could he?

A wave of fatigue and sleepiness washed over Remy, and he fought to hold it at bay. "Which is why you can understand our shock when she suddenly stopped talking," Roshan said. "I mean, this was a woman who used to fight with the servants so loudly that we could hear it from out in the hallway. And then one fine day, bas, nothing, full stop."

Remy was on high alert. "Meaning?"

Roshan frowned. "I thought you'd told him," she said to her husband. She faced Remy. "She doesn't speak. She has fallen totally silent."

"Since when?"

"Since . . . I don't know. For at least three or four months. I should've taken her to the doctor then, only. But we didn't know anything was wrong until the coughing started. And even then, she flatly refused to leave the apartment." She patted her cheek. "Baap re! I had never heard someone cough like that. She sounded like a TB patient."

Remy fought again to control his temper. "But, Roshan," he said quietly, "didn't you think it odd that she stopped talking? Why didn't you try and find out what was wrong? Insist that she see someone."

"Arre, which general's army can make your mother do something she doesn't wish to do?" Roshan said, her voice rising. "As it is, the only reason we managed to take her to the hospital is because she fainted at home and Dr. Lokhanwala was good enough to make a house call."

Remy turned to his cousin, but Pervez stared back at him impassively. A disconcerting thought wormed its way into Remy's head: By promising the couple the third-floor flat after Mummy's death, had he unwittingly given them less of an incentive to take good care of her? He remembered how anxious he'd been to get away the last time he'd been here. Had his impatience made him reckless?

Pervez stirred, as if he'd read Remy's mind. "Listen, cuz," Pervez said. "I didn't call because I didn't want to worry you all the way in America. I'm hoping she'll be home soon."

Remy bit down on his lower lip to keep from crying. He had tried to foist his family obligations onto the couple, and this was his punishment. In any case, after he returned to Columbus, he would have to continue relying on Roshan and Pervez. *At least you are here now*, he said to himself. He would soon be able to assess his mother's situation in person.

How had Mummy sounded when he'd called her on Christmas Day? He tried to remember. Subdued, come to think of it. But he had called from the car while he and Kathy were driving to Kathy's mom's house, and he'd been distracted. Still, he didn't remember Shirin coughing. Even if she had, she would've brushed aside his concerns, blamed it on the pollution in the city. And he would've happily bought that excuse.

He finished his drink and pushed back his chair. "Thanks for the juice. But I'll take my leave now. I want to go see her at the hospital."

"I have the day off, so if you give me time to get dressed, I can take you," Pervez said.

"No, no," Remy said. "That's okay. I'll get a cab."

Pervez gave him a penetrating look, then shrugged. "Whatever you wish."

REMY TOOK THE two flights of stairs back up to his mother's apartment. The hostility in Roshan's voice as she'd spoken about Shirin had shaken him. *But you are her own flesh and blood, and you struggle with her*, he reminded himself. *Why did you expect a couple of distant relatives to succeed where you'd failed?*

Still, he felt a deep misgiving about having promised them the apartment after Mummy's death, realizing now that they had no motivation to keep her alive. *You idiot*, he thought as he let himself into his mother's flat.

It was something Dina Mehta, the family lawyer, had said that had planted the seed that had made Remy approach Pervez. Cyrus had bought the third-floor apartment as an investment and had leased it to executives from HSBC Bank. But after his father's death, Dina had informed Remy that the lease was up, and Dina had suggested a rent reduction to someone who would provide care for Shirin instead of looking for another corporate tenant. Offering the apartment to Pervez and Roshan had seemed like an elegant solution to all their problems. Roshan could send meals for Mummy, accompany her to doctors' appointments, and run errands for her. In exchange, the couple could move into one of the most prestigious neighborhoods in the city.

But the longer Remy had sat in Pervez's crowded, pitiful room, the sorrier he had felt for him. As Pervez described how his nephews had cheated him out of inheriting his late mother's flat, Remy heard himself say, "And after Mummy's passing—provided, you know, it all works out—I could put the apartment permanently in your name. Like, I would never leave you stranded, you know?"

Seeing the incredulity on their faces, Remy had wondered why none of the fairy tales he'd read as a child ever described the pleasure felt by the wish-granting genie or the fairy godmother. Even though Daddy was dead, Remy had felt Cyrus's approval when he'd left that gloomy one-room flat. What, after all, had separated him from Pervez except for the whimsy of fate? Not only had Pervez's father died when he was young, but Faroukh had possessed none of the drive and vigor of his younger brother. If the roles had been reversed—if Remy had been born to Faroukh instead of to Cyrus—well, he hoped that someone would've been as kind to him.

He had called Kathy after he'd offered up the arrangement, fully expecting her to support his grand gesture. But, to his surprise, Kathy had disapproved. With real estate prices in Bombay being as high as they were, he had rashly thrown away a small fortune without consulting her, she said. They had exchanged words; Kathy had reminded him that they could have kept the third-floor flat for them to stay in whenever they visited Bombay. He had heard what Kathy was too polite to say: that without Cyrus's buffering presence, she had no desire to stay with Shirin. But Remy couldn't go back on his word. And if Kathy had seen Pervez's shabby flat, she would've agreed with him. They were more than comfortable, between Kathy's salary as a pediatrician and his flourishing ad agency. Not to mention the fact that he would inherit Mummy's flat someday. That alone was worth a ton of money.

Now, for the first time, Remy thought perhaps Kathy had been right all along.

CHAPTER FOUR

BOMBAY LOOKED UNCHANGED from three years ago except that there was more of everything—more people, more traffic, more noise, more construction projects. Remy covered his nose with his handkerchief—the air was brown with smog, and even in his wealthy neighborhood, the sidewalks were so crowded or broken that he was forced into the road. The humidity pasted his shirt to his back. How had Mummy made her way around this dusty city? He wished he hadn't sold Cyrus's car after his death, as she'd insisted he do. He should've hired a driver for her instead. Imagining his mother battling these streets made him feel terrible; also, he sure could've used a driver and an air-conditioned car right about now.

He hailed a cab, and within minutes they were caught in a traffic jam. As they crawled along, he spoke to the driver in Hindi, bemoaning the slow pace. The man turned around and gave him an incredulous look. "What are you saying, sahib?" He laughed. "This is nothing. You should see in the evening. It must not be this way in your desh, correct?"

What was it that revealed he was an outsider, a foreigner in this bewildering city? Daddy used to tease him that even his Hindi now had an American accent, and he supposed that was true.

He had the driver drop him off on the main road, outside the imposing stone arch that led to Parsee General Hospital. He walked the lane that led to the hospital grounds, trying to gather his thoughts. Was it really just earlier today that Monaz had dashed his hopes so cruelly? Time was already beginning to blur. It was hard not to blame some of this on Bombay itself, as if this unpredictable, wily city had it in for him and was attacking him personally.

You're not making any sense, he chided himself.

The gardens around the hospital were beautiful, lush with trees and flowering bushes and birdsong, a welcome change from the grime of the streets. He took in the grandeur of the century-old stone building as he approached its entrance. *For a small community, we Parsis sure have left our mark on the architecture of Bombay,* Remy thought. The solidity of the structure stood in contrast to the flimsy, cookie-cutter skyscrapers that kept springing up elsewhere all over the city.

Once inside, he bypassed the reception desk and climbed the stairway that led to the second floor, cursing himself for forgetting Shirin's room number. He strolled down the sunlit verandah, flanked by patient rooms on one side and open windows on the other. He peered into each room, hoping to spot his mother. Most of the patients were frail and old. *A dying community*, Remy thought. *Soon to be extinct.*

The Zoroastrian faith forbade conversion; if he and Kathy eventually did adopt, he wasn't sure whether their child would even be considered a Parsi. He and Kathy, agnostic themselves, had never discussed in what religion, if any, they would raise their child.

Some of the patients waved at him as he walked by, and he waved back. Almost all had family members fussing around them. Young ward boys buzzed past him, carrying water pitchers and bedpans. After he'd walked the entire length of the hallway, he stopped a passing nurse and asked for Shirin Wadia's room. She led him back the way he'd come, to where a white-haired woman lay in bed, looking up at the ceiling. He turned to the nurse to say there'd been a mistake—that this shrunken, emaciated woman wasn't his mother—then stopped. It *was* her. He recognized the gesture she made as she scratched the bridge of her nose.

He nodded his thanks at the nurse and then stood in the doorway, studying his mother, waiting for the thumping of his heart to recede. He had the awful sense that years from now, when he lay awake in the accusatory dark, this memory would be tucked into his heart like those folded notes Shirin used to send with his school lunches: he was the man who had failed to recognize his own mother.

After a few minutes, he entered the room. And now, he realized why he hadn't known it was her.

She had always dyed her hair black, and that's who he'd been looking for—a dark-haired woman, with features as sharp and lethal as her intellect. No wonder he hadn't recognized the gaunt face, the bewildering reality of white hair and dull eyes. How could she have possibly aged so much in three years? He looked at her dirty toenails sticking out from under the thin cotton blanket—why hadn't someone clipped them, for Christ's sake? Pity, monstrous pity, flooded Remy's heart, followed by guilt. As he stood, he looked for some sign of recognition from her, but there was none.

He licked his lips, swallowed. His mouth was dry. "Hi, Mummy," he said at last. "It's me, Remy. I've come home."

CHAPTER FIVE

ON THE LONG flight to India, Remy had braced himself for the inevitability of his mother's scathing comments, the critical eyes looking him over and ready to find fault. He had been sure she would disapprove of his plans to adopt; she would shame him for his unconscionable three-year absence. What he was unprepared for, couldn't have imagined, was the deadness in Shirin's eyes, the weight loss, the gray, papery skin, bruised from where they'd been drawing blood. When had this decline started? Had it been slow—the drip, drip, drip of age—or had it been a swift decline due to her illness?

He pulled up a chair and told her how glad he was to see her, described the long international flight from Newark, and made up a story about how sad Kathy had been to miss out on a chance to see her on this trip, but Shirin said nothing. After several minutes of keeping up a one-sided conversation, Remy fell silent, running out of things to say. "I'll be back, Mummy," he said, and stepped out of the room.

He stopped the first nurse he saw. "Excuse me," he said. "I . . . Is there anyone here I could talk to? About my mother's condition?"

The young woman stared at him for a moment. "Who's your patient?" she said.

"My patient?" Remy said. "I'm not a doctor."

"Yes, yes. But what is the name of your patient?"

"Oh. Shirin Wadia."

"Dr. Bilimoria is rounding. Usually, he comes in the mornings only, but he's still here today for another case. I can request him to stop by."

"And he's her doctor?"

But the nurse had already started walking away, and Remy returned to Shirin's room. He took in the oxygen tank in the corner, the rusty metal bedside table, upon which sat a jar of Vicks, a bottle of eau de cologne, and a glass of water. Pervez had mentioned that they'd hired a private-duty night nurse. But who kept Mummy company during the day? There was enough money in her bank account to pay for a day nurse.

He heard a low rumbling sound and realized that it came from his mother's chest, that she was trying to suppress a cough. But a harsh, wet cough exploded out of her anyway, and it went on and on, causing her thin body to shudder. Shirin's face turned red with exertion, and Remy wanted to shut his eyes and ears against her obvious suffering. He lifted her head and torso, careful not to tug at the IV in her arm. Their eyes met, and a look passed between them before she turned her head away so as to not cough on him.

"Oh, Mama," Remy whispered. "This sounds terrible. I'm so sorry." He reached for the water glass and held it to her lips while propping her up with one arm. "Take a sip, Mummy," he said. Her back felt as hollow as a wooden bowl under his hand.

After the coughing subsided, he lowered her again. As he pulled his hand out from under her, Shirin reached for it and held it to her chest, all the while gazing at him wordlessly. There was a different light in her eyes, and he felt that she had recognized him. But he wasn't sure.

"Mummy," he said, and his voice cracked, and he didn't dare say another word. He stood beside her as she continued to look at him. Then her eyes closed, and a few minutes later he heard a snort and then a soft snoring.

There was a rustling sound, and a bald older man in a white coat breezed into the room. "Hello," he said, extending his hand. "Dr. Rumi Bilimoria here. And you are . . . ?"

"Oh, hi. I'm Remy. Shirin's son."

"Ah, yes. The one who lives in America."

"Yes." Remy had the wild thought that maybe Shirin had spoken to the doctor. "How did you know?"

"Oh, I forget. That lady—I think it's her niece?—who admitted her to the hospital had mentioned a son in America. But she had indicated that there was some family problem and that we should not expect a visit."

Remy stared at the doctor, appalled by his tactlessness. "Well, I'm here," he said at last. "And I was hoping to find out what exactly is wrong. Is her fever under control?"

Bilimoria held up a finger as he pressed his stethoscope to Shirin's chest to listen to her breathing. Then he leaned into her ear and said loudly, "So, Mrs. Wadia? How do we feel? Medicines are helping?"

Silence. Bilimoria gestured for Remy to step out of the room with him.

"Your mother was completely dehydrated when they brought her in," Bilimoria said. "Seems like she was not eating or drinking much. She had pneumonia in both lungs. She's on IV antibiotics, but we're not out of the woods yet. She's still getting a fever at night."

"I see." Remy bit his lower lip. "But . . . she'll be okay?"

"I hope so. We're doing our best." Bilimoria gave him a curious look. "She's only been in the hospital for three days. You came that quickly?"

Remy flushed. "Well, to see her and for other reasons," he said evasively.

Bilimoria looked as if he were about to ask something else, but then he pursed his lips. "Okay," he said. "Well, good to meet you."

"Um, one more question," Remy said. "Do you . . . ? Can you give me a rough idea of, you know, when she might be discharged? Because I'm only in India for another week or so." Without meaning to, he looked at his watch, as if his plane were departing imminently.

Bilimoria frowned. "Your mother is still getting a fever every evening."

"I understand. Sorry. I'm just anxious to . . . Never mind."

"Your mother's an elderly woman who lives by herself."

"She's not elderly. She's only seventy—"

"An *elderly* woman who lives by herself," Bilimoria continued. "She wasn't able to take care of herself at home. What she will need is for someone to keep an eye on her."

"But can't we . . . ? Once she's off the IV, everything else can be done at home, correct?"

Bilimoria raised his bushy eyebrows and stared intently at Remy. "Listen, deekra," he said at last. "We don't run on an American schedule here. Your mother is on antibiotics. She requires oxygen off and on. And the niece said"—Bilimoria cleared his throat—"that they couldn't manage her at home. Said she was, you know, a little hard to control."

Remy flushed. "In America, they discharge patients as soon as possible," he muttered. "To avoid the risk of an infection."

"In America, I've heard they also send patients home the same day after a double mastectomy," Bilimoria replied. "What can I say? I guess we are more humane in this country. I will not discharge her as long as she's getting these fevers."

Remy nodded, chastised.

"If you want my medical advice," Bilimoria said, softening, "I think under the circumstances and looking at the full picture, it's good that we keep her here until she has fully recovered." A glint came into his eyes. "And it looks like you can afford the hospital fees, no? Now, if you'll excuse me." He gave Remy a quick nod and moved away.

Remy watched the doctor's retreating back. "And the reason she's not talking?" he called after him. "That's normal?"

Bilimoria stopped, walked back to Remy. "I don't have an explanation for that. It could be general weakness and exhaustion. Or, maybe she's just given up. People do that when they have nothing to look forward to."

Remy felt the doctor's indictment spear through his body. He watched as Bilimoria entered another patient's room. An elderly Parsi woman using a walker ambled past him, and Remy stepped aside to let her pass. "Sukhi raho, deekra," the woman said. "God bless."

After he had regained his composure, Remy went back into Shirin's room. "So what do you think, Mummy?" he said conversationally. "Do you like Dr. Bilimoria? He seems really happy with your progress."

Shirin turned her head and looked him dead in the eye. *She heard me*, Remy thought. *There's nothing wrong with her brain.*

Then another thought: *She knows. She knows I'm lying.*

WHEN THE DINNER tray arrived, he cut up the chicken cutlet and fed it to Shirin. Each time he held the fork to her mouth, she turned her head away. After four attempts, he spooned a bit of the mashed potatoes. "Okay, Mummy," he said. "Let's try this, okay? Just a little bit, accha? It's mashed potatoes. Your favorite, remember?"

At last, he got her to accept a bite. But instead of simply swallowing

the soft food, Shirin chewed it, swirling it in her mouth. "Chalo," he
said finally. "Swallow."

She did. In this slow, laborious way, he managed to get her to take
a few teaspoons of food before she pursed her lips and refused more.
Remy felt a growing desperation. He could hear the rumbling as the
cough gathered in her chest. Shirin looked exhausted, as if the effort
of eating had worn her out. "Mummy," he said, "does anything sound
good to you? Any food?"

She moved her lips and said something wordlessly. He leaned in.
"Mama?" he said. "I'm sorry. I couldn't hear you."

She tried again. "Kho."

Kho? Kho? Who or what the hell was that? Remy panicked, his
eyes searching the doorway, imploring someone to come in and help
him decipher the word.

The look of irritation on Shirin's face echoed his own frustration.
Her lips are so dry, he thought. He dipped the edge of a napkin into a
glass of water and dabbed them. She opened her mouth to let the water
trickle in. "Okay," he said. "Let's try again. Please?"

But Shirin didn't repeat herself. Instead, her eyes darted to the glass
and then to him, and Remy knew to offer her some water. He held the
straw to her lips with one hand, supporting her neck with the other.
Shirin took two sips and then began to cough.

A NURSE CAME and switched the IV bag, then coaxed Shirin into
swallowing a couple of capsules. Remy sat beside his mother while she
napped. He heard the constant rattle in her chest, observed the new
lines on her face. Weight loss had made her front teeth protrude. Maybe
Bilimoria was right, Remy thought. In a country where the retirement
age was sixty, maybe seventy *was* old. Occasionally, a cough woke
Shirin up, but after it subsided, she fell back into a deep slumber.

Jet lag made Remy's own eyelids heavy, and he dozed off.

He felt a tap on his shoulder, imagined it was a crow tapping him with its beak, and woke up with a start. An anxious-looking woman stood by his side, looking at him questioningly.

"Hi," he said, rubbing his eyes. "Can I help you?"

The young woman looked from him to the now-awake Shirin. "I'm Manju, the night nurse," she said. "And you are?"

"Oh. Sorry. I'm Remy. Shirin's son."

Suspicion clouded the woman's face. "I don't understand. Madam is having no children."

Remy had the strangest feeling that his long absence had resulted in his erasure. *This is what death must feel like*, he thought. Or rather, this must be what it was like to never have been born, a blank space that didn't even register as absence. "You're wrong," he said, softening his words with a smile. "I'm her son. I've come from America to see my mother."

"Accha?" Manju's face lit up, as if she herself were the recipient of good fortune. She spun around to look at Shirin. "You see, madam? Your baba has come all the way from Am'rica to see you."

Shirin stared unseeingly at a spot between the two of them. But Remy was not fooled. *She hears everything*, he thought. *She sees everything*. Behind the blank facade, his eagle-eyed mother was still very much alive.

CHAPTER SIX

As he left the hospital, Remy thought of phoning Dina Mehta, who still managed Mummy's finances, to inform her that he was in Bombay, but it was all he could do to get into a cab and give the driver directions to the apartment.

Remy smiled bitterly as he remembered that it was Mummy's irrational hostility toward Dina that had hastened his return to Columbus after Daddy's death.

He and Mummy had worked tirelessly and in unison during the last week of Daddy's life. Knowing that his time with his beloved father was drawing to an end, Remy had stayed awake around the clock the last three days, refusing to let the nurse attend to his father—emptying the catheter bag himself, lovingly giving Cyrus a sponge bath each morning. Shirin had sat by her son's side, leaving the room only long enough to cook dinner, and it had taken him a few days to realize that his mother was making all of Remy's favorite dishes. On the day that he realized this, when she'd served him the chicken fried rice that he'd loved as a boy, he'd embraced her and sobbed in her arms.

He had not cried in his mother's presence since he turned twelve, when their dog Biscuit had died. Mummy had wept inconsolably that day, but the very next afternoon she had erupted at Remy for some minor provocation, leaving him bewildered. Still grieving Biscuit's death, he had flinched at each ugly word that had escaped her lips. But after a few moments, something in him hardened, and he became a tree. Ever since that day, whenever Shirin was in one of her explosive moods, he had stood tall and immobile, would imagine her words as a swirl of wind that circled above his head, leaving him unmoved and unbowed. He would bend in the gale of her anger but not break. No more flinching, no more sobbing, no more cowering.

But Daddy's death was a giant eraser that had wiped clean the slate of ill will between mother and son. Remy had assumed that they would cremate his father, but Shirin said that Dad had wanted his remains disposed in the Parsi way. Remy was surprised—even though his father had always been proud of being a Zoroastrian, he was not an orthodox man—but he had acquiesced. During the four days of the funeral ceremonies, Remy hadn't left his mother's side. They had greeted the long line of white-clad mourners together; he held her hand when the professional pallbearers wrapped Daddy's body in a white sheet and staggered toward the Tower of Silence. The ancient Persian tradition of allowing tamed vultures to feast on the flesh at the Tower of Silence was no longer viable, the vultures long dead from diclofenac poisoning. There were new ways to disintegrate the bodies, but Remy didn't—couldn't—allow a picture to form in his mind.

After they came home on the final day, a tight-lipped Shirin immediately began to straighten the house, stripping the sheets from the rented hospital bed. Remy instinctively understood that staying busy was her way of containing her grief, lest it spill out uncontrollably. And so he stopped himself from stopping her, although he would've preferred to have left his father's impression on the pillow, his imprint on the mattress, a little while longer.

He wandered around the large apartment, thinking it had never felt so silent and empty before. Dad had been a blazing fire of a man, and he had filled the house with his oversized personality and presence. Remy shivered from the sudden cold left in his wake. Now, he and Shirin moved through the house like two solitary flames—slender, flickering, trying to hold the darkness at bay.

He helped his mother load the sheets into the washing machine and warmed up the food friends had sent, while marveling at the fact that despite his lifelong devotion to his father, he took after his mother in appearance—they were both tall and slim, with pale, angular faces, thin lips, and light-brown eyes. Daddy had been three shades darker than the two of them, a short muscular man with a kindly, broad face.

They ate in the living room. Remy reached for the television remote to break up the awful silence in the house, but Shirin reminded him of the Parsi rituals of mourning—no TV or movies or music allowed during the first month; she would have to wear the widow's white for at least that long. He opened his mouth to argue, then thought better of it. He would do everything in his power to hold on to this new Shirin, the gentle mother he'd always longed for.

FIVE DAYS LATER, Remy came home drenched in sweat, frustrated from the hours spent arguing with the bank branch manager, who had insisted that Remy's signature was not an exact match with his old one on the joint account Cyrus had opened for his son and himself several years earlier. At times like this, he detested India and its idiotic rules and regulations, the unexpected roadblocks, the inability of petty officials to use their common sense and judgment. He went directly into the kitchen to pour himself a glass of cold water and then joined his mother in the living room.

"Everything went okay?" she said. "Was Mr. Basant there? Was he helpful?"

He shook his head, his mouth twisting with contempt. "He was useless. Absolutely useless."

"But he's such a nice man."

In his irritable state, he noticed immediately that she had sided with a goddamn bank manager rather than with her own son. *Typical*, he thought. "He's totally incompetent," he said. "He said my signature didn't match my old one, from donkey's years ago." Without meaning to, he'd lapsed into his schoolboy English.

"You have no idea how strict the Reserve Bank rules are these days. These poor people don't have a choice," Shirin said.

"Then maybe we should forget about the fixed deposits," he snapped. "You know, just let the bank keep all of Dad's hard-earned money."

Shirin's eyes narrowed. "A week after Daddy's death, and you're already talking about money? Have you no shame?"

"Wait, what?" Remy was incredulous. "You think I'm doing this for *me*? I'm trying to leave as much—"

"But of course. It's *your* money. Why do you think your father put the fixed deposits in your name instead of mine? How many men would cut out their own wives from a joint bank account?"

Remy shut his eyes. It was as if they were back to where they'd started. Where they'd always been.

"Mummy, please. Let's not do this," he said. "For what it's worth, I spoke to Kathy on my way home this evening. We both agreed that the money should stay in India. For, you know, your upkeep. I am not taking a penny with me. Okay?"

He looked at her, hoping she had not detected the lie. He didn't need Dad's money, was happy to leave it here, but he had not called Kathy today and they had certainly not discussed his parents' finances. In fact, earlier in the day, he had even contemplated having Mummy accompany him to the States when he left. That persistent hope, the immigrant's dream of braiding the disparate strands of his life together, still crackled like a fire within him. When his parents had visited him in Columbus, Remy would experience a happiness so ferocious that it felt primal. He would be overcome by a profound pleasure at the sight of his parents and his wife gathered around the dining table as they devoured Shirin's prawn fried rice and chicken Manchurian. The tug of the outside world, usually so strong, fell away, and he looked forward to coming home each evening to simply be under the same roof with the three of them—his past and his present conjoined for a few glorious weeks.

Now, Remy realized he'd dodged a bullet. The cold fact was that on every one of those trips, he and his mother would quarrel. Kathy and Dad would rise to his defense, which, in turn, made Mummy lash out even more. They were like oil and water, his mother and he, and Dad's death would not alter that equation. Remy would set up things so that she was comfortable and then go home to Kathy. Once a year, he could return to see Shirin.

"Okay, Mummy?" he repeated. "All of Daddy's money stays here."

"Yes, it's better that way," she said, in a tone that sounded like she was doing Remy a favor. "We get a much higher interest rate than you do in America."

That night, they again ate in the living room in front of the blank TV, unable to face each other across the dining table, the old, wretched formality and stiffness regrowing between them. They made desultory talk about how hot it was, how unlivable the city was becoming, before they finally lapsed into an awkward silence. After a few moments,

Remy reached for the remote and turned on the TV. He braced himself for Shirin's reproach, but she said nothing. She, too, must have realized how impossible it would be to get through the evening without this welcome distraction. He flipped through the channels and settled upon a Jackie Chan movie.

"Your daddy loved him," Shirin said, and Remy was grateful for the affection he heard in her voice.

"I know."

"What am I going to do here without him?"

The tears came to his eyes. "It's going to be a huge adjustment," he said. "I'm so sorry."

Shirin gave a sarcastic laugh. "'Sorry,' he says. Arre, if you are really sorry, you'd take your old mother back with you."

"Back where?" Remy asked, stalling for time, as if he didn't know exactly what she was suggesting.

"Where? To your big house in America, where you live with your doctor wife."

"I'm sorry," he said politely, as if he were talking to a stranger. "That's . . . It's not possible at the moment."

Mummy's lips pulled in that thin, disapproving line he remembered only too well. He tensed, ready for her recriminations, but instead she turned her head away, a profile in disappointment. On the television, Jackie Chan continued with his acrobatic ballet of violence, but neither of them watched.

TWO DAYS LATER, Remy had gone to meet the lawyer Cyrus had chosen as the executor of his will. Dina Mehta strode into the room, a tall, light-skinned woman with short curly hair and a warm smile. Her cotton sari was as impeccable and crisp as her accent. "Good to meet you, Remy," she said, peering at him over the top of her rimless glasses. "How are you? And how is your mother?"

He noticed the slight gap between Dina's front teeth as she beamed at him, the kind eyes, and took an immediate liking to her. Thank God Dad had chosen this woman as his lawyer, rather than some dull fool, like that idiot branch manager. "We're okay," he said. "You know, under the circumstances."

"Of course, of course," Dina said ruefully. "Your father was a dear man. I am still in shock. We shall all miss him terribly."

Remy's eyes filled with tears. Dina rang a bell on her desk, and a young woman appeared. "Can you get us chai, Sheila?" she said.

"You have read the will, yes?" Dina said to Remy.

"Yes, I have. I wanted to meet to see what all I need to do before I go back. I live in America," he added.

"I know that. I know all about you. Your father was very proud of you. He spoke of you often." She cleared her throat as Sheila set down the tea and left. "But before we begin, there is something we need to discuss. About my fees . . ."

Remy tensed. "I thought Dad had spelled that out in the will? Are there additional expenses?"

"No, no, no. You misunderstand. I had told Cyrus I wouldn't—" Dina broke off, then started again. "Basically, I am not charging your family the ridiculously high amount your father has specified. I had tried telling him, but he wouldn't budge. But, please, it will be my honor to help you gratis."

Remy leaned forward. "I don't understand?"

"Your father was an old family friend. When I started my own firm years ago, he was of great help to me. This is the least I can do."

Had Dad mentioned Dina's name to him? For the life of him, Remy couldn't remember.

"I hope you will convey this to your dear mother," Dina said. "I—I don't want her to be upset or worried about her financial future or anything else."

Remy heard Dina's stumble, and an unease came over him. How could this lawyer have possibly guessed Shirin's outraged reaction to the news that Dina was the executor of Cyrus's will? That Shirin had thrown a fit when she'd heard what Dina's fees would be?

"Do you . . . ? Do you know my mother?" he asked.

A quick laugh. An anxious look. "I . . . Not well. That is, we've met a few times over the years. The thing is, Cyrus and I have known each other since our college days. So naturally, I have an acquaintanceship with your mother."

A tingling started at the base of Remy's spine. Something was not adding up here.

And then his suspicion was replaced by a painful thought: *Why didn't Daddy marry someone like Dina?* Soft-spoken, warm, maternal. How different his own life would have been if he'd had Dina for a mother instead of Shirin, who was probably pacing around the house right now, awaiting his return and spoiling for a fight.

"So that's settled," Dina said. "In which case, shall we continue? I have made a list of things that we need to attend to immediately."

"Yes, of course," he said, straightening in his seat. "That's exactly what I was hoping to do."

"How long are you in Bombay? When do you leave?"

He looked her in the eye. "As soon as I possibly can," he said, enunciating each word.

She held his gaze for a minute, then nodded imperceptibly and looked away. "Understood," she said, and he thought, *She knows about my difficulties with Mummy. Daddy must've told her.*

Dina glanced at her watch.

"I'm sorry," Remy said. "Your assistant had said you'd slotted me in for a full hour."

"No, no." Dina laughed. "I was just wondering—would you like to do this over lunch? We can just go to Gaylord. My treat."

"That would be great," Remy said. "I've been running around all morning."

They crossed the street to the restaurant.

"I used to come here with my dad when I was a kid," Remy said. He looked around and was immediately comforted by the displays of chicken puffs and colorful pastries in the bakery section, the familiar sight of the uniformed waiters bustling around, the lunchtime excitement. He could almost picture his father beside him, pulling out a chair for him.

"When we would leave, Daddy always bought a cake to take home."

Dina smiled. "I know. Cyrus loved this place. He sure had a sweet tooth."

"Both my parents did." Remy smiled bashfully. "We all do."

Remy ordered the prawn curry that Daddy always got. Dina got the Waldorf salad. After the waiter had left, she sat back and looked at Remy. "So have you given any thought to your mother's care? You know, who will look after her in your absence, that kind of thing."

He cocked his head, puzzled. "Well, Mummy doesn't need looking after as such. She's pretty with it, touch wood."

"I know. But, believe me, things can change in a minute. Look at how suddenly your father took ill . . ."

Remy realized how little he knew about the woman sitting across from him. "Are you . . . ? If you don't mind me asking . . . do you have a family?"

Dina gave a short laugh. "Everybody has a family, no?"

"I mean, are you married?"

"Married? No." She smiled ruefully. "I never found the right man. Rather, the one I did was taken." She smiled again, and Remy had a strong feeling that she meant Dad. He reddened and looked away.

"Anyway," Dina continued, "I think you should make some arrangements for your mother, beta. She was used to your father managing their finances."

"What do you suggest?"

Dina looked at him thoughtfully. "You know the third-floor apartment that your dad purchased a few years ago? I manage the lease for it, and I just learned that HSBC is going to let it lapse. So the flat will be vacant soon."

"And . . . ?"

"So give it some thought. I'm not a financial planner, but it seems to me that most of Cyrus's money is in fixed assets. Interest rates are good, so why touch those? We can find a new renter immediately so that your mother has some liquid cash each month. But I'm thinking, instead of finding another corporate client, what if we lease to an individual? Maybe a family or a couple who can, you know, keep an eye on your mother, give her whatever help she may need, in exchange for a reduction in rent."

"She'll never agree to it," Remy said. "You don't know my mother. She—she can't tolerate anyone for more than a few days."

"I understand," Dina said. She sighed. "Well, then, let's just hope for the best, shall we? We'll come up with an alternative plan."

Dina ordered a malai kulfi for dessert while Remy went to the bakery and brought back two chocolate cream éclairs. "Like father, like son," Dina said with a smile.

When they were done, Dina glanced at her watch. "I'm due to appear in High Court in a half hour," she said. "Can I drop you off somewhere?"

"I'm fine. But, please, allow me to pick up the check."

"Nonsense," Dina said cheerfully. "You're my Cyrus's son. It's the least I can do."

Remy thrilled to Dina's obvious affection for his father. "Did you . . . ?" he started. "Were you and my dad ever—" He cut himself off.

Dina nodded, as if she'd been expecting the question. "No. Not really. I mean, we sort of dated when we were in college, if you can call it that. You know. I mean, we were just kids. And it was different back then. There was none of this kissy-koti stuff. It was a more formal time. A more innocent time. In any case, I left for London for my LLB immediately after graduation. And by the time I came back—well, that ship had sailed."

"I'm sorry."

To Remy's enormous relief, Dina threw back her head and laughed. "Don't be," she said. "It's all ancient history. Mostly, I am grateful for Cyrus's lifelong friendship."

"I wish he'd married someone like you instead," Remy blurted out. "You'd have made him happy."

They looked at each other, shocked. Then Dina reached over and covered Remy's hand with hers. "You must be more tolerant of your mother, dear," she said quietly. "She has had a hard life."

Before he could respond, Dina rose to her feet. "I'm so sorry. I do have to be in court. But I'll be in touch soon, I promise."

Remy walked around Churchgate after he said goodbye, slicing through the tidal wave of commuters who poured out of the railway station with the arrival of every train. He figured he'd seen more people on the street in the past half hour than he saw on the streets of Columbus in a year. The thought made him reel. How far he'd traveled in his thirty-three years! At this moment, America felt as distant as the moon, and just as luminous. Its light beckoned him home, and yet until he got his mother's finances in order, he would have to remain here, trapped in a city where he was mourning the passing away of one beloved parent, and tiptoeing through the minefield of his relationship with the other.

A man came toward him from the opposite direction, grinning broadly and waving. "Ae, Remy," the man called as he drew closer. "What a bloody coincidence! How are you, cuz?"

Remy blinked, trying to place the stranger. "Pervez?" he said at last. He hadn't seen his cousin in at least fifteen years.

"Yes, of course. The same." Pervez laughed, covering his mouth as he did. But the next instant, he looked stricken. "I'm so sorry about Cyrus Uncle," he said. "My condolences. I couldn't come to the funeral, even. Roshan and I were out of town, you see. We just got back last night."

Remy remembered the wedding invitation from a few years ago, recalled Mummy telling him not to bother with mailing a gift from America, that she and Dad would present the couple with an envelope from Remy and Kathy. "They can use the money," she'd said dryly. "Better than some useless toaster or blender."

Now, Remy looked at Pervez curiously. "And you . . . You live around here?"

"Nahi, yaar. We rent a small flat in Andheri. I can't afford to live in Churchgate! But my bank is located here. Long commute, but cannot be helped. I was just returning to work from my lunch break."

Remy swallowed, suddenly embarrassed. Dimly, he remembered a childhood birthday party at his home, to which Pervez had been invited. The boy had taken in the large, sunny flat, the pile of presents, the huge chocolate cake, and asked Cyrus, "Are you a king?" Cyrus had guffawed, while Pervez's mother, dressed in a simple white sari, had smiled and shushed her son. Remy couldn't recall Pervez being at any of his other parties.

"I'm in town for a few more weeks," he heard himself saying. "Maybe we can . . . Maybe I can visit? I'd love to meet your wife."

Pervez looked terrified. "At my apartment? No, no, boss. It's not suitable for"—a beat—"people like you."

They had parted that day with vague plans to see each other before Remy left for America. But a week later, Remy had found himself sitting in that bleak apartment, armed with an offer he was certain Pervez would not be able to refuse.

CHAPTER SEVEN

BENDING TO PICK up the letters that the postman had dropped through the slot in the door, Remy noticed that some of the floor tiles were cracked. The apartment had been immaculate in Cyrus's time; clearly, Mummy had neglected its upkeep as much as she'd neglected her own health.

He changed into his nightclothes and then, suddenly ravenous, ate the dinner Hema had prepared for him. He flipped through his mother's mail as he ate. An envelope from the electric company said FINAL NOTICE, and he frowned as he opened it.

Mummy had not paid her bill in four months. Was there not enough money in her account? But that was impossible. He'd made sure that there were ample funds in her checking account each month.

He went into his parents' bedroom and noticed a watermark, and that a chunk of the ceiling plaster was missing. The watermark looked old; why hadn't it been fixed? Remy remembered Pervez's apartment, how spiffy everything had been. He'd have to have a candid talk with Pervez and Roshan, maybe threaten to back out of his promise to leave the third-floor apartment to them. His stomach roiled at the thought of a confrontation.

He sat at his father's old desk and pulled open the drawer where Dad used to store the utility bills. There was a stack of unopened envelopes. He tore open a water bill. It, too, was unpaid. *What the hell?* he thought. It was a miracle that her utilities had not been cut off. Tomorrow, he'd take the stack to the hospital and pay bills while he sat by her bedside.

He felt around for his father's bronze letter opener in the back of the drawer, the one he'd given Daddy as a birthday gift one year. The teenaged Remy often visited his father's engineering firm during his summer vacations, sitting in Cyrus's air-conditioned office, drinking bottle after bottle of Coke. He had noticed his father slitting envelopes with his index finger; the next day, Remy had taken the bus to Cottage Industries and bought the letter opener with the carved handle. Daddy had kissed him after he'd received it, thanking Remy not only for the gift but for his thoughtfulness. Now, Remy felt the cold metal against his hand. There was an envelope atop the opener, and he pulled that out, too.

To Remy, it said. *Love, Dad.*

Remy stared at the envelope in confusion. Daddy's handwriting was so shaky it was almost unrecognizable. There was an ink stain next to Remy's name. Dad must've written it with his beloved Parker fountain pen, the one that Remy had taken back to America with him after his death. For the last three years, Remy had signed every new contract for the agency with that pen. But when had Daddy written this, and why had Mummy not given it to him?

He slit open the envelope. The first thing he noticed was the date: *Feb. 3, 2016.* So Daddy had written it a few days before he'd fallen into his coma, just before Remy had arrived to say his final goodbye. He straightened the crease and read:

> *Dear Son—*
> *I am sorry.*
> *I tried.*
> *Never cld.*
> *Be btter than me.*
> *Love forever*
> *Yours,*
> *Dad*

Remy read the note three times. What was Daddy apologizing for? For dying? What was "Never cld"? Cold? Could? Never could? I tried but never could? Never could do what? And had Daddy hidden the note in the drawer? But why would he, since it was addressed to Remy? Surely, Dad had known as he wrote it that Remy was on his way to India. So that only left Mummy. She had deprived him of his father's last communication. He would've never thought her capable of such injury. The sheer cruelty, the selfishness of this act, took his breath away.

He fell asleep that night holding his father's note to his chest. *I'll ask her tomorrow*, he thought as he drifted off to sleep. *Maybe there's a good explanation for this.*

And then he remembered: his mother had stopped speaking.

CHAPTER EIGHT

Remy reached Parsee General early the next morning. Dr. Bilimoria and his team were already in Shirin's room when he arrived, the residents shushing Remy as the doctor listened to her lungs. When Bilimoria was done, he looked up and mouthed, *No change*.

After they left, Remy got a report from the night nurse: Shirin had had a slight fever again. She was still mostly uncommunicative.

"Madam only ate one, two bites this morning," Manju said. "I tried, but what to do? She stubborn." She grabbed her purse. "Okay, sir. I will take my leave. I'll see you this evening."

"See you."

After Manju left, Remy removed Cyrus's letter and held it up to Shirin. "Mummy?" he said. "I found this in Dad's desk last night. It's addressed to me. How come I never saw it?"

For a heart-stopping moment, Shirin appeared to focus on the sheet of paper. Then her eyes went blank and a look of exhaustion came over her face. She turned her head to the wall.

That's it? Remy wanted to yell. *You're not going to react? You're not going to tell me what Daddy was trying to say?* He felt his anger spread like a slow-burning fuse, extinguishing the sympathy he'd felt toward his mother the day before.

The hours crept by slowly. Remy wrote checks for the delinquent bills, hoping the payments wouldn't arrive too late. He had wanted to pound on Pervez's door this morning and demand an explanation, but had thought better of it. He would talk to his cousin when he was less angry.

He answered a few work emails on his phone, but the connection was so slow that he gave up. The first intimation of how different this visit would be from past ones had come the night he'd arrived, when he'd stopped at a booth at the Bombay airport to get a domestic SIM card installed into his phone. On each of his previous trips to India, Cyrus had loaned him a spare phone, one of the countless ways in which he had always made Remy's visits easier. This time, there was none of the extravagant hospitality, none of the giddy joy with which Daddy had marked his arrival. No one had filled the freezer with packs of ice cream and kulfi; no one had brought home a box of freshly baked chicken patties, a snack Remy couldn't find in America. On this trip, only disappointment awaited him at every turn—first, the blow that Monaz had delivered, and now, this unexpected detour to the hospital.

At lunchtime, a server brought in Shirin's tray. Remy lifted the lid. Baked fish and insipid-looking French beans. Red Jell-O for dessert.

"Mummy," he said, shaking her lightly. "Wake up. Time to eat."

He raised her bed, then cut the fish into minuscule portions and held up a forkful to her mouth. Shirin pursed her lips. "Come," he cajoled, trying to gently pry her mouth open, his thumb on her chin. "Come, Mama. You have to eat *something*."

She held her mouth shut. *Skin and bone, and amazingly, she can still fight*, he thought. He eyed the Jell-O. "You want some jelly?" he asked. "You love jelly, right?"

"Kokh," Shirin said. "Kokh."

There was that word again. Shirin's voice sounded creaky, like a door that was being opened after a hundred years. But he could see in her eyes the effort she was making to enunciate.

Kokh. Remy repeated the word out loud: "Kokh?"

Coke. She was asking for Coke?

"Coke?" he said. "You want a Coke?"

An imperceptible nod, so slight that he might have imagined it. But something else: A new light in her eyes. Relief on her face. A connection. He had guessed right. A small triumph.

"I'll be back in a jiffy," he said. He leapt to his feet, glad to do something for her, but also relieved to get away from her bedside.

He walked to the nurses' station. "Excuse me, sister," he said, remembering the manner in which they addressed nurses here. "Is there a cafeteria or store nearby that sells soft drinks?"

The woman looked up at him. "For you, sir?"

"No. For my mother. Shirin Wadia? I . . . She asked for a Coke."

The nurse looked beyond his shoulder. "Dr. Bilimoria, sir," she called. "The patient's relation has a question, sir."

Remy frowned. Why the hell would she trouble the doctor to give directions to the store?

"You again," Bilimoria said, but he softened his words with a grin. "What is it now?"

Before Remy could reply, the nurse interjected, "Sir, he wants to give his patient a Coca-Cola. I just wanted you to give permission, sir."

"Coca-Cola?" Bilimoria peered at him. "Where is the nutrition in that? If she's drinking, let's give her Complan or Ensure."

"You don't understand. She specifically asked for Coke."

"She spoke to you?" Bilimoria said.

"She did."

"But it is not good for her health."

Remy glared at the doctor. "My mother has been unresponsive until now," he said. "Why can't I give her the one thing she asks for?"

His voice must've been louder than he'd realized, because heads turned. *Control yourself*, Remy said to himself. His right hand was shaking so badly he shoved it into the pocket of his jeans. But he kept his eyes locked on the doctor's face, wanting to stand his ground.

"Okay. Do what you think is right." Bilimoria shrugged. "Just don't overdo it," he said over his shoulder as he walked away.

The nurse gave Remy an earful about how nobody dared to speak to Dr. Bilimoria as rudely as he had. But he caught little of it, because another truth was ringing in his ears: he would never have a Hollywood-style reconciliation with his mother. Still, he vowed to himself, in the short time that he was here, he would make himself useful. He would indulge her, spoil her, atone for the fact that he had stayed away for the past three years and let her fall into this decrepit state.

And he'd do his best to get her to tell him why Daddy had written that letter.

As REMY WALKED toward the store, he grinned as he recalled how he and Mummy used to sneak in cold drinks behind Cyrus's disapproving back. He had long since quit drinking soda; his mother obviously hadn't.

He remembered how, when he was six, he had insisted on celebrating the three-month anniversary of his birthday. Cyrus tried to explain that that wasn't how it worked, that one didn't have anniversaries of birthdays, but Remy was insistent. Usually he was an obedient, well-behaved child, but choking on the injustice of having to wait all year for another birthday, he'd thrown a fit and demanded another chocolate cake. It embarrassed him now to think of it.

Finally, Cyrus relented and brought home a small cake. Shirin made chicken sandwiches and stuck two cans of Coke in the freezer. That afternoon, she pushed back the couch and chairs and spread a quilt on the living room floor. The three of them sat there, feasting on sandwiches and macaroni salad, Remy and Shirin drinking their Cokes while Cyrus sipped his beer. Shirin affixed six candles to the cake, and his parents sang "Happy Birthday" to him for the second time in three months.

Remy smiled. None of his friends had had such indulgent parents. Jango, he suspected, would've been greeted with a slap if he'd had a similar meltdown and asked for a second birthday celebration. Mummy and Daddy had been great in that way. There had been many such sweet moments in his childhood, and some of them had involved his mother. Why, then, did he not remember them as well as he did the sad occasions?

He made his way to the main road and was transfixed by the sight of a shirtless construction worker swinging an axe to break up rocks for a nearby building project. *How can a city filled with forklifts and bulldozers also rely on a tool this crude?* Remy wondered. But this was the essence of Bombay, this city of duality and wild contradictions, of skyscraper and slum. Chalta hai. It was a phrase with which every Bombayite—although he supposed he should refer to the city's inhabitants as Mumbaikars now—was familiar. Chalta hai. It'll do. Or anything goes. If ever there was an informal slogan for the city, this was it. Thus, a scrawny man harnessed all of his strength to smash rock with an axe while two feet away, a portly man sat at the traffic light in his silver Mercedes-Benz. As Remy watched, a construction worker in a blue sari swept the rocks into a metal bowl that she balanced on her head and carried to where a new, gleaming skyscraper was going up, each apartment selling for millions. She swayed as she walked, as graceful as any high-priced model on the catwalk. Turning his head, Remy noticed a stray dog sitting smack-dab in the middle of the street, forcing cars to go around it. *Bombay*, Remy thought, *where even the dogs have attitude.*

Remy thought of Roger, who Kathy had brought home four months ago. The dog had belonged to one of her patients, a three-year-old boy with Tay-Sachs disease. After the boy's death, his distraught parents had mentioned that they were giving Roger away, because he was running around the house searching for his young companion and they found the animal's grief unbearable.

"I don't understand," Remy had said. "I would think they'd want to hold on to the dog. Because, you know, he belonged to their son."

Kathy's eyes were cloudy. "Grief distorts thinking," she'd said. "The dog's pain reminded them of their own loss. In any case, I couldn't bear the thought of the poor thing going to the pound. Do you mind?"

Of course, he didn't mind. Kathy's kindness and generosity reminded him of his own parents'. Cyrus would've done the same thing. Shirin had spent years feeding the street dogs in their neighborhood each evening, despite the complaints of their neighbors. "Wah," their ground-floor neighbor had once grumbled to Remy, "these animals eat better than I do. Chicken, eggs . . . wah."

At a little cake shop, he purchased two cans of Coke for Shirin and bottled water for himself. He was about to pay when he spotted the tray of jelly rolls, and he remembered how his mother had bought him a slice every time they walked past their neighborhood bakery. In her own scattershot way, Mummy had tried to spoil him and love him. *And now it's your turn*, he said to himself, *to set aside old animosities.* This is how he'd communicate with her: in the language of sugar. He would pull out all the stops before he left; he would lavish time, attention, and sweets on her and hope that she would know that, despite everything, he cared.

"I'll take a slice of the jelly roll," he said.

As he headed back to the hospital, Remy remembered again that he still needed to call Dina Mehta. Maybe he should see if she was free for a visit this evening? He hesitated. He liked Dina, but what he really wanted to do tonight was see Jango and Shenaz, assure them that he didn't hold Monaz's change of heart against them. Jango Dalal was his oldest friend, the yin to his yang. Remy had been an artistic, dreamy child, scribbling his poems in the margins of his schoolbooks, and even in second grade Jango had been tall and broad-shouldered, a bruiser of a kid. Even though he was the new boy in school, Jango had taken it upon himself to protect Remy from his teasing classmates.

If he returned to his apartment, Pervez would invite him for supper, and he didn't want to spend the evening with him and Roshan, angry as he was about the unpaid bills and their overall neglect of Shirin. The fact was, he had little in common with them. Roshan had grown up in small-town Nasik and had gone to a Gujarati medium school. Pervez still had a chip on his shoulder about growing up poor and made up for it by constantly talking about the success of his toy company. Remy needed to spend the evening with old friends, people with whom he shared history and memories and cultural references. Nepean Sea Road kids. Cathedral School alumni. If that made him a snob, so be it.

He dialed Jango's number as he entered the hospital gates.

"Hey, it's me."

"Remy, what's up, man? How is Mum?"

"She's okay. About the same."

"Shit. Sorry. What a turn of events!"

"Yup." Remy cleared his throat. "Anyway, listen. I just wanted to ask—any chance you'd be free some evening this week?"

Jango spoke before he could finish. "What about tonight? Can you come for dinner?"

Remy looked up to the sky in gratitude. "I'd love to. But are you sure I won't be disturbing? Why don't you check with Shenaz and—"

"Oof. Enough of this formality, yaar. America has ruined you, I say. It's just dinner, Remy, not a marriage proposal."

Remy grinned. "What time?"

"Eight? Eight thirty? What do you want the cook to make?"

"Jango," Remy said happily, "I don't care what we eat. I . . . just . . . I'll be happy to see you. All I ask is that you pour me a Scotch."

"Done. See you soon. Come hungry."

A YOUNG MAN was mopping the floors with phenyl when Remy reentered the hospital, and he covered his nose against the familiar musty smell as he went up the stairs.

Shirin was wheezing in her sleep. *She would be more comfortable if they gave her supplemental oxygen*, Remy thought, eyeing the gas cylinder in the corner. He would ask the doctor tomorrow. He pulled up a chair and studied her face and felt a sensation at the base of his throat, which spread to his chest. He examined the sensation and gave it a name: love. Now that Mummy was in this weakened condition, she had lost her ability to hurt him. The wariness that he'd felt around her for most of his life fell away. In its place, there was finally room for love.

He stared unseeingly out of the room and into the hallway, full of grief. When he looked at her again, her eyes were open and she was gazing at him. "You awake, Mummy?" he said, faking good cheer. "Excellent. Your Coke is waiting for you."

He raised the hospital bed, adjusted her pillow, then opened a can and stuck a straw in it. He held the straw to her lips. "Sip, Mummy," he coaxed. "No, no, you have to suck in . . . *In*, not *out* . . . That's better. Can you taste it?"

She took a few sips, and it was obvious that even this effort exhausted her. Then she signaled to him with her eyes, the slightest flutter of the eyelids, and he knew to remove the straw from her lips.

"Mummy, look what I found at the bakery. A jelly roll. Remember how you used to buy me a slice every time we went out? Would you like a bite?"

He broke off a small piece and held it to her lips, which remained shut. He felt a sudden urge to force her to try it, hoping that the taste would ignite a memory, act as a kind of communion between them, a signal from the present to the past. That hope must have made him press harder, because Shirin turned her head away and made a loud, terrible bleating sound that made Remy's hair stand up.

"Mummy, it's okay," he cried. "You don't have to eat it. I'm sorry. God. Please, stop."

He put his hand on Shirin's bony shoulders, but she kept shaking her head and making that sound. Remy was stunned. Did she also have some kind of dementia? What else would explain such odd behavior? He tossed the slice into the trash can. "There. See? It's gone."

As if he'd flipped a switch, the wailing stopped. The agitation drained out of Shirin's body, and once again, her eyes were blank as they rested on Remy's face. He bit his lower lip, trying to regain his composure, telling himself not to take the rejection personally. But he felt none of the tenderness he'd felt earlier, and couldn't escape the feeling of her pushing him away as inexplicably as she had in his boyhood.

When he spoke, his voice was stiff. "You'll just have to tell me what you want in the future. Okay, Mummy? Okay?"

She looked at him, motionless, expressionless. It was as if she were sleeping with her eyes open.

He stayed at the hospital until Manju came at seven.

"Has she done the pee?" Manju asked as soon as she arrived.

"I think so. The . . . They were in here a couple of hours ago and changed the diaper."

"Good." Manju opened a cloth bag and pulled out a fresh coconut, flipped it into a glass, and let the water drain. "I bring this every evening for madam," she said. "It is good for health. It is from our own trees."

"Your own trees?"

"Yes, sir. I live in Malad. Faraway suburb. But we have a small plot with coconut trees."

"You carry this in all the way from Malad? How long does it take you to get here?"

"Almost two hours, each way. I catch the auto rickshaw to the railway station and then take a train and a bus. Then I walk here." She smiled at the look on Remy's face. "Don't worry, sir. I am used to it."

"Well, thank you. But I must start paying you for the coconuts."

"No, no, sir. Why to charge for something that grows free?"

"Thank you again." Remy looked at his watch. "Well, I think I will get going. It's been a long day. Are you . . . ? May I give you my phone number? If you need something at any time, please call."

"No problem, sir. You go peaceful. I take honest care of your mother. You keep no tension."

"Thank you."

He kissed his mother goodbye.

"One question, sir," Manju said. "You are living close to the New York?"

"No, not really. It's about a nine-hour drive from Ohio. Why?"

Manju looked around the room furtively, then riffled through her purse. She removed a bundle of hundred-rupee notes, tied together with a rubber band. "I have a brother," she whispered. "He lives in the New York. But he . . . He is white."

"What?" Remy said, puzzled.

The woman moved closer to him. "He is working in a restaurant there . . . How you say? . . . Like the ghost. Without the papers."

"Ah." Remy nodded. White . . . like a ghost. Which, if he was illegal, he may as well be. As far as most Americans were concerned, their food was planted, harvested, and cooked by invisible hands. By ghosts. "The correct word is 'illegal,' Manju," he said.

"No, no, no, sir," she said, shaking her head. "How can that be? I was there when he was born in our hut. I was nine years old—I helped with the delivery. He is cent percent legal."

Remy swallowed, moved by Manju's earnest indignation. She was right. *What a thing*, he thought, *to refer to a human being as "illegal."* But the gulf between them was too wide—the politics of immigration, the legalities of US jurisprudence, the xenophobia that had gripped the country—too difficult to explain. "I understand," he said. "But why do you ask?"

"I want to send Sunil some money, sir," she said. "But how? I saved for one full year. What if my money is getting stolen?" She waved the bundle of notes toward Remy.

He looked at the bills. A big sum of money for her, the result of sacrifice and thrift. But converted into US dollars, it was a pittance. "Keep it," he said. "Before I leave, give me a phone number for him. I . . . I'll figure out a way to get him some cash. I'll make sure he gets it. Okay?"

He gathered his things, ignoring Manju's fervent thanks and blessings. It would cost him so little to help this "white" boy. He could even send him a few hundred dollars each month and barely notice its absence. Remy's own path to citizenship had been easy, but he could imagine the obstacles this poor, uneducated boy was facing: Moving from one roach-infested apartment to another. Lying awake at night, mute with homesickness or fear at being nabbed in a workplace raid. Bearing the inevitable racial taunts on the streets. Being exploited, humiliated, unable to ask for a raise from his Indian or Pakistani bosses, who would hold the threat of deportation over him. Unable to enjoy the glories of New York—the magnificence of Carnegie Hall and Grand Central Station, the expansiveness of Central Park, even the carnival glitz of Times Square. Manju was right. Her brother would move through the streets of Manhattan as an apparition—unseen, unnoticed—if he was lucky.

"Good night," he said. "I'll see both of you in the morning."

Maybe Kathy and he could visit New York later in the year and look up Manju's brother, Remy thought as he searched for a cab. Back home, in their cosseted life on their cul-de-sac, it was easy to pretend that life in the US was pretty and benevolent; hearing a story like Sunil's blew open that myth, laid bare the fact that the comfort and luxuries enjoyed by the few—the fancy restaurants, the manicured lawns, the beautiful monuments, the movable feasts, the supermarkets fat with bacon and cheese and gourmet breads—were built on the backs of brown-skinned ghosts.

And even though the particulars were different, it was the same story in India, of course. The lives of the Indian upper-middle class were made possible by the callused, exhausted hands of the working poor—hands that swept floors and kneaded bread and tilled the earth and washed cars and cleaned shit and pampered the flesh of the rich. Except these hands belonged not to foreigners, but to fellow citizens.

He got into a cab and stared out the window. For a second, his vision went cloudy and the dust and the sun and the crowds disappeared. Instead, he saw the bleached bones of the city, saw them crack under the weight of all the secrets and stories they had to carry.

BACK AT THE APARTMENT, Remy removed Cyrus's letter from his pocket and reread it. The words now took on a different meaning than they had the night before. *I am sorry. I tried*, Cyrus had written.

Daddy had scribbled this note with his last ounce of strength. Knowing him, he was apologizing for not being able to greet Remy at the airport as he'd always done, for taking to his deathbed before his beloved son made it to India. Poor man. He had probably placed the letter in his desk, sure that either Remy or Shirin would find it. Maybe Mummy had not even known about its existence, tucked away as it was at the far end of the drawer. After three years, who knew if she'd even remember its provenance?

Remy ran his finger over the *Love forever*, and then placed the letter in the zipped section of his suitcase. He would carry his father's final words back to America with him. Maybe it was just as well that his father's message would remain a mystery. Love itself was a mystery, wasn't it? By all accounts, he should've been closer to his mom than his dad. And yet Remy's bond with his father had been unassailable.

He glanced at the clock and decided to take a quick shower. He wished he could go for an evening run to clear his mind, but he'd be late for dinner at Jango's. If he could find the time in the next few days, he would go jogging at Priyadarshini, the beautiful nearby park that overlooked the sea.

CHAPTER NINE

———→———

JANGO REMEMBERED THE way Remy liked his Scotch—on the rocks, with a dash of soda. Remy took an appreciative sip. "You could be a bartender, yaar. This is excellent."

"Yeah, right. In my ample spare time."

Jango had started out as an actor but had soon switched to working behind the camera. Remy was a little unsure as to what he did exactly these days.

Remy looked around the enormous living room. "So why isn't Shenaz here? Where is she?"

"I told you. It's a surprise." Jango glanced at the clock. "She will be back soon."

Remy took another sip of his drink, feeling more like himself for the first time since he'd arrived in Bombay. He exhaled, getting rid of the tension in his shoulders.

"Saala, you're as skinny as ever," Jango said. "Does Kathy starve you or what?"

"Well, Kathy's pretty health-conscious. We have a protein shake for breakfast and a salad with dinner every evening."

Jango made a sound of mock disgust. "How terrible, yaar. Imagine, chewing on lettuce like a bloody goat when you could have a nice fried batata vada or a juicy mutton chop. I'm telling you: divorce Kathy, and I'll get you married to a plump, semiliterate, voluptuous Parsi bhen from Udvada."

Remy sputtered Scotch onto his shirt. "Look what you've made me do."

"Ae, fucker, don't blame me. Blame that boner you have at the thought of that sexy Parsi chickadee."

Remy burst out laughing. "God, Jango. You haven't changed a bit. Same wretched third-grade humor."

Jango sat back and smiled affectionately. "Just trying to cheer you up, my Remy. What a couple of days you've had. Bad news upon bad news. Shenaz feels awful for what her idiot niece did to you."

"She shouldn't. We know you guys had our interests at heart." He hesitated. "One lesson I've learned, Jango: If something is not meant to be, you shouldn't fight it. Because if you do, you may not like the outcome."

"Glad one of us has become wise with age, yaar. For me, it all gets more confusing the older I get." Jango fell silent. "So how do you find Bombay? It's a fucking madhouse, no?"

The front door opened, and Shenaz walked in.

"Remy," Shenaz cried. "Hi, darling. I'm so sorry to hear about Shirin Auntie. How are you, my love?" She set down the paper bag and flung open her arms. They hugged a long time and only broke apart when Jango interjected, "Okay, you two. Break it up before Remy gets another hard-on."

"Jahangir," Shenaz said. "You are shameless." She was the only person who called Jango by his real name. She took a pink cake box from the bag and presented it to Remy. "Chocolate cake from La Patisserie. Your favorite."

"Oh, Shenaz. *That's* where you went? To the Taj?"

"Of course. I wanted to do it on the first night you arrived, but I knew you'd be too tired to enjoy."

Remy found himself on the verge of tears, the events of the last forty-eight hours finally catching up with him. Pervez and Roshan were family, but they were not friends. Mummy was family, but being so nonresponsive she was almost corpselike. Bombay felt empty without Daddy in it. But to be with Jango and Shenaz felt like a homecoming. "Thank you," he whispered. "I'm so overwhelmed."

Shenaz beamed. "Oh, come on, Remy," she said. "It's such a small thing."

"Yeah, stop this bullshit," Jango said, picking up Remy's glass to replenish it. "Don't worry. You're not here with your American wife, where you have to be all polite." Jango switched to a falsetto: "'Oh, thank you, my darling. Oh, pardon me, my dear.'"

"He's as crazy as ever." Remy laughed. "Still crazy after all these years."

Shenaz rolled her eyes. "What else is new? Okay, you ready to eat? I've made your favorites—dhansak and papdi with mutton. And, oh, fried Bombay ducks on the side."

Remy groaned, pretended to clutch his chest. "Shenaz, will you run away with me?"

With the generous table spread out before them, Shenaz said, "Oh, by the way, I hope you don't mind—I gave Monaz your mom's address. She wants to drop you a card." She shook her head. "I'm still ready to kill her for what she did."

"Don't," Remy said, taking Shenaz's hand in his. "I mean, this is good news, right? That she will marry her boyfriend?"

"Boyfriend? Ha! They hardly know each other. Still, I guess it's a good thing. Otherwise, I would've lived the rest of my life in fear of my older brother finding out."

Remy looked at her curiously. "You mean you'd have never told him? About his grandchild?"

"Remy, you've lived abroad for too long. You've forgotten how conservative this country is when it comes to sex and all. Phiroz would've disowned Monaz for sure."

"But won't he anyway? For marrying a non-Parsi?"

"Who knows? Maybe he'll come around, once the baby is born." She shook her head. "Okay, enough. Let's talk about something more cheerful."

Remy noticed that Jango kept his arm around his wife for the rest of the evening; he was a jokester, but he was fierce in the care of those he loved. He was very much like Dad in that regard.

REMY WALKED THE few blocks home from Jango's. He was astonished by the amount of traffic even at that hour. *The city that never sleeps*, he thought. *Take that, Frank Sinatra.*

It was a nice night, cool and breezy, a crescent moon in the sky. *What is Mummy doing right now?* he wondered. *Can she see the moon from her hospital bed?* He felt a shivering loneliness and wished they were on the balcony of their apartment, looking up at the sky together. His reaction surprised him; he couldn't remember ever having had such a desire before. But, of course, the feeling was new because this version of Mummy was new—bedridden and defanged. He could love her now, in the way one loved small, harmless things.

But do *you love her?* Remy asked himself as he walked. *Or is this some weird combination of pity and guilt?*

He dodged the scooter coming toward him and decided that it didn't matter. Love, pity, sympathy, tenderness—these were just words. What counted was action, the fact of his physical presence. What mattered was that he was here and that he was willing to help her. He was in Bombay tonight, looking up at the lights of the buildings he passed, each apartment a rectangle of individual family sagas. How many of the people in these rectangles led happy lives? How many were lucky enough to be free of money problems, as he was? How many had marriages as wonderful as his own? How many of them had married their best friend, as he had? Not too many.

Of course, there were unhappy people everywhere on earth, and if you catalogued all their griefs and disappointments, every place could be considered a museum of failures. One could argue that this was the universal human condition. But Remy sensed a special brand of sadness in Bombay. You expected the poor to be burdened: the servants and the migrant workers, the farmers and the ragpickers, the masses desperate to make ends meet. But here, even his parents, who'd had everything going for them—good looks, money, education—had seemed as miserable as those with nothing to call their own.

Oh, bullshit, Remy chided himself. *Take Jango and Shenaz. They seem perfectly content and in love.*

He walked on, arguing with himself. What about Pervez and Roshan? They seemed happy enough, and they'd certainly overcome their humble beginnings, thanks to him. But he didn't want to think about that right now.

He reached the building, sweaty from the walk. He rode the elevator and let himself in the apartment. For a moment, he stood still in the silent dark. In that moment, he felt acutely the absence of his father and mother, and had to remind himself that only one of them was dead, that his mother was a mere cab ride away and that he'd see her in the morning, armed with a fresh supply of Coke.

CHAPTER TEN

REMY LOOKED OUT at the early morning sky, trying to piece together the fragments of his dream. After a few minutes, he gave up, but he kept tracing the path of the sun. Of all natural phenomena, sunrise was the most predictable and yet, he believed, the most extraordinary. Dawn was the miracle that made every other miracle possible, but it was also the one that humans took most for granted. Millions of people literally slept through life's greatest magic show. In Bombay, the orb burned as bright as a nugget of gold, whereas in Ohio it often hid behind cloud cover, like a wedding ring one had misplaced somewhere in the house.

He called Kathy and caught her up, then took a shower. When he came out, the house phone was ringing. It was Pervez, checking to see if he needed anything. He detected a slight stiffness in his cousin's voice and knew that he was offended that Remy had not spent the previous evening with him and Roshan. To appease him, Remy invited them out to dinner that night. It would be better to talk about difficult matters in a neutral atmosphere, how they needed to step up their game after he left.

He was getting ready to leave for the hospital when the doorbell rang. *That must be Hema,* he thought. *Why hadn't she used the house key?* But it was a scared-looking Monaz who stood in the hallway.

"Oh, hi," he stammered. "What are you doing here? How did you—"

"Sorry, Remy Uncle," the girl said. "I got your address from Shenazfui. Can I please come in? I just need two minutes of your time."

Is it prudent to be alone in the apartment with a strange girl? Remy thought. But even as he stood blocking her way, Monaz's face grew teary. *Oh, hell, she is a mere child, a girl in distress. How can you turn her away?*

He stepped aside to let her in, and she sat down on the couch.

"You want something to drink? Something to eat?"

"No, no, I'm okay, uncle." She looked up at him, and her eyes were large and pleading. "I just need a favor. You see, I told Gaurav about you yesterday. And he—he's insisting on meeting you."

"Meeting me? Whatever for?" Remy looked around the room helplessly. "I . . . Monaz, I'm not trying to be rude, but now that the adoption is off, I have no role to play in your life. My mother is in the hospital, and that's where I'm needed. I'm sorry, but—"

"You don't understand," Monaz cried. "Gaurav wants to talk to you. I don't know why. But he says he won't tell his parents about us until he's met with you." Her face scrunched up. "Please, Remy Uncle. Please. Just meet with him. As a favor to me."

Remy knew he should call Shenaz and ask her to intervene. But Shenaz would be mortified by her niece's cluelessness, and he wanted to spare her the embarrassment. "Monaz," he tried again. "I really don't have the time."

"It will just take fifteen minutes or so. Gaurav is so close by, only."

"Where is he?" he asked wearily.

Monaz leaned forward. "He's waiting at Café Strand. It's a two-minute walk from here. Please. This won't take long. Please. I beg you."

Remy sighed. "Fine," he said.

AT THE CAFÉ, Gaurav Advani pushed his mirrored sunglasses onto his head as he stood to greet Remy. "Hi, uncle," he said. "Thanks for taking the meeting."

Taking the meeting? Remy thought. *What is he? Some Hollywood mogul?*

"I only have a few minutes," he said curtly.

"No problem," Gaurav said. He turned to Monaz. "You go on to college," he said. "I'll meet up with you later, okay?"

Monaz looked as surprised as Remy felt. "I'm not staying?" she said.

Gaurav smiled. "There's no need. You don't need to miss your classes. This is a man-to-man talk."

The girl looked uncertainly at Remy, who felt a sudden, overwhelming protectiveness toward her. "Let me give you my phone number," he said to her. "Call if you need anything." He didn't like the way Gaurav had dismissed Monaz. He would make sure that Gaurav saw that Monaz had his support.

"What will you take, uncle?" Gaurav said after they settled into the booth. "Breakfast? A cold drink?"

"I'll have a coffee," Remy said. "Black."

Gaurav grinned. "Americans drink their coffee black," he said to no one in particular. He snapped his fingers to draw the waiter's attention, and the gesture was so arrogant that Remy felt an unexpected revulsion. He knew Gaurav's type, had gone to college with young men who smoked their foreign cigarettes and drove their foreign cars, all paid for by their daddies. He felt sorry for Monaz, that she was going to marry someone so obviously entitled and rude.

"Monaz said you wanted to see me?" Remy said. "How can I help you?"

Gaurav waited until the waiter had served them. "I did," he said. "You see, when I approached Monaz a few days ago and offered to marry her, I had no idea she had an arrangement with you to adopt the baby, uncle. The silly girl conveniently forgot to mention this important detail to me."

"And . . . ?"

Gaurav lit a Dunhill. "So, uncle, if there is a solution to this mess she got herself in, why should I get involved? I just wanted to meet with the man who will be raising my baby in America."

Remy felt a slow anger travel through his body. "'Why should I get involved?'" he repeated. "Because you're the one who got her pregnant."

Gaurav looked surprised, and Remy realized that he had expected a different reaction—gratitude, maybe? The young man opened his mouth to speak, but Remy cut him off. "Do you not wish to marry Monaz? Do you not love her?"

"Love her? Arre, Remy Uncle, how can I love her? I hardly know her. We met, what? Three or four times before we . . . y'know."

"Before you had sex? With a girl you had no feelings for?" Remy heard the contempt in his voice, and he assumed Gaurav did, too.

"Please don't lecture me," Gaurav said. "I . . . I was trying to do the right thing by your niece, but—"

"She's not my niece."

"Yeah, okay, whatever. All you Parsis are related in one way or the other, isn't it? What with the inbreeding and all."

"Wow," Remy said. "Wow. You are some piece of work." He would

beg Shenaz to intervene if Monaz was crazy enough to insist on marrying this guy.

"Sorry."

Remy controlled his temper. "How do you think your parents
would react to Monaz, if you introduce her?"

Gaurav frowned. "Not well. My father is a real estate developer.
He . . . I think . . . He wanted a *suitable* match for me. Someone from
our own community, you know? Monaz's parents . . . I don't think
they are wealthy."

Remy felt a rising sense of panic. "Who's in your family?" he said.

"I have my parents, my grandfather, and four older brothers. Three
of them are married, and they and their wives live with us. A joint
family system. We are Sindhis, so we have our own customs and ways.
Monaz, being a Parsi, will have to adjust. If I'm forced to marry her,
that is."

Remy could see the future that awaited Monaz as clearly as if he
were watching it unfold on a screen: A haughty, disapproving father-
in-law, territorial fights with the sisters-in-law, a husband who stayed
out late and thought he was entitled to an affair or two to compensate
for his loveless marriage. Monaz would end up one of those nervous,
obsessive women whose life revolved around her child, a half-Parsi
child who would never be treated as an equal in their household.

"And if my wife and I agreed to adopt the baby," he said slowly,
"would you concede all rights?"

Gaurav grinned happily. "Definitely," he said. He ran his fingers
through his thick hair. "You have to understand, uncle. I'm only twen-
ty-one years old. I'm not ready to settle down. My whole life is going
to be disrupted if I get saddled with a child."

"Next time, use a goddamn condom."

Gaurav flinched. After a moment, he asked, "So, uncle, are you still
interested in taking the baby to America?"

"Maybe. I need to talk to my wife. And to Monaz, naturally. But I will have a lawyer draw up an ironclad contract saying that you relinquish all rights."

Now that it appeared as if he might have his way, Gaurav's demeanor changed. "Sure, sure. Whatever you need, uncle. The only thing is, I don't want my parents to find out."

They won't, Remy thought. *If we end up adopting the baby, you'll never hear from us again.*

"So what are you going to tell Monaz?" Remy finally asked. "She— she seems to think she loves you."

"Oof. That crazy girl. She's been pestering me ever since she found out about the pregnancy. If she had known earlier, I would've gladly paid for an abortion."

Remy knew he had to leave before his distaste for this boy showed on his face or he said something that would make Gaurav change his mind. He got to his feet, took out some bills from his wallet, ignored Gaurav's "No, no, no, I got this," and placed the money on the table. "You can pay for my coffee," he said. "This is just for the tip."

As he could've predicted, Gaurav said, "It's too much."

"That's okay," Remy said. "I can afford it." He turned to leave, then stopped. "You need to talk to Monaz yourself. This is *your* responsibility, you understand? And be gentle with her. You have done enough damage as it is. Do you get me?"

He waited until Gaurav nodded. "Got it," he said sullenly.

Remy didn't know he'd been holding his breath. "Okay. If Monaz still wants to pursue the adoption, it will be her choice. But if she does, I'm serious about you signing a contract. That's the only way I will get involved. Are we clear on this?"

Again, Gaurav nodded, displaying none of the earlier cockiness.

Remy resisted the urge to feel sympathy for him. "You'd better rehearse how you're going to approach Monaz," he said. "Break the news gently," he reiterated. "She—she has family who cares very much about her." He straightened. "I'm one of them. You said it yourself—all of us Parsis are related one way or the other."

"Okay, uncle," Gaurav muttered. "Nice meeting you. Good luck with everything."

A DISORIENTED REMY stood on the sidewalk outside the restaurant, overwhelmed by the sudden turn of events. Most of all, he was stunned by his own ferociousness, the way he'd talked to Gaurav, and the almost paternal protectiveness he'd felt for Monaz. He watched distractedly as a motorcycle carrying a family of five—a little boy standing in front of his father, two children riding pillion, squished between their parents, the wife with her arms around her husband's waist—sped past him, weaving in and out of traffic. He felt like he was the only person standing still in this dizzying, mad metropolis of millions.

He felt breathless as it hit him: he and Kathy might become parents after all. If Gaurav refused to marry Monaz, she might have no recourse other than to give up her baby for adoption. Surely, the girl would not change her mind a second time? Hope lit up within him. But hope was dangerous and premature. In order to squelch it, Remy reminded himself that Monaz was going to be devastated, bereft not just of the man she thought she loved—a man who was unworthy of her, although she was too naïve and inexperienced to know this—but also of the baby she was carrying.

Yeah, Remy thought. *There is no room for hope in the museum of failures. Even if it hangs on the walls for a moment, it usually comes crashing down.*

CHAPTER ELEVEN

———————

AT THE HOSPITAL, Remy told his mother that Jango and Shenaz had sent their best wishes, but Shirin showed no sign of recognition. He managed to get her to take two bites of the yellow daal and rice at lunch, but Shirin kept chewing until he told her to stop and swallow. To his surprise, she did. He pulled out a slice of the chocolate cake that Shenaz had sent home with him last evening. "Try this, Mummy," he said. "You remember La Patisserie at the Taj, right? Where you used to buy my birthday cake every year?"

Was that a flicker of interest in her eyes? He couldn't be sure. He took out a small morsel with the fork and touched it to her lips. The tip of her tongue darted out, and then she opened her mouth a tiny bit, looking for all the world like a baby bird. Eagerly, he gave her another forkful. He looked up to the ceiling to give thanks, knew that he would remember this moment.

"Remember that strawberry cake you once ordered for my twelfth birthday, Mummy? And how Temul's grandson put his entire hand in it? I was so angry that day. But I consoled myself with your fabulous chicken sandwiches. I tell you, I still miss them."

Shirin's hand fluttered on her chest, and she mumbled something. "What, Mama?" he said. "What did you say?" He put his hand on hers and felt the congestion in her lungs.

When Shirin spoke, he could see the brown of the chocolate on her tongue. "I . . . make . . . for . . . you."

Had he heard her right? "Thank you, Mummy," he said finally. "That's a promise. When you're feeling better, you make them for me, okay?"

Shirin took two more bites of the cake and then turned her head. Already, he knew to stop. "I'll put the rest of it in the fridge. You can have more later."

By the time he returned from the common room, Shirin was fast asleep.

HE STEPPED OUT into the hallway as soon as he heard the heightened buzz that announced that a doctor was rounding. How quickly he had adapted to the rhythms of hospital life. He waited impatiently as Dr. Bilimoria's team visited the man in the next room. When the doctor emerged, Remy strode up to him, ignoring his startled look.

"She ate," he said triumphantly. "And—and she spoke to me. I swear, she did."

Bilimoria seemed unimpressed. "Good. What did she eat?"

"I . . . A few bites of chocolate cake."

"She needs to eat nutritious food," Bilimoria said, emphasizing each word. "Not empty calories. Part of the reason she's not bouncing back is generalized weakness."

Remy heard the judgment in Bilimoria's voice. He stared at the older man helplessly, unable to explain the significance of the event, how it had allowed him to share a rare, sweet moment with his mother. Jubilation flattened into shame.

Bilimoria turned to a nurse. "So how was the patient overnight? Any fevers? Oxygen level stable?"

Remy felt redundant and foolish as they studied Shirin's chart. How did a few crumbs of chocolate cake measure against details about Mummy's oxygen level and whether her lungs were clear?

He watched from the doorway as Bilimoria woke up Shirin and listened to her heart and lungs. His mother lay there, eyes open but unresponsive.

Bilimoria walked into the hallway and snapped at a nurse. "Is someone making her sit up in a chair and walk every day? Staying in bed will only fill up her lungs with fluid. And even in bed, is someone making her change positions every two hours or so?" He looked at Remy. "You should remind the night nurse to do this, all right? Very important to avoid bedsores. Also, encourage her to get her out of bed each day. At the very least, to do soo-soo and potty."

Remy flushed. Why had he forgotten to check for bedsores? When Dad was dying, he and his mother had been diligent about turning him.

"Is there any progress, Doctor?" he asked. "Any improvement?"

"Her lungs are still congested. But there was no fever last night, which is good news." Bilimoria gave him a curt nod and turned away, then stopped. "It's good you came," he said with a smile. "Good that you're here. It will make a difference."

"Thanks," he whispered, and then stood in place as Bilimoria and the residents left, a swarm of white coats fluttering past him. Remy was so stunned by the change in Bilimoria's attitude that he forgot to ask the obvious: What kind of difference? And to whom?

HE STAYED IN the hallway while a nurse and a ward boy turned Shirin in bed, steeling his ears against Shirin's moans as they moved her. When he went in, she was lying on her side, and he smelled the talcum powder they had sprinkled inside her diaper. He recognized the smell immediately. He had not used it in decades, and yet there he was, back in his childhood, standing with his arms raised above his head while she applied the powder to his armpits. "Hands up," she used to say as if she were a character from the Hollywood Westerns that Daddy had adored, and Remy would giggle and oblige.

"Are you comfy, Mummy?" he whispered, and she opened her eyes. His mouth went dry at the coldness and anger in them. It was a look he remembered only too well. "I'm sorry if they moved you roughly," he said. "Next time, I'll—I'll tip them lavishly and make sure they are gentler."

But even as he spoke, he thought, *Who is going to keep up with the tips after I leave?*

IN THE AFTERNOON, he walked to the small floral shop he had passed yesterday and ordered a basket filled with the most fragrant flowers they had: roses, sprigs of jasmine, and Cestrum. He could smell their perfume as he carried them back to the hospital.

In Shirin's room, he set the basket on the dresser. He wanted it to be the first thing she saw when she opened her eyes and he was surprised at himself, at this new desire to please his mother. Had it always been there, this affection, hidden in the crevices of his stony heart?

He remembered what Kathy had once told him—that even abused children loved their parents.

But Mummy had not really been abusive, had she? *Had she?* Well, yes, a few times. There had been that weird period when she would surreptitiously pinch him, but it had been short-lived, thank God. There was that time, when he was eight and she had said those awful words: *I wish I had never given birth to you.* He couldn't remember what he'd done to make her say this. It was as if he'd walled off those words, so that they existed on their own, a sentence floating in space. He did remember that she'd apologized an hour later, had covered him in kisses and begged for forgiveness and struck herself in remorse, which had frightened him even more than the careless words. And he had forgiven her, of course, but that sentence had haunted him ever since. It had made him feel like an interloper, a gate-crasher, someone who had forced his way into a place where he was not wanted. Except that that "place" happened to be his life.

His therapist had frowned when Remy told him about the incident, had said it was the key to understanding Remy's self-image. He had gone to see the therapist after he had been married for three years. Kathy had a fiery temper, and each time she'd gotten angry, Remy had reacted the way he'd done his whole life—cowering inwardly and falling silent.

"For fuck's sake, say something," Kathy had said during one of their fights. "What're you thinking?"

"Nothing."

"Nothing? Remy, I'm not Shirin, okay? I'm not your damn mother."

His cheeks had stung with anger. "This is why I don't tell you anything about my past. You just fling it back in my face, see?"

Kathy had looked at him, her eyes brimming with tears. "Oh, Remy," she'd said. "You should see your face right now. I'm . . . I won't ever abandon you, honey. You need to go talk to someone about all this."

He had turned away from her, hating her for reminding him of those awful two weeks when Mummy had left. Remy had been sent away to Lonavala with their old neighbor, but even when he had returned to Bombay, she was not home. For a week or so, it had just been him and Dad in their apartment, and the gloom and fright of that time had entered his body and penetrated his very bones.

Well, Remy thought as he finished positioning the floral arrangement and then left Shirin's room, *Kathy was right—the weekly therapy sessions did help*. He'd learned to argue with her cleanly, honestly, fairly. And once he did, a strange thing happened: they stopped picking on each other and drew even closer than before.

He sat on a wooden bench in the hallway, waiting for his mother to wake up. The afternoon sun felt strong and steady, like a fatherly hand cupping his back. It was snowing in Columbus, Kathy had told him this morning, and as depressing as things were here, he was glad to be missing part of the Ohio winter. He looked up as an elderly man shuffled toward him. "Sahibji, deekra," the old man said, "who is your patient?"

Remy had already learned that this question was an icebreaker among the fraternity of relatives of the hospitalized. "Good afternoon, uncle," he replied. "It's my mother."

The old man nodded absently. "My wife is in there," he said, pointing with his chin to one of the nearby rooms. "Sixty-eight years of marriage we are having."

"Wow," Remy said. "Congratulations."

"Thank you." The old man's face contorted. "But she is very sick. The doctor says there's no hope."

"I'm so sorry."

"I'm Mehernosh, by the way." He sat down beside Remy with a thud.

"Nice to meet you. I'm Remy."

"Remy," Mehernosh repeated, as if committing the name to memory. "Unusual name for a Parsi. Is it short for Rohinton?"

"No. It's my real name. My parents named me after a Frenchman they used to know."

"I see," Mehernosh said, a faraway look in his eyes. "You know," he added after a second, "my late father used to say, nothing lasts forever. He was so right."

Remy nodded, not knowing how to respond.

Mehernosh gave Remy a sideways look. "You are having a family?"

"I have a wife."

"Long live, long live," Mehernosh blessed. "A long, healthy life to both of you, deekra."

"My mother is in this room." Remy pointed. "I'm here all day. If I can help you in any way . . ."

"Thank you very much." Mehernosh eyed Remy silently. "But you are not from here? You are a foreigner?"

Remy had indeed felt like an outsider from the time he'd arrived in Bombay, but something in him rebelled at the label. "I live in America, uncle," he said. "But, you know, I grew up here. Bombay born and bred."

Mehernosh nodded. "My daughter is settled in America also. In Seattle." He sighed. "This is the destiny of our Parsi community. So many of us have lost our children to America."

"I'm sorry," Remy said, feeling as if he were apologizing for the entire Parsi diaspora, fighting the urge to take the old man's hand.

"No, no, why sorry? It is good to go wherever there is opportunity. After all, that is what brought our Persian ancestors to India, correct? My Jessie has a good life in the States."

Remy remembered what Cyrus had once said about his living in America. He had met Kathy by then, and a new future had opened up, as if someone had parted heavy drapes and let in the sun. Cyrus owned one of Bombay's largest engineering firms, but he had long accepted the fact that his moody, artistic son would never take over the family business. "Stay away," Cyrus said on the phone. "Build your life there. Don't let anyone curtail your dreams. Your happiness and success will be my reward, Remy. And don't worry about your mother—I will talk to her. She'll come around. You'll see."

The damp spot of grief that had taken root in Remy's chest ever since Cyrus's death expanded. He missed his dad. How much easier this trip would've been if Cyrus were still alive. Remy had always thought of his father as Indiana Jones, armed with a metaphorical machete, cutting down every obstacle in his son's way, domestic or bureaucratic. Remy glanced at the trembling old man beside him and felt sorry for the unknown Jessie in Seattle. It was obvious that Mehernosh loved his daughter, but Remy knew that Jessie didn't have the kind of dad who would've set himself on fire before allowing a single hair on his child's head to get singed. Nobody he knew did.

Parsi fathers, Remy thought. *Sentimental and loving, wearing their hearts on their sleeves.* He was generalizing, of course. He'd heard stories about Parsi men who were alcoholics, abusive, cruel. He had gotten lucky twice in his life—first with Dad and then with Kathy. So much undeserved good fortune. Maybe his thorny relationship with Mummy was simply the law of averages.

His phone rang. He saw that it was Shenaz, and his stomach lurched, wondering if Monaz had contacted her, whether she was calling to tell him that the adoption was back on. He smiled apologetically at Mehernosh, rose from the bench, and walked a few feet away.

"Hi, darling," Shenaz said. "How is Mom?"

"More or less the same," he said. "She ate a bit of your chocolate cake."

"That's wonderful. Give her a hug from me, okay? Listen, I'm planning tonight's menu. What do you want to eat?"

He debated whether to mention the strange meeting with Gaurav and decided against it. This was a delicate situation—he would give the girl the time she needed to grieve and make up her mind.

"Shenaz, I can't come tonight," he said. "I promised Pervez I'd take him and Roshan to dinner."

"Ae, tell him to fuck off, yaar. You'll have a better time with us."

He smiled. "I know. But I already made plans."

Shenaz huffed. "Fine. But I'm telling you, you better come tomorrow night."

Was there any feeling greater than an attractive woman demanding your company? "I'll be there tomorrow. I promise," he said.

CHAPTER TWELVE

———✗———

WHILE PERVEZ DROVE and they made small talk, Remy rehearsed what he would say to them at dinner: They would have to step up their game after he returned to America. One of them would have to check in on his mom daily. They would have to make sure her bills were paid on time, and if she took ill again, they would have to inform him immediately. And, yes, they should indulge her—have fresh flowers delivered every week, bring her desserts when they visited. He would make it clear that they weren't to spare any expense for her care.

He waited until after they'd finished their soup, then started in, feeling as if he'd struck the right tone—firm but not accusatory.

Roshan was immediately defensive, complaining again about how querulous Shirin had been. But Pervez stopped her and apologized. He had been too busy with work and had let all of Shirin's care fall on Roshan, and that had been a mistake, he said. He had not liked the way Shirin had treated his wife, and this had angered him. But his lack of involvement hadn't been fair to Roshan, it hadn't been fair to Shirin, and it most definitely hadn't been fair to Remy.

"I'm sorry, boss," Pervez said. "After everything that you've done for us, I don't blame you for being angry."

"I'm not angry," Remy began before stopping himself. He had the upper hand; he would be foolish to concede now. "Well, okay, I am," he said, with a smile that softened his words. "Just a little bit." He broke off as the waiter set down their food. They had ordered a spread of chicken fried rice, green beans, fried shrimp, and Manchurian chicken, and the waiter served each dish with the precision of a Swiss clockmaker. Remy would've preferred to have helped himself, but he knew the tradition at restaurants in India, and allowed the man to portion the dishes on each of their plates.

The waiter left, and Roshan pushed away her plate. "I have lost my appetite. After everything we have done for Shirin, to be accused of neglecting her is too much. You've forgotten that she's no saint."

"Roshan," Remy said, "I know what a handful my mother can be. But you knew the situation when I made you the offer. I was very honest."

"Three years ago," Roshan said loudly. "You haven't been back in *three years*. You had promised you'd visit every year."

Remy wondered how to explain the pressures of work, growing his business, helping Kathy's mom after her hip surgery—all of which had postponed his returning to Bombay. How he hadn't intended to stay away for this long, the years falling fast on one another, like playing cards.

"I should have," he said. "I'm sorry I didn't keep my word." He gestured toward Roshan's plate. "Come on. Please eat. This is a social dinner." Seeing that she was not appeased, he tried again. "Look, I'm not blaming you. I'm just saying . . . my mother is getting older. The two of you are her only relatives in Bombay. I'm just asking you to step up. As a favor. A kindness."

He heard the sniveling quality in his voice and hated himself for capitulating so quickly. But what choice did he have? He would be leaving soon, and at this late date, there was nobody else to whom he could assign Shirin's day-to-day care. Other than Roshan, everyone that he knew worked full-time jobs. And Pervez was his father's nephew—it was unthinkable to go back on his word about the flat.

"Okay, enough," Pervez said to Roshan. "Drop your nakhra and start eating. We also made a promise to Remy, no? You yourself have said many, many times that we owe him every good thing in our lives. Without Remy, we would still be living in that broken-down room at Andheri. And I would still be slogging at that bank." He took a sip of his beer. "I have to tell you, cuz. You have surprised me with your devotion to your mother. I mean, the last time you were here, you couldn't wait to leave town."

Remy forced himself to meet Pervez's eyes. "I know," he mumbled. "But I didn't anticipate . . . I . . . Mummy is so weak and helpless now."

He stared at the tablecloth, trying to control his emotions. When he looked up, Roshan was looking at him sympathetically.

"It's good," Roshan said as she picked up her fork. "It's good that you came. It's always important to . . . let bygones be bygones."

"Thank you. I'm glad I came, too." Suddenly, Remy was grateful to Monaz, despite the fact that he had no idea where things stood between them now. Without her, he wouldn't have been here when his mother needed him.

"Tell you what," Roshan said. "You sleep in tomorrow. I'll go in the morning to visit Shirin."

"You don't have to," he said. "As long as I'm in town, I can spend the days there."

"How much longer are you staying?"

He hesitated. "I'm guessing until next week? I have an open ticket, but this is still peak season, so flights are difficult to book. And it would be great if I could bring Mummy home and get her settled before I leave."

"You're getting dark circles under your eyes," Roshan said, in her blunt manner. "You take rest tomorrow. I'll go to the hospital around ten. You can relieve me in the afternoon. Now, come, let's discuss something more cheerful than all this dookh-dava talk."

Remy grinned to himself at Roshan's use of the old-fashioned term *dookh-dava*, which literally translated to *illness-medicine*. Sad talk. Somehow in English, it lost its quaint, humorous edge.

But then, he thought, *something always gets lost in translation, doesn't it?* Even to Kathy, who knew him so well, it would be difficult to explain the roller coaster of emotions he'd felt since he'd arrived here. For a second, he thought about confiding to the couple his real reason for coming to Bombay, but immediately dismissed the thought. The last thing he needed was for Roshan to take his temperature daily about the situation with Monaz. He wouldn't be able to bear their curiosity—or, worse, their pity, if things fell apart yet again.

CHAPTER THIRTEEN

THE NEXT MORNING, there was a knock on the door, and Monaz stood leaning against the wall in the hallway. Remy could tell that she had been crying.

This time, he let her in wordlessly and watched as she took the same spot on the couch, her hands twisting in her lap. His heart sank. There was nothing in Monaz's demeanor that indicated that she was at peace with her decision.

"Something to drink?" he asked by rote.

"A glass of water, please."

He opened the fridge to get her some cold water but, at the last minute, decided on the glass of orange juice that Hema had squeezed for him yesterday. Monaz took it from him without saying anything, as if she'd forgotten what she'd asked for. She took a sip as he sat watching her.

"Did you force him to change his mind, uncle?" she asked.

"What?"

"Gaurav. Did you convince him to ask me to give up my baby?"

He exhaled, exhausted by this girl and her pathetic love life. *He's a selfish prick*, he wanted to say. *Can't you see how miserable he'll make you?*

Instead, he said, "Monaz, haven't you wondered why Gaurav wanted to see me? He'd already decided. He doesn't wish to be married, darling."

He forced himself to remain seated when Monaz burst into tears. He was alone in this apartment with a lovesick girl. Any gesture of kindness on his part—a sympathetic arm around her shoulder, say—could get misinterpreted. Remy knew that if he'd remained in India, he wouldn't have hesitated to embrace a girl almost young enough to be his daughter. But his years in America had made him acutely sensitive to personal boundaries and sexual dynamics. He imagined Jango's reaction to this: how he would guffaw and then shake his head and say, "You crazy Americans. Sexualizing everything." Still, he remained seated, only murmuring, "I'm so sorry. I know this hurts."

"I should've never told him about the adoption, about why you were in town," Monaz sobbed. "I love him. I was so happy when he came back to me."

Remy opened his mouth to contradict her, to remind her that she'd known Gaurav only briefly and that she couldn't possibly love that arrogant, self-absorbed narcissist who would hurt her repeatedly. He stopped, remembering what Kathy always said: *Love is chemistry. It's either there or it isn't.* He remembered his immediate reaction when he'd first seen Kathy—how he had felt breathless, like someone had punched him in the gut. The fact that Kathy had reciprocated his feelings was just dumb good luck. Monaz had not been so lucky. "I'm so sorry," he repeated. "You will find the right person, I promise."

"How, uncle?" Monaz said bitterly. "This is India, you know. Nobody will marry a girl who had a baby out of wedlock."

Remy forced himself to look her in the eye. "Well, you do have another option."

"You still want my son? You would trust me? After what I did to you?"

He shrugged. Did he still trust the young woman who sat crying in front of him? Not really. But what choice did he have? What choice did *she* have?

"We may be each other's best chance," he said, and he felt the truth of that statement. In that moment, he longed for Kathy to be in this room with him, knew as sure as anything that if Kathy were here, Monaz would not hesitate to let them adopt her child. Kathy had that solid competence and confidence to which Monaz would respond. But, alas, it was only Remy sitting across from the girl, and he felt inadequate. He knew that if Monaz were to entrust him with her child, he would be a good father, because he himself had had a great role model. But the road to get there suddenly felt daunting.

He glanced at the clock. "The cleaning woman will be here soon," he said. "I . . . I don't wish to talk about these personal matters in her earshot."

"So Gaurav just told you that he'd changed his mind?" Monaz asked, as if she hadn't heard him.

"Yes. He said he lives in a joint family and that the adjustment would be very difficult. Monaz, listen. They are Sindhis. Their ways are very different from ours, deekra. You follow?"

Monaz got a stubborn look on her face. "But *you* married a foreigner. Your wife is American."

Remy sighed. How to describe for her the instant connection between Kathy and him from the moment they'd met at Ralph Addington's house? "Monaz, the difference is that Kathy reciprocated my love," he said as gently as he could. "But . . . you see, with Gaurav . . . it doesn't appear to be the case."

Monaz began to cry again. "He lied to me. He told me he did, when, you know . . . when he wanted to make love to me."

Remy closed his eyes briefly. "Men do that sometimes," he said, irritated at Monaz's naïveté. Why was he the one having this conversation with her? Where was her mother, for heaven's sake? "It's not right, of course, but it happens."

Monaz blew her nose, then looked at him. "What should I *do*?" she asked.

Remy considered her question. "Have you talked to Shenaz since, you know . . . since Gaurav changed his mind?"

"No. Shenazfui is angry at me as it is. For how I treated you." Her face crumpled again.

"I'm not," Remy said. "I . . . It's not your fault. There are no hard feelings here, Monaz. I mean, I'm disappointed, of course, but I'm sympathetic to what you're going through. This is not an easy decision."

Monaz gave him a long, penetrating look, then nodded. "What they said about you is true—you are a very nice man, Remy Uncle." She pocketed her handkerchief. "Do you have a picture of your wife? I'd like to see it."

He sat on the couch next to her, keeping a good distance. He scrolled through his phone and said, "This is Kathy." It was a beautiful picture of her, out in their backyard, the autumn sun behind her, lighting up her dark hair. Fifteen years of marriage, and Kathy's good looks could still make his heart quicken.

"She's lovely," Monaz said, and he nodded proudly, showing her a few more pictures.

"I think—I think she would be a good mother to my son," Monaz said, her voice cracking, and Remy felt a splinter in his heart as he realized the enormity of Monaz's dilemma, of what was being asked of her at such a young age. How the hell did one know at nineteen whether an irrevocable decision was the right one, whether the choice would create a lifetime of regret and sadness, or relief and certainty? Would giving up her baby open up a new, bright future for Monaz, or would it permanently wall off some essential part of her spirit?

"Listen," he said. "I'm still here for several more days. You don't have to decide anything today. My suggestion is you talk everything through with Shenaz. That is, if you're sure you can't confide in your parents?"

Monaz was shaking her head before he finished his sentence. "No way, uncle. My father will kill me if he knows that I . . . did what I did with Gaurav."

"Okay. Then at least talk to your aunt and uncle. They care about you." He rose to his feet. "I'm sorry, Monaz, but I have phone calls to make before I leave for the hospital."

She got up, too. "I hope your mother gets well soon," she said. And before he could react, she flung herself at him and hugged him. "Thank you for being so nice, Remy Uncle."

He was aware that Hema might let herself in at any moment, but Remy found himself hugging her back. "It's all right," he whispered. "It will all work out. You'll see."

He picked up the phone to call Kathy as soon as Monaz left, then thought better of it. There was no reason Kathy should follow Monaz's every mood swing. Kathy's job was already tough, and he always tried to shield her from any bad news until he'd fixed the problem. "Our house address is Codependency Central," Kathy used to joke.

His phone rang two hours later. "Wow," Jango said when Remy answered. "That's quite a development, yaar. Shenaz just called and gave me the news. Are you happy?"

"I don't know. I don't want to be, until she decides for sure."

Jango made a dismissive sound. "Of course she'll decide in your favor. There's zero chance of her keeping the child."

Remy hesitated, unsure of whether to bring up a sensitive subject. "Are you certain . . . ? That is, are you and Shenaz not tempted to adopt the child, Jango? I would totally understand it if you wanted to."

"No, yaar," Jango said. "We are so set in our ways. I know it sounds awful, but neither Shenaz nor I have that parental instinct. I mean, we love indulging other people's children and all, but we enjoy our freedom and independence too much. I guess we're just selfish."

"Not at all. Kathy and I were in the same place just a few years ago. Then, I don't know, something changed in her. Now"—he lowered his voice—"it's like she's obsessed with the idea of motherhood."

"But you want this also, right?"

"Yes, I think so. Yes."

Somebody spoke in the background, and Jango said, "Listen, I gotta go. Come over directly from the hospital tonight. I'll send the car."

"I can take a cab."

"There's no need. As it is, the bloody driver just sits around catching flies all day," Jango said. "I may as well put the poor bastard to work. Just come straightaway to our house tonight."

As he slipped into Jango's air-conditioned Camry that evening, Remy had to admit that this was a hell of a better mode of transport than a hot, cramped taxi. Half of the taxi drivers in Bombay seemed to light joss sticks in their cabs, making Remy's allergies act up. And the only way to keep out the exhaust fumes and the blare of horns was to roll up the windows, which made the tiny Hyundai taxis even more stuffy. The other half of the drivers blasted loud Hindi music. This car was blissfully silent, and Remy sank deeper into the leather seat and shut his eyes.

Even spending just the afternoon in the hospital room—Roshan had kept her promise to visit Mummy in the morning—had been more tiring than he would've ever imagined. To pass the time, he had scribbled a few lines of a poem, but as always, he had run out of things to say and had tossed the scrap of paper. When they'd cared for Dad at home, the routine had been so different—there had been doorbells to answer and bedsheets to wash and phone calls to make. Now, the only moments of gratification came when Shirin took sips of Coke or nibbled on dessert.

Despite his resolution to indulge Shirin, it worried Remy that she was surviving almost exclusively on sweet things, sugar having become the Morse code with which he communicated with her. And it wasn't just Mummy's condition that made him gloomy. Almost every hospital room he passed housed an elderly patient, a poignant reminder of the dwindling number of Parsis, a community on the verge of extinction. "Take a good look," Remy used to joke with American friends who were curious about his Zoroastrian faith. "I'm a dinosaur. Soon, we'll be gone the way of the Shakers."

Remy had never had much to do with the religion. But as he walked the corridors of Parsee General Hospital, he felt an ancient tug, a longing in his blood, a sense of kinship with the elderly men and women he passed, artifacts of a bygone genteel age. If they did adopt Monaz's son, Remy would perform the boy's Navjote, the religious thread ceremony that initiated children into the Zoroastrian faith. Kathy would support such a move.

"WE HAVE REACHED, SIR," Jango's driver announced.

Remy awoke with a start. "Great," he said. "Thank you." He pulled out a hundred-rupee note. After the customary refusal, the driver accepted the tip.

Remy walked through the open front door. Jango was behind the bar, dispensing ice into a glass of Scotch. "Come, come. Sit," he said. "Relax. How was your day?"

Remy took the glass that Jango handed to him. This trip would be unbearably sad if he didn't have Jango and Shenaz to lean on.

Shenaz came into the living room. "How are you, my jaan? How is Mummy?"

He shrugged. "She's hanging in there. I didn't go in until the afternoon today, and she seemed a bit more responsive. No fever for two nights in a row."

"Excellent news." She sat next to him on the couch. "Sorry about the continuing melodrama with my niece. She stopped by here after she visited you."

"There's no problem. It's not really her fault. She's so young, and it's a huge decision."

"Yes. But the baby is not waiting for her to hem and haw. It's going to pop out whether she's ready or not."

"So where did you guys leave matters?"

"I told her straight up—it was time for her to make up her mind, once and for all. I didn't have to remind her of how difficult life will be for her and the child if she's an unmarried mother. It's not like in America. There's a lot of social stigma here."

"It's so strange," Remy said. "All this progress—the skyscrapers and the malls and whatnot—it's so deceptive. Because attitudes are no different than when I lived here."

Jango refilled Remy's glass. "And then we have these politicians who want to take us backward, instead of forward," he said. "All this fake nostalgia for a past that never was. To hear them talk, you'd think Indians invented everything, from paper clips to rocket ships. Revisionist history, invented by these damn liars."

Remy sighed. "It's the same thing in the US right now, boss," he said. "Everything is 'America first.' They act as if the rest of the world doesn't exist."

"Well, *that's* not exactly new. Remember when we were kids we used to joke that Americans knew more about outer space than about other countries?"

Remy nodded. When he'd arrived in America in 2003, he had been amazed by the display of American flags everywhere, even at car dealerships, and had found such jingoism mortifying. Two years earlier, he'd read about the horror of 9/11 in the *Times of India*, and he'd felt the same outrage as the rest of the world. He'd understood the groundswell of patriotism that gripped the US in the aftermath of the attacks. But in the weeks and months that followed, it became obvious that the tragedy was being used as a cudgel to beat up the weak— the attacks on Muslims and Sikhs in New York, the brown-skinned civilians bombed back to the Stone Age in Afghanistan, and later, the fantastical invasion of Iraq. But what was happening in America today was something Remy could've never foreseen.

Despite its many blind spots, he'd never imagined the US as anything other than extraordinary, unique, the Alphonso mango of nations. Now, for the first time, it seemed . . . ordinary. He now lived in a country riven by the same tribalism and hatreds that haunted lesser nations. He had always seen American democracy as a giant oak tree, with roots that went more than two hundred years deep. But it turned out the roots were shallow, held in place by custom and good manners, and all it took to lay them bare was one man who refused to play by the rules of civility and democracy.

"Remy?" Shenaz said. "What's wrong, love? You have a terrible look on your face. Please, I don't want you to worry so much about Monaz. She'll come around. You'll see."

He shook his head. "I wasn't. I was just thinking that . . . Never mind." It was impossible to describe the sense of betrayal that he felt from his adopted country. The fact that all this had followed the heady Obama years was particularly cruel, a bait and switch. Obama was native-born, but he was global, almost immigrant-like, in his understanding of America and its place in the world. The first time Remy had heard the young black senator pronounce Pakistan the correct, non-Anglicized way—pah-ki-stahn—he had thought, *He's one of us.* He had sent him a campaign contribution the same day, and his initial faith had been validated over those eight glorious years.

Jango sat across from him, nursing a beer. "Is Gita frying the kebabs?" he asked his wife. "Maybe we can eat those as starters?"

"Munch on the cashews and wafers," Shenaz said. "And leave the dinner menu to me."

Jango grinned at Remy. "See how she bosses me around?" He cleared his throat. "Let me ask you something. If Monaz agrees, will you still take her up on it? After the shit she pulled?"

"I . . . I have to check with Kathy. But I think so."

Jango slapped his thigh. "Then it's decided. We'll have a candid talk with her this week. She cannot leave you hanging like this. Bloody hell, it's *my* reputation on the line."

Remy opened his mouth to reassure Jango, but the doorbell rang. "Saala, who can it be at this hour?" Jango said.

It was Soli, a school friend Remy hadn't seen in over a decade.

"Oh my God," Remy said. "Wow, Sol. You look great."

Soli looked as surprised as Remy felt. "Arre, bossie. What the hell are you doing in Mumbai?" He turned to Shenaz. "I was in the neighborhood and decided to stop by for a few minutes. I hope that's okay?"

"Yes, of course. Come, sit. What will you take?"

Jango was pouring Soli a drink when the doorbell rang again.

"Maybe it's the fellow from Royal Chemist," Shenaz said. "I'd ordered some nasal sprays."

There were four people outside the door. Gulnaz, Remy's old class-mate, stood leaning against a man Remy didn't recognize, along with Joseph and his wife, Sabrina. "Hi, Remy," Joe said, grinning widely. "You look like you've seen a bhoot, man."

"What's going on here?" Remy said.

Jango threw back his head and laughed. "You should see your face, man. I just decided to invite a few school friends to throw you a small welcome-home party. Hope you're happy."

"Remy, this is Hussein, my hubby," Gulnaz said, her dimples showing.

Remy remembered getting an invitation to Gulnaz's wedding a few years ago. Had they sent a gift? Kathy probably had. "Congrats," he said, shaking hands with the tall, gangly man beside Gulnaz. "Great to finally meet you."

"It's my pleasure, Remy. I've heard so much about you."

Remy gave Gulnaz a hug. "Our little Gulu," he said. "Married. Hard to believe."

"Yah. Can you imagine? At my age? Good thing my hubby doesn't have great eyesight."

"Nonsense. He's lucky to have you."

Three other couples arrived next. Remy was the center of attention for several long minutes as everyone asked about his mother, followed by inquiries about why Kathy had not accompanied him. Their ques-tions told him that Jango had not revealed his reason for visiting India, for which he was thankful. He did not want to be subjected to their sympathy or curiosity on that matter.

After the maid brought out the appetizers, Remy settled in with his drink as the others talked over one another, trading quips and jokes. Except for the touch of gray in their hair, it was as if they were all back at Cathedral. Even after all these years, he could see them as they had been in fourth grade, seventh grade, or on the day the results of their high school board exams had been posted. (He and Gulnaz had passed with distinction; Jango had passed in second class.) He grinned as they reminisced about the pranks they'd played during out-of-town school trips—like putting toothpaste on the faces of classmates as they slept on the train—and the crush the boys had on their geography teacher.

But the comfort seeping into his bones was from more than just their shared past, Remy realized. It also came from sharing a culture. He listened as his friends conversed mostly in English, occasionally throwing in a Gujarati or Hindi word or phrase, the signature move of polyglot Bombayites. He loved how easily and lightly Joe and Jango swore, the casual sprinkling of *bhenchot* and *madarchot* into their conversation, their merriment removing the sting out of the cuss words.

Remy recalled a moment from last Christmas at his mother-in-law's house. He was telling Rose about how well his agency had done that year and had rapped his knuckles on the dining table, adding a superstitious "Touch wood." Kathy and Rose had exchanged a bemused look. "What?" he'd said.

"Nothing," Kathy had replied. "It's just that in America we say 'Knock on wood.'" And even though he had chuckled along with them, his wife's correction had stung just a tiny bit, the "we" that excluded him, that separated him from his own wife. Most days, Remy felt as American as Mount Rushmore, but once in a while, these fissures reminded him that even though he had wholeheartedly embraced America, it was never guaranteed that America would embrace him in equal measure.

After all these years, it still made him angry to remember Bill Warner, the account manager at his first job, saying "Namaste, Remy" every morning. Warner said this in a singsong, heavy accent, sounding like no one Remy personally knew. And Remy, who had never greeted anyone with a "Namaste" in his life, who had the clipped accent of his social class, who spoke better English than Bill ever would, but who was fresh out of graduate school and thankful to have landed a job at the largest ad agency in Columbus, had no choice but to grin and say "Fine, Bill. And you?"

It had bothered him ever since, this insult and his complicity. He wouldn't presume to call it racism; Bill was fond of Remy and had been one of his biggest supporters at the firm. Remy had always been aware of the privileges that inured him from blatant racism: his education, his fluent English, his light skin, his bearing, his good looks, his American wife. But what, then, to call how Bill greeted him for the three years he was at the agency? Was there a name for that? What to do with the shame that the memory still elicited in him, the helpless sense of unease that he had felt? It sounded crazy, but it might've been easier to be a target of open, naked racism, because at least then it would've had a label.

The bitterest, most cynical part of Remy was almost grateful for the last three years, when the millions of Americans had made their distrust of foreigners, their xenophobia, crystal clear. He wore this new knowledge like an overcoat over his expensive suits—that despite being allowed to take a sizable bite out of the American dream, he would never completely belong to America. To any country, really. This was the eternal burden of the immigrant, the divided soul. He would always be a foreigner in America, but the irony was, he was also a stranger in India.

He leaned into Gulnaz, who was sitting next to him on the couch, and put his arm around her. "Hey, sweetheart," he whispered. "I'm thrilled to see you looking so happy."

Gulnaz's eyes glittered as she smiled at him. "Can you believe it?" she whispered. "That I would marry? I was so sure I'd die an old maid. But better late than never, right?"

"And"—Remy hesitated—"he's Muslim, right? Was there a lot of opposition from your families?"

Gulnaz looked suddenly serious. "You won't believe this, Remy," she said. "I myself was opposed to my marriage."

The inanity of her statement made Remy burst out laughing. "That makes no sense, darling," he said.

"No, no, let me explain. What I mean to say is, I'm very proud to be a Parsi. Believe me, I didn't *want* to marry out of my faith." She shrugged. "But what to do? I just couldn't resist him."

"How could you? He's lovely. And he clearly adores you."

"And he's more like us Parsis than you'd think, Remy. Bindaas. Happy-go-lucky. I mean, look at him, drinking like a fish. Plus, he's resolutely nonvegetarian, just like us bawas."

Catching Hussein's quizzical look from across the room, Remy laughed. And then, because it felt so good to be with old friends and away from the gloom of the hospital, he laughed some more. He saw Jango stare at him with concern, and he flashed him a thumbs-up sign.

Gulnaz took his hand in hers. "And you're okay, jaan? Managing with Mummy?"

"I'm okay." He shrugged. "It is what it is."

She squeezed his hand. "I'm so glad you're here."

So was he. Somehow, Shenaz and Jango had known that he'd needed this, the company of old friends. He had a large circle of devoted friends in the US, and in many ways, they knew him, the adult him, better than these people ever would. As lovely as this gathering was, there was something—what was the word?—juvenile about it. The hilarity, the silly jokes and puns, as if they were forever trapped in fourteen-year-old bodies. Would he even choose these people as friends if he'd met them today? And yet there was something to be said for friends who knew you before your identity was formed, when you had only half emerged out of your shell. Who had seen you cry when your debate team lost the citywide championship, who knew the name of the first girl you'd fallen in love with. Remy felt himself grow sentimental, as was often the case after the second Scotch. *One more drink,* he said to himself, *and I'll stop.*

Dinner was lavish: white sauce with shrimp as big as a child's fist, sali boti with apricots, spinach with cottage cheese, and Parsi-style fried chicken. "Mera khoda," Soli gasped. "Is this a party or a wedding feast?"

"Eat, eat." Shenaz grinned. "Please, fill your plates."

Soli patted his belly after they'd finished eating. "I'm fully fed up," he said, and they all cracked up, instantly remembering the expression was one of their math teacher's many malapropisms.

They took a break before Shenaz served dessert, and Remy seized the chance. "Excuse me," he said. "I want to make a quick call to Kathy before she starts her workday."

"Go into the bedroom," Jango said. "Nobody will disturb you there."

He shut the bedroom door, reached for his phone, and saw that he had three missed calls from the same number. Why had he not heard it ring? Shit. He'd turned off the ringer at the hospital so as not to disturb Mummy.

"Sir," the female voice said when he phoned back, "I've been calling and calling. This is Manju, the nurse. Please come quickly. Madam is not well."

"What's wrong? She was fine when I left."

"I know, sir, but what to do? Very high fever she is having."

Remy's heart began to thud. "Has the doctor been in?"

"Just the junior doctor. They are trying to reach the senior."

"Okay," he said. "I'll be there as soon as I can. Do me a favor. Tell my mother I'm on my way."

"She is not hearing, sir."

"*Tell her.*"

Everyone fell quiet when he went back into the living room. "Something wrong, boss?" Jango said.

"I had a call from the hospital. Mummy has a high fever. Can I get a cab or . . . ?"

Jango was already on his cell phone, calling his driver. "Shekhar is still downstairs. He will take you. I'll come along."

"No. I . . . Please. I want to go alone. I'll call if there's need." He turned to the group. "I'm really so sorry. I . . ."

"Remy," Gulnaz said. "*Go.*"

THE RESIDENT WAS yelling in Shirin's ear, trying to get her to respond. Remy pushed past the head nurse, went to his mother's bedside, and took her hand. He was startled at how hot it felt. "Mummy, it's me. Remy. I'm here, okay?"

Shirin let out a low moan. Her face was flushed and sweaty.

Remy looked at the resident. "What's the plan? And what is wrong?"

"We're not sure. We've given her medicine for the fever. We're about to start a new IV antibiotic."

"Why haven't you done so already?" Remy's tone was sharp.

"Sir," the man said, "we're waiting for the pharmacy to send it."

Remy turned to his mother, who was muttering something. "Mummy? What is it? You want something? Some ice?"

"Cyrus," Shirin said. Her voice was raspy. "Cyrus, my Cyloo. I . . . I want . . . Cyloo."

The resident caught Remy's eye. *Who?* he mouthed.

Remy shook his head. "My father."

Shirin tried to pull her hand out of Remy's grasp, agitated. "Cyloo," she said again. "My darling. Miss you."

Remy felt a regret so sharp it displaced his fear. The human heart was a goddamn mystery, and every person was ultimately unknowable.

He had always believed that his parents had had one of the worst marriages he'd known. But here was Shirin, crazed with fever, declaring her love for her husband. How greatly he had misunderstood the strange, complex dynamic between his parents.

When Dad was away on a business trip, Shirin often used to put out a third plate when she and Remy ate lunch. "It's for my imaginary friend," she would say. As a kid, Remy hadn't thought that it was peculiar that his mother had an imaginary friend. Now, he realized that this had been her way of coping with Dad's absence, and a cavern opened up in his heart.

Remy stood helplessly by the bedside, longing to call Kathy to ask her medical advice. But he didn't want to leave the room. He looked over his shoulder to where Manju was standing behind him, nervously twisting the ends of her sari. "Pour some cologne water into a bowl," he ordered. "Then dip a washrag in it and place it on her forehead." It was the way Shirin had tended to him whenever he'd had a high fever.

Shirin's breathing slowed as the cool rag hit her forehead. "Son," she muttered, although Remy had to lean in to make out what she was saying. Her eyes were open but unseeing. "My son. Gone so far away."

"It's okay, Mama," Remy said. "I'm right here. I'm not going anywhere. I'm by your side, I promise." He had never meant anything more. He felt feverish himself, burning with a long-suppressed tenderness for his mother. There was no place he'd rather be than here, right next to her, holding her, feeling the heat emanating from her body, registering each tremor. It was the purest, most concentrated feeling he'd ever known, every fiber of his being alive and purposeful, wanting to be of use to her. His mother was floating away from him—he could feel that in the ebb and flow of her grip—but he kept holding her as he wondered what had gone so wrong, whether this was just a flare-up of the fever or something more serious and final.

He watched as they wheeled in a new IV pole and flushed the needle before starting the new meds. Shirin didn't even flinch, lost as she was in the fog of her mind, repeating Cyrus's name over and over. "It's okay, Mummy. It's okay," Remy said. "I'll be right by your side."

She turned her head slightly and looked directly at him. There was a puzzled look in her eyes as she struggled to focus on him.

Though I walk through the valley of the shadow of death, I will fear no evil; for thou art with me. The long-ago words, learned in school, flew into Remy's head, and he fought against the urge to say them out loud.

"Remy," Shirin said, a new tone of wonder in her voice. "Rem . . . Deekra. My son."

Remy swallowed a few times and then began to cry.

THE SUN APPEARED to take its own sweet time rising the next morning. Remy's back was sore from having spent the night in the chair next to Shirin's bed. Manju had risen periodically from the cot on the far side of the room and begged him to switch places with her, but he had refused, not wanting to leave his mother's side. *For thou art with me.* He was no god; he was merely a man—and a prodigal son, to boot. But he was *her* son. And he was here, by her side. He hoped that this was enough.

Manju had opened the room's door a few minutes earlier. Outside, the sky was beginning to lighten, a pale pink spreading across its skin. He could hear the low grumbling of the pigeons and the strident cawing of the crows.

It was a new day. And the fever was down, and his mother was alive.

Remy ran his hand across his face, as if to erase his fatigue.

His phone vibrated. Kathy. He glanced at his mother, who appeared to be fast asleep. "Hey," he whispered to Kathy. "Hold on a minute."

He motioned to Manju to sit next to Shirin, then stepped into the hallway. "Hi, honey," he said. "Sorry for not calling last night. It's been quite a shitstorm here."

He started to shake as he recounted the events of the previous night. He cradled the phone between his ear and shoulder and held himself to stop the tremors.

"Babe," Kathy said, "I'm so sorry this is happening. You were so excited when you'd left for India, and now . . . all this."

"I'm all right. I'm just glad I'm here for her. I can't imagine her facing this alone." He gulped. "And Kat. Just to know her love for my dad . . . it was . . . worth everything."

"That's good." And now he heard the exhaustion in Kathy's voice. "How are you, love?" he asked. "How is everything back home?"

"I'm fine," she said quickly. "Everything is fine. You just take care of yourself. And her."

He closed his eyes in gratitude, even as he wondered if he would be this selfless if the roles were reversed. But, then, there was no danger of Kathy having to fly eight thousand miles away to care for family. Kathy's mother, Rose, lived just seven miles away.

Kathy was saying something, and he forced himself to listen. "Stay a few extra days if you need to," she said. "When you come home, there should be no regrets, you hear? I want you to have closure."

Closure? he thought after they hung up. How lucky, how *American*, to be able to see life as something so pristine and tame that it could be shaped into a narrative with a beginning, a middle, and an end. In India, they understood the inherent messiness of life, the endless bleeding of one story into another, from one generation to the next. The idea of closure was a fairy tale, the Muzak of the human condition. As Remy sat on the bench outside his mother's room, on the morning after a long, dreadful night, the concept rang hollow, lipstick on a pig, a refusal to face the existential reality of life—its brokenness and its unpredictability.

He nodded off. He woke up to the sound of someone clearing his throat. It was Dr. Bilimoria, peering anxiously at him.

"Hard night?" Bilimoria said. "I heard."

Remy nodded.

"But she pulled through," Bilimoria said. "She is stronger than she looks. Fever is down, according to the five o'clock report."

"But can it happen again? I mean, she was doing so much better the last few days."

Bilimoria shrugged. "Anything can happen. But so far, she's responded well to the new antibiotic. So let's stay positive."

"Are you keeping her on it?"

"Yes." He cleared his throat. "Most patients would have recovered by now. But given her age, I suppose—"

"She's only seventy, for God's sake." Remy was suddenly irritated. "And Parsis have one of the highest life expectancies in the world. Look at the patients here. Most are well into their eighties and nineties. I don't understand why we're treating her as if . . ."

Bilimoria eyed him carefully. "I'm going to tell you something, okay?" He turned to the residents. "Start rounding with the next patient. I'll be there in a minute."

Remy tensed as Bilimoria sat down next to him. "She had come to see me," Bilimoria said. "About a year ago."

"Who?"

"Who? Your mother. She had pneumonia then, too. So there is some scarring on her lungs. At that time, I had prescribed a nebulizer and other treatment. I also lectured her about nutrition and all. But I could tell she had no interest."

"Why the hell not?"

Bilimoria looked at him sternly. "Would you?"

"Would I what?"

"Would you want to keep living if you lived all alone? If your only child didn't wish to have anything to do with you?"

Remy flinched, his newfound love curdling into resentment at Shirin for sharing these private details with a stranger. He thought back to that little boy crying softly in bed, seared by his mother's acidic words. He remembered Daddy being driven half crazy by her cruelty—how she'd steal his business papers or car keys from the coffee table and hide them for a day, how she'd take his wallet and swear she'd never seen it, only for it to show up days later under their mattress.

"You have no idea," he said now to the doctor. "You have no idea what antics—"

Bilimoria raised his hand to cut him off. "Son, I am not judging you. I'm sure there were good reasons. There always are. I'm just trying to tell you that your mother has lost the most important tool for recovery: the will to live. Do you understand?"

Remy nodded, unable to meet Bilimoria's eye.

"Okay," Bilimoria said after a moment. He got to his feet and ran his fingers over his bald head as if he had forgotten the absence of hair. "I'll change one other medicine," he said, "and I'm putting her on a steroid for a few days. That should help with her breathing and control the fever." He looked at Remy. "Any questions?"

Remy rose. "No questions." He stuck out his hand. "Thank you, Doctor."

Bilimoria took his hand and held it. "No mention. I'm sorry if . . . I just wanted you to have the full picture. So we know what to do next."

"Agreed." Remy suddenly felt lighter, as if he and Bilimoria were now a team.

"Deekra," Bilimoria said, "one more thing. Don't forget to take care of yourself also." A hint of a smile. "Go home, shave, bathe, eat breakfast, get rest. Don't worry. Your mother is tougher than she looks."

REMY PAID MANJU overtime wages to stay longer with Shirin while he ran home. He called Jango from the cab to fill him in and was gratified to hear his friend exhale. "Saala, we were so worried. We almost came to the hospital this morning."

"No, she's better. The fever is down."

"Great news. So . . . any plans for tonight? No pressure, but if you want, you can drop by. It's just Shenaz and me at home."

Remy hesitated. He had still not contacted Dina Mehta, and the longer he waited, the more awkward it would get. After all, it was Dina's expert management of his affairs that had allowed him to stay away so long. But after the kind of night he'd had, he wanted to be with people his own age. He could see Dina later this week.

"Can I let you know after I return to the hospital? I want to see how she does the rest of the day. If she's not well, I'll spend the night there. And I don't want to ruin another evening for you, like I did yesterday."

"Why do you talk such rubbish, yaar?" Jango said, exasperated. "You think setting an extra plate is going to bankrupt me or what? Everybody understood why you had to leave in a rush. Anyway, come tonight if you can. Just take care of yourself. And if you need anything, ask for help like an ordinary human being. Understand?"

"I do," Remy said, thankful for Jango's gruff kindness. He was incredibly grateful that two young boys, so unlike each other, had become lifelong friends.

CHAPTER FOURTEEN

WHEN HE RETURNED to the hospital after having showered, Shirin was sitting up in bed, taking a few sips of Coke from the can that Manju was holding. Remy felt a jolt of apprehension. *Does she drink water at all?* he wondered. *Or is she living on this stuff?* Then, remembering how sick she'd been last night, he thought, *What does it matter?*

"Hi, Mummy," he said. "Feeling better?"

She looked at him, and he saw the faintest of smiles on her face, so slight that he may have imagined it. But then she raised a bony hand and lightly patted the bed. Heart thumping, he sat down next to her. Manju, too, looked wonderstruck, as if she'd witnessed a statue come to life.

Manju. Remy was thankful that she had been here last night. It was always good to have a companion in the foxhole. He opened his wallet and took out several crisp notes. "I want you to take a cab home," he said. "And you can start later tonight. Is this enough money for you to return by cab also?"

The woman gasped. "Sir, too much money. I cannot take."

"Please," he said. "You were a great help last night. I don't want you to struggle with catching trains and all that. Go home and get some sleep."

"Sir," Manju giggled at his cluelessness, "at this time, it will be faster to go by train. Too much traffic."

Of course. Still, he held out the cash. Manju had no idea how small the amount was when converted into dollars. "As you wish," he said. "But, please, accept this as a token of my appreciation."

"It's my duty, sir," Manju said as she took the bills. "I will go and come back quickly-quickly this evening."

"Manju, please. Don't rush." He lowered his voice. "Who knows what tonight will bring?"

THEY HAD MANAGED to bring down Shirin's fever, but last night's spike had clearly taken a toll. When the lunch tray came, Remy had an idea. "Let's take a few bites of the custard first, Mummy," he said. "Okay? Dessert first. But then you have to eat some of the real food. Promise?"

He spoke as he fed her, coaxing her along, his voice alternately stern and cooing. Shirin happily ate a third of the custard but chewed slowly on the mutton, her eyes steady on his face. At last, unable to bear it, he said, "Okay, Mama. Swallow or spit it out." He held a kidney tray to her lips, and she spat out the cud. He felt nauseous at the sight but didn't look away. He would go buy her some protein drinks later.

After lunch, Remy carried on an upbeat conversation, determined to keep her engaged. He racked his brain for topics, searching for inspiration. Why hadn't he brought a small music player to the hospital? Surely, some Kishore Kumar or the Beatles would've cheered her up?

An hour later, there was a light knock on the door. He looked up to see Monaz, and his stomach dropped. Was this girl stalking him? What gall, to show up here unannounced. He hadn't even mentioned Monaz to his mother, nor the real reason for his sudden arrival in Bombay. He leapt to his feet, shaking his head slowly in warning, as the girl walked toward him. She gave him a reassuring smile.

"Mummy, this is Shenaz's niece," he said, playing for time. Shirin gave the girl a thin smile.

Monaz approached the bed, bent, and gave Shirin a quick kiss on the cheek. For the first time, Remy spotted the bulge under her cotton shirt.

"Hello, auntie," Monaz said. "How are you feeling?"

To Remy's surprise, Shirin's smile grew wider as she swept her eyes from Monaz to Remy. *If I didn't know better, I'd swear that she knows*, Remy thought. All his life, he had feared Shirin's preternatural sixth sense when it came to matters pertaining to him.

"What brings you here?" he asked the girl, who gave him a nervous look.

"I wanted to talk to you about something," she said quietly.

Remy sighed. "Take some rest, Mummy," he said. "I'll be right outside your room."

"Monaz," he began after they sat on the bench in the hallway. "I don't mean to offend, but you can't just barge in like this whenever you want. Not to the apartment, and certainly not at the hospital. My mom doesn't even know why I'm here—she doesn't know about you or the baby."

"Oh God. I'm sorry. But I have some good news and didn't wish to wait."

How to make her understand that he couldn't surf the waves of her moods and whims? That he had his hands full trying to get his mother well enough to take her home? That he was too old to play games with an irrational, lost girl who couldn't make up her own mind?

"Don't you want to hear my news?"

"What is it?" Remy looked at Monaz with weary eyes.

"I've decided, uncle. I'm giving you and Kathy custody. I won't change my mind again, I swear."

"Monaz, if you need a few more days to think . . ."

"I don't. I've thought, and I've thunked. But the baby will not stop growing while I think."

"That's true." A small hope flared in Remy's chest. "If you're serious . . . That is, if this were to proceed, I'll have to insist on a contract. You know, something in writing."

Monaz pulled a sheet out of her purse. "I know. I already wrote it out. See? I even signed it."

Despite himself, Remy was moved by Monaz's obvious sincerity and eagerness to make amends. "What about Gaurav?"

"What about him?" Monaz's mouth was set in a firm, bitter line. "You think he gives a damn?"

He opened his mouth to offer his sympathies, but she spoke first. "There's one more thing, Remy Uncle. I have one condition. I know it's asking for a lot, but there's no way for me to have this baby in India and have it remain a secret. Take me to America with you. I'll come back after my delivery. That way, nobody here will ever find out about my pregnancy."

CHAPTER FIFTEEN

———✗———

REMY'S MIND WAS reeling after he walked Monaz out and returned to Shirin's room. His mother was sleeping peacefully, the tiniest thread of drool escaping her mouth. Afraid of awakening her, he resisted the urge to wipe it. It was too late to call Kathy. Instead, he went back out into the hallway to call Dina Mehta. If Kathy agreed to Monaz's stipulation, he would have Dina draw up a legal document. He was reaching for his phone when he heard shouting from two rooms down, followed by a keening sound. "Banu," a male voice yelled. "Darling, no, no, no."

Remy hurried toward the noise. Mehernosh was hunched over his wife's bed, his upper body racked with sobs. "Please, my love," he was saying. "Please, please. Don't leave me."

Four nurses crowded around the bed as Remy watched. One of

them rubbed Mehernosh's back. "It's okay, uncle," she said. "She was suffering, poor thing."

Mehernosh looked up and spotted Remy. "Deekra," he called out, but Remy stood rooted in place. "Deekra, help me," the old man implored, one arm outstretched, and Remy had no choice but to enter the room. He glanced quickly at the dead woman and looked away, focusing on her bereaved husband.

"I'm so sorry, uncle," he said.

Mehernosh's face was a tableau of suffering, his eyes bloodshot. "What do I do now?" he cried.

This is how it feels to lose a life partner, Remy thought. He had been devastated when Daddy had died, but the loss of a spouse was different. Mehernosh looked as if he were being shredded by grief. Remy put an arm around the old man. "I'm sorry," he murmured.

A doctor entered the room. "Are you his son?" he said to Remy.

"Me? No. Just a . . ." Remy straightened. "Just a friend."

The doctor nodded and set his stethoscope on the dead woman's chest. After a moment, he looked up. "Condolences for your loss, sir," he said. He turned to the head nurse. "You can call for the hearse now."

At the word *hearse*, Mehernosh started crying again. "Oh, my love," he said. "What will become of me now, all alone?"

"Is your daughter coming from America?" Remy asked.

Mehernosh shook his head. "Her husband had a fall." He sighed. "I told her that her first duty was to him. My niece and nephew are on their way."

Remy waited until the relatives arrived, then slipped out of the room. What a difference a day made. He could have been in Mehernosh's shoes last night. *But would you have been as cut up if Mummy had died?* he asked himself. The answer was . . . yes and no. No because unlike poor Mehernosh, he had a wife to whom he would soon return. Yes because Mummy would've been taken from him when he was on the cusp of learning to love her rather than fear her. The fact that she'd called out for Dad was something he would treasure the rest of his life, the knowledge that underneath the hostility and the long angry silences, a quiet love had burned.

He checked on his mother. She was still asleep. He went in the hallway and called Dina.

"So good to hear from you, Remy!" she exclaimed. "How is your dear mother?"

Her voice, warm and friendly, immediately made him feel lighter, like the glow after the first long sip of Scotch.

He told her he was in Bombay and that his mother was in the hospital, letting her assume, for now, that Shirin's illness was the reason for his visit.

"I'm very sorry to hear this," Dina said. "Let's hope for good news soon."

"Yes," he said. "But Dina. How are *you*?"

"Oh, I'm fine. Getting old, but plugging along. Tell me: How can I help?"

"Well, I was wondering if I could stop by one of these days. To, you know, say hi and also go over all the accounts and make some changes. Mummy is definitely going to need long-term care."

"Of course."

"And . . . And I also need your advice on a different legal matter. I can explain more in person."

"Sure. Hold on while I look at my calendar." When she returned, she said, "This week looks very bad during the day. But . . . are you ever free in the evenings? For dinner?"

"I usually leave the hospital after seven. Is that too late?"

Dina laughed. "No, it's perfect. I typically eat around eight. Tell you what. Why don't you come to my house tomorrow night? I'm sure you're craving some home-cooked Parsi food."

Touched by her invitation, he didn't mention how frequently he was eating at Jango's. Dina was clearly treating him as a family friend. "That would be lovely," he said. "I'll bring dessert."

"So much like your dad." He heard the smile in Dina's voice. "I tell you, that man never once came to my office without bringing a cake or some other dessert. I'm on P.M. Road, right behind the Bombay Store. Do you know where that is? I'm in Trumbal Apartments."

CHAPTER SIXTEEN

———✦———

LUCKILY, THE CABDRIVER knew the location of the Bombay Store. Many of the taxiwallas around here came from the hinterlands, and Remy was always amazed at how little they knew of the city. He walked past the glittering shop, wishing he had the time to go in and pick up a few gifts for his in-laws, but he didn't want to keep Dina waiting, especially on a weekday.

He felt himself relax as soon as Dina's elderly cook led him into the living room. The handloom prints hanging on the white walls, the blue ceramic bowls, the tasteful furniture—all gave the apartment the feeling of an inner sanctum, a refuge from the noise and chaos of the streets below. Brahms's Violin Concerto in D Major played on the stereo. Remy recognized it immediately—it was one of his father's most cherished pieces of music.

"Remy," Dina said as she walked into the room. "So good to see you again." She was wearing denim pants with a light-blue linen shirt, and the outfit made her look younger than she did in the starched cotton saris that made up her work attire.

He leaned forward and gave her a quick kiss on the cheek as he handed her the box of pastries. "You have an exquisite home," he said.

Dina's face lit up. *She has such an animated, transparent face,* Remy thought. He couldn't help comparing it to Shirin's impassive visage, and he felt the old, familiar ache. How different his childhood would've been if he had been brought up by this cultured, elegant woman instead.

"Come sit," she said. "What will you take? Some wine? Beer? Something stronger?"

"Wine would be great," Remy said. Somehow, asking Dina to make him a Scotch felt impolite.

Remy took in the spacious living room, his eyes alighting on a painting in the corner. He walked over to take a closer look. "If I didn't know better I'd say this is a Husain," he said.

She came up to him and handed him the glass. "That's perceptive of you," she said. "Most people only recognize his signature horses. This particular piece is hardly ever featured in the catalogues."

He studied the painting, the blackened face of the mother cradling her child, the tragic, bent posture, the luminous colors. "Is this . . . ? This isn't an original, is it?" he asked.

"I wish. No, it's a limited-edition print. Only fifty of these. I bought this from the earnings on my very first case. Even before I had this apartment, I had this print." She lowered her voice. "I actually do have a very small original, over here. I was very lucky to buy it when I did. Now, it would be unaffordable."

"It's funny," Remy said after they'd finished admiring the original. "Your taste is so similar to my dad's—in music, in art, what have you."

Dina flushed. "Cyrus was a big influence on my life," she said. "Do you know I went to my first-ever classical music concert with your dad and his mother?"

"You knew my grandma?"

"Not too well. They used to invite me to concerts occasionally, that's all. Which was a big treat for someone like me."

"I don't understand why Daddy didn't marry you. You were obviously so compatible." The words were out of his mouth before he could take them back. He stopped, stricken. "I'm—I'm sorry. That was incredibly rude."

"Don't be." Dina looked down at her hands, then looked up. "We had a big fight when I . . . He didn't want me to go to London for my studies. But for me . . . You see, I came from a lower-middle-class family. My father was a clerk at Central Bank. So the scholarship was a once-in-a-lifetime chance. I defied Cyrus and went. I thought he'd wait for me." Dina smiled, but her eyes were pensive. "I was so naïve. I understood so little. Your grandma definitely didn't want him to marry me, a girl from my background. By the time I returned, Cyrus had moved on. And then once he met Shirin years later, he was a total goner. Head over heels in love with your mother. Shirin was so beautiful. A real looker, as we used to say. And she came from money. So . . ." Dina shrugged.

Remy felt personally culpable for what had happened decades earlier. "I'm sorry," he said again.

Dina shook her head. "It's all water under the bridge, dear boy. I just wish Cyrus and Shirin could've been happier together. I had really hoped for that."

Remy drained the rest of his wine, and Dina got up immediately to refill his glass. "Something very strange happened two nights ago," he said. "I didn't want to tell you on the phone, but Mummy had a very high fever. I—I was sure that we were losing her. But in the midst of all that, she kept moaning Dad's name over and over. Kept saying, 'Cyrus, Cyloo, my darling.' It was very gratifying. So, you know, in their own way, I think they did care about each other."

Even though Dina's back was to him, Remy saw her body tense, and he regretted his words, salt on her wounds. He looked at her inquiringly as she finally turned and handed him the glass. How foolish he'd been to believe her when she'd said she had hoped for his parents' marriage to work out.

Dina sat down on the couch across from him. "She called out for Cyloo? What else did she say?"

Seeing her love for his father made Remy reluctant to say more. "That was about it. She calmed down after a while."

"I see." Dina's hands clenched in her lap. "Well, I suppose one never knows what goes on behind closed walls."

"True," Remy said, wanting to get off the subject. He told her quickly about Monaz and the proposed adoption. "I was wondering if you could draw up some papers for me."

"Sure. But if she changes her mind, the contract won't mean a thing. No court in India will rule against the birth mother."

"There's one more thing. She told me yesterday that her offer was contingent on her coming to America with me and staying with us until she gives birth."

"Wow," Dina said. "This girl is a smart cookie." She frowned. "But you're leaving soon, no? It'll take months to get her an American visa. Does she even have a passport?"

Remy smiled. He'd raised the same issues with Monaz, but she had interrupted him. "I have a ten-year tourist visa, uncle," she'd said. "I was supposed to go to the States with my parents two summers ago, but my mother broke her ankle and we didn't go. So I have all my papers. I even have some savings that I can use to pay for my ticket. I'm sure Shenazfui will help me if I'm short."

"Don't be silly," Remy had said. "If we do this, I'll buy your ticket. But you understand, I have to talk to my wife first."

"Of course, uncle. Please tell her that I'm a very honest and responsible person. I will cook and clean for you until the baby arrives. I make good Parsi food. I won't be a burden, I promise."

Despite his reservations, Remy had warmed to Monaz's words. The adoption would feel so much more intimate, so much more like a family affair, if Monaz was with them in the final months of her pregnancy. He and Kathy would be present when her—*their*—son was born.

"She has a visa and a passport," he told Dina. "She's thought of everything."

"Except using protection to prevent getting pregnant," Dina said. There was a bitterness in her voice that startled Remy. "Sorry. It's one of my pet peeves—these girls who allow themselves to be used by men. I've seen many such cases."

He had broken the news to Kathy late last night his time, catching her before she had left for work. Kathy had been shocked, then flustered. "The guest room is in such disarray," she'd blurted out.

"I think that's the least of our worries, hon," he said quietly.

"And I don't like the thought of having a stranger in the house for the next four months. I mean, we don't know her habits or tastes, or anything else about her."

But Remy did. He had met Monaz less than a week ago, and already he felt a sense of kinship. What Gaurav had said was true; the Parsis were such a small and distinct community that they were all related, by culture if not by blood. There were differences between his and Monaz's upbringing, of course: she had grown up in small-town Navsari in a modest home, whereas he was raised in luxury in the most cosmopolitan city in India. Yet Remy knew that Monaz, too, had eaten dhansak for Sunday lunch; that she'd gone to the fire temple on Navroz, Parsi New Year; that she'd watched *The Sound of Music* a dozen times; that on her birthday, her parents had placed a garland around her neck and applied a red tili on her forehead.

"You'll like her," Remy had said, and it was true. "She's an odd combo of gullible and smart. I mean, she fell for a real asshole and completely bought his bullshit. But look how she's trying to engineer her way out of India."

Kathy sighed. "I just . . . I feel like she's manipulating us."

Remy closed his eyes briefly, struggling for the words to tell his wife she was wrong. Kathy was thinking as an American—he needed her to see Monaz in the Indian context. "I can see why you'd think that, honey," he said. "But it didn't feel that way when Monaz proposed it. She's scared. Desperate. Her parents will never speak to her if she carries her baby to term here. Men will hit on her, because they'll think she's a loose woman, damaged goods. An unwed pregnancy is a real no-no in India still."

"Jesus. It's like they're stuck in the 1950s."

"You've been here, Kat. You know what it's like."

But Kathy had only visited when Dad was alive, and Daddy's wealth and status had protected her from seeing the real India, Cyrus not so much as permitting Kathy's feet to touch the ground. Their visits had been a swirl of dinners and parties and trips to seaside resorts, where they got massages on the beach. Kathy had only experienced the postcard version of India, glimpsed out of air-conditioned cars. She knew nothing about the gossip and scandal, the social isolation and ostracizing that awaited unmarried women who had a child.

"I was also thinking," Remy continued, "it might be nice to get to know Monaz a little bit, you know? Let her get to know us, too, so that she feels good about her decision. I don't want this adoption to feel like a transaction. And this way, we can be there for the actual delivery."

Kathy had sighed. "Okay. Bring her back with you. We'll make it work. The time will go by fast. Just make sure the contract guarantees that she will return home after the birth."

"Your wife is fine with this arrangement?" Dina now asked.

"Yes. She's sympathetic to Monaz's situation," Remy said.

"And your mother? She approves?"

Remy gave Dina a knowing look. "I haven't told her yet. I have no idea how she'll react."

Dina lifted a bowl of cashews and offered them to Remy. "It's hard to know, beta," she said. "Hopefully, she'll be happy for you."

Dina's cook came into the living room. "Dinner is ready, madam," he said. "Shall I serve?"

They managed to keep the conversation alive as they ate, the hours passing quickly as they tossed stories back and forth like a beach ball. Dina was poker-faced as she recounted an unusual case: a multimillionaire client wanting to sue his ex-wife for breach of contract and negligence over the death of their pet parrot.

"What did you do?" Remy asked.

Dina arched an eyebrow. "Do? I told him the judge would revoke my law license if I took on such an absurd case. I mean, the backlog of serious cases before the courts is unimaginable already."

"So you convinced him not to sue?"

"No." She smiled wryly. "He hired one of those . . . What do you call them in America? . . . Ambulance chasers. That's a wonderful term, by the way. American English is so evocative."

Remy grinned. "It is, isn't it?"

When the clock chimed eleven o'clock, Remy looked up, startled. "I'm so sorry," he said. "I can't believe I stayed this late, and that, too, when you have to work tomorrow."

Dina smiled. "Don't be. I've so enjoyed talking to you. You're every bit as smart and sweet as your father always said you were."

Remy felt a bright ache in his heart. Why hadn't Mummy ever praised him as effortlessly as Dina did? In her presence, under her amused and appreciative eye, he indeed felt intelligent. Then he felt guilty for comparing the two women again. The guilt itself was a new experience; most of his life, Remy had collected mothers, had always felt wistful when he'd compared Shirin's miserly love to the fawning of the other women in his life. The first time he'd met Kathy's mother, he had tried winning her over with a fervent ruthlessness, had so turned on the charm offensive that by the end of the evening Rose had proclaimed him part of her family and labeled him the son she'd never had.

The night streets were still bustling when he left Dina's house and he decided to walk for a bit before getting into a cab. It was not as cool tonight, and he prayed that this was not an intimation of warm weather to come. He was almost certainly going to be in Bombay longer than he'd intended, given the situations with Monaz and his mother. Luckily, the advertising business was typically slow in January, and in Eric, his creative director, he had a reliable and brilliant second-in-command. Still, as lovely an evening as he'd had with Dina, he had not accomplished what he had needed to. He had intended to eventually steer the conversation to discussing Mummy's legal and financial situation, but the evening had gotten away from him.

His mind flashed back to hearing about Daddy's college romance with Dina. Dad had been so encouraging about Remy's going to America for his MFA that it was hard to believe that he had tried to talk his girlfriend out of accepting a rare scholarship abroad. And to have dated other women while Dina was away? To have listened to his mother when it came time to select a bride? Remy's paternal grandmother had died when he was very young, but the few memories he had of her were not pleasant ones. He remembered her chastising him for running around her apartment and falsely accusing him of stealing money out of her purse. Why on earth had Dad taken her advice?

A man coming from the opposite direction hocked and spat on the sidewalk, and although Remy swerved instinctively to avoid the bullet-like trajectory of his phlegm, he remained preoccupied in his musings: All children believe that the world begins with their birth. But to be an adult was to acknowledge the endless circles of life that began before one's time and would continue long after, to realize that one's story was shaped and written by unknown others. His own history had begun so much earlier than his actual story began. Cyrus's choices, made for reasons he wasn't alive to defend or rationalize, had bled into his own.

Remy looked around, and for a quick moment, he saw beyond the row of parked cars, the storefronts shuttered for the night, the dog raising its leg to pee on the tires of a parked scooter. Instead, he heard his ancestors whispering in his ear, telling him of their disappointments and triumphs, their joys and failures. No matter how many years he spent in America, the fact remained: he was built out of the clay of this city, out of its imperfect earth.

Back home, he didn't have time to think about such things. In America, he had been a young man in a hurry, determined to be worthy of Kathy, who had taken a chance on marrying an aspiring poet. It was one of the reasons he had changed careers after graduation. In Bombay, he could afford to be an idealistic, mopey dreamer. But Daddy's wealth wouldn't get him far in America, and seeing how hard Kathy worked in med school had fueled Remy's ambition to be successful in his own right. It was abundantly clear that an MFA in poetry wasn't going to allow him to support a family.

The poetry had abandoned him anyway. He had written a well-received chapbook, *Falling Room*, for his master's thesis, had started at his new job at Columbus's largest ad agency two weeks after graduation, and then—nothing. The muse had fled. Perhaps it was punishment for the Faustian bargain he'd struck, trading his gift for a steady paycheck. Perhaps being with Kathy had chased away the melancholy that had inspired his literary work, and replaced it with contentment. Contentment, the enemy of art. He had given up his rich inner life for other rewards: the Clio he'd won two years ago, the kitchen renovation this past summer, the presidency of the local Rotary Club. Occasionally, he caught a glimpse of the thin, moody fellow who had wandered around campus that first semester at Ohio State, but it was like spotting the flash of a red sweater belonging to a friend through the trees in the woods. Before he could wave, that boy was gone.

But tonight, walking the streets, listening to the sounds of Bombay, smelling the salty air from the nearby ocean, Remy felt the tug of the past again. This was the power of India: it whittled you down, stripped you, made you believe not in the promise of the future as America did, but in the firm hold of the past. In America, a man could become what he dreamed; in India, dreaming could undo a man.

But that's not true, he argued with himself. *You are free. You escaped this museum of failures. You are the one who got away.*

THAT NIGHT, as he slept, he saw the faces of women: Kathy, Monaz, Shirin, Dina, and Rose. They were bodiless, just their faces flitting by, like playing cards being dealt on top of one another. Mothers, wives, daughters—all of them competing over his divided self. He groaned, struggling to find his way out of the vision.

He was startled out of his sleep by the ringing of bells.

CHAPTER SEVENTEEN

---✤---

THE DOORBELL HAD been ringing, but Remy kept incorporating the sound into his dreams. Then his phone rang, and he was wide awake and scrambling to his feet. Shit. He had overslept, and now he had to let Hema in even as he had to pee urgently. He rushed to the front door while answering his phone.

"You still in bed?" Kathy said. "Isn't it late there?"

"Yeah," he said as he unlocked the door. "I overslept."

"Oh," Kathy said. "I just needed—"

"Hey. Can I call you back in like five minutes?"

"Sure." Kathy's voice was amused. "Go pee."

He smiled to himself and went into the bathroom, checking his phone. Two messages from Jango and one missed call from Dina. She had called at 7:14 a.m., and he had slept right through it. He hadn't even had that much to drink last night. Why on earth was he so tired?

"Hi," Kathy said when he called back. "I just had a quick question. Do you remember that letter to the Chathams you were helping me with the day before you left? I can't find it. Do you still have a copy on your laptop by chance?" The Chathams were a young couple who had lost their six-year-old daughter. He had helped Kathy compose a condolence letter.

"I don't know," he said. "Let me check. Hold on, okay?" He had edited Kathy's letter a mere ten days ago. And yet that memory felt impossibly distant and unreal, as if his life in America had happened to someone else.

HE FOUND THE email and forwarded it to her. "I don't understand why you didn't mail it as soon as it was written," he said.

There was an abrupt silence. "Well," Kathy said, "things haven't exactly been easy around here, you know."

Remy heard the tightness in his wife's voice. "I know," he said quickly. "I'm sorry."

"And now I have to get the house in order before you bring Monaz."

"Honey, don't," he said. "Monaz is . . . She's a teenager. She's not going to care about the guest room being neat and all that."

"But we're not teenagers, Remy," Kathy said. "I'm not going to welcome a guest into a messy house. Also, she's pregnant—I want her to be as healthy and comfortable as possible. In any case, don't worry about it. Jerry is going to stop by and help me rearrange some furniture."

Remy was grateful to his brother-in-law for helping his wife in his absence. And yet he couldn't help but feel left out, stranded in Bombay.

"Although I'd much rather have you helping me than Jerry," Kathy said, and Remy knew that she'd read his silence accurately.

"It's hard being here," he said quietly. "I miss you."

"Me too," Kathy said. "But we'll get through it."

Kathy described her long workday to him, and he sat back on the bed, interested but distracted. He was going to be late getting to the hospital today. Still, he didn't dare interrupt. He reminded himself of the number of times Kathy had traveled to Bombay with him and dealt with the culture shock, how she had tolerated his mother's erratic behavior during his parents' visits to Columbus, how she had learned to cook Parsi food, how she'd even attempted to learn Gujarati in order to impress his parents, although they both spoke fluent English.

"Remy," Kathy was saying, "there's one other thing. I hate bringing it up, but I do need to know. I had planned to throw a surprise birthday party for you. But I'm telling you now so that I know. You'll definitely be home by your birthday, right?"

"Definitely," he said. "But, Kat, you don't have to do anything."

"Yeah, right. After the fuss you made for me last year?"

He'd taken Kathy to Cedar Point for the weekend and surprised her by inviting twenty of her friends and family members to join them. Kathy had joyfully ridden the rides from morning till dusk. To Remy's amazement, she had gone on the stomach-churning Corkscrew roller coaster three times. He himself had chickened out after the first ride.

"How are the girls doing?" Remy asked. The "girls" were Kathy's older sisters, Karen and Liz—hardly girls, but it was how they nevertheless referred to one another, the three of them so close.

"They're fine. We'll all miss you at Uncle Albert and Aunt Regina's anniversary party this weekend."

It grounded him, hearing about the routine happenings, the celebrations occurring halfway across the world. At the same time, it made him feel ghostly, distant, as if he were stranded in outer space and Kathy were beaming an image from Earth to him.

There was a light knock on his bedroom door, and he opened it. "Sir," Hema said, "shall I start breakfast?"

He nodded, waited until Hema left. "I miss our life," he said, his voice low. Then, not wanting to infect Kathy with his sadness: "See?

This is your punishment for marrying an immigrant. You should've married that beefy football player at OSU who was lusting after you. What was his name? Biff? Hogan? Rambo? Whatever. He would've been happy to lie on the couch and eat nachos for the rest of his life, and never step foot out of Ohio."

Kathy laughed. "I'm happy with my skinny Indian dude. He'll be home soon enough."

He was smiling when he got off the phone. As always, Kathy had recalibrated him. For the umpteenth time, he was grateful for that rarest of gifts: a happy marriage. Indeed, Daddy's most fervent prayer had been answered. "More than anything, I wish for you a good wife," he used to say when Remy was still living at home. "Choose wisely. Believe me, ninety percent of life's happiness comes from selecting the right life partner."

At that time, Remy would see the wistfulness in his father's eyes and think, *There's no way I'll ever marry. The last thing I want is to be unhappy like you. Like the two of you.* His parents' marriage had had two temperature settings: heated bickering and frosty silence.

Saturdays were the worst. Every Saturday morning, Shirin would visit Mount Mary Church in Bandra, leaving Remy at home with his father. When he was a child, Remy had asked to accompany his mother, but his father forbade it. Like most Parsis of his generation, Cyrus was a secular man, tolerant of all faiths. But something about his wife going to a Catholic church in a faraway suburb irked him. Shirin often returned home afterward tired and snappish.

"You couldn't have come home sooner?" Cyrus would say. "Leaving your son alone the whole day?"

"I watch him every evening after school, and you're complaining about keeping him one day of the week?" Shirin's eyes would narrow as she'd address the cowering boy: "Didn't I tell you to just do your homework and not disturb your father? Rotten boy, for troubling your father."

Decades later, the word *rotten* still produced a sour feeling in Remy, reminded him of a blackened banana with fruit flies hovering around it. But as he set his phone down to charge, Remy remembered what Dina had shared with him last night. He had always blamed himself for his parents' shitty marriage. Now, for the first time, he understood that their problems had preceded his birth: Daddy had never gotten over his love for Dina; Mummy had never forgiven Cyrus for this.

Hema looked up when Remy poked his head into the kitchen. "I'm going to take a quick shower," he said. "Can you delay making breakfast?"

"I will wait, sir."

The sour feeling remained as he turned on the hot water geyser and stripped, and he forced himself to think about Kathy. "I'm happy with my skinny Indian dude," she'd said. She'd always been this loving, from the first time he met her at Ohio State.

REMY WAS RENTING a small studio apartment close to campus, and his prized possession was a Technics stereo, a gift from his father. He spent his days attending classes and studying at the library, in love with the scholarly hush of the building. At noon, he'd sit shivering under an enormous oak tree in the Oval, munching on a sandwich, sketching and writing in his notebook. Some of the undergraduates were still wearing T-shirts and shorts as they chased Frisbees, but Remy, raised in tropical Bombay, felt the October chill through his blue jeans and the red sweater he'd purchased at Target on his second day in Columbus.

He was enchanted by the slant of the fall light, its texture and hue different from any he'd ever seen. The scarlet and gold of the trees reminded him of playing Holi on the streets of Bombay as a boy and coming home bathed in color. He loved hurrying to his classes under the big autumnal skies, white patches of clouds against the blue denim of the sky. The air smelled like crisp apples, and he inhaled deeply. *I'm in America. I'm walking on a campus in America*, he would repeat to himself, his astonishment at his good fortune never waning.

In the evenings, he walked some more, sometimes taking the Olentangy Trail, at other times wandering for hours along High Street. He marveled at the friendliness of his fellow students, how everyone smiled and said "Whassup?" or "Hey" as they passed. He stood in front of the mirror and practiced that jaunty upward nod, so quint-essentially American, and repeated "How you doin'?" until he was satisfied he'd mastered the gesture and the intonation of the informal greeting.

Often, he picked up dinner from one of the many restaurants near campus. His favorite was a small rotisserie chicken joint, owned by an elderly Greek couple. They welcomed him like a grandson, and he felt most at home there—something about their slow and precise move-ments, the care with which they filled his container with rice, feeling familiar and precious. Always, he tipped them; always they refused, shooing him out of the restaurant when he'd insist.

At home, he turned on the stereo before pouring himself a chilled Coke and tearing into his dinner. All evening long, R.E.M. and Savage Garden and Bob Dylan kept him company as he ate and washed his dishes, then settled in to read the poets who were new to him: Jorie Graham and Claudia Rankine, Maggie Anderson and Yusef Komunyakaa. He reveled in the pleasure of discovery, that heady feel-ing of reading a line that made him catch his breath, even while it fueled his own competitive juices. He wanted to savor those poems, tear them apart to see if he could find the beating heart at their center, analyze them, memorize them, internalize them. He wanted to keep them for himself, while also wanting to share them with everyone he knew.

He didn't know many people. His fellow grad students were friendly; his professors accessible. After his public life in Bombay,

where everyone in his neighborhood knew who he was and whose son
he was, nobody recognized him in Columbus. Remy loved this feeling
of anonymity, the invisibility he felt as he walked around campus at
dusk, soaking up the quiet, muffled quality of human life here, compared to the noisy parade that was Bombay. America, for all its glam-
our, its razzle-dazzle, appeared muted and subdued, compared to the
shouting exuberance of street life in Bombay.

On a Friday night, he walked toward Ralph Addington's house.
Once he left behind the rowdiness of the High Street bars, the side
roads were hushed and still. In the amber glow of the streetlights, a
long row of maples stood like town criers bursting with today's news,
bearing the weight of weather, carrying the forecast in their slowly
turning leaves. The only sound Remy could hear was the sound of his
shoes on the sidewalk. As far as he could see, there was not another
soul out on Seventeenth Avenue. In Bombay, the streets wouldn't be
this empty even at four in the morning. But he was already getting used
to how Columbus rolled up its carpet at dusk, and that there were far
more cars out than humans. *The ancient empty street's too dead for
dreaming.* The line from the old Dylan song swam through his head,
as sweet and familiar as breath.

Everything about this country—the chilly autumn air, the unlim-
ited number of books he could check out from the library, his long,
solitary walks, the passionate, heated discussions in his seminar on
the Modernists—everything was lighting a fire under him, so that he
felt gloriously, ravenously alive, burning like a rag on fire. His own
poems poured out of him at an astonishing rate. At night, he dreamed
in streams of words, saw them unwinding like endless scrolls of paper,
and when he awoke, he wept in frustration at being unable to remember them all.

Ralph Addington was in his poetry workshop, a lanky boy with
red, tousled hair and an easy smile. He had introduced himself to

Remy on their first day of class, and Remy had liked him immediately, as soon as they discovered that they both loved Patti Smith. Before the start of their second class, Ralph gave Remy a yellowing, dog-eared copy of *The Cantos of Ezra Pound*. "Welcome to America," he said with a smile. The price of the old book—six dollars—was written in pencil on the first page, and the fact that Ralph had bought him a used copy appealed to Remy's romantic notion that they were penniless grad students. Later, he'd find out that Ralph's father owned eight hundred acres of farmland in southern Ohio, making him one of the wealthiest landowners in the state.

In America, he'd learn, the sons of the rich dressed in torn jeans and constantly complained about being "broke," whereas in India, the children of the poor desperately tried to dress above their station and never talked about their poverty. Remy had almost bankrupted himself that first semester by treating classmates to lunch or drinks anytime they said they were broke, before Ralph pulled him aside and explained that being broke was not the same as being poor. Six weeks into the semester, when Ralph said he was throwing himself a birthday party that Friday night and that everybody would be there and that Remy should definitely check it out, Remy couldn't come up with a reason to refuse.

So here he was, carrying a six-pack of Molson and standing in front of a three-story Victorian. Dozens of students were milling around the front porch, hooting with laughter and talking all at once. Abandoned beer bottles were strewn across the front lawn, and as Remy strolled up the front walkway, he caught the sweet smell of pot and tobacco. It occurred to him that with so many people here, Ralph wouldn't miss him if he turned around and went home.

"Hey," a guy called out to him from the porch. "Aren't you in Prof Lincoln's class?"

"Yeah," Remy said, climbing up the stairs, feeling overdressed in

his denim jacket, white shirt, jeans, and leather loafers. "Good to see
you." He looked around. "Have you seen Ralph?"

The man jerked his head. "He's in the kitchen, I think."

Ralph was pouring vodka into the punch bowl when Remy entered.
"Remy," he cried, and hugged him exuberantly, as if they were brothers. "You made it, dude."

Remy grinned awkwardly, still clutching the six-pack. "Here you
go," he said. "Happy birthday. I forgot your actual gift at home." His
mother had sent him to America with dozens of small Indian curios to
present to new friends.

"Hey, man, beer's gift enough," Ralph said loudly—too loudly. His
face was red and sweaty, and he was clearly drunk. "Do you know
everybody here?" he said, sweeping a hand across the expanse of the
crowded kitchen.

"Not really," Remy said. Had Ralph forgotten how new he was to
Ohio State?

"Me neither." Ralph snorted with laughter. He poured the punch
and handed Remy a glass. "Here's to new friends."

"To friends." Remy knocked back the drink. Despite its benign
pink color, the punch tasted like rubbing alcohol. He looked down at
the checkered floor, forcing himself not to choke or cough. When he
finally looked up, he was staring directly at a woman who stood across
the kitchen island from him. "That's some messed-up shit," she said.
She smiled.

Remy blinked. Her smile was so dazzling, its wattage so strong,
that he took a half step back, as if he had been seared by it. "Yes," he
said at last, feeling blind, stupid. Surely, he couldn't be tipsy with one
glass of punch, even if it was 90 percent alcohol.

"It packs a punch," he said, smiling at his own cleverness.

She groaned. "Oh God. That's awful."

He felt miserable, a failed punster. But then she smiled again, and
the world righted itself. "Where're you from?" she asked.

"Bombay. I've only been here a month and a half."

"Wow. You're a long way from home. Well, welcome to the US of A."

"Thanks." He wanted to say something witty or funny, something that would make this girl stay and talk to him. But he felt tongue-tied, gauche.

She nodded, grabbed a beer, and walked away. She stopped and looked over her shoulder. "I'd stay away from Ralph's concoctions if I were you. Beer is safer. Hell, arsenic is safer."

REMY STAYED IN THE KITCHEN, feeling disoriented, spun around, an intense longing tearing through him. He wanted to find the woman again, but he was afraid to move. Afraid to leave the kitchen and go looking for her and find out that she had left and he'd never see her again. (His heart did an awful dip at the thought.) Afraid that he'd find her in the living room with her arms around her handsome American boyfriend. Afraid that she'd be sitting alone and he wouldn't know what to say. He'd had girlfriends in college in India, but they were kind, waiflike girls who had hung on his every word. Now, he dismissed them as inconsequential, silly, made of paper. Whereas this woman? She looked like steel. Until she smiled, that is. Then, she was sunlight. It had scorched him to look at her.

Remy felt out of breath. It was hot in the kitchen, and he needed to feel the cool evening air again. He grabbed a beer from the cooler and made his way back to the porch, looking at the clusters of people in the living room to see if he could spot her again. There she was, surrounded by a knot of students, laughing. He felt a jolt of pure misery. No way for him to extract her from that crowd. His leather shoe caught on a raised floorboard, and he tripped. He straightened immediately but, self-conscious, looked sideways at her. She raised her eyebrows at him, then raised her bottle slightly in acknowledgment of his clumsiness. It was such a subtle gesture that only he would notice.

Still, infused with shame and misery, he went out to the porch, waiting for his heart to beat normally again.

"Hey, man," someone said to him, "I just wanted to say I loved your poem this week." And when Remy stared at him blankly: "I'm Dustin? I'm in your poetry workshop?"

"Oh, yes. Hi."

"You okay?"

"Yeah. I'm fine. Just . . . It was hot in the kitchen."

Dustin stared at Remy, then began to laugh. "Oh man," he said. "Don't tell me you drank that punch?"

"Yes. Ralph offered it to me." Remy smiled. "Although 'offered' might not be the right word."

"Jesus. I'm sorry. You're Remy, right?"

"Right."

Dustin cocked his head. "And that's . . . Indian?"

"Well, I'm Indian. But the name is French. It's a long story."

Dustin slapped him on the back. "Well, c'mon. Let me introduce you to some others."

Somebody lit a joint and passed it to Remy, who took a hit before passing it to the blond woman on his right. The conversation drifted to professors and thesis advisors, and Remy understood that Ralph had invited grad students from other departments as well. Dustin's older brother, Justin, was getting a PhD in physics. Remy leaned against the railing as he listened to their conversation, aware that every moment he spent out on the porch was a moment away from the woman in the living room.

He heard someone turn off the stereo and then the tuning of a guitar. A male voice started to sing a tune he didn't recognize, and a chorus of voices followed. Remy smiled at Dustin and excused himself wordlessly, heading back to the living room. She was still there, thank God, sitting on the couch between two others. He stood in the doorway. After a few songs, a space opened up on the futon directly across from her, and he grabbed it. They were singing "Blowin' in the Wind"; he closed his eyes and sang. He knew the lyrics as well as if he'd written them; Daddy had taught him the song while driving along Marine Drive with the car windows down, had explained Dylan's cultural significance to him.

When he opened his eyes, her eyes—what color were they? blue? purple? violet? he wasn't sure—were warm on his face. He looked back, a dizzying whiteness falling over him, a ringing in his ears that made other voices fall away. She kept her gaze on him. When he finally looked away, she did, too. It took all his effort to pay attention to the people around him. They were calling out requests for the guitarist.

"'Gentle on My Mind,'" Remy heard himself say.

The singer turned to him. "Don't know that one."

"You don't? Glen Campbell?"

"I don't know the chords."

Remy held out his hand for the guitar. The man gave him a quizzical look before handing it over. Remy tuned it, then sang it for the woman sitting across from him. But she wasn't looking at him. Disappointment made him fumble a line, but he recovered and finished the song to applause.

After that, there was no way to talk to her, not with all the sing-alongs. He took a beer that someone handed him and sucked it down. In any case, he had come to America to get an education, not to fall in love with the first woman who talked to him. He turned his attention to the girl sitting next to him. "What are you studying?" he asked in between songs.

"Art history," she said. "You?"

"I'm getting an MFA in creative writing. I'm Remy, by the way."

"I'm Janice. Are you a writer?"

"A poet." His eyes darted to where the woman he really wanted to talk to sat, a few feet away.

"Cool," Janice said. "I thought you were a music student. From how beautifully you sang and all."

He was about to thank Janice when he heard the girl with the violet eyes chuckle. He turned his head to see her staring at him, covering her mouth with her hand. Her eyes shone with mischief.

Remy turned resolutely back to Janice. "Thank you," he said. "You're kind."

He went to get yet another beer, then returned to the futon. Someone lit another joint, and he watched it going around, saw Violet Eyes suck in her cheeks as she took a hit. But instead of passing it to the boy next to her, she leaned forward and looked directly at him. He reached out to take the stub from her, their fingers brushing as he did. He held her gaze as he inhaled. Why had she skipped passing the joint to the person next to her and given it to him instead? Was this some kind of a signal? He couldn't tell. He turned to Janice and passed the reefer to her.

Later, much later, after many of the couples had drifted to the second floor and Janice had disappeared, he moved to a newly vacated armchair. The pot had relaxed him, and he sat with one leg dangling over its arm, twisting his lanky body into the chair.

"Hey." It was Violet Eyes. "What's your name?"

He looked over at her, his head foggy. "I'm Remy."

He waited for her to introduce herself, but she didn't. "So you're gonna be a poet, huh? Set the world on fire with your words?"

Somebody in the room snickered. Remy ignored it. "Why not?"

"Why not, indeed? You look a little like Rimbaud anyway."

Remy made a dismissive sound.

"Or is Rilke? I can't ever tell them apart. Anyway. No matter. Reny, Rimbaud, Rilke. What's the difference?"

Remy pushed himself off the armchair, and went to sit next to her. "What's the difference?" he said. "For one thing, my name is Remy, not Reny. 'M,' not 'n.'"

"'M,' not 'n,'" she mimicked. She smiled. "You're cute."

He stared at her, terrified by the sudden rush of feeling. She was petite, with short dark hair and those enormous blue-violet eyes, and he wanted to scoop her into his arms and not let go. The feeling was so intense that his skin tingled, as if he were actually holding her. Was she flirting with him? Hell if he knew. Everything that she'd said so far had been slightly off-kilter. Remy felt his youth, his inexperience, more acutely than ever before. All around them people were necking, holding hands, nuzzling. But the two of them sat apart. "So," he said, hearing the huskiness in his voice, "what are you studying?"

"I'm in med school. Second year."

"Are you pulling my leg?"

"No. Why would I?"

"I don't know. I just thought . . . How come you know about Rilke and all, then?"

"Oh, come on. Have *you* heard of tonsils?"

"Of course."

"Well, are you a medical student?"

"Touché." He smiled at her. "Do you realize I don't know your name?"

"Is it my fault that you haven't made the effort to find out?"

Remy opened his mouth, then shut it. He looked at her in dismay. Because, without warning, he had to pee desperately. "I have to use the loo." He stood up. "The restroom, as you Americans say. Promise me you won't leave?"

She smiled but didn't answer.

He used the small bathroom off the kitchen, finished as quickly as he could, knowing he wouldn't be able to handle his disappointment if he returned to find her gone, like a butterfly that had landed on his shoulder and then flitted away. He dried his hands on his jeans as he stepped out.

She was standing outside the door. His face lit up. "I'm so glad—"

She stood on her tiptoes and kissed him. It was a long, firm, tender kiss, which stirred every part of Remy. His arm went around her waist, and she opened her mouth to him. Remy was aroused, but more than that, he was moved. The kiss lingered; it felt more sensual than sexual. There was a hint of a promise in it—not just the promise of the moment, but something steadier than that. It was madly exciting but strangely familiar; it felt like coming home.

He broke apart first, to stare at her. Her eyes shone with an emotion he couldn't read. Remy made a small sound, then bent down to kiss her again. They stood there, lips pressed together, until someone finally said an exasperated "Excuse me," and they moved to a corner of the kitchen, where they stood smiling at each other.

"I'm Kathy." She stuck out her hand, and after the intimacy they had shared, the incongruity of the gesture made Remy laugh. He took her hand and held on to it, keeping his eyes on her face the whole time. "Hi, Kathy," he whispered.

"Hey, you two," someone shouted. "Go get a room, will ya?"

He listened to the whoops of laughter, but they barely registered. *I don't care what happens next*, Remy thought, *as long as she doesn't snatch her hand away*. It would be like losing some part of his own body if she did.

"Wanna go out on the porch?" she said. "We can . . . chat there."

"Sure." Not letting go of her hand, because some part of him still thought she was a sprite that would disappear, he reached into the cooler and pulled out two beers. He tried to open the bottles with one hand, but she laughed and said, "It's okay. I'm not going anywhere."

They found a papasan seat on the porch. An emboldened Remy put his arm around Kathy, and she snuggled into him. He felt a starburst of joy in his heart. Why had he thought this woman was steel? She was as soft as cotton. No, that wasn't right. Cotton was ordinary, common. Whereas Kathy seemed luminous, incandescent.

"What're you thinking?" she asked.

He kissed the shiny hair on the top of her head, then rattled off the first lines that came to him:

"*Bread does not nourish me, dawn disrupts me, all day I hunt for the liquid measure of your steps.*"

Kathy gave him a look he couldn't decipher, and he suddenly felt dorky, uncool.

When she spoke, her voice was neutral. "Who wrote that?"

"Neruda."

"Who's your favorite Indian poet?"

He thought hard. "I'm not sure. In Bombay, we mainly studied British poets. Some American. I . . . I mean, I've read a few on my own, of course."

"I want you to recite Indian poetry to me sometime," she said, and his stomach twisted painfully.

"You mean I'm not a one-night stand?"

She turned her face up to him. "Let's hope not, Remy," she said.

They kissed again, more passionately this time. Her mouth smelled of beer and pot, a dry, burning smell that ordinarily would've repelled him, but each time they kissed, he felt as if she were breathing life into him. He felt the friction of her jeans against his thigh, and he shifted slightly to accommodate the tightening in his groin.

"I have a roommate," she whispered, "who has her boyfriend over tonight."

His eyes widened as he understood her meaning. "I don't."

"Did you drive here?"

He shook his head. "No. I'm on Thirteenth Avenue. Not far. I walked."

He had the strong feeling that even though Kathy had taken the initiative this far, she would not invite herself over. "Would you like to see my place?" he asked.

Kathy didn't reply.

Maybe he had misunderstood her and been too forward. He didn't know the rules of American courtship. He braced himself for the gentle letdown, the wistful rejection, and then he felt Kathy's hand slip into his.

"Yes," she said.

He glanced at his watch as he got up from the chair. It was 1 a.m. "Let's go," he said, helping her up.

And so, with their arms around each other, Remy and Kathy stumbled into the jingle-jangle morning and followed each other home.

CHAPTER EIGHTEEN

———→———

HOME. As he sat down to breakfast, Remy sighed. It wasn't just Kathy he missed. He would've loved being home for Uncle Albert and Aunt Regina's anniversary party. He loved his in-laws, the boisterous Sullivan clan, how Rose interacted with her three daughters at family gatherings—caressing them when they walked past her, laughing uproariously when she beat them at poker, making each girl's favorite dessert. After all these years, he still marveled at the fact that a chance meeting with Kathy had turned into something so rich and deep and life-transforming.

Despite Hema's protestations, he carried his plate into the kitchen when he was done eating. This was an aspect of Indian life he couldn't get used to: the dependency of the rich on their servants to perform the most basic, routine chores. He was already struggling with letting Hema do his laundry each day. He washed his own underwear by hand each morning before throwing the rest of his clothes into the washing machine. He would be damned if he let her pick up his dishes, too. "I have to leave in a few minutes," he said. "I'm late for the hospital today."

"How is memsahib, seth?"

He made a face. "Still very weak."

"Not to worry, sir," Hema said. "You don't take any tension. I will make an offering to Sai Baba's shrine on my way home today. You'll see. She'll be home, fighting-fit, soon."

He thanked her and went back into the bedroom. He had no idea if Hema actually believed her own words or had said them simply to prove her fealty to him. From what Roshan had said, Mummy had been mean to every servant who'd worked for her. Surely, Hema had experienced her wrath, too.

AT THE HOSPITAL, Manju was waiting for him in the hallway. "You stayed?" Remy asked. "I'm sorry I'm late."

"Sir"—Manju sounded breathless—"where have you been? She is very upset you didn't come on time."

"She's aware that I'm not here?" Remy increased his pace as he strode toward Shirin's room.

"Sir, she is demanding her cola."

Remy stopped walking, gave a startled laugh. "*That's* why she's asking for me? Because she wants her Coke?"

The irony escaped Manju. "Yes, yes," she said. "You didn't bring?"

No, he hadn't stopped at the store, intent as he'd been on getting to his mother as quickly as possible. He opened his billfold. "Can you run out before you leave and bring back two bottles?"

He walked into Shirin's room and noticed the difference immediately. Instead of the usual listlessness, her face was alert, her eyes narrowed and focused on him as he crossed the room. When he bent down to kiss her cheek, there was a slight, almost imperceptible stiffness in her body. *She is angry*, he realized incredulously. All the running around he was doing, the endless hours spent trying to lift her spirits, the rush to get to the hospital each morning, and she was angry at him because of the goddamn Coke.

A week ago, he would've been stung by this. Now, he saw it as a small victory.

Or maybe it has nothing to do with me, he reasoned. *Maybe it's the change of medicine. Hell, maybe she's better because of the sugar and chemicals in the damn Coke.* He grinned at the last thought, picturing the look on Dr. Bilimoria's face if Remy's whimsy turned out to be fact.

He glanced at Shirin and blinked. She was smiling at him. What the heck?

"Mummy," he said, "your Coke is coming, okay? Manju is getting it. I'm sorry I came empty-handed."

Her eyes fluttered in acknowledgment. Then she pointed to her throat. "Thirsty," she said.

"Oh God," Remy said, biting his lip. He poured water into the glass, stuck in a straw, and lifted her head so she could take a sip. She drank, keeping her eyes on him the whole time. After she was done, she croaked, "Thank you."

Remy wished Manju had witnessed this moment. Like an old Polaroid, his mother was being restored, bit by bit, life seeping back into her.

He sat beside her, stroking her hair. An overwhelming feeling of tenderness swept over him, and it puzzled him, the extraordinary fact that the most ordinary and universal of emotions—love for his mother—should feel so fraught and precious. Her eyes kept searching his face, and he had the strange sensation that she could read every thought in his head.

At last, the communion he'd always wanted, the closeness he'd craved, was his, but just as he was on the threshold of leaving her behind and starting a new chapter as a parent himself. This time, the parting would be hard. *It's not dark yet, but it's getting there.* The line from the Dylan song swept into his head. A feeling of sweet regret cut him, like an evening breeze.

But it's not dark yet, he reminded himself. *You are still here.*

Manju walked in and immediately began fussing—fluffing Shirin's pillows, raising the hospital bed, and making Shirin sip the Coke. As she did, she gave Remy the morning report: Doctor sahib had already rounded. Shirin had eaten one full piece of toast and a little bit of egg. Manju had wanted to wheel his mother into the shower, but Shirin had refused, and so Manju had given her a sponge bath. They were almost out of talcum powder, and could Remy please buy some more?

Remy nodded, but he was only half listening. It was almost as if he and his mother were alone in the room, a wordless conversation going on between them. Here, in this sparse hospital room, was exactly where he belonged.

CHAPTER NINETEEN

———✂———

"Good morning," Shirin said as he walked into her hospital room the next day, and just like that, Remy heard the surf and felt the syrupy warmth of the morning sun.

Two days after Remy's Navjote ceremony Cyrus had taken his family to Goa for a week. Remy was still glowing from the head priest's praise at how well he'd recited his prayers, and Cyrus had swept his hand across the expanse of the Arabian Sea and said, "See this, son? Two days ago, the sea was half this size. But because you memorized your prayers so perfectly, God doubled it for you to enjoy." And seven-year-old Remy had believed him.

It had been a wonderful holiday, with none of the frostiness and tension that usually marred his parents' relationship. On their first full day, Cyrus had impulsively hired a fisherman to take them for a ride in his wooden boat. Remy could still recall his parents' profiles against the clear blue sky, Mummy's shoulder-length hair fluttering in the breeze, Dad sitting with his arm around his wife, while behind them the bare-chested fisherman steered the boat. Remy had felt seasick for the first few minutes, but Cyrus had shown him how to roll with the waves, and as his queasiness lifted, Remy had gazed at his father in awe, thinking that his daddy was as wise as God.

The next evening, they'd taken a sunset cruise down the Mandovi River. "Will we see dolphins?" Remy asked as they'd boarded the ferry, but Cyrus shook his head no.

"But I want to see dolphins."

"On another day," Shirin said. "It's too late in the evening. The dolphins have to go to sleep with their mummy and daddy. They get tired, too, you know?"

"Why? What work do they do all day?"

Shirin pretended to be shocked. "Arre wah. What work? Do you think it's easy, swimming all day? Remember when you went to Juhu Beach last summer?"

"Yah?"

"Didn't you get tired after swimming at the hotel pool?"

Remy nodded soberly. "Good night, dolphins," he yelled, leaning over the railing, Shirin holding him from his waistband. "Good night, fish." He turned to his mother. "The waves get tired, too," he said. "But when do they rest?"

She smiled, pulling him back onto her lap. "Very late at night, when it's dark," she murmured, nuzzling his hair.

They heard the furious beating of drums, and a troupe of Goan folk dancers came running out. "Mummy, look. Fairies!" squealed Remy, then he watched in delight as several of the passengers jumped up to join the dancers. The music reminded him of the night of his Navjote, when he'd danced with Zenobia, the girl who lived in the next building.

He turned to say something to Daddy just as one of the female dancers sashayed up to his father, extending her arm. To Remy's great surprise, Daddy leapt to his feet. His father looked so strange, dancing with the male and female fairies.

"Mummy?" he protested, but Shirin was laughing, clapping to the Konkani song.

The sky above them turned the color of honey and, later, it burned red, as if someone had built a bonfire. The sun itself grew smaller, a red marble that rolled behind the distant shore. Remy grew sad as it disappeared, wanted to call it back. "Mummy, look," he cried, jack-knifing in her lap. "The sun is melting away."

"It will be back tomorrow by the time you wake up," Shirin said. "I promise."

But despite the festive atmosphere on the boat, the melancholy feeling lingered, and Remy learned his first lessons in loss: That his sorrow was in proportion to the happiness he'd felt earlier in the evening. That you only miss what you value.

They let Remy sleep in the next morning. After Cyrus finally got him dressed, father and son walked hand in hand to join Shirin for breakfast at the hotel's rooftop restaurant. Shirin was dressed in a checked shirt and dark pants, her hair tied back with a silk scarf. A glass of watermelon juice sat in front of her as she looked out at the sea. Even though the restaurant was brimming with guests, Shirin looked serenely, supremely alone. Peaceful. Remy's breath caught at the sight of her; he thought she was the most beautiful woman in the world.

"Mummy," he cried, when they were almost upon her, and Shirin turned her head and smiled.

"Good morning," she said, and the morning sun sparkled on the rim of her glass.

The boy blinked, took a picture with his eyes. If he'd had to caption the picture, he would've labeled it PERFECT HAPPINESS.

"GOOD MORNING, MUMMY," Remy replied now, careful not to share the sweet memory her two words had triggered. Each day, Shirin spoke a little more, but Remy still treated her like a feral cat that he was trying to tame, afraid of spooking her.

"Where's Manju?" he asked, before recalling that she had asked him if she could leave a little early this morning. Still, it looked as if the nurse had dressed Mummy before leaving, although she'd forgotten to comb her hair. "Come, let's get you out of bed," he said, the memory of the Goa trip lingering, struggling to reconcile the beauty of the young woman who had turned away from the sea to smile at him with Shirin now. *What a monster time is*, Remy thought, *laying waste to everything in its path, destroying youth and beauty, even tarnishing memory.* Maybe that was the only thing humans had to fear—the steady ticktock, the relentless current. Because, ultimately, what was death, even, other than the ceasing of the clock?

He lifted his mother into a chair, then ran the comb gently through her hair. "Remember when you used to do this for me?" he said as he worked to remove the knots. "Times change, huh, Mama?"

A smile bloomed on Shirin's face. With concentrated effort, she raised her right hand from her lap and touched her chest. "I remember," she said.

"Remember when I didn't want to wash my face when I was a kid? Remember the game you invented?"

Shirin looked at him blankly. He gave her a moment, then prompted. "Powder . . . ?"

"Powder," she finished.

"Exactly. You used to rub your hands across my face, chanting 'Powder, powder.' Why that worked, I don't even know. Do you?"

There was no verbal response, but Remy noticed a softening in her expression. *She knows I'm trying*, he thought, even though he wasn't exactly clear whom he was trying to please. It certainly didn't matter to Mummy if her hair remained uncombed. *But it matters to me*, he thought. *It matters to me.*

He and Mummy had been separated by so much—distance for sure, but also by the pain of unpleasant memories. Well, he would try to write over old memories with new ones. He was in advertising, for God's sake. Who knew better than he did the power of nostalgia and how memories could be manipulated? This is what he would do while here: fill up tiny vials of memory to take home.

With his back to her, he removed a few strands of her hair from the comb and wrapped them in a tissue. Something of her, something of this time, to carry to America.

CHAPTER TWENTY

——————✗——————

REMY HAD SPENT his boyhood keeping secrets from his mother, so when Kathy suggested that it was time to tell her about Monaz and the baby, his first instinct was to recoil. "I don't think it's the right time," he said. "What with her health being what it is, I can't take the risk. Who knows how she'll react to the news?"

There was a long silence. "Hello?" he finally said.

"Yeah, I'm here," Kathy said. Another pause. "I guess I'm just wondering who you're actually protecting. Shirin or yourself?"

He had not slept well the previous night, and the stress of spending entire days in the hospital was getting to him. So he was immediately defensive. "That's a shitty thing to say, Kat. You know how involved I've been in my mom's care. I can't have her have another setback."

"Have another setback?" Kathy's tone was incredulous. "Why, for God's sake? It's not like you're confessing to being a serial killer, right?

We're adopting a sweet, innocent baby. Why on earth would that set Shirin back? If anything, it might give her something to look forward to."

Remy felt cornered. Many Parsis seemed to have a gut-level aversion to the notion of adopting another's baby, and he didn't know if Mummy was one of them. Or what if Mummy got excited at the prospect of a grandson? He had no plans to take her to America with him. How would she handle that rejection? Now that they had reached some kind of equilibrium, he was trying so hard to not rock the boat.

"Remy?" Kathy said. "Are you really not going to answer?"

"Listen, you're just going to have to trust me. I know my mother—I'll judge the timing of it, okay? I'll tell her when the time is right."

"Jesus. You're about to get on a plane soon with an unknown girl. You don't think Shirin will find out? You are forever telling me how small and close-knit the Parsi community is. How can you keep such a secret from your own mother?"

"Wait a minute—"

"No. No, Remy. We're not going to start our life with our baby in secrecy and shame. I'm not going to do it."

His temper spiked. "Do you even hear yourself?" he said. "This is between me and my mom. Don't you think I know the situation better than you?"

"But this involves me, too, doesn't it? Or am I not going to be consulted on any of it?"

"What the hell are you talking about?" A thought occurred to him. "Are you upset about Monaz coming back with me? Is that what this is about?"

"There you go, twisting my words. Forget it, Remy. Do what you like. But I personally can't imagine keeping such a huge secret from *my* mom. She would be devastated."

Remy bit down on his tongue to keep from saying what came immediately to mind: *Well, aren't you lucky. Not having to worry about your mother's reaction, knowing she would support you no matter what. Not having to carry around all the baggage that I've had to.*

"Listen, even my dad was not keen on the idea of adoption," he said. "He told that to me once, I remember. And Mummy is much more old-fashioned than he was. So, yeah, I have no idea how she will react. But I suspect it won't be good."

"Maybe she'll surprise you."

"Maybe." He sighed. "Okay, can we please change the subject now? I'll tell her in the next few days, I promise. I just have to find the right moment."

THE NEXT MORNING had been gray and overcast, but the sun had burned away the smog and left behind a shimmering afternoon. Remy stood in the hallway, looking out the open window, as a nurse bathed Shirin. The warmth felt good on his face. As he stared at the lush gardens, noticing the arch made by two bougainvillea bushes bending toward each other, he replayed yesterday's conversation with Kathy. An idea presented itself.

He made a quick call to Monaz, leaving a message about changing their lunch plans, then walked rapidly toward the nurses' station. He grabbed one of the wheelchairs near the station and wheeled it back to his mother's room, ignoring the nurse's call of "Sir, may I help you?"

He waited outside until the nurse exited Mummy's room. Shirin was lying on her side, visibly tired. He sat and let her rest, wondering if he should abandon the idea. But a breeze swept into the room, making Remy long to be outdoors.

"Listen, Mummy," he said. "It's a beautiful day. How about we go outside?"

His mother did not reply. He was debating what to do when a ward boy walked past the room. Together, they lifted Shirin; she was so light and tiny, and as they positioned her, she slumped in the chair, and

Remy felt a throb of fear. But convinced that the fresh air could only help her spirits, he wheeled her toward the elevator.

"Beg your pardon," a female voice said as he was about to open the metal grates of the old-fashioned lift. "Doctor has to give permission for the transport of the patient." The head nurse stood in front of him.

Shirin lifted her head ever so slightly, as if interested in seeing how her son would navigate the situation. The movement gave Remy the courage he needed.

"It's okay," he said. "She's my mother. I take full responsibility." He rolled Shirin into the elevator and hit the ground-floor button.

REMY PUSHED THE wheelchair gingerly down the outdoor ramp. He heard the insistent chirping of a bird and felt his spirits soar. Red bougainvillea shook in the breeze as he steered Shirin toward a stone bench on the lawn. Even though she couldn't have weighed more than a hundred and five pounds, tops, Remy was a bit breathless by the time they reached their destination. He realized he'd been bracing for a confrontation with the hospital staff for violating their rules; he had half expected someone to chase after them.

He locked his mother's chair and sat on the bench facing her. He wished he could identify each of the trees around them, but mostly he was thankful for this rare splash of green in this dusty city. "It's peaceful here, Mummy, isn't it?" he said, noticing that Shirin had lifted her head and was squinting into the sun. He removed his own sunglasses and placed them on her nose. "There. Is that better?"

Shirin tilted her whole face toward the sky. Even though he was unable to see her eyes, he felt her relax. A thrill ran through him. *She's enjoying this*, he thought. He had done the right thing by bringing her outdoors. His mind skipped ahead, debating whether they could do this each day.

His phone rang. It was Monaz.

"Listen, there's been a slight change of plans. We're sitting in the front garden," he said. "Can you join us here? . . . I'll keep a look-out . . . Okay, see you soon."

An elderly couple walked past them, the man holding the woman at her elbow. "Sahibji," Remy called out.

The couple turned to acknowledge the greeting, and as they did, the woman stumbled.

Remy rose immediately. "Are you all right, auntie?" he called.

In response, the old man grimaced and mouthed, *No.*

Remy glanced at his mother, who looked secure in her chair. "I'll be back in a jiffy," he told her.

"May I?" he asked, walking to the couple and taking the woman's other arm. He led them carefully toward the entrance of the hospital.

He hurried back to his mother after he'd finished assisting the couple. Shirin had removed the sunglasses and was holding them in her lap. The softness of her expression told him that she'd approved of his actions. Both Mummy and Daddy had always been helpful to others, and had instilled in him the same obligation. It was Mummy who had first taught him the expression "There but for the grace of God go I."

"Are you tired?" he asked his mother. "Do you want to go back in?"

Shirin shook her head.

"Mummy, do you remember Monaz, the girl who visited you a few days ago? Shenaz's niece? She's going to stop by here in a few min-utes. We . . . She wants to say hello . . ." His voice trailed away as his courage ebbed. Maybe he should break the news about the adoption to his mother when they were alone. What if she said something nasty to Monaz about her pregnancy? It was thoughtless of him not to have anticipated this.

Monaz arrived carrying a white box, which she placed on the stone bench between herself and Remy. "Hi, auntie," she said. "I brought chicken patties for us from RTI. Fresh and hot, they are.

Will you eat one?" She picked one up in a paper napkin and placed it on Shirin's lap.

Remy stood up to help his mother, but Shirin raised the patty to her mouth and took a bite, all on her own. He stared at her, remembering his many futile efforts to get Shirin to eat. Monaz had solved the problem in five seconds.

The girl gave him a triumphant grin and offered one to him. The three of them sat in silence, munching on their lunch as if this were an ordinary picnic. Remy was stunned by the sheer normalcy of the moment. *Youth is a superpower*, he thought. Without Shirin saying a word, he could tell that she liked Monaz.

Shirin nodded at the girl and said, "How many months?"

Remy almost dropped his lunch, but Monaz appeared unfazed. There was no trace of the confused, nervous teenager Remy had come to know. "Five months, auntie," she said. "But it's that obvious? I wear these baggy kurtas, hoping it won't show."

"Kathy and I are hoping to adopt Monaz's baby, Mummy," Remy said in a rush. "I . . . I wanted to tell you. Ask for your blessings," he added, feeling ridiculous. It sounded stereotypically Indian, as if he were parroting a line from a Bollywood melodrama. He had not even sought his parents' permission to marry Kathy.

Shirin gave him a wry look, before turning her attention to Monaz. "They will take good care. My son is . . . a kind man."

Her words lifted a dreadful weight. Kathy had been right to force him to come clean. This made so much more sense than the cowardly way he'd been thinking of dealing with the situation, after he was safely back in America.

"Thanks, Mummy," he said. "I feel so happy right now."

Shirin smiled, then began to cough, a harsh and prolonged fit, her face turning red with the exertion. Remy looked around, angry at himself for not having brought a drink, but Monaz dug into her backpack and fished out a water bottle. She helped Shirin take a few sips, rubbing her back as she drank. Remy felt certain he was witnessing the birth of a friendship between his mother and the mother of his future child.

"Thank you," Shirin croaked.

"Not at all, Shirin Auntie. You remind me so much of my grandmother."

Mother and son exchanged a quick, bemused look. Remy felt his chest fill with lightness, although some part of him still wondered how much Shirin understood.

"Mummy?" he said cautiously. "So you're okay with us adopting?"

Shirin stared down at her hands. When she finally looked up, her eyes were filled with tears. "Your daddy and I had always planned on a houseful of children." She turned toward Monaz. "What is your due date?"

It occurred to Remy that Shirin was talking in full, intelligible sentences. The new drugs that they'd started Mummy on since the scare last week were clearly working.

"May fifteenth," Monaz said. She turned to Remy, silently asking his permission to disclose their arrangement.

"I'm going to take Monaz back with me, Mummy," he said, trying to sound casual. "That way, you know, she can deliver the baby in America."

A strange look crossed Shirin's face. "Your parents don't know?" she asked.

Monaz flushed. "No, Shirin Auntie. My father is very old-fashioned. They would be . . . They would disown me."

His mother fell silent. When Remy glanced at her, her face was blank. But Remy suspected that she was upset that he was taking a stranger to America while leaving her behind.

Shirin shivered. "Let's go in, Mummy," Remy said immediately. "You're cold."

He was about to wheel her back when she raised a finger to stop him. "You can stay at my flat anytime you want," she said to Monaz. "We have an empty guest room."

Monaz leaned over and gave Shirin a kiss. "You are so sweet, auntie." She took a step back. "Can I call you Granna?"

Shirin smiled but didn't respond.

Remy gave Monaz a quick hug. "I'll talk to you soon," he said. "Thanks for lunch."

"Bye. See you both soon."

He wheeled Shirin toward the hospital building. He felt guilty when he noticed the tracks the wheelchair made on the grass. He was trying to figure out how to navigate up the ramp by himself when Shirin twisted in the chair and looked up at him. She covered Remy's hand, which was resting on her right shoulder, with her own.

"Son," she said, "get me out of here. Take me home. I want to go home."

BOOK TWO

CHAPTER TWENTY-ONE

———→———

BOMBAY WAS SHIVERING, going through a cold spell. Everybody was bundled up in sweaters and woollies. Remy had chuckled when Hema came to work this morning wearing a knit sweater under her sari and complaining of the baraf—ice—which in the context of a tropical city was merely a metaphor. Amused, he pulled out his phone to show her a picture of Kathy and him shoveling their driveway after a blizzard. Hema had looked at him as if he'd suddenly turned into an astronaut or a space alien.

He had invited Gulnaz to lunch today and she, too, was wearing a sweater. At twenty-two degrees Celsius—seventy-two degrees Fahrenheit, Remy's phone told him—he was delighting in the weather, happy to be escaping the harsh Ohio winter. But Gulnaz looked at him in horror when he answered the door in a T-shirt. "Are you mad?" she said. "Aren't you freezing? Or has living in America turned your brain into yogurt?"

"Welcome, Gulnaz," he said. "And, no, I'm not cold. It's a balmy seventy-two degrees here. It's currently five degrees in Ohio."

"Ae, forget this Fahrenheit nonsense. Talk in Celsius, na, like a normal person," Gulnaz said as she walked into the living room. "Why must you Americans always be out of step with the rest of the world? You haven't even embraced the metric system yet."

Remy grinned. "The perks of being the world's sole superpower, darling."

Gulnaz looked around. "Where's Mum?"

"In her room. Want to come say hello?"

"In a minute." Gulnaz took Remy's hand in hers. "Tell me. How are you? How are things since you brought her home?"

Remy considered her question. On the one hand, things were easier. Shirin was a lot more communicative. He was grateful not to battle rush-hour traffic. Gladys, the day nurse he had hired, was cheerful and competent. Monaz often stopped by in the afternoon after her classes, regaling Mummy with stories about her professors. Sometimes, she would stay for dinner, studying in the guest bedroom until it was time to eat. Both Remy and his mother had grown to enjoy these visits.

On the other hand, Remy missed the hustle-bustle of the hospital—talking with the relatives of the other patients, chatting with the nurses and doctors who came in to check on Shirin. He worried constantly about Mummy getting sick again and having to rush her through the traffic-clogged streets, where no one ever pulled over to let an ambulance through, simply because there was nowhere to move. Their large flat was peaceful, tranquil, and comfortable, but he no longer ended his days going over to Jango's house and decompressing over drinks and conversation. Instead, he had to settle for friends stopping by for lunch or tea.

"Chalta hai," he said, using that all-encompassing Bombay expression. "It's mostly fine. We're managing."

"Are you lonely?"

Remy was startled by Gulnaz's perception. "Yes, of course. I miss . . . my life. My Kathy."

"And your mother? How are things between the two of you?"

Remy shrugged, unsure of what lay behind Gulnaz's questions. As a boy, his relationships with his friends and classmates had been based on common interests—cricket or a love of limericks, movies, and pop songs. It would not have occurred to him to discuss his family troubles with them. But Gulnaz had lived three buildings down from him until her family moved to Hughes Road when she was sixteen. Had everyone known about his strained relationship with his mother?

"Remy," Gulnaz said, "I'm not trying to pry, yaar. It's just that . . . I don't know if you remember. One time—I think we were in the third standard or something—I had come over to your place on a Saturday, and your mom had just come home. I think she'd gone to Bandra or somewhere. And I . . . well . . ."

"And what? Did something happen?"

Gulnaz looked at him curiously. "You honestly don't remember?"

He shook his head. "I'm sorry. I don't."

"She . . . You were bragging a bit about having stood first in class that term. You know how competitive you and I were with each other at school. Your report card was on the table, I remember. And, my God, my mother would've ordered boxes of jalebis to distribute to the whole neighborhood if I'd had such good grades. But she . . ."

"She what?"

"She got really angry at you. Said you were being a show-off and that you had to learn to be more humble. I—I never forgot the incident, because it was so bizarre. I mean, most of our parents were so proud of our achievements."

A worm of memory tickled Remy's brain, but it was so faint that he wasn't sure if Gulnaz's words had planted it there. "I honestly don't recall," he said.

"I remember it vividly," Gulnaz said. "Your dad came into the living room and got really upset at your mom. And then he took the two of us to Kailash for ice cream. To celebrate your success, he said."

"He was great like that, Dad," Remy said. "And I have no idea why my mother got so angry. But she was always after me to be modest. I dunno—maybe she was afraid of the evil eye or something. Except she wasn't superstitious like that. Anyway," he added, "that was a long time ago."

"Yes, of course," Gulnaz said immediately. She took a step toward Remy. "All I'm saying is, you are like a brother to me. If you need any-thing while you're in Bombay, just ask, okay? I took care of both my parents until the end. I know how hard this is."

"Thank you, Gulu. You've always been so kind. You haven't changed at all."

"Arre, I'm an old fart. Why the hell should I change at my age?"

"I'm sorry I haven't stayed in touch in recent years. I've been a lousy friend to you. No excuses, but my life there is so busy that—"

"For God's sake, Remy, stop." Gulnaz looked at him seriously. "I've always understood why you had to distance yourself from your life here. And in any case, I used to often run into Cyrus Uncle at the fire temple, and he'd catch me up. He was so proud of you."

"Dad used to tell me when he saw you. He was happy whenever that happened."

"I loved Cyrus Uncle," Gulnaz said. "Remember how he used to take all of us neighborhood kids out for Chinese food?"

"I do. Those were good days."

"Do you go?" Gulnaz asked. "Have you been since you got here?"

"Go where? For Chinese food?"

"No, silly. To the fire temple."

"No, I—" Remy shook his head. "You know I'm not religious."

"Do you at least still wear your sadra and kusti?"

Remy hesitated, taken aback by the intensity with which Gulnaz was looking at him now. "I wear my sadra. It acts as a nice undershirt for me. But, to be frank, I don't even own a kusti."

"I see." Gulnaz didn't try to hide her disappointment. Then she perked up. "Let's go now. I will buy you a new kusti from the shop outside the agiary. Let's go give thanks for your mom's recovery."

"Now? What about lunch?"

She made a dismissive sound. "We'll be back in a jiffy, yaar. My driver will drop us off right at the entrance. Come on."

"Really, Gulu," he protested. "There's no need."

Gulnaz stood in front of him with her arms crossed. Remy shook his head at this sudden turn of events. He checked in on his mother, then went into his bedroom to fetch his wallet, a little disconcerted by the change in his friend's behavior. He hoped that her guilt over marrying outside the faith had not turned her into one of those religious loons.

Gulnaz's car had tinted windows, and Bombay looked softer, almost benign, as they rode to the fire temple. "You remember Turtle?" Gulnaz said. "He died last year. Got hit by a car."

"Oh no," Remy said. The beggar had been a fixture through Remy's childhood. A neighborhood boy had given the poor, disabled man the nickname, and it had stuck. A congenital defect had left Turtle with stumps for arms and legs. He used those stumps to push himself around the city streets on a wooden skateboard. Every morning, after he arrived at the bus stop, one of the nearby men flipped him onto his back, so that he faced skyward and could thank those who dropped coins into the tin cup beside him. At the end of each day, a woman came to pick him up. Remy would sometimes watch them crossing the street—the woman stretching out her hand to slow down the traffic, Turtle racing on his skateboard to get to safety. Remy had never known who the woman was. Mother? Wife?

"God. I haven't thought about him in a long time," Remy said.

"His real name was Sukendar," Gulnaz said. "I only found out a few years ago. I actually got him admitted into one of those shelters. He was getting up in years, you know? But he was miserable there. Said he missed the hustle-bustle of the streets. That bus stop had become his home."

This was one of the things about Bombay, Remy thought—the everyday interactions between social classes, the small attempts made by people like Gulnaz to change the lives of the poor. In Bombay, poverty was omnipresent, with none of the housing segregation that was a feature of cities like Cleveland and Chicago. Here, people lived cheek by jowl, alongside one another, slums and makeshift hutments springing up under the shadows of glittering skyscrapers. And so even while the affluent denizens of those buildings complained incessantly about the "nuisance" caused by the hutment dwellers, it was not uncommon for the more kindhearted residents to "adopt" a homeless family on their street, providing clothes for the children, say, and meals for the family.

"How did you find out his real name?" Remy said.

"I asked," Gulnaz said. "I got tired of just walking past him. Years and years of basically ignoring him, thinking I was a good person just because I always gave him money. So one day, I squatted next to him and we chatted. You remember that old movie *Sholay*? Well, he had the whole film memorized. Word for word, scene by scene. Remy, can you imagine what his IQ must've been?"

Remy sighed. All this human potential going to waste. Who would Turtle have been if someone like Gulnaz had entered his life earlier? Who would he have been if his childhood poverty and his disability had not become his destiny? When Remy was three or four, he had believed that every old person with white hair whom they passed on the street was poor and needed their help. He'd tug at his father's shirtsleeve and look up beseechingly, wanting Daddy to give them money.

Once, while shopping at the dry fruits store during the Diwali rush, Cyrus had run into an elderly Parsi friend. The two men were chatting when Remy said loudly, "Daddy, please give this poor uncle some money, na? You're just talking and talking, but not helping." The older man had looked quizzically at a red-faced Cyrus, who stammered out an apology and explanation. The old man had then laughed uproariously, patted Remy's head, and said, "God bless, God bless. May Ahura Mazda always look upon you favorably, beta."

Well, fortune had definitely smiled on him. But what about the unlucky millions like Turtle? No god had abandoned Turtle; it was his fellow humans. And that included himself. *What have you done,* he asked himself, *to change things in the place where you were born? You've acted as if you have no responsibility, just because you were lucky enough to escape. But how does that absolve you?*

"Gulu," he said. "I . . . Can you recommend some organizations doing work in the city that I could support? I'd like to send regular contributions. I mean, it's not going to change everybody's life, but it's something, right?"

"Yeah, and it will change a few lives," Gulu said immediately. "I can definitely come up with a list of local charities."

"Thanks," he said, squeezing her arm.

IN THE NARROW shop attached to the fire temple, Gulnaz bought Remy a kusti, the long strands woven out of lamb's wool that Parsis tie around their waist. She also bought two small offerings of sandalwood. At the entrance, she gave Remy a red velvet cap to cover his head, then wound a scarf around her own. They walked into the foyer of the temple, dipped their fingers into the bowl of water, and dabbed their eyes. The liquid felt cool against Remy's skin.

A familiar smoky smell greeted them as they entered the large sanctum, Remy's eyes slowly adjusting to the dark. In the quiet wood-paneled room, the noise and bustle of Bombay fell away and Remy felt an immediate sense of tranquility, as if he'd entered a plush, private club. He understood why people like Gulnaz sought refuge in this place every day. "Let's step into the courtyard and do our kusti beside the well," Gulnaz whispered. "Then we'll come back in."

"You know," Remy said, "I don't think I remember the words." His Navjote had been so long ago.

"Not to worry," Gulnaz said. "I'll pray, and you just follow along. The main thing is that you must wear your kusti at all times, Remy. It will help guide you through the troubles you are facing."

They stood before the well, and Remy followed Gulnaz's lead, remembering the emphatic beat and the intonation of the short prayer, although he couldn't remember all of the words. The fact that they were reciting it in a dead language didn't help. He felt awkward, hypo-critical, as if watching the ritual from a remove, but halfway through, something tugged at him and he found himself moved by his friend's obvious sincerity. More words came back to him in fragments, and his hands knew what to do when he looped the strands of the kusti around his waist three times. *Muscle memory*, he thought.

After, Gulnaz led him into the main hall and toward the inner sanctum that only the priests were allowed to enter. A dastur clad in white stood praying in front of a giant silver urn, tending to the holy fire that was kept alive day and night. The priest nodded at Gulnaz, then approached them with a long-handled silver spoon bearing ashes from the fire. Gulnaz took a pinch and offered up the pieces of sandal-wood. The man moved back to the urn and fed their gift to the blaze.

Gulnaz smeared some of the ash on Remy's forehead before plac-ing the rest of it on hers. They sat side by side on a mahogany bench, watching the priest. Leaning into Remy, Gulnaz pointed at a spot to his right. "That's where I'd run into your dad. He never sat down. He always stood when he prayed. And I tell you, Remy, he had the most beautiful voice. It was like he sang those prayers. All these priests could've taken lessons from him."

"That sounds like Dad."

"He was so generous. He always gave money to the priests before he left. Every single time. I mean, who does that?"

Everyone in the neighborhood seemed to have a memory of Cyrus that softened their faces when they spoke about him. How was it that only Mummy hadn't appreciated Daddy? Yeah, she'd cried out for him that night at the hospital, but it was too little, too late.

He had a sudden absurd thought: *I wish I'd been old enough to have warned him against marrying Mummy. Maybe with a different spouse, they could have each been happy.*

He shook his head to clear it of such ridiculousness, and sank farther into the bench, enjoying the rare quiet and solitude. "You come daily?" he whispered to Gulnaz.

"Yes."

"I can see why. It's . . . so peaceful here."

"Naturally," Gulnaz said immediately. "God is here."

Remy wished he shared Gulnaz's conviction; that he, too, could sit in this dark, hushed room and feel God's presence here. Cyrus had been pained by Remy's agnosticism, had felt personally culpable. "I should've insisted on you going to the fire temple with me more often," he'd once said, sitting in Remy's kitchen in Columbus. "It's my fault, for letting you move to America without giving you an ironclad faith."

"What difference does it make, Dad?" Remy had said. "I try to be a good person."

"You are," Cyrus had said. "You are good. But, son, faith is like an armor. It's for your own protection. This world can be an unforgiving place. Faith helps a man from getting buffeted around."

Be better than me, Dad had written to him. At this moment, Remy found it impossible to live up to that stricture. *I will never be as brave or large-hearted as Daddy*, he thought, missing his father with a fierceness that shook him. He envied Gulnaz for having spent more time with Cyrus in recent years, for getting to hear him pray in his sonorous voice. He would give five years of his life for five extra minutes of that. He wished Daddy and he were tangled in a theological debate right now. He wished his father could say something—one true thing— that would mitigate the confusion Remy felt about his mother, that he could advise him about whether to trust this new détente between himself and Shirin.

Remy recalled the times he'd been furious at his mother during one of his parents' visits to Columbus, after Shirin had said something particularly cutting to Kathy, and Cyrus would ask Remy to go for a drive. They'd get in the car, Remy's hands tight around the steering wheel, and Daddy would search for the right words before he spoke, glancing worriedly at Remy to appraise the level of his anger. When Cyrus would finally speak in his low baritone, he'd ask Remy to understand his mother's frustrations, explaining that Shirin was one of those unfortunate women who only knew how to express their grief by turning it into anger.

"What the hell is she sad about?" Remy had once snapped. "We wait on her hand and foot."

"She knows we're leaving for Bombay soon. She is going to miss you terribly."

"Why doesn't she just fucking say that she's sad, then?"

Cyrus had shaken his head. "She doesn't know how. People are . . . People are complicated, Remy. They don't always react like you expect them to. Try and understand her."

"But, Dad," Remy had cried, "you're giving me all this advice, but you can't tolerate her bullshit either. I've seen you lose your temper with her."

Cyrus had given him a dejected look. "You're right. I suppose I expect you to be a better man than I am."

"I miss him," Remy said to Gulnaz now. "It's been three years, but I still miss him."

"Don't think that pain will ever go away," Gulnaz said. "It never will. Same thing will happen after your mom goes. It's like there will always be this ache in your heart. In any case, you can always talk to your dad, you know. If you can't talk to God, talk to him instead. He will help you."

"Gulu," he said, "thank you for bringing me here. This place is truly a kind of escape. A refuge."

"You're welcome." Gulnaz smiled. "You know what your dad told me once? Something I've never forgotten. He said that spirituality is a muscle; you have to exercise it daily."

"Dad said that?"

"He did. Wise, no?"

"I guess."

Gulnaz guffawed, thumped Remy on the back. "I guess," she mimicked. Then she grew serious. "Try coming here regularly while you're in town. You'll see. You will feel better after each visit. Okay, now let me pray in silence for a few minutes."

When they finally left, Remy glanced back. He imagined he saw Cyrus, solid and strong, eyes closed, hands folded, a look of concentration on his face as he stood before the holy fire. *What had Daddy prayed for?* he asked himself. *Peace in his marriage? Good health?* But even as he wondered, he knew the answer: all of Cyrus's prayers would have been for Remy.

Nobody would ever love him as unconditionally as his father had, not even Kathy. As he walked out of the fire temple with Gulnaz, Remy felt comforted and orphaned by this thought.

CHAPTER TWENTY-TWO

REMY SAT IN the living room with a contractor, discussing the work he wanted done in the apartment: the fallen ceiling plaster replaced, a fresh coat of paint throughout the flat, some of the floor tile repaired. "The main thing is, boss, I need you to start soon. Put us at the top of your list. I'm willing to pay extra."

The man smiled. "They told me you're from foreign, sir. You must to be anxious to return home?"

Was he? Yes and no.

"I'm here for at least another week," he said. "I want to oversee the job."

Mummy was too weak to supervise the workers. And there were other obstacles to a quick return to Columbus. Remy had been unable to locate two seats on a flight, even in business class. It was still peak season—thousands returning to the States after visiting family in India over the break.

Also, he was dragging his feet on the arrangements he needed to make with Dina and Pervez. Because for the first time in his adult life, Remy was enjoying his mother's company. Sometimes, when she'd tell him a story from her own childhood—about her beloved father, say—he felt like she was filling a well of longing that he hadn't known existed. All four of his grandparents had died either before his birth or while he was young. He was thirsty for family stories.

At lunch two days earlier, Shirin had said, "You know, the other surgeons in town hated my papa."

"Why?"

"Because he used to let his patients pay whatever fees they could afford. He would say he became a doctor to help people, not fleece them. The other doctors were afraid he was going to bring their prices down." Shirin smiled. "But they couldn't say much, because he was the best orthopedic surgeon in the city. He once did hip surgery on a man who had been in a wheelchair for seven years. No other surgeon would touch his case. Papa got the man walking again. The patient was an ordinary bank clerk, but he came to the house with the largest bouquet of flowers I had ever seen. I was seven years old. But I can still smell those roses today."

"Dad once told me he cried like a baby when Grandpa died," Remy had said while taking another serving of okra. "He said he cried more than when his own father passed."

A look had crossed Shirin's face that Remy couldn't decipher. "Yes," she'd said at last. "Papa loved your daddy like his own son. They were close."

THE CONTRACTOR HAD been gone an hour when the doorbell rang and Monaz and Shenaz stood, grinning, at the door. They were holding a bottle of hair dye, a footbath, and a brown paper bag.

Shirin's makeover had been Monaz's idea, after she'd seen an old picture of Shirin with dark hair. Remy led them to his mother's bedroom, watched as Monaz gave his mother a hug and explained why they were there. Shirin flashed Remy a startled look, but she didn't protest, reluctant to dampen the girl's obvious excitement, as there was a growing bond between them. Just the other day, Shirin had once again offered Monaz the guest bedroom after her return from America.

"Come on, Granna," Monaz said. "Let's make you young again. You will feel so freshum-fresh once we're done."

Remy made a quick trip to the chemist, to pick up Shirin's medications. When he returned, Gladys greeted him. "Madam is in her bedroom," she said. "She wants you to come see her."

He stepped into the room and gasped. The mother of his youth had been restored. She was sitting at the edge of her bed. They had trimmed her toenails and cut and dyed her hair. They had also showered her and put her in a fresh outfit.

Shirin rolled her eyes. "These two chokris have had fun trying to turn a pumpkin into Cinderella."

Despite her self-effacing remark, Remy could tell that she was pleased at the transformation. "Nonsense, Mummy," he said. "You look absolutely great." He turned to Shenaz. "I don't even know how to thank you. I mean, this is nothing short of a miracle."

"It's all Monaz's doing," Shenaz said. "She's the miracle worker." She put her arm around her niece.

Remy asked them to stay for lunch, but they refused. "I promised this girl lunch at Copper Chimney. Then we have a check-up with the ob-gyn. After that, I'm taking her shopping. She's going to need some new clothes for her trip to America."

"There's no need," Remy protested. "Kathy will take her shopping soon after we get there." He had a sudden thought. "Should I . . . ? Do you want me to go to the doctor's appointment?"

Shenaz shook her head. "We'll be fine."

Monaz gave Shirin a kiss. "I'll see you soon, Granna," she said.

It's as if she's made her way into our family, Remy thought. But, then, why not? She was about to gift them her most precious thing.

"You are welcome any time," Shirin said. Her voice was weak, and Remy frowned. The makeover had clearly tired her out.

"Tell you what, Mummy," he said after their guests had left. "Why don't you take a short nap before lunch?"

"You won't be hungry?" Shirin said, and Remy heard the reflexive maternal concern. Why had he ever believed that she didn't love him? Had he been wrong about her all those years, or was he deluding himself now? It felt impossible to know whether this was a temporary cease-fire, a truce brokered by a crisis, and whether he could trust it.

"I can wait," he said softly, although he went into the kitchen and grabbed a few crackers.

THEY ATE A late lunch in the dining room. Remy helped Gladys clear the dishes, then went back to sit with his mother while Gladys served them Parsi bread pudding. Shirin took one bite and said, "It's not sweet enough."

"Oh my God," Gladys said. "Hema added so much sugar already. Not good for your health, madam, to eat so much sweets."

"Gladys," Remy said, "it's all right. Please bring my mother whatever she asks for. Maybe some of that caramel sauce? Warm it for thirty seconds or so."

He, too, was rattled by the prodigious amount of sugar Shirin consumed. But, then, who was he to argue with the resurrection he had witnessed? A couple of weeks ago, he couldn't have imagined sitting with her in her own apartment and sharing a meal. "Let me," he said, when Gladys came back with the sauce, and he spooned it over the pudding.

"You don't have a sweet tooth anymore?" Shirin asked. "You used to love sweets."

"I still do," Remy said. He patted his belly. "But I'm getting a bit of a paunch. Kathy makes me watch my weight."

"Don't be silly. You take after my side of the family. My father was even skinnier than you. Now, the Wadias . . ." She coughed, took a sip of water, and gave him a sideways look. "Your daddy developed a paunch in his fifties."

He nodded. "I have something to ask you," he said after a moment. "Why did you stop talking? Roshan said it was even before they shifted you to the hospital."

Shirin was quiet for so long that Remy began to feel uneasy, the companionability between them still tenuous.

"I'm sorry . . . ," he began, but Shirin shook her head.

"I wasn't well," she said. "I felt so weak and breathless it was an effort to do anything. Even talking took energy."

"That makes sense," Remy said.

"But that wasn't it," Shirin continued. "It was also, what was left to say? Who was left to say it to? Everyone was gone. You were calling less and less. I decided I was done with this world, done talking to it."

"You *decided*?"

Shirin's lower lip jutted out, and Remy had a sudden flash into how she must've looked at age seven. "It happened gradually . . . I don't know. Who can say?"

"Mummy, were you aware of my presence at the hospital? During, you know, those early days?"

Shirin looked directly into his eyes. "Does the heart ever stop feeling its own beat?"

GULNAZ VISITED AGAIN two days later, drove Remy to the fire temple, then stayed for lunch. After she left, Remy took a nap. When he awoke, he went to his laptop and spent several hours giving feedback to his creative team on the ad campaign it was about to pitch to the Wexner Medical Center. He sent an email to Eric thanking him for his work on the project, then wandered into his mother's room. It was around seven in the evening, and Shirin and Manju were on the balcony. Manju stood as soon as he entered and disappeared into the kitchen. Remy took Manju's seat, across from Shirin, and the two of them sat watching the sky turn dark. In the distance, the moon was rising, but a portion of it was cut off by one of the buildings. "It's a beautiful evening," Remy said.

Shirin smiled but kept silent. She had been much more alert at lunchtime, enchanted by Gulnaz's constant prattle. Remy was accustomed to these cycles of conversation and silence, the ebb and flow of his mother's energy level. "Did you enjoy lunch today?" he asked.

"She's a good girl," Shirin said in reply.

"She is." Remy fidgeted with his hands. "Are you okay with us having visitors? You know, having my friends stop by?"

Shirin shrugged.

"Gulnaz was telling me that when we were kids she used to come over on weekends to study with me. I had forgotten. She and her parents lived in Norman Building for years, remember?"

Shirin looked at him and blinked. "I remember."

Remy shivered. *She knows*, he thought. *She remembers the same incident that Gulnaz was telling me about. Why am I the only one who doesn't?* The silence between them stretched taut.

"Where did you go with her?" Shirin spoke so low that Remy had to lean forward to hear her.

"Today? Oh. We went to the agiary. Gulnaz insisted."

"Daddy used to see her there sometimes. Once, he brought her home for lunch." Shirin smiled, a hairline smile. "Of course, it was on a day I had nothing special prepared. Just chutney sandwiches."

There's nothing wrong with her brain, Remy thought. In the hospital bed, Shirin had looked small, like a shell discarded on a beach. But that shell had teemed with life, with memories and emotions.

"I'm sure Gulnaz didn't mind," he said. "Your chutney sandwiches were the best."

Shirin's head jerked up. "You remember?"

"Yes, Mummy, of course. My mouth is watering just thinking about them."

"Take me to the kitchen. I will make some for you. I will—"

"Mummy, it's okay. Maybe in a few days, accha? When you're a little stronger. In any case, they have already made dinner for tonight."

"Before you go back. Before you go, I will make them for you."

"Fine," Remy said, humoring her, knowing she would be out of breath before she could even finish grating the coconut for the chutney.

"They're still allowing her into the fire temple?" Shirin said abruptly. "Now that she's married to a non-Parsi? That, too, a Muslim."

The novelty of hearing his mother talk in full sentences had not yet worn off. Bringing her home had clearly been the right thing to do. "Well, *I* married a non-Parsi," Remy said. "And I've never had a problem."

"That's different. You're a man. The rules are different."

Remy shook his head. "Such double standards. In any case, there was no issue. The priest greeted Gulnaz like an old friend."

Shirin scowled. "Fardoon. That crook. He will let Satan into that place of worship if you bribe him enough."

There it was—the bitterness, the abrupt mood change. The dastur had seemed like a decent man. Everybody knew that the priests were poor, dependent on tips to supplement their salaries. And maybe he didn't even know that Gulnaz had married. In any case, how was it their business? Remy had a sour taste in his mouth. He willed himself to steer the conversation back into neutral territory. "When was the last time you went to the agiary?"

"Me? I don't go. I used to just say my prayers at home. Even before you left for America, I had stopped going, remember?"

"We went on Navroz each year, didn't we?"

"On Navroz and on your birthday. It was important to your daddy, so we went to Banaji Agiary in Fort on those two occasions. Other than that, I never went."

Remy wondered if this was connected to Cyrus's increasingly urgent admonishments to his son to develop his faith. Maybe his father had been fearful that Remy was unconsciously following in his mother's footsteps. But there was a difference: Unlike Remy, his mother was devout. Shirin had prayed for an hour before dinner every evening of Remy's life.

Why hadn't Pervez and Roshan brought Mummy's prayer book to the hospital? It might have given her some solace. For that matter, why hadn't it occurred to him to do this since he'd brought her home? Remy felt chastised. Hell, if *he* hadn't thought of it, how could it have occurred to Pervez that the unresponsive woman they'd dropped off at the hospital was capable of reading the Avesta?

"I'll be right back," Remy said.

He went to the wardrobe in his mother's bedroom, and as he opened it, he remembered how he hadn't been allowed to touch her prayer book as a boy, that Shirin had always kept it out of his reach. Once, she had caught him standing on a stool to get to the top shelf. He had stiffened when she'd entered the room, braced himself for a smack on his buttocks at the very least, but she had simply lifted him off the stool and crooked her finger at him. His humiliation at being caught had taken away the mystique of riffling through her wardrobe, and he'd never attempted it again.

Now, he could reach the shelf easily. His fingers encountered a glass bottle—it was an unopened bottle of Tata's Eau de Cologne, the once light-golden liquid aged to a brass brown. How many years had she hoarded this bottle? He remembered the summer nights lying in his parents' bed, his small body blazing with fever, recalled the coolness against his forehead of a rag doused in the cologne and dipped in ice water. His mother had believed that this was a tried-and-true method to break a fever, and indeed, he had resorted to the same technique in the hospital with her, hadn't he? He set the bottle on her bedside table, then felt around for the prayer book.

He found it immediately and lowered it from the shelf. As he did, a piece of paper fell from it, and he bent to pick it up. It was a pass-port-sized picture of him, but it was too dark in the room to see it clearly. He turned on the overhead light. It was him, except his image was distorted. The boy in the picture was a grotesque version of him-self, his arms twisted, his mouth deformed. He had Remy's eyes, but they were hazy, as if some essential light had been snuffed out. Looking at the photo was like looking for his reflection in a foggy mirror and not finding it. Remy turned the picture over in confusion. *Cyloo C. Wadia, age 6*, it said in his mother's handwriting. *Jan. 5, 1986.*

Remy blinked, confused. The date made the boy in the picture two years older than he was. But who was he? A cousin he'd never met? And why did Mummy have his picture in her prayer book?

Cyloo. She had cried out for Cyloo that night in the hospital. Remy shook the prayer book, hoping for an explanation to fall from between the leaves. Maybe a picture of Remy? Or a note? Anything that would dispel this cold feeling spreading through his body. But the yellowing pages of the book held no other clues.

He walked slowly back to the balcony. The moon had floated up in the sky, and it lit up Shirin, who sat looking at it, her hands in her

lap, the moonbeam an interrogation. In the distance, he could hear
the faint sound of the waves from the nearby sea lapping against the
rocks. There was something so still and ghostly about the sight of his
mother sitting alone on the balcony that it stopped Remy in his tracks.
He was seized by an inexplicable feeling of dread, the unease settling
deep within him.

Remy shook his head. *Stop being dramatic,* he said to himself.
There's a simple explanation for this. The deformed boy in the picture
was probably some distant relative whose poor, hapless mother had
asked Shirin to pray for a miracle cure. Hence its placement in the
prayer book. *Why on earth would Mummy carry your picture in a
holy book?* he asked himself. *You, who have had every advantage and
none of the misfortune that twisted this unlucky boy's features?*

But his heart was hammering as he sat down in front of her, and
for a second he wondered if he was getting sick. He rubbed his hands
before holding out the picture to her. "Mummy?" he said, trying to
sound casual. "Who's this?"

Shirin glanced at the picture and then turned back to stare at the
sky, her face impassive.

Remy waited, and when it was clear that she was ignoring him, he
felt a spurt of insult that turned into anger. "I asked you, who is this?"
he repeated, his voice tight with injury. Tears sprang into his eyes.
"Mama, please. I have the right to know. Who is this boy?" His voice
had taken on a whiny quality he despised.

Shirin turned her head slowly and looked at him. In the light of the
moon, he saw her eyes take on a new depth as they flicked to his face.
She opened her mouth once, twice, but no words came. She cleared her
throat. "Let it go, son," she said. "You shouldn't have come."

Remy was gripped by a sudden, nameless fear, as if a pair of hands
had gripped him and dunked him into an opaque sea. "What are you
talking about?" he said. "Shouldn't have come where? To see you?"

Shirin nodded. "Better for you to hate me," she said. "Me, rather than him."

He thought again of Daddy's strange letter. *I'm sorry. Be better than me.* Was that apology connected in some way to this boy? At the hospital, he had tried asking Mummy about the note, but she'd merely looked at him blankly. And once they'd come home, he'd let the matter drop and not grilled her about why she hadn't given it to him.

Remy slipped from his chair and fell to his knees, a penitent looking up at a distant goddess. "Mummy, please," he said, the tears falling from his eyes. "I beg you. Answer me. Look at this picture, Mummy. *Look.*"

To control his tremor, he used both hands to hold the picture inches away from her. But Shirin's face was a mask, impenetrable.

Finally, after the longest time, she ran her hand through his hair. "My Remy," she said. "Always, such silky hair. Better than any daughter I could've had."

He kneeled with his eyes closed, afraid to move as she continued to stroke his hair. He remembered those hands running through his hair whenever he'd been sick or injured on the playground. Strong maternal hands that only emerged when he was vulnerable or ill. The rest of the time, she withheld them from him, or wielded them to pinch him when no one was looking, or to threaten him with the wag of her finger.

"Why didn't you?" he said after a while. "Have a daughter, I mean?"

"Why?" she said. "When I had two perfectly wonderful sons."

THE COMMENT MUST have quickened Shirin's own breathing, as she began to cough and cough. Remy helped her take a few sips of water, rubbing her back as she drank, even as his hair stood on end. He knew her lungs were still not clear, but right now, he couldn't help but wonder if this long coughing jag was an act, a way of taking back what had slipped from her lips. His body felt hot and cold, jumpy with impatience but also numb with shock. *Two sons? Two wonderful sons?* Who was the other boy who had a claim to her heart? Surely, not the deformed boy in the picture. Where was he now? Something seemed to be getting jumbled in Mummy's brain, a crossing of wires that made her misremember some poor, unfortunate relative, who bore a passing resemblance to Remy, as her son. Her second son. Or, rather, her first son, given the date on the photograph. If Remy had an older brother, wouldn't he have remembered? Wouldn't they have told him? Daddy had always said that they were not just father and son, but best friends and confidants.

Remy sat back in his chair. He would ask Mummy about the photograph tomorrow, after she was rested. Hopefully, her memory would right itself in the morning, the drug-induced confusion would lift, and he'd find out the true lineage of the boy in the photograph. Probably the progeny of some poor widow living in one of those Parsi chawls, who had come to their apartment decades ago, asking for help with the medical expenses for her disabled son. Cyrus agreeing to send a monthly check. Shirin salvaging the poor woman's pride by keeping the photograph and promising to include her son in her daily prayers. All the while keeping Remy in the other room, so that the widow's envy would not darken the light of Remy's strong, athletic body. Remy and an unknown boy, examples of the random whimsy of life.

He picked up the photograph from where it had fallen on the floor and examined it closely. It was uncanny, but the boy had his own distinctive eyebrows, arched, almost girlish. Their eyes were the same shape and color, but illness made the boy's look vacant. He tucked the picture back into the prayer book.

"His name was Cyrus. Cyloo. My firstborn."

Remy said, "Mummy, don't talk nonsense. You're just confused. Cyrus was your husband."

Shirin looked at him sharply. "A mother can never forget her child. Even when the world demands that she do."

It's definitely the drugs, Remy thought. *Or maybe she has a fever.* He leaned over and felt her forehead. It was cool to his touch.

"Son," Shirin said. Her voice was raspy. "I never wanted to tell you. But you are about to become a father yourself. Maybe it's time for you to know the truth about your family." With that, she began to cry, which led to another coughing fit.

Manju came out to the balcony with a spoonful of yogurt to coat Shirin's throat. After Manju left, and Shirin's cough had subsided, Remy leaned forward and took her bony hand.

"You were always such a loving boy," Shirin said. She looked out at the moon. Struggling for composure? Remy wasn't sure.

When she turned back to him, her eyes were clear. "You had a brother. Two years older than you. He was named for your father, but we called him Cyloo."

Remy's breath caught in his chest. "Tell me," he said quietly. "Please. Tell me everything."

CHAPTER TWENTY-THREE

A YEAR AFTER Cyrus Wadia married Shirin Sethna, he was offered a promotion and a transfer to the city of Jamshedpur. As a senior executive at Tata Steel, Cyrus had often visited the city, and he enticed Shirin with descriptions of Jamshedpur's broad boulevards, its green spaces, and its place as the only city in India that was run not by a local government, but by a corporation renowned for its efficiency and civic responsibility.

Shirin, Bombay born and bred, was aghast. "How can you compare that backwater to our Bombay?" she said. "What would I do there all day while you're at work? I would be bored out of my mind."

"Think, Shirin," Cyrus said. "A thirty percent pay raise. Plus, the cost of living is cheaper there, and they provide many perks. I tell you, we can save so much that I'll be able to start my own engineering firm in a few short years."

Shirin was not convinced. She went to see her father. Framrose heard his daughter out, a sympathetic look on his face. After she'd finished, he pushed his glasses back on his nose and said, "So what do you want me to tell you? To leave your husband?"

"Daddy!" Shirin exclaimed. "Of course not. I love him."

"Good. And that is why you must follow him wherever he goes. That's the Indian way, beta. I thought your late mother and I had taught you this."

Shirin went to Jamshedpur with a heavy heart, but within three months, she had adjusted to the rhythm of life there. The Wadias became members of the prestigious United Club, where they soon made friends with the other executives and their wives. Shirin became particularly close to Jasmine, the wife of Cyrus's second-in-command, Behram. Jasmine was warm and loud and funny, and the two women soon started meeting for lunch three days a week. The men played billiards together at the club on Saturday afternoons. Shirin grew to appreciate Jamshedpur and its well-planned streets, its ample greenery, the hilly countryside that framed the town.

Most of all, she loved their spacious, sunny bungalow and the gardens around it. Jaiprakash, the gardener, had a five-year-old son, Chotu, and four days a week Shirin taught him how to read and write. She loved watching Chotu's face open with wonder as language blossomed in his head, and shared in his jubilation the day he learned to write his own name.

So when Shirin found that she was pregnant, her first thought was about how wonderful it would be to read to her son, to feel his breath on her face as he sat on her lap and helped her turn the pages of a book. Her time with Chotu had convinced her that she was carrying a boy.

A jubilant Cyrus declared he didn't give a damn about the baby's gender but that, by golly, if it was a son, he would teach the little bugger to drive a car by the time he turned twelve.

"And if it's a girl?" Shirin asked, laughing.

"If it's a girl, I'll put fresh flowers in her hair every day and teach her to dance. Like this," he said, twirling Shirin around.

"Such a double standard. Many girls are driving in Bombay now, you know."

Cyrus grinned. "I will teach my children to drive and dance and whistle and play cricket and . . . everything."

"Arre wah," Shirin said to the walls. "We haven't had one child yet, and already he's talking about children."

"*Children*," Cyrus repeated. "A full cricket team. With their mother's good looks and my—" He caught her eye. "And their mother's brains."

They went over to Jasmine and Behram's house for dinner that night. On the way there, Cyrus stopped at a sweetmeat shop and bought an assortment of mithai. "To sweeten your mouth," he said as he presented the box to Jasmine. "In celebration of our good news."

As they made their way to their car that night, Shirin stumbled over a cobblestone. Cyrus's hand shot out to grab her. "Careful," he said. "Precious cargo you are carrying."

"Oh Lord." Shirin laughed, shaking off his hand. "You make me sound like one of your shipping containers."

But Cyrus didn't laugh. "Those containers transport steel," he said. "Whereas you . . . You are carrying the most fragile cargo on Earth. Our baby."

Shirin rolled her eyes. "Are you going to treat me like this for the entire nine months?"

"You bet," Cyrus said. "You bet."

THE PLAN HAD been for Shirin to go to Bombay for her delivery. But five days before she was to leave, everything changed.

It was a quiet afternoon. The cook had left an hour earlier, and Shirin was alone, reading on the couch. When the first spasm came, she assumed it was indigestion. When it hit a second time, she rose to take an antacid. But the third spasm knocked her back on the sofa. She sat still, hand on her belly, unsure of what to do. She should've never eaten the dhansak, she thought, that heavy stew of lentils and chicken. *Breathe*, she told herself. *Breathe*.

The deep breathing calmed her down enough that she picked up the novel again. The next spasm made her jerk with pain, and the book landed on the floor. Shirin was suddenly petrified. The house phone sat across the long living room and looked impossibly far away. She felt a gush and raised her head to look below her torso. Her pants and the sofa were awash with fluid; her water had burst.

She screamed. Pain and terror mixed together, and she kept screaming. The baby was coming, and she was alone and couldn't reach the phone.

"Memsahib. Memsahib." She heard a male voice, but it was muffled, far away. She twisted her head in its direction and saw the gardener peering at her through the sliding glass door.

"Mali," she cried out. She pointed to her belly. "Call for an ambulance. Now." Sweat dripped into her eyes and made her vision blurry.

A few minutes, which felt like hours, passed, and then there was a hard knock on the front door. She closed her eyes, praying that the cook had left it unlocked. When she opened her eyes, Jaiprakash was standing over her, and the look on his face scared her. "The phone," she gasped, pointing.

It took a half hour for the ambulance to arrive. The pain was unlike anything she'd imagined.

The baby had begun to crown before they wheeled Shirin into the delivery room. She looked at the unfamiliar faces at the unknown hospital and wondered why her own doctor was not present, why her husband was not here. And then she turned her head, and there was Cyrus, bug-eyed, hurrying toward her, his face reflecting the terror that she felt.

"Shirin," Cyrus said, taking her hand. "It's all right. I'm here."

She closed her eyes and moaned.

WHERE THERE SHOULD have been a weight, her arms felt light. Barren. Shirin opened her eyes to a dark, silent room. She screamed. Cyrus came rushing in, his face haggard, his eyes red and heavy-lidded from fatigue.

"The baby," she gasped. "Is my baby dead?"

He nodded yes.

Then he shook his head no.

"It's alive," he said.

It.

It's alive.

She never forgave him for this.

THE DOCTOR WAS GRIM-FACED. Something had gone wrong, he said.

Wrong. Wrong. Wrong.

The word echoed in Shirin's ears, accompanied by the thudding of her heart. The rest of what he said floated around her, disconnected, dislodged from all logic or meaning.

Forceps delivery. Umbilical cord around his neck. Starved of oxygen.

Starved. Her baby was starved.

"I want to see him," she said loudly. "I need to feed him."

The doctor exchanged a look with Cyrus. "Maybe it's better if you don't, Mrs. Wadia. It will make the parting more difficult. In any case, he's in the observation unit."

She was already struggling to her feet, ignoring Cyrus's urgent "Jaan, don't."

They wheeled her down the corridor, admonishing her to be careful because of the stitches. She ignored their advice in the same way she'd ignored the pain.

When she finally saw him, she cast her eyes away from his bruised, twisted face and limbs. The baby's face had angry red splotches on it, and his jaw and hands looked as if they'd been bent by some giant piece of machinery.

She took a deep breath and looked again, and noticed the perfect moon-shaped fingernails. Something gnawed in her breast, a little mouse. It was love. She looked up at Cyrus, tears in her eyes.

"He's beautiful," she said, and noticed him flinch.

It was to punish him for the flinch that she named her son Cyrus. The namesake of the man who had referred to their son as *it*.

CHAPTER TWENTY-FOUR

IN THE FIRST few months after they returned home from the hospital, Shirin could see that Cyrus was making an effort to connect with his son, to hold him and play with him. But Cyloo would scrunch his face when his father lifted him from the crib, would scream until he was red. Shirin tried to explain to her husband that Cyloo did this with everybody, that it was not personal, but Cyrus looked shattered. Soon, he took to merely peering at his son when he returned home from work, and asking, "How is the little one?" Often, he didn't wait for an answer before going into another room.

Shirin was so exhausted by evening time she trained herself to pay scant attention to her husband's behavior. For three months, they argued about the need for a nanny, Cyrus begging her to hire someone so that they could resume some semblance of a social life—go to the club on occasion, say—but Shirin refused to be away from her son.

Finally, Cyrus answered the loud knock on the door on a Sunday afternoon, let in an older Catholic woman named Rita, and introduced her as their new live-in nanny.

Shirin was about to object when Cyloo let out a shriek and Rita scooped him up, rubbed his back, and said, "Okay, little man, calm down." She spoke to Shirin. "You are massaging the little fellow like this daily, right?"

"No," Shirin said, wondering why no one had told her to do this.

"Very important to do," Rita said. "See? You must go around and round like this. Important for blood circulation."

Shirin turned to Cyrus. "Yes," she said.

In the sixth month, her father came for a visit. As Framrose met his grandson for the first time, his eyes filled with tears. He ran his hands lightly over the infant's spine and limbs, his thumb pressing down at regular intervals. "Nothing can be done," he said when he had finished his examination, and although Shirin had been told the same devastating news by other doctors, she broke down upon hearing her father say it.

That night, Cyrus and Framrose sat at the table, drinking. At one point, Shirin heard her father say, "Such bad naseeb, deekra. Best thing to do is to have another child soon."

Shirin tiptoed out of the room, shaken by the cruelty of her father's words. Cyloo was not the burden they all thought he was. If only they could see him the way she did—his smiles when he passed gas, the way he looked at her as if he knew her deepest secrets, how adorable he looked in the yellow bonnet she'd bought for him. Only she and Rita, it seemed, knew what a treasure he was.

Rita became a substitute for Cyrus, who often traveled to Bombay for work. Shirin asked a few times to go with him; they could stay with her father, she said. But each time, Cyrus looked upset at the prospect, blaming it on the logistics of traveling with a disabled boy.

Shirin knew the truth: Cyrus was ashamed of his son and didn't want friends and colleagues to see what he had sired. The knowledge hurt her more deeply than she could've imagined. Also, she was quietly furious at him. What had possessed him to drag her to this small, isolated place? Would such an accident have happened if they had been living in Bombay? They would never know for certain, of course, but surely the doctors there would've been more skilled and experienced.

One evening when Cyrus came home from work, Shirin allowed him to kiss her on the cheek, say hello to Rita, and go take a shower. She sat on the bed, waiting. When he emerged from the bath, clad only in a towel, his dark hair damp, she stood up and said, "What were you discussing with that doctor who delivered Cyloo? The one who didn't want me to see my own flesh and blood?"

"What?"

"He said something about how seeing Cyloo would make the parting harder. What were the two of you plotting?"

Cyrus shook his head as he slipped into his pajama bottoms. "What bhoot has gotten into you this evening? Why are you making me relive the worst day of my life?"

Shirin recoiled, as if he'd struck her. "The worst day? The day our son was born?"

He grabbed her wrist and pulled her down to sit beside him on the bed. "Shirin, I'm sorry. That's not what I meant. Please, jaan. Don't be like this. You need to understand. What hopes I'd had for my—our— child. Our firstborn. The months spent planning what I was going to do. What I'd teach my child, how I'd show him off. And instead, we are left with this. For the rest of our lives."

She pulled away from him. "Tell me something. And don't lie. Do you love him?"

Cyrus's expression was confused. "I . . . I'm not sure. I'm sure I will, eventually. It's still a shock, okay? Just give me time, Shirin. Try to understand. I need time." And when Shirin looked unconvinced: "Think of what I do for a living. I'm an engineer by trade. I have a God-given ability to solve problems. But I don't know how to fix him."

"There's nothing to fix," she cried. "He doesn't need fixing. Don't you see how perfect he is?"

Cyrus rose to his feet, keeping his eyes on his wife's face the whole time. He chewed on his lower lip. "If you think he's perfect, hats off to you, yaar," he said at last. "But I'll be honest with you. I dread coming home in the evening. Whereas before . . ." He brushed away his tears and left the room.

He could have all the time he needed, Shirin thought, to learn to love his son, to look past the deformities and into Cyloo's soul. In the meantime, she had enough love in her heart to make up for the neglect and scorn that the world would fling her son's way. This was her only job now—to protect and defend Cyloo. She vowed to get it right.

CHAPTER TWENTY-FIVE

THE NEXT PREGNANCY came as a surprise, and she didn't break the news to Cyrus for three days. When she finally did, his face displayed all the conflicting emotions she felt. She waited to take her cues from her husband, ready to be happy if he was. Cyrus smiled a weak smile, then embraced her.

"We need this," he said. "And I promise, you will deliver this child in the best hospital in Bombay. In fact, I want you to consult with an obstetrician in Bombay immediately. Ask your father for a recommendation. I will book the plane tickets tomorrow."

"The doctor said that what happened to Cyloo was a freak occurrence. That it wouldn't happen again."

He squeezed her tight. "Of course not."

Still, they were taking no chances. Cyrus and Shirin and Cyloo and Rita flew to Bombay in the seventh month and settled into Framrose's apartment. Cyrus went back to Jamshedpur a few days later, calling Shirin every morning and night. And Shirin found herself missing her life in Jamshedpur. She had lost touch with her college friends. She endured the visits of a few of her father's friends but when she noticed their morbid fascination with her disabled son, heard their clucks of pity, their ridiculous advice on how to "cure" him—consulting with this sadhu, meeting with that astrologer, offering novenas at the church in Mahim—she decided against any more visitors. She was content chatting with her wise, serious father and tending to her child. *Children*, she reminded herself.

Cyrus returned to Bombay a week before her due date, having secured permission to work out of the main office after the baby's birth for as long as he wished. Shirin was happy to see him, but it was undeniable: having Cyrus there, seeing his anxious face as he eyed her swollen belly, watching him avoid Cyloo, disturbed the rhythm of the past two months. She realized something with a cold clarity—being a mother was so all-consuming that she had little energy left to also be a wife. And perhaps, very little love to spare. The last thought made her cry; Cyrus was a good man and had been a loving husband to her.

Remy's birth went as smoothly as Cyloo's had been tortured. It was as if the past two years had affronted God's sense of fair play. All the nurses in the maternity ward came to ooh and aah over the newborn— his perfectly shaped lips, his long eyelashes, the smooth, delicate skull, the exquisite fingers and toes. Cyrus smothered him in kisses and was reluctant to hand him over to Shirin even for breastfeeding. In fact, he was so open in his instant love for his second son that Shirin had to look away, tell herself to ignore the jealousy she felt on behalf of her firstborn.

Shirin had wanted to name the infant after her father, but Cyrus crouched beside her hospital bed and smiled. "Do you remember that inn in Toulouse where we'd stayed during our honeymoon?" he asked.

She looked at him curiously. "Yes? Why?"

"Remember the name of the owner? How good he was to us, how happy we were there?"

"Of course. Remy Arnette. He was a wonderful man. Why?"

Cyrus picked up his son. "Look at him. He looks like a Remy. Let's give him that name, so that whenever we look at him we will remember that happy time."

A Parsi boy growing up in Bombay with a French name? she wondered. Wouldn't he be teased and bullied by his schoolmates? Wouldn't the servants mangle the pronunciation? *But you named your first son out of spite*, she told herself. *What's the harm in letting Cyrus have this pleasure?* She swallowed her reservations. Cyrus had clearly carried this notion all these years and had hoarded the name for just such an occasion. And maybe he was right. Maybe the commemoration of a happy time would bring them good fortune.

She held out her arms to cradle the newborn. He looked up at her with those big light eyes, so much like Cyloo's and yet so different. "Welcome to the world, Remy Wadia," she said.

WHILE IN BOMBAY, they continued with Cyloo's therapy. Framrose had hired one of the best physiotherapists in the city to work with his grandson, and each afternoon the young man would spend over an hour gently moving Cyloo's limbs, stretching them, and encouraging the toddler to walk. One morning as Shirin sang to three-month-old Remy, Cyloo emitted a high-pitched sound. She looked over to see him stagger to his feet and take three steps toward her before tumbling to the floor. Cyrus had gone to the bank with her father, and when she saw their car return, she ran down the stairs to give them the astounding news. Her husband and her father exchanged a quick look before they smiled at her joy. "Let's hope for the best, beta," Framrose said.

She was determined to do just that when the family flew back to Jamshedpur a few days later. Shirin missed her father but was glad to be home. Her life resumed its patterns: Rita watched Remy while Shirin worked with the new physiotherapist on Cyloo, determined to help him become as high-functioning as possible. The cook came at noon to prepare their meals, and after lunch, Shirin would take a nap, one son on either side of her. She would sip her afternoon tea sitting on the couch in the living room, Remy in her lap and Cyloo leaning against her. Every now and then, Cyloo would reach over to touch the baby's toes or tummy, and Shirin's heart would lurch with joy at what she presumed was Cyloo's attempt to bond with his brother.

After a few months, it was safe to leave the boys with Rita long enough for her to run to the bank or the store; four days a week, she began to take walks at a nearby park. In the beginning, she worried about the boys the entire time she was away, and often cut short her walks. But after Rita repeatedly assured her that she had the situation under control, Shirin began to enjoy her rare moments of quiet and solitude. Sometimes, she'd invite Jasmine to lunch, because she appeared to take Cyloo's deformities in stride and was madly in love with Remy. Jasmine had grown up with an uncle who was mentally challenged, and she had an easy, nonchalant way around Cyloo that pleased Shirin. Indeed, Jasmine and Rita were the only other people who seemed to love both boys equally, and Shirin began to think of the three of them as a sorority of sisters.

For Remy's first birthday, Shirin wanted to throw a party at home, but Cyrus convinced her to host it at the United Club. That way, someone else could cater the affair and they could relax, he said. That way, he could invite his work colleagues without feeling guilty about adding to Shirin's chores.

Cyrus had taken the day of the party off from work, and they slept in. They were enjoying a late breakfast on the balcony when Cyrus stretched and said, "How much extra should we pay Rita for tonight?"

"Pay her extra for what? Are we taking her to the club with us to watch the boys?"

"No, of course not," Cyrus said. "I meant for watching Cyloo while we're gone."

"You want Cyloo to stay at home with Rita? You want to keep him away from his own brother's celebration?" Shirin was incredulous.

Cyrus glared at her. "Do you think it matters to Cyloo? Do you think he even knows? He's going to freak out in front of so many people. And doesn't Remy deserve one damn evening where he's the center of attention, for a change?"

"What do you mean?" Her voice wobbled. "I pay attention to him all the time."

"Until his brother screams or cries. And then . . ." Cyrus shook his head, not finishing his sentence.

"Daa. Da?" Remy tottered into their room, as if on cue. He had begun to walk at nine months, a fact that had made Cyrus inordinately proud.

"What is it, my baby?" Cyrus rose from the table, scooped him up, and hugged him tight. "What does my raja want?" He threw Shirin a look and walked into the living room, cooing to his son.

As always, Shirin felt conflicting emotions. Cyrus often referred to Remy as a raja, a king. But what did that make Cyloo? A pauper? He may as well have been, given how little attention he got from his father.

She carried her resentment to the United Club that evening. It grew when she realized that Cyrus had invited all the senior and junior executives to the party, the very people he'd stopped inviting to the house after Cyloo's birth. It simmered as she watched her husband showing off Remy, rubbing his back as they walked, lifting him up so that he was eye level with Cyrus's boss, laughing each time a female associate pinched Remy's cheeks and squealed, "Oh my God! You are *tho* thweeeeet."

It was true—in his navy-blue sailor suit and white Keds, Remy looked adorable. Even as Shirin felt a throb of pride at her son's luminous beauty, she felt a corresponding guilt at the thought of her other son, at home in his pajamas. She glanced at her watch. What was Cyloo doing right now? Rita had probably strapped him in his high chair and was feeding him mashed food with a teaspoon. Would his eating ever improve? They had tried feeding him bits of chicken for the first time a month ago, but he had coughed and she, terrified, had pried his mouth open and removed the food. Cyloo, with the same beautiful eyes as his brother, had looked at her tearfully as she'd forced his jaw open, all the time afraid that he'd bite her, as he did when he was scared or frustrated.

The live band was playing "Stayin' Alive," and then it segued into "How Deep Is Your Love." Shirin found herself humming the chorus. How deep was her love? Deeper than outer space. Deeper than the five oceans piled on top of one another. That deep. For both her sons, of course. But, yes, perhaps a tad bit deeper for Cyloo. Because he was the pauper prince, the exiled brother, banished into the forest by his father.

She watched as Cyrus matched his stride to Remy's steps, the boy holding on to his father's index finger. *They are a complete unit. They don't need me*, she thought. But instead of being hurt, she felt liberated. Remy would always be a steady flame in her heart, but Cyloo was the bonfire. Shirin remembered something the nuns at her school used to say: *You go where there is need.* Remy would have everything that he wanted, the world opening up like a treasure chest to a handsome, intelligent, able-bodied boy.

Until a few years ago, Shirin herself had been part of that privileged society. Her father's wealth and her own beauty and intelligence had made the world seem like a benevolent place, one she could slip into as easily as a favorite armchair. But as she watched her husband stroke the back of her son's head—a gesture that once would've cracked her heart open—Shirin realized something: that without knowing it, she had joined the ranks of the world's shunned and neglected, the invisible and unseen. If they couldn't see past Cyloo's deformities to his spirit, to his soul, then she was happy to relinquish her membership in such a superficial society. By treating her son as less than human, they had diminished their own humanity.

She didn't owe any of them one damn thing. Not even Cyrus. She had given him what he wanted—a golden child, a mirror that reflected back his own, unspoiled image. A sweet, loving boy who had burrowed into his father's heart from the instant he appeared, who seemed determined to make up for every loss that Cyrus had suffered with his firstborn. *Every* perceived *loss*, Shirin thought, correcting herself. Cyrus could've learned to love his son if he had seen Cyloo as a *person*, rather than as a shameful secret.

As if she had conjured him up, Cyrus stood before her, smiling. Some of her thoughts must've shown, because for an instant, his smile froze. She watched as he willed himself to ignore whatever he'd read on her face and reached for her hand.

"Dance with me? It's been so long since we've had a chance."

Shirin was about to refuse, but the pleading look in his eyes made her acquiesce. He led her toward the stage and whispered a request to the musicians. It was such an old song—"Save the Last Dance for Me"—that the band members had to consult with one another before they launched into it.

As they swayed to the music, she felt Cyrus's breath, as warm as the cognac he'd been drinking, as he sang the lyrics into her ear. She felt her body soften toward him, her earlier resentment drifting away. She wanted them to fetch Remy and have the three of them waltz home, adrift on this cloud of tenderness and music, wanted them to enter the house, relieve Rita for the night, lock the door, and be a family, the four of them.

Cyrus had a heart of gold. That was the first thing the old match-maker had told her father: "I tell you, Framrose, you can look far and wide, and you'll never find a boy like him. He has a heart of gold, believe me." And the auntie had been right. On their first date, he had given money to every single beggar who had come up to them—had done it absently, as if generosity was as natural as breathing. Shirin had noticed because he was so unlike the other men she had dated, who had tried to impress her with how aggressively they shooed the urchins away. And that evening, as they'd sat on the parapet at Marine Drive and watched the dark waves of the Arabian Sea, he had not shuf-fled and fumbled like a schoolboy but had simply asked, "May I put my arm around you?" She had nodded, and a few minutes later, had surprised herself by leaning her head on his shoulder.

This was the man she was dancing with tonight, who was holding her close—so close—as if he knew that if he let go of her for even a moment, she would leave him and fly away to her firstborn son.

Remy fell asleep in Shirin's lap as Cyrus drove them home. She kissed the top of her son's sweet head, felt a tremor of love run through her. *My Remy*, she thought. *May you always be this bright ray of sun-shine.* She had Cyloo's faded moonlight and Remy's golden daylight. In other words, a perfect galaxy. What more could she ask for?

Cheered by the thought, she put her hand on Cyrus's thigh. "Did you have a good time?" she asked.

"Yes." A beat. "You obviously didn't."

"No, no, that's not true. I did. It was a good party."

Cyrus took his eyes off the road to glance at her. "Really? Then how come you spent half the evening sulking, as if you were a new widow or something?"

After the earlier sweetness, Shirin was shocked by the bitterness in Cyrus's voice. What had happened to the man with the heart of gold? Was she responsible for the tarnish? "I'm—I'm sorry," she stammered. "I didn't realize . . ."

"That you looked like you were at a bloody funeral? Everybody was looking at you. Everyone noticed."

"Cyrus. I did my best. You know I'm a shy person. I don't have your personality. Gregarious."

"Yah, well, maybe if I'm so outgoing, it's because I have to cover for you. All the time."

She blinked back her tears, stared out the window at the dark. In her arms, Remy stirred, and she adjusted her body so that his head wouldn't loll.

"Nothing to say. As usual," Cyrus said.

Shirin was quiet for a long time. Then: "I can't—I won't. Pretend. Like you. That we don't have a second son. I won't let him become invisible. I won't."

Cyrus let out a cry. "One evening. One motherfucking evening. Away from the moroseness, the gloom. One evening to be carefree and young. To enjoy our other child. That's all I asked for."

"I'm sorry . . ."

"You seem to have forgotten, Shirin. You are a mother, yes. A very good mother, in fact. But"—Cyrus's face crumpled—"you are also a wife. You've forgotten that part."

She knew that anything she said would simply lead to more fighting, so she didn't try to console him. He wanted her fully, the way she'd belonged to him before the children. Yet Shirin knew that the woman she'd been was gone. She was now divided into parts, many parts, a small piece of her belonging to each of the four men in her life—her father, her husband, her two sons. If she *had* to choose, if Cyrus forced her to, she knew who she would choose.

As if he knew what she was thinking and was afraid to push her, Cyrus, too, fell quiet. They drove home the rest of the way in silence, the sound of Remy's breathing filling the car.

CHAPTER TWENTY-SIX

THEY REACHED AN uneasy equilibrium in the second year of Remy's life. Cyrus got another promotion, and Shirin was happy for him, allowed him to take her out to a nice restaurant to celebrate. The promotion meant that he would be traveling even more than before, but it didn't really affect Shirin's life much, because she had Rita's help in raising her two sons. Every morning, the two women would divide up their duties: Shirin would bathe one boy while Rita bathed the other; one of them would feed Cyloo while the other made breakfast for Remy.

In an effort to revitalize their flagging sex life, Cyrus offered to get a vasectomy. Shirin was noncommittal. What would've revived her interest would have been his embrace of Cyloo. But almost four years after Cyloo's birth, she knew that it would never be. It was the bitterest of life lessons—the realization that you cannot force someone to love what you do.

Cyrus was away the day Cyloo tottered over to where Remy was playing with his blocks on the floor, and tried to pick up a block with his gnarled hand. Shirin walked into the living room a few minutes later to find her sons sitting side by side, Remy patiently trying to place the blocks in his brother's hands. She was so overcome with emotion that she dropped the fruit bowl she was carrying. Two identical pairs of eyes turned to look at her.

The physiotherapist said it was good for Cyloo to interact with his brother, and Shirin encouraged her sons to play together as much as possible. But Cyloo was given to screaming in frustration after a few moments of play, and Remy often came to her in tears, complaining about his brother being mean, knocking down the tower he had built.

They celebrated Remy's second birthday at home, with none of the festivities that had marked his first. Cyrus took the day off, and for lunch they had the traditional Parsi meal for auspicious occasions— fried fish, yellow daal with rice, and a side of sweet yogurt. For dessert, Shirin made sev, sweetened vermicelli garnished with golden raisins and toasted almonds. She loved making sev; it brought back happy memories of past celebrations. Cyrus, too, enjoyed her home cooking, preferred it to the rich restaurant meals he was forced to eat while entertaining clients.

A month after Remy's birthday, Shirin decided on a more ambitious menu for Navroz, Parsi New Year: patra ni machhi—pomfret slathered with green chutney and steamed in banana leaves—for the first course, followed by chicken pulao with dhansak daal. They would have bread pudding for dessert. She was in the kitchen giving instructions to the cook when she heard a hair-raising scream. She ran into the bedroom, thinking Cyloo was hurt, but it was Remy, covering his cheek, a trickle of blood on his face. Cyloo sat next to him, pointing at his brother, grinning vacantly.

Shirin dropped to her knees. "Remy," she yelled. "What happened? Why are you bleeding?"

"He. Bit. Me." Remy was sobbing hard, his voice outraged.

"Bit you? Who bit you?" Shirin asked, although she knew the answer.

"Bhai. Bhai bit me."

Rita came into the room and cradled Remy, leaving Shirin to deal with Cyloo. "Is it true?" she said to him. "You bit your brother?"

In response, Cyloo grinned. Vacuously. Stupidly. Maliciously.

"You nasty boy." Shirin's hand flew from her body and struck Cyloo on his head. *Thwat.* "You evil boy." Another hit, this time to his cheek. She had no control over what her hand was doing. *Thwat.* Even harder this time.

Cyloo was howling, but Shirin, unable to bear the sound of Remy's grief, wasn't satisfied. She raised her hand even higher and struck Cyloo a fourth time.

Rita was yelling at her to stop, but the voice that Shirin heard clearest over the commotion was Remy's. "Mummy, please," he screamed. "Stop hitting my brother." He broke away from Rita and wedged himself between Shirin and Cyloo.

Shirin's hand froze in midair. She looked from one boy to another. Cyloo was still howling, but Remy had stopped crying, although his eyes brimmed with tears. "Come here," she said to him. "Let's go clean your face."

She washed his cheek with soap and water, pressing a towel against it until the bleeding stopped. Remy didn't cry as she poured Dettol on a piece of gauze and held it against his face. She carried him to her bed and sat him down, telling him to hold the gauze in place.

She was about to pick up the phone to call Dr. Mistry's clinic when Remy said, "Mummy?"

She turned around. "Yes, my darling?"

He looked at her with those big, wounded eyes. "Thank you for loving me so much."

Shirin felt those words enter her like a blade. She went back to the bed and sat on her haunches before him. "I love you so much, my darling," she said. "I'm sorry that I spend so much time with your brother. It's only because . . ."

"I know," Remy said, nodding his head. "Daddy told me. It's because Cyloo is not well."

She took his hand in hers. "But both of you own my heart. No matter what happens, I want you to remember this, always. Promise?"

"Promise," he said.

DR. MISTRY CAME to the house that afternoon to take a look at Remy's cheek, and he prescribed an antibiotic ointment. The bite didn't look infected, but Shirin should keep an eye on it, he said. Luckily, Remy had received already his tetanus shot a few months earlier, so he should be fine.

"What do I do to keep this from happening again?" Shirin asked.

"Keep them apart the best you can."

Cyrus returned that evening from a six-day business trip to Dubai. He went pale when he heard what had happened. Shirin managed to calm him, doing her best to downplay the incident. "It's Navroz," she said. "Everybody's fine now. Let's not ruin our evening. We've made all your favorite dishes."

It might have ended there if Remy had not started a fever in the middle of the night.

REMY FELT APPREHENSIVE as his mother's breathing grew shallow while she continued to relay her tale. "Take a break, Mummy," he said, and went into the kitchen to open a bottle of Coke.

"Shall I warm up dinner, sir?" Manju asked as soon as he walked in.

"Give us a few more minutes," he said. "I'll let you know. But, please, you go ahead and eat."

He gave Shirin two puffs of her inhaler and then offered her the Coke. After a few sips, she seemed better. "What happened then?" he prompted gently.

Shirin looked at him. "You started a fever in the middle of the night," she repeated.

REMY'S FEVER HAD not come down for two days. Dr. Mistry was puzzled, since the bite had not looked serious. It was likely from delayed shock, he said. *Relax*, he told Cyrus. *It's nothing.*

Still, Cyrus decided to work from home to keep an eye on Remy. Even though Remy was better on the third day, Cyrus stayed home again. His friend Dina Mehta, who was acting as legal counsel for Tata Steel on a difficult case, was flying into Jamshedpur that afternoon, and they had invited her to stay with them while in town.

Shirin knew that he and Dina had dated while in college, but Cyrus assured her that he had married the woman he loved. Shirin had no reason to doubt him; she had met Dina on several occasions and despite the two friends' obvious affection for each other, Shirin hadn't detected the slightest romantic interest on Cyrus's part. It had been her idea to have Dina stay with them, rather than at a hotel.

Dina stayed for three nights, she and Cyrus riding to work together in the mornings and returning home in the evenings. On her first night, Cyrus suggested that Rita feed Cyloo in his bedroom while they ate in the dining room, but Dina spoke up. "Oh, nonsense. Let's all eat together, na?" she said cheerfully. And throughout the meal, she paid equal attention to both children, nodding and glancing at Cyloo as she spoke, including him in the conversation. Cyloo watched her, enamored.

Shirin, too, warmed to Dina. *Maybe Cyrus will learn from her example*, she thought as Dina spoke about growing up with her cousin Adi, who was mentally challenged. There was not a hint of pity in her voice. Shirin glanced at Cyrus, who was nodding as Dina spoke. When she caught his eye, he looked away, as if ashamed.

After dinner, Shirin served the Parsi custard she had made. Remy finished his portion and said, "May I have another slice, please?" There was something so courtly and earnest about his tone that Dina cracked up laughing.

"Oh my God," she spluttered. "He's a Little Lord Fauntleroy."

As if to prove her right, Remy jumped off his chair after dinner, swept his hand with a flourish, and said to Dina, "Ladies first."

Cyrus guffawed. "My son, the flirt."

After Dina left, the house felt empty. Even though she'd only been there in the evenings, she'd brought a new rhythm to their lives. By finding something to admire in each boy, simply by *seeing* Cyloo, she had altered their family dynamic. The realization forced Shirin to notice all over again just how much Cyrus favored one son over the other.

THE HOUSE WAS full of stacked boxes, and Shirin had to work hard to make sure the boys didn't bump into them. Cyrus had gotten yet another promotion, and they were being transferred back to Bombay. The big move wasn't until a few weeks later, but they had already transported some of the furniture, and Shirin had started packing the rest. It was hard to believe how much stuff they had accumulated during their five and a half years in Jamshedpur. Shirin had mixed feelings about the move back—on the one hand, she was sad to leave the tranquility and isolation that their little bungalow afforded her. And she would miss Jasmine and Behram, not to mention Rita. On the other hand, it would be nice to start again in the new flat that Cyrus had purchased, and to be in the same city as Daddy.

She had just gone into the shower when she heard a deafening scream. She came out with a towel wrapped around her body and found Remy doubled over.

Rita was apologetic. "I . . . I just left them alone for a moment," she said. "I went into the kitchen to warm their milk. Before I could stop him, Cyloo kicked Remy in the stomach."

"Cyloo," Shirin said, shaking him roughly as she gripped his shoulders. "Why do you do this? Are you a mawali? A thug? We don't kick and bite in this house."

"Mummy," Remy said, his eyes puddling with tears. "I'm scared of him. I hate him."

Shirin gathered Remy to her side. "No, baba. We don't talk like that about our brother. Understand? He—he doesn't mean it. He's a child, you see?"

"But he's older than me."

"I know. I know, Remy. But . . . in a way . . . he's not. I'm sorry, my baba."

She separated the two boys, brought Remy to her bed to lie down with her. After a few minutes, Remy rolled over to look at her. "Mummy?" he said. "Can I ask you something?"

"Of course, my darling."

"Is Cyloo a monster? Like Godzilla?"

"Remy," she said, shocked. "No, of course not. How can you think this? He's not a monster. He's your brother."

"Then why is he so mean?"

Shirin pulled the boy toward her. "He's not trying to be mean. He loves you. Do you understand?"

Remy looked at her dubiously with those big eyes, but he nodded yes. Shirin tried to be satisfied with that. But after he fell asleep, she lay awake, heart thudding. She hoped that Remy would forget about the incident before Cyrus came home from work.

For the first time since Cyloo's birth, Shirin felt despair. "Why, God?" she said out loud. "What did I ever do to you? Why did you give me this challenge?"

But even as she asked the questions, she knew that the challenge was not her disabled son. The real challenge was her husband, from whom she had to keep secrets.

Well, she thought, *maybe things will be better once we move back to Bombay.* In his new job, Cyrus wouldn't be traveling as much. Perhaps that would bring a new stability into their lives. She would redouble her efforts to find better medical treatment for Cyloo, therapies that might make him more functional. Today's incident was probably because he was sensing the change in their lives. What a disruption the absence of familiar objects must have caused for Cyloo. Unable to speak or express his feelings, what recourse did he have but to lash out at someone smaller than he was?

Shirin decided to explain this to Remy when he woke up. For all their differences, there was a bond between the brothers—she was sure of it. Remy often walked over to his brother and gave him a kiss; Cyloo grinned each time. Shirin thrilled when this happened and did her best to encourage such moments. They were blood; their story would continue long after she and Cyrus were dead.

Bombay, she thought. *A fresh start.*

THAT SUNDAY, she and Cyrus packed the kitchen together. Shirin was reaching for a wineglass when Cyrus said, "So you didn't tell me about Cyloo kicking my son in the stomach?"

She almost dropped the glass, but recovered. "They're *both* your sons," she said automatically. And when he didn't reply: "How did you find out?"

Cyrus wrapped a bowl in newspaper. "Not from *you,*" he said. "Were you planning on not telling me?"

"You want me to tell you every time one child hits the other?" She tore off a sheet of paper and wrapped the glass in it. "They are brothers. They will fight. It's normal."

"It's normal? That's why Remy was traumatized even the next day? That's normal, hah?"

Shirin blinked in astonishment as she realized that Cyrus was furious.

"Cyrus," she said. "They are children. What do you expect me to do?"

He looked at her for the longest time. "Nothing," he said at last. "I expect you to do nothing."

CHAPTER TWENTY-SEVEN

THEY HAD GIVEN Cyloo a light sedative for the flight to Bombay, and he was still snoring in the wheelchair when they reached baggage claim. While they waited for their suitcases to arrive, Shirin looked up to see a petite woman hurrying toward them. She wore a white sari with a blue border, and Shirin thought she looked like one of those nuns who worked at Mother Teresa's homes. Her flushed, sweaty face told Shirin that it was hot outside.

The woman gave Shirin a quick smile. "I—I'm so sorry, ma'am, but I need to disturb Mr. Wadia for a moment. It's urgent. I know you just landed and all, but . . ."

Shirin sighed. They had barely set foot in Bombay, and already Cyrus's work was calling. "Of course," she said. She turned to Cyrus. "Don't worry. I'll get the suitcases. The coolie will lift them off the conveyor belt."

As she waited for the bags, Cyrus and the woman huddled a short distance away, Cyrus glancing in Shirin's direction occasionally. She smiled to let him know it was okay, that she didn't resent the intrusion. In any case, she was distracted by Remy, who said he was thirsty *and* had to pee.

"Two minutes," she said. "Hold it, and we will go to the loo before we drive home, accha?"

She took Remy to the bathroom on their way out while Cyrus instructed the porter to hail a cab, and begin loading their suitcases. When she stepped outside, she saw that Cyrus had placed Cyloo in the young woman's car, along with a couple of their bags. Shirin frowned. She understood that Cyrus needed to complete his conversation with his colleague, but why take Cyloo with them instead of sending him home with Remy and her?

"He'll be more comfortable in an air-conditioned vehicle," Cyrus explained, as if he'd read her mind. "See you at the apartment. If you reach there first, ask the security guard to carry the bags upstairs. You don't lift any of the bags, you hear?"

"Won't you be right behind?" Shirin asked, but he was already climbing into the car, and they had taken off before she had even put Remy in the taxi.

She reached the apartment building before Cyrus did. She prayed that Cyloo didn't do potty in his diaper, knowing that Cyrus would be mortified.

A half hour passed, but there was still no sign of her husband and her oldest son. Shirin opened all the windows to air out the new apartment, which still smelled of fresh paint. She longed for a cup of tea but was too tired to unpack a box to find a pot. She opened a packet of Marie biscuits and shared it with Remy. She went to the newly installed phone to call her father, but there was no dial tone. *They haven't connected the phone yet?* she thought with irritation.

Remy was tired and on the verge of a tantrum, so she put him to bed and lay down next to him and told him a story. Halfway through, they both fell asleep.

A small noise woke her up. She opened her eyes to see Cyrus beside the bed, looking at her. There was a strange expression on his face, and she shot up, scared.

"Cyrus," she said, taking his hand. It was clammy. "Where did you go for so long? I was starting to worry." She looked around. "How did Cyloo behave in the car? Do you need help with him?"

He gestured to the living room, and she followed him there. But the room was unoccupied. "Where is Cyloo?" she said.

"Shirin. Sit down. I have something to tell you. Sit."

Cyrus's face was tense, his eyes hooded. Shirin was suddenly terrified. "Where is Cyloo?" she repeated. "Is he hurt? Did you have an accident? Cyrus, tell me."

"What? No. *No.*" He held her by her shoulders, forced her onto the couch. "Sit. He's okay. He's better than okay. He's where he belongs. Where we should've put him from the start."

"I don't understand. Can you please not talk in riddles? You're really scaring me. Where is he?"

"With people who will take excellent care of him. Who have lots of experience with disabled boys. He—he didn't even cry when I dropped him off. I'm sorry I had to do it this way, Shirin. But I knew you'd never agree. See, we are about to begin a new chapter in our lives. This way, we can have a fresh start. We're still young, Shirin. We can still—"

Shirin screamed.

Cyrus recoiled. "Stop. You'll wake up Remy," he hissed, and when she didn't stop, he covered her mouth with his hand. She clawed at him, striking him over and over again. But he kept his hand there until she went silent.

"Are you my enemy?" she said as soon as she could speak. "Are you my mortal enemy from a past life? Do you hate me so much that you would kill my soul but keep my body alive? Why is my son with strangers? Why? When he has two healthy parents!"

"Because he also has a brother," Cyrus snapped. "A boy who is being abused, bitten, punched. Not to mention neglected by his mother."

She began to sob. "How do you know? You're gone all day. I love Remy. I do my best for him. He knows I love him. I tell him every day."

He pulled her toward him. "Shirin, of course you do. You're a great mother. But there's only one of you. You've dedicated nearly five years of your life to caring for Cyloo. You deserve better, my darling."

"So what is he? A piece of tissue paper that we can simply discard? Cyrus, have you gone mad? Do you think I will allow this? Do you think my father will stand for his grandchild being raised by strangers? This is kidnapping. I will charge you with kidnapping. My father will hire a lawyer and—"

"Framrose knows. He agrees with me. That if we are to survive as a family, this is our only chance."

"Bullshit. *Bullshit*. Daddy would never be part of such a scheme. I will divorce you before I give up my Cyloo."

Cyrus looked at her sharply. "Don't ever use the word 'divorce' in this house. Nobody in my family has ever gotten one. And how are you going to manage alone in this city as a single mother of a disabled boy?"

"Not 'boy.' '*Boys*.' I will take both of them with me."

"Shirin. Talk sense. I will lose my life before I part with Remy. You know that."

She began to sob again. "Please, Cyrus. Don't do this. We will stay out of your way. You won't even have to see him when you come home. I'll keep him away from you."

Cyrus looked hurt. "You think I'm doing it for that reason? Haven't you heard a word I've said? I gave him away for Remy's sake. So that he can grow up unencumbered. And for your—no, *our*—sake. So that we can be a normal couple again." His voice assumed an urgent tone. "Shirin, think. Cyloo is developmentally stunted. You think he knows the difference between being here or somewhere else? The other day, it was a kick. Before that, a bite. One of these days, he might do something more dangerous. What if he lights a fire, say? Or—"

"How is he going to light a fire? He can't even hold—"

"And what about us? As we grow older? Do you want to be fifty years old and wiping the butt of an adult man? Because *we* will grow old, but Cyloo will never grow up. Why should poor Remy be burdened by this responsibility for the rest of his life? Shirin, I'm telling you, this will hurt like hell for a while, but it's the right thing to do. It hurts me, too—believe me. I'm just trying to save my family, that's all."

Shirin didn't speak. After a very long time, she raised her head and looked at him with dead eyes.

"What family?" she said.

REMY FELT AS if he were listening to a horror story, a hallucinatory tale hatched by Mummy's dehydrated brain. None of this could possibly be true, could it? Could Daddy—kind, loving Daddy—have ever done such a thing? It was impossible. And yet she hadn't hallucinated the picture of the young boy that he had found.

A thought struck him. "One minute," he said, and rushed to his bedroom, fishing out the envelope he'd tossed in his suitcase. "This letter," he said to her when he returned. "Daddy wrote it to me before he died. What was he apologizing for?"

Shirin stared at him, and Remy had the eerie feeling that she was receding away from him, like the moon, which had climbed higher into the sky.

"I should have destroyed it," she said at last. "I never wanted you to find it. Even though he begged me to tell you what he had done. He wanted to make things right between you and me, you see. Those were his last words to me, asking me to tell you, spoken two days before you arrived."

Just like that, he knew she was telling the truth. That the story was not a figment of her imagination, but a harrowing recollection. She had kept Daddy's secret at her own expense. Year after year, on Cyloo's birthday, say, on a million occasions, she'd bitten down on the words that would've forever altered Remy's life, that would've rewritten his narrative. What kind of fortitude, what kind of self-control did this take? The decades of secrecy, suppression, and silence had taken their toll. The secret had erased the loving, kindhearted mother Shirin had been and left behind the shrewish, brittle shell that Remy had known most of his life.

Remy looked at his mother with new eyes. She had loved his father enough to protect Cyrus from his son's contempt. She had loved Remy enough to protect him from his disillusionment about his father. If he had not stumbled upon the photo, she would've taken Cyrus's secret to her grave. But why did he have no memory of having had a brother? Was this normal? Or had he suppressed the memory? He didn't know.

"Mummy," he said. "Where is Cyloo now?"

Something happened to Shirin's face, as if it had suddenly turned to rock. "Ask *her*," she said finally. "Go ask her. She knows."

"Who?"

"That witch. Dina Mehta. She knows everything. Ask her how she killed my son."

CHAPTER TWENTY-EIGHT

REMY STOOD OUTSIDE Dina Mehta's apartment building and looked up. He had arrived uninvited, without calling, not knowing if she was home. He wanted the advantage of surprise, wanted to fish the truth out of her before she could reel it back in. The truth—unadorned, uncovered, unembellished. Truth, buried or hidden, was still the truth: that's what he had to tell her.

Dina had an honest face, probably a great liability for a lawyer. *But*, he reminded himself as he entered the lobby, *she* is *a lawyer*. The sincerity, the compassion, the maternal affection she had shown toward him, was most likely an act. If Mummy was right, that is. And, God, how he hoped that she wasn't, that he could end this night with at least one of his idols still standing.

He had left his apartment after asking Manju to feed Mummy her dinner. Confused and agitated, he had walked toward the main road, searching for a cab, caked in sweat. As he walked, he had felt an anger that burned as pure as oxygen, propelling him forward, making him hate this ugly, vile city, its perfidy and betrayals. He wanted to get on a plane tonight and fly away, leave behind Bombay to choke on its own noxious fumes. But even as he longed to escape his life here, he also wanted to confront it, look it squarely in the eye, once and for all, for the first and last time.

From childhood on, he'd been groomed by his father to leave India, Remy realized now, and he'd spent his childhood in a golden fog, a dreamy prince whose feet barely touched this soil. Cyrus had plied him with American comic books and novels, had taken him to Hollywood movies, had raised him on American folk music and rock and roll. In some strange way, only his conflicts with his mother had kept him tethered to reality. And most of these conflicts, he now realized, had occurred because Remy came to his father's defense against Mummy's inexplicably mean behavior toward Dad, and she, in turn, raged against Remy for siding with his father.

Remy felt like sobbing, right there on the street, but anger chiseled through his grief, and there was a cab at the traffic light, and he surprised the driver by opening the back door and getting in, ignoring the man's protestations that he was done for the day, and asking to be driven to P.M. Road in a voice made quiet by fury. The man had given him a fearful look and obliged.

Now, he rode the elevator to Dina's flat, unsure of what he would do if she wasn't home, afraid of what he'd do if she was.

He rang the doorbell, and the cook opened the door and let him in, then went into the bedroom to fetch Dina. She was in a housedress and slippers when she came out, and Remy felt a pang of guilt for not having called first.

"What is it?" she asked. "Is your mummy all right?"

"She's fine." His voice was jagged, laced with curtness.

"That's good. Well, come sit."

But Remy remained standing. As soon as the cook left the room, he dug into his shirt pocket and held out Cyloo's photograph to Dina. "Who's this?" he said without preamble. "And please don't lie to me."

Dina stared at the picture for a beat. A muscle moved in her jaw. He heard the faint sound of traffic in the otherwise quiet room. When she looked up, her eyes were clear and unburdened. "Sit down, son," she commanded, her voice flat. "And let me make you a drink. You are going to need something strong."

She returned with two glasses of cognac, handed one to Remy. She took a sip, then motioned for him to do the same. He tried to calm the churning in his stomach. Some part of him had hoped that she would've asked why he'd dragged out the photo of an unknown boy.

Dina took another sip, eyed him over her glass. "I had always argued with your father that you should know," she said.

"Know what?"

She spoke over him. "You should've heard it from him. About your older brother. Cyloo. The one they gave away."

"*They* gave away?"

"Remy. You have to promise you'll listen before you interrupt." Her voice cracked. "Because I don't know if I can tell this story more than once."

"Your father came to see me a few weeks before your family was to return to Bombay from Jamshedpur," Dina began. "He stopped by one evening, without calling. Much like you, tonight, as a matter of fact. It's uncanny, actually. Even the look on your face . . .

"Anyway. He knew I had done some pro bono work for a Catholic orphanage in Bandra. It was run by the Sisters of Charity, and they did great work. Most of the children there were not just orphaned, but also disabled. Cyrus asked me all kinds of questions—about their standard of care, how the children were treated, and all that. I assumed he wanted to make a donation. You know, in honor of Cyloo. It made sense to me. He asked me to take him there, so he could see the place for himself. I said sure, after you return to Bombay, we can go sometime. Take Shirin, too. But, no, he wanted to go the very next day, on Saturday. He had to return to Jamshedpur on Monday, you see.

"So we went. The nuns knew me, of course, and we got a tour of the place. Cyrus spoke to many of the kids—I remember that. As usual, he'd brought a huge box of sweets for them. Ladoos and jalebis for all the kids. They loved him. He spoke to the head nun about paying for a new roof that the home needed.

"It was on the way home that he told me the real reason for the visit. Begged me to help. I yelled at him. I said no. I told him what he was suggesting was wrong, unforgivable. But the drive from Bandra was long. By the end of the trip, he'd taken a promise from me. And you know the main reason I relented and agreed?

"I saw the look in his eyes, saw the love he had for you.

"Cyrus really believed that he was saving your life."

CHAPTER TWENTY-NINE

REMY WAITED FOR the elevator and then, unable to stand still, took the stairs to the street. It was late at night, but he needed to clear his mind before he went home. He needed to rearrange the kaleidoscope in his head, get the broken pieces to organize themselves into a new reality. Up was down, and down was up. Everything he'd believed about his mother and father had to be rethought before he could face Shirin again.

He stubbed his toe against something hard, tripped, but regained his balance. He looked at the object and realized that it was someone sleeping on the sidewalk, fully covered in a bedsheet, like a corpse. Remy muttered an apology and kept walking, but the man flung back his sheet and rose to his feet. "Saala chootia," he called. "Watch where you're going."

Remy stopped walking. "Sorry," he said.

Under the streetlight, Remy saw the man's face tighten with rage. "Sorry?" he said, approaching Remy. He was wearing a sleeveless undershirt. "You have eyes in your head or what? Or for rich men like you, do we homeless people not exist?"

"Look," Remy said curtly. "I apologized. I didn't see you. It's dark."

The other corpses on the sidewalk, a row of them, stirred. Suddenly, Remy was hyperaware of his surroundings and sensed a new vulnerability. Half a dozen men started to rise. Remy watched them saunter toward him as if in slow motion and then was surprised at how quickly they had surrounded him.

"What, seth?" one of them said. He looked like an ordinary street dweller, the kind his father would've hired to run errands, the sort who wouldn't normally look Remy in the eye. But under the anonymity of the night, the man's eyes blazed with hatred. "What are we? Animals? You hurt one of us and keep walking?"

Something exploded in Remy's chest, fury at having thoughts about his family dislodged from his head by these ruffians, irritation at their theatrics, their faux insult over a minor mistake. "Get away from me," he shouted. "I said it was an accident. The sidewalk is for walking, not sleeping. If you—"

"Arre, chup." A hand hit him hard on his back. "Where do you think we should go? Or are you inviting me to your house to sleep with your mother?"

Remy swung around and hit the first jaw that he saw. He felt the crunch of bone and the corresponding vibration in his shoulder. There was a howl, followed by a moment's silence, and then a pair of hands caught the front of his shirt and someone hit him in the face. He staggered backward but resisted dropping to the ground, knowing that they'd kick him senseless if he did. He could hear their breathing and smelled the sweet, metallic scent of his own blood.

"Stop. *Stop.*" An older man forced his way through the crowd, pulling people away from the tight knot that had formed around Remy. "Arre, bhenchot, I said stop. This is Dinabai's nephew, I tell you."

They stepped away from him.

"Dinabai's nephew?" a man said.

"He should've said," someone else grumbled sullenly.

"We didn't know."

"Chalo, sahib. Let's get you upstairs," Dina's cook said. "You can wash up and rest."

"No." Remy pulled away from the man's grasp. He straightened, rubbing his face. "It's okay. No need to trouble Dina."

"But, sahib . . ."

"No. I'm fine. Thank you for your help." He debated whether to give the cook a tip but thought better about opening his wallet on the street. He nodded and hurried away, ignoring the man's entreaties to let him call a taxi.

He only felt safe when he got to the main road. He found himself walking in the opposite direction from his home, heading automatically toward his old South Bombay haunts—toward Elphinstone College, where he'd earned his BA in English, toward Jehangir Art Gallery, where he used to hang out during his college years. He passed the few paan and cigarette shops that were still open at this hour. Manju must've put Mummy in bed by now, and he had no place to be. He'd keep walking until he found a restaurant that was open, where he could go and wash up, and maybe get a drink.

His phone rang. Kathy. He hesitated, then silenced the call. Talking to Kathy right now would make him come undone. He was in shock; he needed to digest what Mummy and Dina had told him. Also, he was afraid of Kathy's judgment. What kind of family—no, say it—what kind of father did what Cyrus had done? Kathy would be horrified, and despite the fact that he hated his dad at the moment, he wouldn't be able to bear this. Nor would Kathy comprehend why Mummy had held on to such a secret.

Remy understood. She had wanted to spare him exactly what he was going through: the collapse of every childhood belief, the dumb, infantile, good guy versus bad guy binary in which he'd compartmentalized his life. But those equations—Daddy = good guy and Mummy = bad guy—had always had a missing value, hadn't they? He simply had not known about the X factor, the absent brother.

Fuck. A brother. How many times in his childhood had he complained about being an only child? Why had no one—not even Grandpa Framrose—ever told him? Theirs was a small family, but surely someone, some distant relative, maybe, had known about Cyloo. Had Pervez's mother not known, for instance? How in the world had his parents gotten away with keeping such an important secret from him?

Remy walked until he reached Delhi Darbar, a restaurant he remembered from his childhood. The man behind the counter gave him a startled look but led him to a table. He ordered a Corona and a tandoori chicken, then headed to the washroom. He stared at himself in the mirror—took in the unruly hair, the bleeding cut on his lower lip, the dissolute look. He had flown to India to adopt a child, and here he was, looking like a schoolboy who'd gotten into a fight, as if he were the one who needed tending.

Then he remembered the whole sordid story again and began to cry. The fact was, he did need tending. And the only one who could help him now was the elderly woman waiting for him at home, a woman who had once fallen silent because she couldn't bring herself to voice the unspeakable. And whose every word he now wanted to cling to, in whatever time they had left with each other.

CHAPTER THIRTY

———→———

SON.

I know what you're thinking.

I know you're trying to reconcile what Shirin told you with what you've learned from Dina, parsing both stories, looking for inconsistencies. I see you searching for that elusive loophole, so you can put a finger in it and rip it wider, until you can climb back into sanity. Back into innocence.

I'm sorry I cannot take you there. Every word of what they've told you is true.

I tried to confess so many times. Once, when we were taking an evening walk in that park near your house. Once, when you and I went to the mall in Columbus on Christmas Eve to buy that scarf for Kathy. Or when you'd get frustrated with your mother and I'd ask *you to take me for a drive. Each time, it was never the right time. Sometimes, the words came right up to the edge of my lips, and I had to lick them away.*

I never intended to die without telling you. By the time I wrote to you, I was too late. I begged Shirin to give you my letter, but I underestimated her love for you, her need to protect you. Her utter selflessness in allowing you to continue hating her, instead of me, even after I was gone.

Face to face with you, what could I say? That your father, the man you adored, was a selfish, weak monster?

That the deed that once had seemed so imperative and urgent, so utterly right, had felt more and more unnatural and horrifying as time went by? That the earlier surety, the moral clarity, now felt like murder?

That I didn't want truth to wipe out love?

One thing I knew for sure: That I had to save you from the poison fumes that I had pumped into our home. That I had to get you out of Bombay intact, without the knowledge of your dead brother. Shirin, of course, could have told you at any time, but despite the bad blood between us, I was confident that her love for you would protect me.

While you were still with us in Bombay, I had just one goal—to give you the life for which I sacrificed your brother. And, Remy, I tried.

Remember those happy afternoons at Hanging Gardens?

Remember when we let you celebrate your birthday twice in one year, or those birthday parties where you were the only boy in your school who got to invite his entire class?

Remember how I stayed up with you all night while you studied for your board exams, making that god-awful combo of coffee and tea to keep you awake?

Remember those evenings at Chowpatty Beach, you and I eating plate after plate of dahi puri and kulfi?

Remember that stroll down Marine Drive five days before you left for America and what I told you then? That you should not come back home after your degree, that Mummy and I would be fine here, that it was my responsibility to take care of her and not yours. That I hadn't raised you to be an Indian boy—pigeon-chested and deferential and burdened by family obligations—but to be like an American kid—confident, ambitious, and independent.

Remember when you brought Kathy to India for the first time and I filled the freezer with eight different flavors of ice cream, all because you told me she had a sweet tooth?

Remember, remember, remember?

I remember it all, from the moment I first set eyes on you until the last time I sensed you near me, the light fading in my eyes.

Then, as now, you were the king of my kingdom. Not the prince. Not the heir-in-waiting. The king.

Remy, listen to me. Don't blame the women. Especially your mother. All the distance you felt from her, all the hateful, cruel words she breathed into you were aimed at me. You were the target she hit because she couldn't reach the true object of her loathing. You were collateral damage in a war you didn't know was being fought in your name.

Son, I destroyed that woman. And I had chance after chance to make it right, to whisk Cyloo away from that place and bring him home. Don't ask me why I didn't take it. Don't ask me why I allowed year after year to go by until the calamitous end. For a long time, I deluded myself that it was because of you. The thought of you being saddled with caring for your severely disabled brother long after Shirin and I were dead used to drive me insane. But there was also another, more selfish reason: I was rising fast at my job, and I didn't want word to get around that I had a defective son. That was pure, ugly ego. The thing I feared most was the look of pity, the soft, wet sympathy in the eyes of my peers. And after your birth, my destiny was clear to me: If I was to touch the sky, it had to be with you flying beside me. Otherwise, the wealth, the success, the achievements would all be meaningless. With one damaged son, and then a wife who shrank away from me, you became my raison d'être, my reason for breathing.

In the end, how many of my peers even came to my funeral? Most of them were old, feeble men, swirling in the currents of their own lives, who had no idea that I was a man who had murdered his own child.

I'm rambling. There is so much more I could say, but I have held your ear for far too long. The time for making excuses is long past. I have done enough damage as it is.

Remy, listen.

Put down that beer and go home. To her. Your one remaining blood. Be good to her in the time you have left here. Because, believe it or not, you were always more her son than mine. I know you think your traits of seeking joy, of good cheer, of kindness, you inherited from me. But that's exactly who Shirin was when I married her. That's who she was—a loving, joyful woman—until I robbed it all from her.

Although you owe me nothing, I will ask for one final favor:

When you board that plane to Columbus with Monaz, leave us behind. Clear your head of this foul history. The sins of the father must never land on his son's beautiful, slender shoulders. Raise your own son as an American boy, raise him without all this history. This is why I'd once told you I was against adoption—I knew better than most the power of the past to destroy the present. Leave us behind,

Remy. This story must die here, on these corrupt shores, where it was born.

Remy, my golden boy, listen to your father one last time.

Don't look back.

Because the only way to destroy the museum of failures is to burn every shameful secret that it has ever held.

CHAPTER THIRTY-ONE

REMY TOOK A final gulp of the Corona and flagged the waiter.

The streets were quiet. *Well, quiet by Bombay standards,* he thought. *In Columbus, this much traffic would be considered rush hour.*

Manju opened the door before he could fit the key into the lock. She held her finger to her lips.

"Madam has just fallen asleep. She wanted to wait for you, but I gave her the cough medicine, which made her sleepy."

"That's fine," he whispered back. He didn't have the courage to face his mother tonight.

HE WOKE UP early the next morning and sat at the dining table, nursing a cup of tea. He heard Manju go into his mother's bedroom to check on her and then tiptoe back out.

"She's still sleeping."

"Good. She had a rough evening."

Manju's face was blank, but he wondered how much she'd heard, and whether she'd taken in his bruised upper lip and smelled the alcohol on his breath last night. *Those who serve us know so much more about us than we know about them,* he thought. He glanced at Manju's thin, worried face, the hair pulled back into a single braid, the frayed collar of her white nurse's uniform. This was not the face of an RN in the States, making sixty grand a year.

Learning about Cyloo's existence made him curious to know more about the woman who stood in front of him. How commonplace it had been when he was growing up to hear his parents' rich friends talk with derision about the dysfunctions of the poor—alcoholism, domestic violence, drug abuse. *Well,* Remy thought, *they've got nothin' on my family.*

"Who's in your family, Manju?" he asked. "Are you married?"

She looked at him, startled by his sudden interest. "Yes, sir," she said. "We are having a four-year-old boy."

"Accha? What is his name?"

"Porosh, sir."

"Porosh? Unusual name. I've never heard it before."

"Yes, sir. My husband's father gave the name, sir."

"And what does he do, your husband?"

Manju looked embarrassed. "He's home, sir. He lost his job four months ago. Good-paying factory job it was, sir."

Remy exhaled. "I'm sorry." He would give her a generous bonus when he left.

"It's good in a way," Manju said. "One of us is at home to put Porosh to bed. Before, we were both working night shift."

"Manju," he said, "won't you sit down? You don't have to keep standing."

"Oh, that's okay, sir. I'm used to it."

That's just it, Remy thought. He saw a snapshot of Manju's life: standing at her job, standing in the crowded trains to get to the job, standing in long lines to pick up the government-rationed sugar and rice. A city full of standing women—working, commuting, eking out a living so that their sons could go to a slightly better school, so that their unemployed husbands could get their daily drink, so that their daughters could maybe go to college, so that they could afford a dowry for those girls. *This* was what held the world together, this unsung army of silently suffering standing women.

"Well, you don't need to stand now." Remy smiled. "Come sit and let me pour you a cup of tea. There's plenty here in the pot."

"No, no, sir. I'll do it. You take rest." Manju pulled up a chair across from him. After a few sips, she asked, "It must be different where you are, no, sir? People like you can talk to . . . people like us. Like, equal and all."

"Manju," he said carefully, "you are an accomplished nurse. You have been very good to my mother. You are smart and competent. I own my business in America, but for many years, I, too, worked for other people. Just like you. You understand?"

She nodded, but he could tell that she was not convinced. And, despite his pretty speech, neither was he. The affluence of the apartment they were sitting in disproved his words. Where did she live? Probably in a dingy room in some wretched chawl, where she shared a bathroom with other families.

"Sir," Manju said earnestly, "if my son studies hard, he, too, can become a big man in America?"

He had to turn away from the hope in her face, a bright, shiny mirror he couldn't look into. How could he explain the politics of immigration to her? How would she react if he told her about the immigrant babies being ripped out of the arms of breastfeeding mothers and

locked up in cages? "It's not easy," he murmured. "As you know, from
your brother's story."

Seeing her downcast face, Remy added, "But India is coming up
these days, Manju. Maybe your son won't have to leave."

"Too much problems here, sir. People just fighting, fighting.
Everybody cares about your caste and religion and how much money
you are having. Bas. There's no humanity here."

Remy smiled grimly. Just over Christmas break, a group of white
teenagers had beaten up an Asian student near Ohio State. He had
always hoped that India would become more like America. Instead,
things seemed to be going in the opposite direction.

"Anyway," he said, "was Mummy . . . agitated . . . last night? After
I left. Did she eat?"

"No, sir. I'm sorry. I did my best. She refused."

"Not to worry." He looked at the clock. "Well, tell you what. Let's
let her sleep for another hour. I'll go call my wife. Then we can wake
her up."

"Very good, sir." Manju picked up both cups. "Give your wife my
salaams. Your mother speaks so highly of her."

He had never known his mother to be fond of Kathy. Shaking his
head in wonder, Remy went into the bedroom to call his wife.

KATHY SOUNDED EXHAUSTED. She'd had to tell the parents of a six-
year-old girl that their daughter had bone cancer. He listened quietly
as she spoke. This was their ritual—they always made time to tell each
other about their day—and even across the phone lines and two oceans,
they were determined to carry on that custom as best they could.

"Enough about me," she said finally. "What about you? How's
Mom?"

"She's better." No way was he going to lay anything heavy on
Kathy from this distance, especially after the kind of day she'd had.

"And Monaz? Have you talked to her? When can you guys leave?"

He answered absently, debating internally how and when he'd reveal his family history to Kathy. He still had so many questions himself. Now wasn't the time.

"Remy, what's wrong?" Kathy said. "You sound so far away."

"I am," he said. "Eight thousand miles away." And when Kathy didn't chuckle: "I'm sorry. I'm just tired. Also, it's very hard, you know? To see Mummy in this condition."

Kathy sighed. "I get it. I'm dreading the day when something happens to my mom. Listen. I've said this before—when you return, I want you to have no regrets, okay?"

"Thanks, Kat," he said. But he was thinking, *No regrets?* Right now, his entire life was one big regret.

He hung up and went into Shirin's bedroom. Manju was helping her out of bed. He glanced at his watch. "Almost nine," he said. "Shouldn't the day nurse be here by now?"

"Gladys had said she'll be late today," Manju said. "It's okay. I will stay until she comes."

"Thank you," he said. How lucky he was to have found not just one, but two competent and responsible nurses. Manju and Gladys made a good team.

"Good morning," Shirin said to Remy.

"Good morning, Mummy," he said. "Did you sleep well?"

She shrugged, a slight movement of her right shoulder. "Chalta hai."

She sat with her feet dangling from the bed, reminding him of the early days in the hospital. *That's not true*, Remy corrected himself. *She looks significantly better than when I arrived.* Even as he felt a moment's satisfaction, his heart sank. What would happen after he left? Would she drift back into the comatose state in which he'd found her?

"Was Dina home?" Shirin said.

"What? Oh. Yeah. She was home." He stared at the floor. "She told me . . . everything."

Mother and son exchanged a long look, a silent promise to talk after Manju left. "Let's get you cleaned up," Remy said with a smile.

Shirin smiled back.

Remy's heart flooded with love. That was what it felt like: a warm, watery gush that swept away every lingering pebble of resentment he had harbored. *I am free*, he thought. *Free of the hurt I've carried around all these years.* All his life, he had foolishly believed that love had to be declared—expressed and made visible with words and gifts. But in one day, Shirin had taught him a transformative lesson: love was also restraint. What it must have cost her all these years to hold her silence, to not reveal the secret that would've turned him against his father.

He helped Manju wheel Shirin into the walk-in shower. Cyrus had renovated the bathroom years ago and, in anticipation of old age, had made it accessible. *But he wasn't supposed to get sick and die so soon*, Remy thought, and the lump in his throat was proof that despite all the ugly revelations, he loved his father. But this love now felt different, more tempered. He had always idolized Cyrus, seen him as someone he could only aspire to be. Now, he remembered Cyrus's admonishment in the letter: *Be better than me.* For the first time in his life, Remy thought: *I already am.*

It was unimaginable that his parents had not divorced after Cyloo's untimely death, that they'd continued to live under one roof. That they'd traveled together for years, made several trips to the States to visit Remy. How had they managed to fake it?

Well, what choice did they have? he thought. With one son gone, they had to stick it out to protect the other.

Remy thought back to the family trip they'd taken to the Grand Canyon in 2012, how his parents had seemed genuinely happy. At one point, Mummy had stumbled and Daddy's hand had shot out to steady her. Cyrus had held his wife's hand for the rest of the hike. He and Kathy had exchanged a look at this rare intimacy between his parents.

Humans, Remy thought. *Who can figure them out? Complex, contradictory creatures, impossible to pin down or reduce to their best or worst traits.*

Gladys arrived and brought him and his mother breakfast in Shirin's room. Remy balanced his plate in his lap. Shirin caught his eye. "What happened?" she asked, gesturing toward him and touching her lower lip.

"Nothing," he said. "I just tripped."

Shirin stared at him intently and then, unexpectedly, grinned. "That daakan didn't hurt you, did she?"

"Who?" Remy said automatically, although he knew who she meant. Dina Mehta. Who, he supposed, his mother had every right to consider a demon, a witch. He smiled weakly. "No, Mummy."

Shirin was quiet for a moment. Then: "I don't hate anyone. Not even her. Everybody had their reasons."

Gladys was looking back and forth at them, a quizzical expression on her face. Remy got up.

"I need to run an errand," he said. "I'll be back in a half hour or so." He gave Shirin a kiss, smoothed her hair, and left the room.

HE ENTERED TIPTOP PHOTO STUDIO, located in a lane a few blocks from his mother's apartment. He took Cyloo's picture out of his wallet, picked out a simple wooden frame, and paid while the salesclerk inserted the photograph into the frame.

As he walked home, he spotted a roadside vendor selling fresh coconuts and, tempted, stopped to buy one. The man scalped the top of the fruit, inserted a straw, and handed it to Remy. "You want the malai?" the vendor asked after Remy had drunk the sweet water. He nodded.

As Remy ate the scooped, translucent meat of the coconut, he spotted the gray hairline of the sea from a gap between two buildings. It was always there, the sea, a silent witness to the human theater of this island city. Its omnipresence reminded Remy of his first visit to Seattle. He had gone for a run on a damp, foggy Sunday morning. But the fog had lifted as he ran, and at one point he'd turned around, and there behind him, squatting like the Buddha, like God himself, was Mount Rainier, in all its majestic, snowcapped glory. Remy had stopped, thunderstruck, feeling as if he were staring at the face of God. The fact that the mountain had been there all along, watching him from behind the curtain of the morning fog, had made its sudden appearance seem more mystical.

Here, the nearby Arabian Sea had kept an eye on his parents, on their human frailties and their superhuman strength; it had watched silently as their story had played out, and without judgment had folded their saga into the other family dramas being enacted each day in this city of millions.

He paid the coconut vendor and resumed walking, wishing there was a nearby public entryway to the sea, so that he could sit by its comforting waters and allow his mind to replay last night's harrowing revelations. He needed time alone to process it all. But he was also anxious to return home to his mother.

It was yet another bright day, the sun having burned away the smog that pressed over the city like a thumb. As Remy walked, he pulled the picture frame from the paper bag and stared at his brother's face. He saw his own reflection in the glass, superimposed over his brother's. *How symbolic*, he thought.

He checked himself and reined in that old poetic impulse. There were things in life so deeply grievous that it was immoral to turn them into symbols. Cyloo had been a real person, a flesh-and-blood boy who, if he hadn't been starved for oxygen for a few fatal moments during his birth, would probably be walking beside him right now, on this very street. A thirty-nine-year-old brother, so akin to him in appearance they would've been mistaken for twins.

Remy sensed Cyloo's presence next to him now, like a phantom limb. Last night, his head reeling with the evening's revelations, all his sympathy had been with his mother. But now, he felt the full weight of his own loss. To think that Dad had thought he had done this for *him*. As if Remy would've ever chosen this cleaving, this amputation. He was a man without a shadow. No wonder there had always been something a little blurry, a little unsubstantial about him. He had gone through his life with a chunk of himself missing and hadn't even known it.

It bothered him that he didn't have the slightest recollection of his brother. He knew people who claimed to have memories of themselves as toddlers. Remy strained to remember anything about Cyloo—his laugh, his voice, even the pain of being bit by his older brother. But his mind was a clean white sheet.

His phone dinged. It was a reminder to check seat availability for their flight. When he'd set this alarm, his world had been different, neatly divided into two camps: The father whom he admired and adored. The mother whom he feared and resented. This was the story he'd always told himself about himself: he was a boy scarred by the cruelties and volatility of his mother, who had grown up to be a man who had put half a globe between him and her.

And now? Now, he wanted to hurry home to Mummy, to spend as much time as he could with her, let her know that he understood every angry gesture, every hurtful word. And that he forgave her, even as he asked for her forgiveness.

Shirin was sitting at the dining table, sipping her orange juice. In her clean cotton dress, smelling of soap and talcum powder, her hair tied up in a small bun, she looked petite, doll-like.

"Hi, Mummy," he said. "How are you feeling?"

She reached for his hand as he pulled up a chair. "Better," she said.

"Good."

"You went for a walk?"

He took out the picture frame and set it on the table. "I went to get you this," he said. "To put on your dresser. So that you can look at Cyloo even when you're in bed."

She turned his gift over in her hand, looked intently at Cyloo's picture before setting it down. "This is a single frame. I need a double. So that I can look at both my sons. One with each eye."

Remy felt his chin wobble. In order to cover this up, he leaned over to hug her. He held her tight, as if he'd never let go. Under his arms, he felt the lightness of her bones, the faint throb of her blood, the ticktock of her mortality.

CHAPTER THIRTY-TWO

———→———

YOU ARE TAKING a nap after coming home with the framed picture.

I had never expected to see you again, but there you stood, one fine day, in my hospital room. And now, even though the parting is inevitable, or maybe because of it, I don't want you out of my sight for even a second. I know you have to return home soon, and I know you will take the sun with you when you go. That is a disappointment that will have to be faced, in a lifetime littered with disappointments. But while you are here, I feel mad with hunger and greed. I don't want to share you with anyone—not with your friends when they visit, not with Gladys or Manju, not even with the fruitwalla who delivers the oranges each morning and with whom you make small talk daily.

But, my boy, I will let you rest. Just knowing you are in the next room breathes life into me.

The last time you visited, you left angry. And every day that you were here, I'd had a quarrel with myself—whether to give you Cyrus's letter or not. You were so distraught about Cyrus's illness there was no question of giving it to you while he was alive. And after? It was just you and me in this house, half of our small family gone. Day after day, you went on one errand after another—going to the bank and the insurance company and God knows where else, trying to get all of Daddy's papers in order. For the first time in our lives, we were at peace with each other, soldiers-in-arms, united by the solidarity of bereavement. With everything that you now know, you may wonder why I was so broken by Cyrus's death.

The truth is simple: I loved your father. Or, more accurately, I felt for him a stew of every human emotion imaginable: hatred, love, anger, guilt, sadness, compassion, remorse, regret. Sometimes, one ingredient in the stew was more powerful than the others. I can imagine how exhausting it was for you and Cyrus to live with such a volatile woman, who never could make up her mind about whether to strike down or pity the man she had married. But, Remy, can you imagine how exhausting it was for *me* to live with such a woman?

Sometimes, when you were a teenager, I used to think how I could've helped you remember that you'd once had a brother. Such a simple thing—a few words to jog your memory, words that would shatter the glass dome of secrecy the three of us lived under. But I couldn't do it. You had made your choice. Sworn allegiance to your father and learned to distrust and fear me. Perhaps even to loathe me. That last thought was like a hand twisting my organs.

I won't lie—sometimes, I used to wonder about your obtuseness. Didn't you wonder why I went to Mount Mary Church, all the way across town, every Saturday? Why Daddy never accompanied me? Why I always came home in a foul mood? And I used to think: *Why doesn't he have the slightest memory of his brother?*

In the beginning, when we first arrived in Bombay, you asked about your bhai, but Cyrus always had a bright, glib answer. And how he distracted you from the pain he had introduced into our home! He stayed home those first two weeks after we returned to Bombay and took you all over town—to the Prince of Wales Museum, to Victoria Gardens, to the aquarium, to the Elephanta Caves. The cover-up was as intricate as one of Cyrus's engineering drawings; Cyloo's erasure was complete. We lived a distance from my father; we had moved to a new apartment building where no one knew us; there were few relatives who had ever met Cyloo.

And you were only three years old, Remy, as bright as a penny, and with all the promise of your own life ahead. What young boy spends his time picking through the welts on his mother's heart?

Once, only once, did I come close to telling you the truth: the day I realized Cyrus was planning on sending you away to America. "Are you crazy?" I yelled at him. "I will never let Remy go. You have already killed me once. Are you trying to kill me again?"

"I'm not sending him away. He'll be back after his degree."

"Liar. *Liar.* How many Parsi boys and girls come back once they've gone to America? Tell me."

He shrugged. "Remy's not like the others. He knows he has good prospects here. By the grace of God, I can help him get whatever kind of job he wants when he returns."

"Please, Cyrus," I begged. "Just have him join you in your business."

"Shirin," he said. His voice was kind. "Our son is an artist. He wants to be a poet, not an engineer like his father. Remy has real talent, his professor said."

"I will tell him," I said. "I will tell him about Cyloo. About what you did. If you send my only son away, I will not protect you anymore."

I saw fear leap into his eyes. But a second later, Cyrus was calm again. "You do what you must," he said. "I will not let you blackmail me. And I will not stop Remy from following his heart."

Your heart, your heart. Cyrus was willing to risk you not returning to us, risk his own loneliness and loss, in order to give you what you wanted. And just as I'd predicted, your heart wanted America. America, in the shape of Kathy.

I knew what you'd seen in her the instant I met her, could see how she'd changed you with her forthrightness, her wide American grin, her toughness, softened by the fact that she was head over heels in love with you. She took my moody, sensitive, introverted son and changed him into an outgoing, confident man. I saw how she teased you and made you laugh. It had been so long since I'd heard your laugh, spontaneous and helpless. "Kathy's a real live wire, Dad," you'd said when you told Cyrus about her on the phone, and I had no idea what that meant until I met her.

Then, I was grateful, so grateful. I loved how playful the two of you were with each other, even when you swept your father into that closed circuit of love and left me out. Me, charmless and awkward, standing outside your orbit. Cyrus's world was so much larger than mine, he understood Kathy's jokes and references so much faster than I did. He never struggled with her Americanisms, her intense curiosity, the desire to explore every aspect of Bombay.

I had always harbored the faint hope that you would return home and marry a nice Parsi girl, but now I came to see that your father had planned your exit exactly right, had hoped for exactly the outcome you'd delivered—an American bride and a future on distant shores.

Even when Kathy and I clashed during our visits to Columbus, even when you inevitably sided with her, even when Cyrus scolded me for my behavior toward our daughter-in-law, even when I could tell from Kathy's guarded eyes that you had told her about your childhood with me, some part of me was always grateful to her. With her fierce devotion to you, I knew she'd protect you. Even from me. Especially from me. Charmless, awkward me.

I just couldn't give the letter to you after Cyrus died, even though I'd promised him I would. What use? You'd had so much stolen from you—your older brother, your mother's attention. I thought, *Let him hold on to the one thing that got him through his childhood—his steady, beating love for his father.*

NOW, AFTER YOUR nap you enter my room, and there is a new tenderness in your eyes, a fresh understanding. Although I regret the reason for this change in you, I thrill to it. I reach out for you with my hand.

"Come sit next to me, Remy," I say.

I clear my throat. I don't know how much of the story you heard from Dina last night—what she embellished and what she left out. But I want you to hear it from me. About what I lost, what was stolen from me. About why I always believed that what happened to my oldest son was not an accident but murder.

Just this once, I want to tell my own story.

I DIDN'T KNOW Cyloo's whereabouts for four months. I begged Cyrus to tell me what had happened to my firstborn, but his stories kept changing: On that first day, he had merely said that Cyloo was with people who could help him. Once, he said Cyloo had been adopted by a family who had taken him abroad for treatment. Then, Cyloo was in a home where he was getting therapy. Always, he stressed that Cyloo was well cared for, getting better care than what we could have given him.

At times, an irrational fear would grip me. Once, I voiced it.

"Have you had him killed?" I said. "Have you murdered my son?"

"Shirin, have you gone mad? How can you even think such a thing?" he said.

"I don't know," I said, and I began to sob. "Otherwise, why won't you tell me? Why can't I see him?"

Cyrus took me in his arms. "Wait a few more months," he said. "He's making progress. When he's better, we will go see him."

"You promise?"

"I promise."

Why didn't I do more? you might ask. Son, I tried. Early on, I took you with me one afternoon, and we went to see my father. I begged him to help. I broke down crying, and I could see how much that hurt him. But he was immovable.

"Your husband is a good man," he said. "Whatever he decides, I trust him completely. Beta, you are still young. Don't throw away your life like this. Cyloo will always be the age he is right now. You have another healthy son. Focus on him."

"I am going to the police," I said.

Daddy looked aghast. "Police? You are married to an honorable, decent man," he said. "You would defile his good name by going to the police? What are they going to do? Do you have any idea what rubbish you are saying?"

If my own father and husband were conspiring against me, what hope could I have that a tobacco-chewing, nose-picking, disinterested police inspector would help me? Cyrus exuded such power and authority that I knew any two-bit officer would either wilt under his influence or be bowled over by his charm.

I went home and took to bed. I didn't get up for three days. I am sorry for neglecting you, Remy. I am sorry that I couldn't follow their advice and pretend that I only had one child. It wasn't just that I loved Cyloo; it was also that I couldn't bear the thought of the world discarding him like a soiled diaper. Some days I felt as if I were insane, cursed with a third eye, which had allowed me to see past his deformed body, to his innocence and lack of malice. Other days, I thought everyone around me was crazy for not being able to have seen his beauty. Most of all, the thought that Cyloo believed that I'd given him up, that I, too, was angry or disgusted by him, made me feel as if someone were peeling the skin off my body.

Then, one morning, I walked into the bedroom while Cyrus was on the phone. He was sitting with his back to the doorway. I was about to move away when I heard him say my son's name. "Tell Dina the check for Cyloo is on its way. She should get it in two days, I hope," he said. I shook, as if a current had passed through my body. As soon as your daddy left for work, I looked up Dina Mehta's address.

I LEFT YOU with the maid, although in those days I was afraid to leave you alone for even five minutes. Ayah held you in her arms as you stood on the balcony and screamed for me, but I gave you a quick wave and got into a taxi.

Dina's office was in Worli then. I entered a large suite with a row of glass-enclosed offices in the back. Even in those days, Dina had a thriving practice. A young woman approached me.

"Yes, ma'am? Can I help you?"

I ignored her. My forehead felt hot, my cheeks flushed. I felt powerful, destructive, demon-like.

"Dina," I shouted. "Come out. Tell me, where are you hiding my son?"

A tremor ran through the office, distressed faces turned toward me. The junior clerks looked fearful, as if they expected me to pull out a knife.

"Call security," someone whispered.

I turned toward that voice. "No security necessary," I said. "Just tell me, where's Dina? Where's that—"

"I'm here." Dina's voice was quiet, but I jumped. She was standing right behind me. "Come, Shirin. Let's go where we can have privacy."

She took my hand in hers, and even in my manic state, I sensed its coolness, its assurance, and, yes, its kindness. She led me to her office and shut the door. She offered me an armchair and sat across from me. Her eyes were warm and sympathetic, but I was in no position to let down my guard. She opened her mouth, but I spoke first.

"Where is he? Where is my son? Tell me, or I swear I'm calling the police. I will have you arrested for kidnapping. I will—"

"Shirin. Calm down. I . . ." She raised her index finger to silence me.

I sat there fidgeting, not knowing what to do, focusing on her finger. She looked away for a moment, and when her eyes fell on me again, there was a new, determined look in them. "Cyrus is going to kill me," she said. "But you have the right to know."

She walked to her desk and picked up the phone. "Have the driver come downstairs with the car," she said. She turned to me. "Come. I will take you to Cyloo."

On the way to Bandra, Dina explained her predicament: How Cyrus had come to her for help. How he'd promised to make a big donation. How he'd told her that Cyloo had been hitting and biting you. How she'd never seen Cyrus that distraught, frantic with worry about your well-being. How he'd pleaded with her to use her influence with the nuns to get a spot for Cyloo in a home for disabled orphans. How he'd convinced her it was important that they do this before Cyloo settled into the new flat in Bombay. How this would give Cyrus, you, and me a shot at a new future. Dina said that she had tried reasoning with him, told him that he was wrong, but that he'd begged and begged. She'd finally agreed and sent her clerk to the airport to whisk Cyloo away.

She said many more things, but I barely heard her. Looking at her clean, handsome profile, all I could think was, *This woman is still in love with my husband.*

CHAPTER THIRTY-THREE

⟶

THE ST. MARY'S Home for Disabled Boys was a short distance from Mount Mary Church, but Shirin had never known of its existence. Dina had tried to prepare her for its clean-but-Spartan appearance, but still, the tears came to Shirin's eyes as they walked down the hallway. The only pictures on the chalky walls were those of Jesus, Gandhi, and Pope John Paul II. Shirin couldn't help but compare the utilitarian, no-frills atmosphere of the place to their own luxury apartment. Her body was stiff with rage as she sat in the administrative office, waiting for Sister Hillary to show up.

"Where do the children sleep?" she asked Dina, who sat with her head in her hand, as if she, too, was realizing how much Cyloo's circumstances had changed.

"They have a large dorm," Dina said quietly. "That way, the boys can keep each other company at night."

"A dorm," Shirin repeated, bitterly. "Like he's in jail. When he could be sleeping in his own beautiful flat in Nepean Sea Road." She had to control herself from spitting at Dina.

Sister Hillary hurried into the room. The white wimple that framed her thin brown face made it hard to guess her age, but Shirin surmised she was in her early thirties. *She looks like a nervous bird*, Shirin thought, and felt herself soften.

A second later, her liking curdled into resentment as the nun ignored her and spoke to Dina. "Miss Mehta," she said. "This is a rare pleasure. What brings you here today?"

"I'm Cyrus Wadia's mother," Shirin interrupted before Dina could speak. "I want to see my son. Where is he?" As she spoke, she was seized by a desperate wildness, fighting the urge to pick up the glass paperweight on Hillary's desk and use it as a weapon if she wasn't allowed to see Cyloo.

Sister Hillary flashed Dina a quick look before focusing on Shirin. "Nice to meet you, Mrs. Wadia," she said. "Thank you for trusting us with Cyloo's care. We love having him here."

The words, intended to calm, only provoked Shirin. "You call yourself an orphanage, but you steal people's children? Even when you know they have their own parents?"

"Shirin, please," Dina said.

Hillary shook her head. "No, it's okay. I understand." She turned to Shirin. "Let me take you to your son," she said. "You can judge his progress for yourself. These children need socialization, Mrs. Wadia."

She led Shirin down a hallway and into a large open room with exercise equipment. There were over a dozen children there, all dressed in white shirts and khaki shorts. Shirin spotted Cyloo immediately. He was in a wheelchair, both arms raised, trying to grab one of the overhead bars, his torso stretching upward.

"Why is my son in a wheelchair?" Shirin demanded. "At home, he used to take a few steps at a time. We were told to encourage him to try to walk."

"We use it mostly to transport him to the gym and for certain exercises, Mrs. Wadia," Hillary said. "I assure you . . ."

Shirin was not listening. "Cyloo," she called as she hurried toward him. He didn't answer, but the therapist working with him heard, tapped him on the shoulder, and folded his arms onto his body before turning him around.

"Cyloo," Shirin said again. "It's Mummy."

She was about four feet away from him. The attendant wheeled him over, and he tilted his head back in his chair to look at her, a gesture so endearingly familiar that her eyes filled with tears. She dropped to her knees so that she was eye level with him. "My Cyloo," she said, throwing her arms around him. "My sweet little boy."

He made a loud, frightened noise and pulled away. Shirin went rigid with embarrassment. Then she was fearful. Had he forgotten her? Were they drugging him? How could he not know his own mother?

"Mrs. Wadia"—Sister Hillary cleared her throat—"give him a few moments, please. He just needs to familiarize himself."

Shirin let go of her son, slowly, reluctantly. But she kept her eyes on him, even though Cyloo was mumbling under his breath and staring down at his folded hands. He looked about the same, despite his ugly haircut. Her Cyloo had beautiful silky hair, and she'd always let it grow a little long; now it was cut too short, almost a buzz cut. His face was thinner. Were they mashing his food for him? What kind of a place was this? Most of the other children in this room were speaking in Hindi and appeared to be children of the poor. Why had Cyrus chosen this bleak place for his son? At least the gym equipment appeared to be expensive and creatively designed.

She turned to the therapist. "How is my son doing?"

"Fine, fine, ma'am. He is a good boy. And he's growing strong. See these muscles?" She touched Cyloo's biceps, and he giggled.

"I like the exercise equipment. It looks new."

Sister Hillary smiled. "It should. All this was made possible by your husband's donation." She pointed in the direction of a wooden plaque on a distant wall. "This whole wing was made possible by the generosity of the Wadia family."

Shirin turned her head away. It was as if Cyrus had plotted to build a whole universe behind her back. "Does he come often to see Cyloo?" she asked.

The smile vanished from Sister Hillary's face. "Um, no. But, then, we know your husband is a busy man." Her face brightened. "But Miss Mehta comes every week. Cyloo looks forward to those visits."

A guttural sound rose deep within Shirin and reached her lips. Hillary looked at her with concern. "Mrs. Wadia, would you like a drink of water?"

"No. Yes. Thanks. I would." Shirin looked from the physical therapist to the nun. "Actually, I'd like to be alone with my son for a few minutes. Is there an office or a room where we could have some privacy?"

"Sure." Sister Hillary sounded reluctant, but Shirin used her hesitation to take hold of Cyloo's wheelchair.

"Please lead us there," she said politely but firmly.

They went down another hallway into an empty office, and Shirin waited for the nun to shut the door before turning to Cyloo.

"Hi, baby," she cooed. "It's your mummy. How are you, my jaan? Are you eating well? Staying healthy?"

Cyloo cocked his head and studied her. Suddenly, unexpectedly, he grinned and waved his left hand. Had he recognized her? There was no way to know.

"We miss you," she continued. "I miss you. Remy misses you." She couldn't bring herself to say Cyrus's name.

"Remmm."

Had he just tried to say Remy's name?

"Remy misses you," she tried again.

"Remmm."

He was repeating Remy's name after her, she was sure of it. She looked around, wishing someone had witnessed this moment. And then the thought came, swift and devastating: Had Cyrus been right after all? Cyrus, who believed that every problem had a solution? Was this the environment that Cyloo had needed? Was he doing better because of the socialization with other children? Had she mollycoddled him too much and stunted his development? Shirin bit down on her lip to keep from crying.

Then she thought, *Now that I know, I can create a similar atmosphere at home.* She could invite other young children to the apartment to play with him. They could even convert the guest bedroom into a gym. She looked around frantically. *Dina.* She was suddenly glad that Dina was somewhere in the building. She would do whatever she had to do—threaten Dina, beg her—but Cyloo was returning home with her. Today. Immediately.

She opened the office door and spoke to the physical therapist who was waiting outside. "Watch my son for me," she said. "Point me toward Sister Hillary's office."

She found Dina sipping a cup of coffee there.

"Dina," she said as soon as she walked in, "I want to get my son out of here. Today. I'm not leaving without him."

"It's not that easy," Dina began.

Shirin bristled at the pity she saw in Dina's eyes. "I don't care. Easy, hard, impossible—I don't care. He's my son. I'm his mother. I gave birth to him. What I say goes."

"Shirin"—Dina's eyes were steady on her face—"you don't understand. Cyrus gave up custody. On both your behalf."

"You will lose your law license, I swear." Shirin was dimly aware of Hillary rising from her desk. "I will take you to court for what you've done. Let's see what judge doesn't return—"

"You don't understand," Dina repeated. "The father's wishes will prevail in court. Also, there's the question of your financial situation."

A spasm of fear gripped Shirin. "You're lying. What do you think—"

"Shirin, listen to me," Dina said. "I know you're upset. And I'm sorry you had to come here without Cyrus. Believe me, he was planning on bringing you here soon. As soon as . . ."

"As soon as what?"

"As soon as Cyloo had made a little more progress." Dina looked into Shirin's eyes. "Can't you see the improvement in him, Shirin? In just a few months? Can't you see how much happier he is here? He doesn't attack the other kids like he used to hit poor Remy. Because he's receiving professional help here."

Poor. Poor Remy. Shirin felt the fight whoosh out of her body. She sat down heavily on the metal chair. She turned to Sister Hillary.

"Tell me the truth. Is my son . . . ? Do you drug the kids here? Do you punish—"

"Never. This is not an orphanage from a Dickens novel, Mrs. Wadia. We follow the teachings of Christ here—we treat our children with compassion and love and respect."

Both women were looking at her earnestly, awaiting her response. Shirin could feel self-doubt creeping in, could feel herself wavering. She had always believed that a mother's love was the most powerful force on Earth. But what if it wasn't? Especially since that love would have to be doled out in secrecy, away from Cyrus's withering gaze.

She began to sob. "I don't know. I don't know what to do."

"Shirin, look," Dina said. "You've found your son. You will see him again. Let's go home. You need to talk to Cyrus. Let him explain things from his side. Maybe the two of you can figure something out."

Cyrus. How would he react to knowing what she'd done, how she'd barged into Dina's law firm? But she couldn't worry about his anger right now. There were other, more immediate things to think about. "As long as my son is here, I will be coming regularly to visit him," she said. "And I'd like to take him out for a few hours each time. Get him some fresh air."

Sister Hillary shifted uncomfortably. "We usually only allow visitors once a month on Saturdays. Today was an exception." Her face softened. "But, Mrs. Wadia, I understand your unique situation. Most of our children don't have parents. In your case, I will do my utmost to accommodate you."

How can a childless nun understand my pain? Shirin wanted to say. Instead, she nodded, grateful for the compassion in the woman's eyes. "Can I take him home for a few days?"

Hillary looked at Dina for help. The silver crucifix around her neck glinted in the sun. "That is impossible, I'm afraid," she said. "The disruption to Cyloo would be tremendous. We can see about you joining us when we take the children on a field trip. And relatives are allowed to visit on the child's birthday. I will do my best to help you, Mrs. Wadia. We are not on opposite sides, believe me."

WALKING OUT OF the wrought-iron gates of the institution without Cyloo was the hardest thing Shirin had ever done. As she got into Dina's car, she pressed her thumbnail into her index finger so hard that her finger bled. But she barely registered the pain, engulfed as she was in this moment that threatened to break her in two.

CHAPTER THIRTY-FOUR

YOUR FATHER WAS waiting for me when I got home. Someone from the orphanage had phoned him as soon as we'd left. I had never seen him look as angry as he did that day. He'd heard about the scene I'd made at Dina's office. But I answered his fire with fire, Remy. Our voices were raised and I beat my fists against his chest. Then you ran into our bedroom and burst into tears.

"Mummy, stop hitting Daddy," you sobbed.

Cyrus and I froze, sleepwalkers shaken out of a trance and finding ourselves standing on a ledge. This is what a mother's love is like, Remy—the grief I'd felt for myself I suddenly felt for you. *Imagine*, I thought, *a little boy watching his parents fight. What damage must this do to his little psyche?* In those days, I was still capable of checking myself from inflicting harm on you.

But as the years wore on, the very sensitivity you showed that day, the quality that made me clamp my mouth shut, began to irritate me. I steeled my heart to your always-hungry face, how you used to run up and hug me the moment I softened toward you. Try as I might, I couldn't help but compare your easy life to your brother's life. I knew it was unfair of me, but I couldn't help it.

But, Remy, there were still many sweet moments between us, weren't there? Weren't there? When you were three, four, five years old? Remember how we used to cuddle together in the afternoons, your little body curled into mine? "My little worm," I used to tease you, and you would giggle and dig in even closer to me. *I still have a son, I still have a son*, I'd remind myself, but then I'd feel a red-hot shame. *I still have both my sons*, I'd correct myself.

Until the day I had only one.

IT WAS A devil's bargain I struck with Cyrus after I discovered Cyloo's whereabouts—every Saturday, he would stay home with you while I spent the day at St. Mary's with Cyloo. Dina had convinced Sister Hillary to bend the rules and allow me to visit weekly. I looked forward to those visits so much that the other six days became mere steps on a ladder I had to climb to get to Saturday. I even got permission from Hillary to bring in home-cooked food, and soon, unable to bear the hunger in the eyes of his friends—yes, Cyloo had friends there!—I began to carry food for the other boys. When you were about six years old, you asked me why I was taking so much food to church.

"It's for the street urchins outside the church," I said.

"Thank you for taking care of the poor, Mummy," you replied, your eyes so clear and solemn my breath caught.

There were days when I wanted to whisper to you that your brother Cyloo was alive, days when I wanted to whisk you away to see him.

But that was the one promise Cyrus had taken from me, in exchange for my weekly visits. Besides, what would this knowledge have gained you, except the fear that we'd give you away, too?

Also, truthfully, I was greedy. Once a week, I wanted Cyloo all to myself. It was hard enough sharing him with others at the home; having to share him with you would have been too much. Because, Remy, even at that young age, you already had the bearing of a prince. I couldn't have borne the gushing of the nuns and the teachers and— God forgive me—I might have resented you for it. You, a thoughtful, loving boy who wore your inheritance so lightly. I know how wrong my thoughts were. But grief and loss can do this, beta. It twists you into a shape that is unrecognizable.

Cyrus understood this, I think. He gave me time—time to untwist myself, to find myself, time to forgive him and make my way back to him. Sometimes, for a few blissful moments, it would happen. You would be indignant about something that had happened at school, and our eyes would meet above your head and we'd both be smiling. Or he would buy me a gift for my birthday, something that I'd paused briefly to look at in the store, and I'd think, *How carefully he watches me! How hard he tries to make me happy.* But then the weight of his betrayal would land on me, and I'd think: *I'd much rather have my Cyloo than this gold earring.* Or: *These flowers are nice, but when's the last time my Cyloo smelled a rose?*

This is what you grew up with, Remy, this ping-ponging mess of a mother, and as you grew older, you learned to distance yourself from me. I could see the fear in your eyes when I was mean to you and the distrust when I was kind. I noticed it all and was unable to change a thing. You learned to dread Saturdays as much as I looked forward to them. I would say goodbye to Cyloo at around four in the afternoon and do my best to leave my sorrow behind during the drive home. But

I'd walk into the apartment to the sound of your and Daddy's laughter, and I'd immediately become resentful.

Still, I was glad that you had your daddy. With you, Cyrus was the man he was supposed to be—the good, strong man he had been, until a cord strangled his firstborn and his dreams. All the hopes he'd once had for our marriage, all the love he'd had for me, he poured into you. I could see it happening—both of you protecting each other from me.

That unforgivable thing I once said to you? About wishing you'd never been born? It burst out of my mouth after Cyloo died. Even God cannot forgive me for this. Slowly, you learned to shutter your eyes, steel your heart, let your love harden into contempt. By the time you were thirteen, you talked to me as if I were a neighbor instead of your mother, polite but distant.

And why not? Cyrus was both mother and father to you. Everybody commented on your closeness; the old ladies in the neighborhood used to bless the two of you as you walked down the street, Cyrus's arm always around your shoulder, as if he were gathering you in, show-casing your bond to the whole world. By age fourteen, you were taller than Cyrus, and that pleased him immensely—he wanted you to out-shine him in every possible way. Why do you think he worked so hard to get you to America? That was the ultimate trophy.

You were seven when Cyrus came to me one evening and asked me to go out with him. We left you with Ayah to go to a movie. Instead, Cyrus drove to Malabar Hill and parked the car on a quiet side street. He turned to me, folded his hands, and began to sob.

"I beg you, Shirin," he said, "take your revenge on me. I will under-stand. I have injured you terribly. This is my paap, my sin, for which God will hold me accountable. But I beg you, don't take out your anger on Remy. He is an innocent victim here. I appeal to your maternal instincts. Please."

He said many other things, but what I remember the most was the grief on his face. It made him look ancient; there was something classical, timeless, about his suffering. *Fallen man*, I thought. He reminded me of those figures from Greek mythology I'd studied in college. But this was no god from antiquity—this was Cyrus, the man I'd loved and married. I couldn't take it—his folded, penitent hands, the tears streaming down his face, the sobs that were the soundtrack to my own endless grief.

"I will do better, I promise," I said. "I love Remy. You know that."

That evening, we went to the seaside and strolled along the beach, holding hands like teenagers. But we were not teenagers. We were scarred, fallen adults, with much to confess and much to forgive. Cyrus's eyes, his words, that evening: Urgent, fevered, filled with regret. And yet a single pulsating hope. That it wasn't too late. That broken, damaged, bereft as we were, we could still somehow be a family again.

I did try harder. I still visited Cyloo every Saturday, but now when I came home, I told Cyrus about the visit and he listened. Three times, he went with me to see him. I could tell that being there made Cyrus uneasy, but he hugged Cyloo and ruffled his hair and participated in his physical therapy session. There was none of the glow, the shimmering pride he felt around you, but I forced, forced, forced myself not to notice.

Cyloo was doing much better. I could understand some of his speech those days, his legs were stronger, and they were teaching him how to hold a spoon and feed himself. Best of all, his behavior had become much less aggressive. I held out the hope that Cyrus would use his influence and convince Sister Hillary to allow us to take him out for the day. Maybe we could take him to a nearby Chinese restaurant in Bandra. My heart ached at the thought of such a simple pleasure.

On the way home from the final time we visited together, Cyrus said to me, "When he's a little older, we will tell Remy about his brother. I would never want him to find out from someone else."

I remember the hope that flared in my chest that day. I remember smiling at him and dreaming of a future where our boys were united again.

FOUR DAYS LATER, Dina Mehta stood shivering outside our front door at ten o'clock at night, her face riven with pain. She had been crying. When she saw me, she burst into tears.

I began to cry, too, although I didn't know why.

I began to cry, too, because I already knew what I didn't know.

CHAPTER THIRTY-FIVE

THERE HAD BEEN a fire in one of the dorms. Faulty wiring, they said. Four boys died before anyone could reach them.

Cyloo was one of the four.

Cyloo was one of the.

Cyloo was one.

Cyloo was.

MY POOR BOY, who had been getting stronger, who had found his mummy and daddy again, who was someday going to be reunited with his brother, died alone in his bed.

I saw.

I saw his body.

Cyrus forbade me.

Said he would go to the home in my place.

I screamed and screamed and screamed.

I don't know how, but you slept through it all.

You slept, my sweet, innocent boy.

You slept, unaware of the carnage that had been committed in your name.

You slept, blameless, oblivious.

We left you with our elderly neighbor Dilnawaz. The next day, we sent you off with her to their bungalow in Lonavala.

DINA AND I sat in the back seat of her car.

Cyrus sat in the passenger seat, next to Dina's driver. He didn't speak a word during that long drive.

I leaned on Dina's shoulder. I think I passed out for a few moments. Or maybe I just wished that I had. I remember thinking, *Dead, dead,* wishing for my death, wanting to claim it, wear it like a shawl. I thought, *This is what it's like to be dead while breathing.* I thought, *It's over, it's over, it's over.*

SISTER HILLARY BEGGED me to not view his body. Said that once I saw, I would never be able to unsee. Cyrus tried holding me back, and I screamed, "Murderer." He withdrew his hands, as if from a fire. Stunned. Frightened.

I saw.

I saw his little body.

I saw what the fire had done to it.

I saw his despised, misunderstood body, his twisted, crippled body, his rejected, shunned body, and I laughed. Cyrus and Dina flinched, but I laughed. Because it was clear that the fire had loved feasting on this body.

Look how it had made his deformed leg disappear, so that he finally looked like a normal boy. A normal, legless boy. Look how it had

kissed his charred left ear and licked his hair. Look how it had climbed
into his pink lungs and turned them black. Nobody, nobody had loved
Cyloo's body as hard as the fire had.

MOTHERFUCKER. BASTARD, *you bastard. May worms eat your face.*
May you rot in hell. Words I never even knew I knew poured out of my
mouth at Cyrus. It was all I had. Everybody had sided with him when
he'd done this monstrous thing—my own father, Sister Hillary, Dina.
And in all likelihood, the police and the courts would have, too. I was a
woman with nothing but words. And I used those words like a machete.

My son's body. Oh, Khoda, what sin after sin had I committed to
have been brought this low? Nine years I'd spent loving my son, from
near and afar. And now, the fire had left so little to love.

They checked me into a mental hospital. They drugged me night
and day. The moment the drugs wore off, I woke up screaming. Only
screaming helped.

Cyrus came to see me daily, wearing a pained expression on his
face, like a necktie that was choking him. He cried, talked, consoled.
Forgive me, Remy, but I didn't ask for you—not once during this time.
All I was trying to do was erase the sight of Cyloo in that bed, one eye
still open, his little ear, which I used to love to fondle, gone.

The drugs they gave me confused my days and nights, scrambling up
love and grief, guilt and blame, life and death. Death. Every time I came
to, like a swimmer cutting the surface of the water, I screamed. But still
Cyrus came back, day after day. Sometimes, I'd wake up to see his eyes
on me, frightened. I'd open my mouth to scream. "Please, Shirin," he'd
say. "Please, my darling. Please, I beg . . ." But I'd scream: "Murderer.
Killer. Bastard. Assassin. You killed him. You killed my son."

I was in the hospital during the funeral. When I came to, more bad
news: Cyrus told me that there had been no ceremony at the Tower of
Silence for Cyloo. Christian rites were performed; he was buried in a

Christian cemetery behind St. Mary's Home, with the three other dead boys. I couldn't believe that my son didn't merit a Parsi funeral. It was like he'd never existed. As if I had never given birth to him.

Remy, I only survived because of you. You had already lost a brother. I didn't want you to lose a mother, too.

When I finally came home, every day was a struggle—to wake up, to move, to breathe. Eating was a chore; looking at meat or fish made me nauseous. I couldn't bear to hear music on the stereo; a cello string, a minor key, would send me into a tailspin. Cyrus was wary and grim-faced around me. He slept in the guest room, and often I'd hear him in bed late at night, sobbing. I knew that what had happened to our son was an accident. But I also knew it was murder. I knew that Cyrus was grieving, too, that he was struggling to hold on to the business, struggling to put on a happy face for you. And I wanted him to suffer, to be destroyed like I was.

Saturdays were the worst—now, instead of going to St. Mary's, I took a cab to the cemetery. I took half a dozen roses each time. There was a gravestone, but Cyloo's name was not on it. Instead, it simply said TO THE ST. MARY'S FOUR. WE WILL REMEMBER YOU FOREVER. I found out later that Cyrus had paid for the marker. What kind of a father doesn't give his son his own gravestone?

I threw that question at him six months after Cyloo's death.

"I knew that seeing his name there would devastate you," he said. "I couldn't bear the thought of you going there and seeing. Seeing . . ."

"Seeing what?"

"Seeing the final, irrefutable proof. That Cyloo is dead."

I looked at him in disbelief. "I don't believe you," I said at last. "It's because you don't want the world to know what you've done. What kind of a man you really are."

He flinched, and I was glad. That's all I wanted to do in those days. Destroy him, the way he'd destroyed me.

Which is why the pinching started, Remy.

The first time it happened, it wasn't deliberate. Cyrus had gone back to work after months of staying at home, and you were inconsolable. You stood on the balcony, crying, long after his car had disappeared, refusing to come inside. In frustration, I pinched your arm. You stopped crying, amazed. It was the first time I had hurt you in anger.

I saw the shocked expression on your face and felt two contradictory emotions: Guilt, of course. But also fury, for the unearned privilege of your life. While my one son lay buried in an unmarked grave, you, at seven years old, were stunned by a pinch. What had you done to deserve such good luck?

I caught myself, ashamed of my resentment toward my only living child. I threw my arms around you and cried. I know I scared you. Everything your crazy mother did in those days scared you.

A week later, I pinched you again. Out of spite. To punish you? Myself? Again, I was racked with guilt.

Cyrus saw the mark on your upper arm the third time I did it. He went pale with anger. "Remy said you pinched him," he said, barely able to get the words out of his mouth.

"He wasn't doing his homework when he came home from school."

"So?"

"So he had to learn a lesson."

"We don't . . ." He swallowed, started again. "We don't abuse children in this family. Is that clear?"

A feeling of mad satisfaction ran through me, as if I could see the next several chess moves I was about to play. "No," I said slowly. "We just let them burn to death."

His hand came so close to my cheek I felt it stir the air. But he pulled back. I felt a twinge of disappointment. The look in his eyes was murderous. That's what I wanted—for him to hit me, to kill me, erase me, put me out of my misery. To place the shell of my body in the grave next to my son.

But I learned my lesson. I began to pinch you in places not obvious to Cyrus. On your thigh. On your belly. On your back. I would change you into your pajamas before Cyrus came home from work. And without my having to tell you, you learned that this was our little secret. At times, I wanted you to confide in your father, but you were a stoic little boy, your earlier, natural joyousness tamped down into a quiet seriousness by your spiteful mother. I would go into the bedroom and bite my arm, slap myself in punishment, but still, I couldn't stop inflicting injury upon your defenseless body. Do you remember that terrible year in your life, Remy? I pray that you don't. The shame still burns on my skin.

It ended as abruptly as it began. You dropped the butter dish in the kitchen, and I, afraid of the shards piercing your feet, yelled as I scooped you up in my arms. I carried you to safety in the living room and was about to return to the kitchen when you stuck out your arm. "Pinch, Mummy," you said.

I felt the air rush out of my lungs. I thought I was going to collapse. You stood there, arm outstretched, as if you were waiting to donate blood. And in a sense, that's exactly what you were doing. You were donating your bruised little body to your sadistic mother. "Pinch, Mummy," you said again, and the last of the evil that had discolored me the past year left. I never hurt you again after that day. I kept assaulting you with my words, but I never touched you again.

ONE LAST SECRET to confide in you, Remy. This recent stay in the hospital scared me. It has made me realize that I will spend my last days here in Bombay, away from you. I'm ashamed to say it, but I'm jealous of Monaz, how easily she has weaved herself into your life, how she will soon enjoy four blissful months in your home, in your company.

The thought of perhaps never seeing my grandson—yes, I've begun to think of Monaz's unborn child as my grandson—grieves me more than I could've imagined.

But now there are no more secrets between us. I thank Cyloo for deciding not to remain hidden anymore and tumbling down from the pages of my prayer book. The other day—was it yesterday or this morning? time is running so fast, I can hardly keep up with it—when we smiled at each other, I felt as if I were taken to a place from before. Before, when we were still the four of us in our bungalow in Jamshedpur, a damaged, banged-up family but still intact. When you used to smile all the time. And each time it was as if your face contained all the beauty and goodness of the world. God had blessed me with a perfect second child. It was my misfortune that I believed that I also had a perfect first son.

But here, I must catch myself. You are now on the cusp of starting your own family. All this happened a long, long time ago. It is the strangest thing—we become so many different people in one lifetime. But in the end, when everything else has been stripped away, only one thing remains.

Let us call it love.

REMY, I PRAY that you have a long, happy life with Kathy and the new baby.

Beta, you have picked at your wounds for too long. You have struggled over the gushy Mother's Day cards that all your friends seemed to pick out so easily. You have wondered why there was none of that natural feeling of love surging through you. How do I know this? Call it a mother's intuition. But, jaanu, you have done many things right. You have married a woman as solid as the earth, who will knock over a mountain to protect you. You will give your son the childhood you didn't have.

Here's what I want to say to you: Do not waste your life hꓸ
father. Forgive him.

If possible, forgive your old mother, too. Not for her sake, but for
yours. I know only too well the price one pays for bitterness.

I know that the time for your departure is approaching. I've heard
you make calls to the airlines for tickets, when you think I'm sleeping.
When you leave here, Remy, leave with your head held high. Leave us
behind—our frailties, our secrets and failures, our shameful, stunted
humanity. This is our story, mine and Cyrus's.

Do not make it yours.

Write your own, beautiful story, emblazed with stardust.

This is the last thing I ask of you.

CHAPTER THIRTY-SIX

REMY FELL QUIET after he related everything to Kathy. For three days, he'd held it all in, unable to share with anyone the dizzying revelations about his brother, the heartache of hearing his mother tell her story a little at a time in her dry, raspy voice. But this morning, he described it all—the scene at the airport when his family had first arrived back to Bombay from Jamshedpur, the Saturday visits to the orphanage, the deadly fire. The only thing he left out was his mother begging his forgiveness for the abuse. That piece belonged to him; that would stay between the two of them.

Kathy was silent long after he'd finished.

"Hello?" he asked at last.

"I'm here," she said quickly. "I just . . . It . . . Oh my God."

"I know."

"I mean, everything we believed about her. All these years." Kathy began to cry.

"I know, Kat. I know."

"I can hardly take this in."

"I know. Me too."

"What're you going to *do*?"

"I don't know."

WHAT HE DID was use his time in Bombay to do everything that would make Mummy's life a little easier after he left. He met with Pervez to go over her finances and to set new requirements for her care. He supervised the painters and the man who came to fix the ceiling plaster. He moved Mummy into his room while the plasterwork was being done in hers, and slept in the guest bedroom himself. He found someone to replace the damaged floor tiles.

And he walked a lot. He always did his best thinking while in motion, had composed some of his agency's most iconic ad campaigns while out walking or running. Now, he roamed the streets of his neighborhood, thinking hard, trying to squeeze out some droplet of memory of his brother. It was disconcerting to be almost thirty-seven years old and find out that your life had been predicated on a lie. It was hard to do what Mummy had asked him to do—to not judge his father, to not feel betrayed by him. It was impossible to not think how his charmed life had been built on the back of his dead brother. It was difficult to not imagine the terror that must've enveloped Cyloo as he lay helpless in bed while the fire swam up his body.

On this particular day, something flashed in Remy's brain, like white light from a camera. An image. Or was it a sound? Remy stopped. Waited for the dizziness to pass. What was it?

Gingerroot.

The word, followed by a giggle. Who was laughing? What was he remembering?

Another flash. A boy's twisted hand, unable to make a fist.

Of course. He was remembering Cyloo's hand from the photograph. *But, no*, Remy thought, *that's not quite it.*

And then he felt it, the tingling, the rearrangement of his own fingers. He was remembering himself as a young boy, trying to imitate his brother's deformity. And someone, probably a servant, giggling, mocking Cyloo, comparing his hand to a claw of ginger. A long-buried memory, proof that Cyloo still lived somewhere deep in his subconscious mind.

Brother, he thought. *Bhai.*

It was a cool day, but Remy felt feverish. He mopped his forehead, determined not to cry on a public street. But some part of him was happy, even triumphant. He had found a way to keep his brother alive. Or rather, he now knew that Cyloo had always lived within him, that he'd carried him in his very bones. From now on, it was up to him to make up for the years his brother had been deprived of. The best way to honor both his mother and Cyloo was to live a large and robust life.

He was on his way home when his phone rang. It was Jango.

"Hi there."

"Hey, asshole," Jango said. "Where the hell have you been? Are you angry at us or something? How come you're not returning our calls?"

"No. No, yaar. Why should I be angry?" Remy said, not knowing how to explain his silence. "I've just been busy. You know, in some ways Mummy needs more care now that we're home."

"But, saala, at least call back, na? Just to let us know if you're dead or alive? Shenaz has been so worried."

"You're right. I'm sorry."

Remy apologized some more, made vague plans to get together soon, and after he was sure that Jango was appeased, hung up. He knew his friends were hurt by his sudden disappearance. Jango, Shenaz, and Gulnaz had been so welcoming and helpful. Why was he freezing them out?

The question, of course, was purely rhetorical because he knew the answer: he was still reeling from the revelations, unable to confide in his friends what he'd learned about his family. How could he possibly tell them what Daddy had done? How would he bear the disbelief that would creep into their eyes, even as it echoed his own? Because, no matter what, he would always be Cyrus Wadia's son, would always feel the throb of his father's blood in his own veins. No revelation was ever going to change that.

But, God, he was so sick of secrets.

He remembered what Gulnaz had told him about his mother's behavior that Saturday decades ago, how she'd been angry when Remy had bragged about his good grades. The story assumed a different significance now. Mummy had returned home from visiting the son abandoned in an orphanage only to hear the other one gloating about his report card. No wonder she'd lost her temper with him. But Gulnaz knew only one-half of the story, the half that was unfavorable to Mummy. *How unforgivable to carry on as if nothing has changed,* Remy thought, *without at least trying to set the record straight.*

ON SATURDAY MORNINGS, Remy and Kathy always had their breakfast of granola and fruit parfaits on the porch. They'd spend the rest of the morning doing household chores. After they were done eating, Kathy would say, "Okay, hon. It's cleanup time. Let's get started."

It's cleanup time, Remy now said to himself.

His stomach dipped at the thought of what he was going to do.

CHAPTER THIRTY-SEVEN

REMY TEXTED MONAZ, asking her to stop by the house after her classes. She came at four, a little out of breath.

"I decided to take the stairs," she said. "The lift was taking too long."

"You okay?" he said. "Are you taking care of yourself? Getting enough rest?"

"Don't worry so much, Remy Uncle." She laughed. "I'm fine. The baby is fine."

He left her in the living room with his mother while he fetched her a glass of lemonade. When he returned, Monaz and Shirin were talking softly, their heads close together. Remy imagined the two of them in his living room in Columbus. Would it make sense to take Mummy back with him, along with Monaz? Would Kathy threaten to divorce him if he asked her for this? Would Mummy be able to withstand the long flight? Was he insane for even contemplating this?

"Come sit," Shirin said.

He handed Monaz her drink, then sat across from both women. His heart pounded as it hit him what he was about to do, what he was asking of the girl.

"Monaz," he said. "Something has happened recently that has changed everything. Changed me. It . . . I have learned an important lesson about the dangers of keeping family secrets. Secrets and lies, they have a way of destroying everything."

He saw Shirin's head jerk up, but she said nothing, her eyes bright and her face unreadable. His hands were clammy with fear.

"Monaz," he began again, "I can't take you back with me without your parents knowing about your situation. I can't be party to that. I just can't. It . . . It would feel like kidnapping. They have the right to know about their grandson."

Monaz let out a cry. Tears filled her eyes. "Remy Uncle," she said, "you don't know what you're saying. My father will be crushed. He will be furious. You don't know him."

Remy sighed heavily and turned to his mother for help. "What do you think, Mummy?" he asked.

"I think this is a mistake," Shirin said. "You cannot impose your will on this child."

He wavered. He came close to throwing in the towel, walking back what he'd said. But then he thought about what Shirin's silence had taken from him. "I'm sorry," he said. "I know I'm asking for a lot. But I can't do it any other way. I can't start a fresh life with my son, knowing that his very existence is shrouded in secrecy and shame. I . . . This is my condition for taking you with me, Monaz."

"He'll kill me," Monaz whispered.

Remy looked at her sharply. "Do you mean that literally?"

"What? No. I mean, my father would never hurt me." Her face crumpled. "But, Remy Uncle, he may never speak to me again."

"Remy, be reasonable," Shirin said.

He ignored his mother and spoke directly to Monaz. "You don't know that. You don't know how anyone is going to react. But if you don't tell your parents, you're depriving them of something. Don't you see? You're depriving them of a chance to rise to the occasion. To transcend their own limitations." All the while, what kept replaying in his head was: *If Dad had told me about what he'd done, I could've decided whether to forgive or not.*

Monaz shook her head. "All this sounds fine and dandy, Remy Uncle," she said bitterly. "Maybe it works this way in America. But you don't know India. You've lived away for too long."

"It's not as if we're going to change our plans," he said. "I just feel that they have the right to know about your son's existence. You're young—this would be an awful secret for you to carry lifelong."

"What did Kathy say?" Shirin asked. "She thinks this is a good idea?"

"She doesn't know," Remy said wearily. He suddenly felt miserable. What if Kathy opposed him on this?

"Maybe you should talk to her," Shirin said. "Before this chokri does anything stupid."

Monaz rose to her feet. "So if I don't do as you wish, then what? You don't want my baby?"

Remy crossed the room, put a hand on her shoulder. "Monaz," he said, "I'm not doing this to be mean. I honestly think this is the right approach. For all our sakes. I swear, it's for your good also."

"You don't know everything, Remy Uncle." She kissed Shirin on her cheek and stood, slinging her backpack over her shoulder. "Bye, Granna," she said, and left.

What had just happened? Had Monaz exited their lives permanently? He wanted to follow her and ask her to clarify.

"That poor girl," Shirin said.

He turned to her. "You think I fu— messed up? Don't you think it's only fair that the grandparents know what's happening?"

Shirin looked at him for the longest time. "I don't know," she said at last. "I'm tired, and I'm old. People always think that we get wiser as we age. But the opposite happens. Everything gets more complicated." She rubbed her face in a weary gesture that broke Remy's heart. "Ask Kathy what she thinks."

THAT NIGHT ON THE PHONE, Kathy was not pleased.

"Have you lost your mind, Remy? You've told me a million times how traditional India is. You're thinking like an American. I mean, what if the father kills her or something? We keep reading about these honor killings and shit."

"Kathy," he said, frustrated. "He's not going to kill her. He . . . He's a Parsi, for heaven's sake. We are not like . . . you know. He's educated and all."

"Okay, fine. But even the thought of him disowning her. That's a possibility, right? And you'd set that in motion because of *your* value system. It's . . . It's almost like cultural appropriation or something."

"Good God, Kat," he said. "How can it be cultural appropriation? To state the obvious, I'm Indian."

"But *are* you? I mean, yes, obviously, by birth. But, Remy, your outlook is American. And your parents were very Westernized. And hers are not."

"I know. And if she were planning on having the baby in India, it would be a huge scandal. But don't you see? By bringing her to America, we're giving Monaz's parents a way out. This way, it's all in the open, but they can wash their hands of the whole situation."

"But you're bullying Monaz into doing something she doesn't wish to. What gives you that right?"

In that moment, he knew what he had to do. "You're correct," he said. "I can't make this decision for her. But I know how to fix this."

"I knew this would be hard," Kathy continued. "But in a million years, I didn't anticipate so much upheaval. Remember how excited we were when Jango called with the news about Monaz? But now? I'm not even sure I want to go through all this. It's just one obstacle after another."

"Kat," he said, "you have to trust me on this, okay? I know what to do."

"What is that?" He heard the wariness in her voice.

"The solution is simple and elegant. I have to tell the truth."

CHAPTER THIRTY-EIGHT

REMY HAD TOLD Shirin that he had invited some close friends over for dinner that night, and she had looked disappointed but held her silence. He could see the struggle on her face—knew that she wanted him all to herself, but that she also realized that it might be a long time before he saw his friends again.

Gulnaz and Hussein arrived at 8 p.m., with Pervez and Roshan following soon after. Remy was still introducing the two couples when Monaz came in with Shenaz, carrying a large platter of her signature chicken cutlets.

"Where's Jango?" Remy asked.

"Looking for a parking spot." Shenaz smiled. "He said to tell you to start making his drink."

Monaz was wearing a loose cotton kurta, but Remy detected the growing bulge. He wondered if Gulnaz noticed. They still hadn't given her the news.

"I'm so glad you came," he whispered to Monaz, who smiled uncertainly. "Don't worry," he said. "I will not let anything bad happen to you."

After he'd laid out the snacks and drinks, Remy poked his head into the bedroom where his mother was resting.

Manju nodded at him. "She's awake."

"Hey, Mummy," he said as he walked in.

She gave him a sleepy smile. "I can just take my dinner here. You go enjoy yourself with your friends."

He shook his head vehemently. "No, no, Mummy. I want you to come out, okay? It's important to me."

"If you insist."

"Good." Remy turned to Manju. "Can you help Mummy freshen up before bringing her into the living room?"

The doorbell rang again. Dina Mehta stood in the outside hallway, looking as terrified as Remy felt. Earlier today, Kathy had told him she disapproved of his idea, that it was ill-considered and impulsive. Now, he wondered if she had been right.

Dina walked in, and there was a silence. His friends looked at the older woman curiously before Gulnaz stood up.

"Hello. I'm Gulu. Please, come sit," she said, offering Dina her own chair, as if she were the host. Remy, noticing, forced himself to move, and introduced Dina to the group.

"Something to drink?" he asked.

Dina shook her head, then changed her mind. "Maybe a little whiskey," she said. She threw Remy an apprehensive look that he pretended not to see.

Manju led Shirin into the room. The three couples and Monaz crowded around her, so that only Dina and Remy remained seated. Dina looked faint. Shirin had not spotted her yet, and she seemed happy to see her son's friends, with the exception of Pervez and Roshan.

"How are you feeling, Shirin dear?" Roshan said, and Shirin replied with a terse "Better."

Dina sat up in her chair. "Hello, Shirin," she said.

Shirin gasped. She turned her head to where Remy sat miserably and looked at him accusingly. Her face took on a bitter cast.

What could Remy say? His high-minded purpose for this gathering suddenly seemed ridiculous, even reckless.

"Take me back to my room," Shirin said to Manju. "*Now.*"

"Oh, no, Shirin Auntie," Jango protested. "You just got here. Sit with us for a little bit, na?"

Shirin pressed her lips, her eyes darting from Jango to Remy. *Ask him,* she seemed to say. *Ask him what this antic is supposed to mean.*

Remy stood up. "Hi, everyone," he said. "I . . . I need to . . ."

His guests turned to him, confused, and he lost his train of thought.

"*Now,*" Shirin said again, growing agitated.

"Mummy, wait. Please," Remy said. "For my sake. Let me explain."

Shirin gave Dina a scathing look. "Why is this woman in my house?"

Remy cleared his throat, stuck his sweaty hands into his pockets. He focused on Monaz, who sat with a perplexed look on her face. "I had an older brother," he said in a rush. "He died. My brother. He was disabled. My father put him in an orphanage. Even though he had parents of his own."

He felt out of breath. He heard the silence, saw Dina's face whiten, registered that Shirin had slumped in her chair. But this was the only justice he would ever be able to get for his mother for what she'd endured—this public recognition among relatives and friends who had judged her. This was his final chance to rewrite the narrative of Daddy as the long-suffering husband and Mummy as the shrew, the volatile, angry woman who harangued her husband and son.

"Gulnaz," he said, turning to her, "you remember the story you told me a few days ago? About Mummy berating me for my good report card? Well, guess what?"

"Stop," Shirin said, covering her ears. "Stop this at once, Remy. I forbid this."

He went and stood behind Shirin, put a hand on each frail shoulder. "It's okay, Mummy. Once and for all, let them all know. What you've suffered. What you've survived."

A nervous energy drove Remy onward, allowing him to disregard their discomfort, to ignore Dina's stricken face or acknowledge Shirin's occasional moan. He was aware only of the words flooding out of him, hot, urgent, and brimming with outrage and righteousness. On and on he went. He left out Dina's culpability, wanting to save her humiliation until the end. When, at last—and he had no idea how much time had elapsed—he fell silent, he turned to her.

"Dina?"

"It's true," she said. "Every word is true. Except Remy left out my role in this tragedy. I was the one who got Cyloo admission to the orphanage. I am the one most directly responsible for his death. And no God will forgive me for this."

Shirin let out a cry. She lifted her head and looked directly at Dina. "Not your fault." Her voice was so weak, they all had to strain to hear her. "You were the reason I got to spend Saturdays with my son."

Dina's face crumpled. "Shirin . . ." she said.

The two women sat looking at each other tearfully from across the room. No one else spoke or stirred, holding their collective breaths. At one point, Dina opened her mouth to speak, then shut it. Shirin continued to stare at her. They were speaking to each other in a secret language that none of the other people assembled could decipher.

Remy had orchestrated this encounter, but now he felt redundant, as if the situation had galloped away from him. When the idea for this party had come to him, he had imagined something more triumphant:

a round of applause for his mother, maybe, or Pervez rising to his feet and admitting how wrong he'd been to neglect Shirin. Something different than this silent, weepy communication between two women who had loved the same man.

He came around and sat on his haunches in front of his mother, his face turned up to her, wanting to rest his head in her lap. He had done his best; he had brought her to this moment; he had freed them. Most importantly, he had demonstrated to Monaz the corrosive effect of lies.

Shirin broke off eye contact with Dina and looked down at Remy. The coldness in her eyes stunned him. "I want to return to my room," she said. "Take me back."

Chastened, Remy escorted his mother. He had forgotten just how harsh and distant Shirin could sound.

He sat beside her on the bed, their faces close.

"Did you mean to humiliate Dina by inviting her? Or did you intend to kill me?"

"Mummy, no. I . . . I wanted to honor you. Your sacrifices. I wanted to let everyone know who you truly are. That was my only goal, I swear."

She stared at him for the longest time, and the longer she looked, the smaller he felt. "I didn't sacrifice," she said at last. "I fought, tooth and nail. Sacrifice implies that I gave him up willingly."

"God, Mummy, I know that. Don't you think I know that?"

"Why did you invite her?"

"Dina? For corroboration. In case they didn't believe me."

Shirin shook her head. "No. You brought her for humiliation." She turned away from him, then looked back. "Enough. Enough pain and suffering. You understand? I don't need anyone's accolades. I don't want their pity. Dina has suffered enough. We all have. Now, send Manju in here, and go be with your friends."

Remy stared at her in incomprehension. A few nights ago, she'd referred to Dina as a demon. What explained this sudden change of heart? And then it hit him: Telling the truth and then seeing his shock and revulsion was what had freed Shirin. Having regained her son, she didn't need anyone else.

"You won't come back out, Mama? To eat with us?"

"I'm tired. You go enjoy yourself. I will see you tomorrow."

"Good night, Mummy. I'm sorry. I love you."

She didn't respond. But just as he was leaving the room, she said, "Remy?" and he turned around.

"Don't you go back out and badmouth your father. It won't help me in the least. Remember one thing: everyone does the best they can. I've had the last three years without Cyrus to learn this truth."

REMY USED THE bathroom to stall for time, to steady himself. He studied his face as he washed his hands, noticed the first gray creeping up on his temples. He had never experienced as deep a sense of failure as he did now. *Everyone does the best they can*, Mummy had said. If so, none of their best had been good enough. He himself had flunked some essential test, hadn't he?

He wished he could go directly to bed and block out the memories of this disastrous evening. He had wanted to demonstrate an important lesson to Monaz about the liberating power of the truth. He feared he'd done the opposite.

Dina stood as he walked back into the room. "I should take my leave," she murmured.

Remy held her hand, a pleading look in his eyes. "No. Please. I beg you. Please stay."

"But why? I've served my purpose."

He looked away, ashamed. "That's just it. I don't want you to think . . . Please, Dina. Stay for dinner. I—I don't know what I was thinking. But, please, allow me to make this up to you."

A look of understanding crossed Dina's face. "My dear boy, you are trying so hard. None of this is your fault. If it will make you happy, I'll stay."

Monaz sat next to him at dinner. She served a piece of fish to Remy before serving herself. She nodded at him, urging him to eat. *She acts as if she's as much my family as she is Shenaz and Jango's,* Remy thought, and was grateful. He loved this girl; being entrusted with her baby would be the honor of a lifetime. He needed to make sure she knew this.

The others did their best to keep the conversation flowing. Hussein entertained them with stories about the howlers his high school students made in their English papers. "Yah, just yesterday I read one that said we should not take our freedoms for granite. *Granite,*" he said. They all laughed, but then they fell back into a labored discourse, each one taking turns to hold it afloat, as if their talk were a banner they had to carry to the finish line.

The finish line came sooner than it normally would. Shenaz yawned, and Jango said, "She's not been sleeping well the last few nights. Chalo, we'll call it a night."

Dina stood up immediately. "I have an early meeting tomorrow. Nice to have met all of you."

"Is your driver downstairs?" Remy asked.

"No. He has the night off. I'll just call for an Uber."

"Nonsense," Hussein said immediately. "We'll drop you off."

"But you don't even know where I live," Dina said with a smile.

"Doesn't matter, auntie. No way you're going home in an Uber at this hour."

Gulnaz stood on her tiptoes and gave Remy a kiss on his cheek. "I'll call you tomorrow," she said, rubbing his back. "You take care of yourself, okay? Forget all this ancient history."

"Thanks, Gulu," he whispered.

Pervez stepped up and gave Remy a hug. "I'm sorry, yaar," he whispered. "We had no idea. My mother never said a word, I swear. Poor Shirin."

"Thanks," Remy whispered back. "She's pretty amazing."

His cousin looked him in the eye. "She is. We will . . . do better. In the future. Okay, we'll take our leave. But we'll talk soon, okay?"

Monaz busied herself picking up the empty glasses as the others left. Shenaz looked at her niece inquiringly. "You coming?" she said.

"You go ahead," Monaz said. "I'll be down in two secs. I need to talk to Remy Uncle."

"We'll go get the car," Jango said.

"I understand now," Monaz said as soon as they left. "Where you're coming from." She looked away, then back at Remy. "I'll go home this weekend. It will be easier telling them in person. And then, soon after I return, I want us to get out of here."

He knew he should be grateful that Monaz had reacted precisely as he'd hoped. But it was a hollow victory. "You're sure you'll be okay?" he asked.

Monaz shrugged. "I think so. But being okay and telling the truth . . . they're sort of different things, right?"

He took a step and embraced her. "You are the most remarkable person I know," he murmured.

"That's not true. The most remarkable person you know is in the next room."

AFTER HE'D WALKED Monaz out, he returned and looked in on his mother. Both she and Manju were asleep. He went to his bedroom and lay down, then buried his head in his pillow and sobbed. He clawed at the fitted sheet, just as he had done as a boy, when despite every effort to steel his heart against his mother's barbed-wire words, he would break down in bed. As a boy, he'd fantasized about how peaceful the apartment would be if only he and Dad had lived in it, how great it would be to joke around with Daddy without Mummy's smoldering presence. And now? More than anything, Remy wanted to savor every minute with his mother. He railed against the injustice of the fact that there was no way to remedy the grievous injury Shirin had suffered. The past remained a published poem that allowed no further revisions.

But you are still here.

The voice in his head was so clear it was as if someone had actually spoken the words out loud. Dad, maybe? But Daddy was dead. Kathy was eight thousand miles away. Dina and Jango and Shenaz couldn't help him. *There's just you*, he thought. *You are the only one who can help her.*

REMY GOT OUT of bed and quietly opened his mother's door. She was lying on her side, her head propped up to minimize her coughing. Manju heard him and opened her eyes, but Remy held a finger to his lips. He slid into Shirin's bed beside her. She stirred, but he kept a light hand around her waist, and after a moment, she covered Remy's hand with hers.

He slept until 3 a.m., when Shirin woke up coughing. His hand was numb from being in one position, but he didn't care. He helped her take a few sips of water. He rubbed Vicks on her throat and chest, remembering the numerous times she'd rubbed the salve on him. As if she'd read his mind, Shirin said, "Vicks and cologne water."

He smiled, the shorthand between them as sweet as a kiss. "Always," he said.

He waited until she fell asleep again and then went back to his room. He woke up again at six thirty, and by the time he had changed into his T-shirt and shorts, it was light.

CHAPTER THIRTY-NINE

—✦—

IT WAS HIS first time at Priyadarshini Park during this trip, and as he slipped in his earbuds and began to run around the track, Remy regretted not having come sooner. Young couples jogged together, the women's ponytails crossing back and forth. Old men sat on the nearby lawn and did yoga or Tai Chi. In the distance, a lone trash collector walked on the big rocks that formed a buffer against the sea, bending to pick up the garbage. An enormous plastic bag ballooned behind him.

He had brought Kathy here during her first visit to India, for the wedding. He had been so proud of this spacious, well-planned park, with its sweeping views of the sea, its immaculate walking paths, the great big trees. But Kathy had been oblivious to his pride. She had enjoyed their run but had not commented on the well-maintained running track or the gardens. Remy saw it from her eyes: The miraculously large expanse of this urban park couldn't compare to the state parks she was used to. The waters of his beloved Arabian Sea looked gray and murky to someone who had seen the sparkle of the Pacific Ocean. The morning air was smog-filled and hazy.

Daddy had made that visit so much fun, though. Remy remembered the huge wedding reception at Bombay Gymkhana, where Cyrus had proudly introduced his daughter-in-law to all his guests, Kathy resplendent in the dark-blue sari Shirin had gifted her; Cyrus insisting that they go for an overnight trip to the holy city of Udvada to seek blessings for the newlyweds; Cyrus taking them to the scrumptious high tea at the Taj Mahal Palace hotel after they returned to Bombay.

Without knowing it, Remy picked up his pace, as if he were trying to outrun the memory cloud that carried the disorienting revelations about his father, new knowledge that would take him years to process, much less understand. His feet pounded on the track until he thought his heart would burst, until sweat fell into his eyes. In his ear, David Bowie's "Starman" gave way to Ferron's "Misty Mountain," and the upbeat tempo of the song made him run even harder.

That first winter in Ohio, Kathy had introduced him to Ferron's music, and Remy had fallen in love with it. They'd played her albums over and over until midafternoon on Sundays, drinking coffee as they stayed under the covers and watched the snow come down in drifts outside the bedroom window. *Those were good days*, he thought, *full of life and music and possibility*.

Another Ferron song played, "Shadows on a Dime," and, as always, the haunting melody produced a hollow, smoky feeling in Remy's chest. A flock of birds flew overhead, and he slowed his pace, his attention snagged by the beauty of their flight. Preoccupied as he was, he was unprepared for the line *Who would I be if I didn't sing?* And even though he'd heard it many times before, the question now made Remy come to a stop.

The runner behind him almost collided with him before changing lanes. "Bad form," the man muttered as he ran past, and Remy, still distracted, waved his hand apologetically. He walked off the track, his mind turning over Ferron's question.

Who was he, now that he was no longer a poet? And why had he tossed off that gift, the salvation of his childhood, as lightly as he had? For years now, he had prided himself for having given up on childish things and becoming a successful businessman. In the early years, Kathy had told him that she wanted him to write full-time, that she would soon earn enough to support both of them. But his ego hadn't let him take her offer seriously. As an immigrant, it had been important for him to stand on his own feet, to be able to look Rose in the eye when he'd announced he wanted to marry her daughter.

All the things—status, money, other people's approval—that had seemed unimportant when it was just him and Kathy cloistered in his book-lined apartment suddenly became important the moment he opened the door and stepped outside. Then, he noticed the tinsel malls hawking the American dream; the TV ads proclaiming that gaudy diamond rings were the best way to declare eternal love; the breathless news reports about the booming housing market; the omnipresent message that a real man was a good provider for his family.

Is this what had happened to Daddy? Remy wondered as he walked toward the sea. The more successful he got, the more important being successful became? Until everything that stood in the way of his ambition, including his disabled child, had to be removed? What if, God forbid, Monaz's baby was born disabled? How would Remy react?

He and Kathy could've adopted in America—if they'd been willing to adopt a black child. Kathy had wanted to adopt from India for the best of reasons, of course: so that they could have a child that looked like Remy. *But,* he thought, *would we have looked here if we knew for sure that we could've found a white baby in America?*

He and Kathy had always prided themselves on their politics; they sent monthly donations to the Southern Poverty Law Center and supported other progressive causes. So why had they not considered a black adoption?

Remy knew the answer: there was a caste system in America, and he had successfully scaled it. The advantages that he had been born to in India had followed him to America. But a caste system depended on dividing people into ever-thinner strata of privilege and status. (This was something white liberals failed to understand, Remy thought, with their lumping together of "people of color." Hell, he had never even known he was considered "Asian" until he'd come to America.) Adopting a black child would've pulled him into the racial cauldron of American life that he'd managed to avoid.

The recent ugliness of US politics had made another thing clear. Remy could sit on three corporate boards, he could drive an Audi, he could employ twelve Americans, but . . . he was an immigrant. He was light-skinned enough that strangers often mistook him for being Italian or Greek, but . . . he was not white.

A brown man and his white wife raising a black child would've drawn attention everywhere they went, strangers at the grocery store trying to solve the puzzle of them. Remy Wadia had no interest in being in a Benetton ad. He had no interest in being an object of someone else's curiosity, at best, and cruelty, at worst.

Remy climbed the dark boulders that buffered the park from the water. He looked to where the dirty morning sky met the crease of the Arabian Sea. He had witnessed the luminescent blue of other oceans and knew that this sea was a poor cousin to those bodies of water. And yet he felt a rare peace. Almost everything else about this city left him bewildered and lost, but the sea was his true inheritance as a Bombayite: Spending countless evenings at the seaside watching the sun smear its fingerprints on the sky. Skipping college during the monsoons and sitting on the seawall at Nariman Point with your back to the city, smoking a cigarette and writing poetry. Taking your first girlfriend to Juhu

Beach and losing your virginity in a small, nondescript hotel there. To be a Bombayite was to carry the salt of the ocean in your blood, so that even decades later, you could leave a restaurant in Columbus and feel a sudden desire for a late-night drive by the seaside, before remembering the landlocked city you now called home.

He sat down on a boulder, staring at the water pooling between the rocks. *Home.* He thought of the deep-green hostas in his backyard in Columbus, how each spring he split them and planted them in different parts of the garden. If only he could do that with himself—plant himself in two different soils.

The trash collector was making his way back, stepping expertly from rock to rock as the wind made the plastic sack balloon behind him. As he drew closer, Remy saw that he was a young lad of maybe nineteen or so. Remy's eyes swept over the boy's dirty face and worn clothes before he looked away.

The boy walked past Remy, then whipped around, bug-eyed.

"Sir?" he said.

"Yes?" Remy said impatiently, because the trash collector was blocking his view and interrupting a rare moment of solitude.

The boy broke into a smile. "You are Cyrus sahib's son, no?" He pointed at his chest. "You don't remember me?"

Remy looked at him. "No," he said at last. "I'm sorry."

"It's okay, sir," the boy said, shaking his head from side to side. "My name is Rajesh. My father washed your father's car every morning. You were having a blue Honda City, correct?"

"Yeah," Remy said, not knowing what else to say. He dug his hand into his pocket to pull out his wallet. Maybe a few rupees would make this boy go on his way.

Rajesh's eyes followed the movement of Remy's hand. "Oh, no, no, sir. I'm just saying hello, only. No money required. Please to give my salaams to your mother, sir."

"I will."

The youth grinned. "Tell her I remember the chocolate she always gave me when I came to the house with my father."

Remy nodded. "I will."

"Okay, sir. I won't disturb. I was just so happy when I recognized you. This government job I have with the municipality? All thanks to your father-mother."

Now, Remy was curious. "They got you this job?"

"They paid the fees for my whole schooling, sir. That's why only I finished high school. These days in Mumbai, even to pick up trash you need minimum high school education, sir. So in a way, they get me this job."

"My father died. Three years ago."

Rajesh's brow knitted with worry. "Sorry, sir. Yes, yes, I am knowing. I was only sixteen, but my own father came home that day crying so hard we were thinking our grandmother die in the village. But he was crying for Cyrus sahib, only." He looked at Remy shyly. "You don't remember me, but I remember you, sir. When you come home with your mother from the funeral place, my whole family come to your door to pay our respect. I remember it very well."

"I'm sorry," Remy said vaguely, all the while thinking, *If you knew how busy my life is, kiddo, how big my world is, compared to yours, you'd understand why I don't remember a small incident like that.* Then he was ashamed.

He stood up, held out his hand. "Thank you for telling me. It means a lot. And give my best wishes to your father."

Rajesh wore a queasy look. Then he grinned, wiped his hand on his pants, and shook Remy's clean, outstretched hand. "Thank you, sir. Most welcome, sir." He flung the trash bag over his shoulder again and began to walk away.

"Rajesh," Remy called, searching for his wallet again. He stepped gingerly over the rocks. "Will you please accept this little gift in my father's memory? Buy something sweet for your family from me."

The boy looked as if he was about to refuse the cash, but suddenly he relented. "You are just like your father, sir. Exact to exact. God bless you and your mother."

Remy sat back down, but Rajesh's intrusion had disrupted his thought process. He reached for his phone and sent Gulnaz, Jango, and Shenaz a group text.

Sorry about last night, he wrote. *Didn't mean to make it an awkward evening for you.*

Gulnaz wrote back immediately: *Don't be. Your heart was in the right place. Loved seeing everybody.*

Thanks, Gulu, he wrote.

His phone dinged. Jango: *In a meeting. Will call later.*

A second later, Shenaz: *Love you. It's all good.*

Remy smiled ruefully. He didn't deserve such good friends. Then again, he wasn't sure that he'd deserved any of the good fortune that had come his way.

HE GLANCED AT HIS WATCH. Shoot. He'd sat here longer than he'd intended. Mummy would be awake by now.

He was navigating down from the rocks when the idea came to him. As he exited the park, he kept ruminating about it. The last thing he wanted was a repetition of last night's debacle, well intended but stunningly flawed.

Yes, he decided, he could carry this suggestion home to his mother like an offering of flowers, for her approval. Unlike last night, there would be no public demonstration, because this would involve only the two of them.

CHAPTER FORTY

JANGO'S DRIVER ARRIVED at 10 a.m. and helped Remy get Shirin out of the rented wheelchair and into the car. Gladys hovered around them, an apprehensive look on her face. "Don't worry," Remy said. "She'll be okay. I can manage."

"I can come along to help."

"Gladys, it's okay. We'll be back in a few hours."

"Her inhaler . . ."

Remy patted the paper bag that sat on the back seat between Shirin and him. "It's here. We'll be fine."

DINA HAD GIVEN him precise directions to the St. Mary's cemetery. When he'd left the park yesterday, he had phoned her to apologize for the dinner party, and then he'd asked her advice about his plan.

"Most of the cemetery is gone," Dina had said. "So is the orphanage."

"Gone?"

"The church sold the property to developers in 2011. The orphanage relocated to Pune."

"But my brother's grave?"

"It's still there. Your dad fought tooth and nail with the diocese for it not to be moved. But I'm warning you—don't expect it to be rolling hills and chirping birds and whatnot, like in America. It's just a small plot of land next to a busy road."

Remy swallowed his disappointment. "Does Mummy know?"

"What? Yes, of course. She went there faithfully for years. Until the last year or so. Most likely because her health didn't allow."

"I see." A beat. "How do you know? You weren't in touch with her."

A long silence.

"Dina?" Remy said.

"Because I went, too. Not as regularly as your mother, of course. But whenever time allowed. And usually there were fresh flowers at his gravesite."

Remy had had to stop walking to catch his breath. "Why?" he said at last. "Why did you go?"

"I'm not sure. Some combination of guilt and remorse and . . . and . . . even love, I suppose. Your brother was a very lovable child." Dina's voice cracked. "I owed Cyloo that much at least. And after your father died? Well, it was my own, feeble way of supporting Shirin. Of letting her know that at least one other person remembered her son."

Why did human beings need to invent heaven and hell? Remy wondered. It was all here on Earth: The stars and the gutter, paradise and inferno. All the contradictions of the world embodied in every single human being.

How juvenile and oblivious his existence had been. He had strolled through the garden of his life, pleased with himself, ignorant of the thorns that had ensnared his parents and Dina. Unaware of this secret communication, written in flowers, between the two women in Cyrus's life, who, in their own way, had destroyed each other.

The world is too big and complex, Remy thought, and he had never felt as small and inconsequential as he did at that moment.

"Beta? Are you still there?" Dina's voice was close, so close, in his ear.

"I'm here." Remy cleared his throat. Beta. Son. She had called him *son*.

"Dina," he said, emboldened. "Can I come see you before I leave? You know, to say a proper goodbye?"

"Yes, of course," she said promptly. "I would love that. When do you leave?"

"Soon," he said. "Soon," he repeated, making up his mind even as he said the words. He would do this one last thing with his mother and leave soon after Monaz returned to Bombay.

His eyes lingered on the street life around him—the fruit carts stacked neatly with piles of oranges and guavas; the sun glistening on the gray fur of the stray cat perched on the hood of a yellow-and-black taxi; schoolchildren dodging traffic, bent from the weight of bulging backpacks. There was more life, more humanity, in one square inch of Bombay than in fifty miles of Columbus, he thought, and suddenly, he missed this city, this hellacious, infuriating, bewildering, beloved metropolis, as if he'd already left.

Remy forced himself back to the present. "So what do you think?" he asked. "You think it's a good idea, what I'm doing?"

Dina was quiet for so long that Remy said, "Hello? Dina? Are you there?"

"I'm here." Then: "Do you know what broken rice is? The dish?"

"No?" he said cautiously.

"It's the fragments of rice, you know, the parts no one wants to consume. Poor people in Vietnam used to eat it. It was all they could afford. But these days, they've fancied it up. They top it with egg and pork and what all, and now it's one of the most popular dishes in Vietnam."

"Okay, but what's that got to do with—"

"Remy, don't you see? A week ago, you were served a heaping of broken rice. Unwanted, unwelcome information. But look at what you're trying to do. You're trying to transform it into something fragrant and good. Does that make sense, what I'm saying?"

"Yeah, I think so," he said slowly. "So you think it's okay? What I'm planning?"

"Who can say except Shirin? Ask her."

Remy gave a weak laugh. "Oh, you bet. After the dinner-party fiasco, I'm not taking any chances."

"I'm sorry, Remy. I know you meant well."

She was consoling *him*? After he'd humiliated her in front of his friends? "Dina," he said, casting around for the right thing to say, wanting to come up with the perfect phrase. "Dina, I can see why my father adored you. You are truly a wonderful person."

It was a lie, of course; Cyrus had never mentioned Dina to him. But the compliment worked. Remy could hear the lift in Dina's voice, and it made him happy. There was far too much sorrow in the world; he wouldn't add to it. What had Mummy said? That people did the best they could. It was as good a life philosophy as any other. When had Mummy gotten this wise? Or had she always been so and he'd been too dumb to know it?

By the time Remy and Dina had hung up, that curious but wonderful alchemy had occurred—by being kind to Dina, Remy had cheered himself up.

AND NOW HERE he and his mother were in Jango's car, driving to Bandra. Remy longed to ask the driver to turn up the air-conditioning, but he didn't, for Shirin's sake. She was looking out the window, taking in the sights.

She must've felt his eyes on her, because she turned to him. "Would you have gone to America if Cyloo had . . . remained with us?"

Would he have left? Would the seductive lure of his dreams have prevailed? Or would a sense of responsibility for his disabled brother have kept him in India? If he had settled in America, who would've looked after Cyloo for the rest of his days after his parents were gone? Would he have ended up in a home anyway? But if Remy hadn't moved, he would've never met Kathy. He felt dizzy at the thought.

"This is what your daddy was trying to protect you from," Shirin said. "From that burden. From having to make that choice."

The road not traveled. If only Dad would've accepted his family situation. If Dad had not placed Cyloo in an orphanage, he probably would've been alive today. Their family would've remained intact. And he and Cyloo would've been close, Remy had no doubt. Daddy would've had no reason to get him out of India. At some point, Remy would've fallen in love with a woman who was not Kathy, and they perhaps would've had children of their own. They would've lived nearby, and he would've been able to stop by daily to visit with his parents and his brother. His children would've known the steady love of their paternal grandparents. Remy would've been there when Dad got his sudden cancer diagnosis and would've been around to help. The thought of such an ordinary life with everyday pleasures and challenges flooded Remy with longing for what had been lost.

"I would have stayed," he said. "I *think* I would've stayed. I mean, look at Jango and Shenaz. They're perfectly happy here."

Shirin frowned. "Don't you ever compare yourself to Jango. You are ten times smarter than any of your friends. Remember all those writing trophies you won in college? I don't think you would've been satisfied with the opportunities in India. You had too restless a mind. Besides, after us, you would've been responsible for Cyloo's care. That's a huge responsibility, darling." She sighed. "It's funny. I understand Cyrus's perspective better ever since I told you what he did. How can this be?"

"I don't know." Remy put his hand on her knee. "But, Mummy, you don't have to excuse what Daddy did. He robbed both of us. He took that choice away from me."

Shirin looked at him tearfully. "I'm sorry."

"In any case, I'm so glad we're finally visiting Cyloo together. We'll have a nice day together, okay, Mummy?"

"Okay," Shirin said slowly. "But . . . the grass is going to be overgrown. I . . . I haven't gone in so long."

Her firstborn was dead, his little body long disintegrated, but she was worried about the condition of his grave. Remy swallowed the lump in his throat.

> I bequeath myself to the dirt to grow from the grass I love,
> If you want me again look for me under your boot-soles.

Unbidden, these lines from "Song of Myself" had come to him.

The driver braked abruptly, knocking Remy out of his reverie. Shirin was looking at him anxiously, as if she were waiting for an answer.

"Don't worry," he said, squeezing her hand. "I will clean Cyloo's grave, if need be. I'm here with you, no? You're no longer alone."

Shirin squeezed back. "Not today," she said.

As THEY LEFT behind the fast lanes of the Sea Link and were deposited back into city streets, the traffic in Bandra felt as terrible as in the rest of Bombay. When Remy was a boy, Bandra had been a posh suburb, home to movie stars, and his head was filled with the stories his father used to tell of an even earlier time, when Bandra was a tranquil oasis, lined with bungalows instead of apartment buildings. In Remy's time, the Goan Catholic families who lived in the suburb gave it a modern, hipster vibe. Remy supposed that Bandra's legendary bohemian atmosphere was still thriving, but as they sat in a miserable traffic jam, all he could see were the clogged, manic streets and the bustling stores and restaurants. A wedding procession ahead, replete with the groom on a white horse and drummers dancing around him, made the traffic move even slower.

"Turn here," he said to the driver, following the directions from Dina. "And then make an immediate right." He glanced at his mother for help, but Shirin was leaning into the back seat, her eyes closed. *It's just as well,* he thought. *The less she remembers of having made this journey alone, year after lonely year, the better.*

THERE WAS NO parking in front of the cemetery, so the driver pulled up as close to the gate as possible, then helped Remy lift Shirin into the wheelchair. "I'll drive around," he said. "You please call when you're ready for pickup."

As Remy wheeled Shirin toward the entrance, she blocked her eyes from the sun, and Remy kicked himself for having forgotten her sunglasses. An elderly guard approached them.

"Can I help you?" he said, and then the old man broke into a delighted smile. "Shirin madam," he said. "Praise the Lord. I am so glad to see you alive and well."

Shirin lifted her head and peered at the man standing before them. "Hello, Mr. Pinto," she said. "How are you?"

"Still here, madam, by the grace of God. And you?"

"Still here also."

Pinto shuffled up to Remy. "Allow me to push, sir," he said.

An elderly guard accompanying them to Cyloo's gravesite had not factored into Remy's plans. "No, it's fine," he said weakly. But Pinto didn't budge.

"Give him a tip," Shirin said to Remy in Gujarati. "To thank him for his offer."

Of course. Awkwardly, clumsily, Remy opened his wallet and pulled out a couple of crisp bills. "For your help," he said.

"God bless you, sir. Shall I show you the spot?"

"Pinto," Shirin said sharply, "it's okay. I remember the way."

"Yes, of course, madam, of course."

It was immediately apparent that the place had fallen off everyone's radar. Weeds grew tall, and the grass was dry and brown. None of the graves had fresh flowers on them. There were no other visitors. As they went down the narrow path, Remy felt a mounting anger. His brother deserved a better resting place than this. Cheated in life, he had also been cheated in death.

With Shirin guiding him, they found Cyloo's gravesite almost immediately. There was a gray tombstone, and Remy felt a fresh wave of outrage. "Wait. He doesn't have his own marker?"

Shirin gave him a puzzled look. "No. All four boys were buried together. Don't you remember? I told you."

"I—I guess not." He looked away, blinking back his tears. "So all these years, when you came here, you couldn't even pray for just your son?"

"Remy"—Shirin's voice was quiet—"I didn't need to come all the way here to pray for my son. Those other three boys here? They were orphans. I knew them. I prayed for all the boys."

"That's all fine and dandy, Mummy, but . . ." He cut himself off, not wanting her to hear his outrage, his disappointment. "Okay, listen," he said. "Let's get a new marker made for Cyloo. We can—"

"No, beta." Shirin was shaking her head. "Let these boys rest together eternally. In any case, what difference would it make now? How many more times do you think I'll be able to visit?"

Remy felt hollow with grief. "Mummy, I can make arrangements for Pervez to bring you here whenever you like. I can get . . ." He caught the sad look on her face. "Mummy, I . . ." But what could he say, really? Between her poor health, the heat, and the traffic, she wasn't going to be able to come back often.

"It is better this way," Shirin said softly. "That my last time here is with my other son. I . . . It would be too lonely to come here alone now. Not after today."

He nodded, unable to refute the truth of what she was saying.

"Remy, listen to me. Let's . . ." Shirin stopped, coughed.

"Do you want some water?"

"No. It's okay," she gasped.

Breathe. Breathe, he thought. Even in once-pristine Bandra, the air was now so polluted.

"Remy, let's not spoil this day with plans. I . . . You have already given me something I never thought I'd get. Both my sons are together with me at last. This is gift enough."

"We left the flowers in the car," Remy said abruptly, remembering. "Oh shit. I can't believe it. Let me call the driver and—"

"Leave it," Shirin said, waving her hands. "Cyloo knows we are here. Better than any flowers. Come, Remy. Sit next to me."

Remy crouched beside her wheelchair, and Shirin put her hand on his shoulder. After a few minutes, unable to bear the strange silence of the place, he leaned forward and began to clear around the gravesite with his hands. As he tore at the clumps of overgrown grass and weeds, he felt the savagery of the action and had the horrible sensation that he was tearing at Cyloo's hair. He stopped. "I . . . I can't," he said, suddenly teary.

Shirin gave him a knowing look. "Sit back, Remy. Don't try and fix anything. Let it be just the way it is. I used to do this frantic cleaning also. But there's no need."

They sat side by side, the midmorning sun on their faces. Shirin kept her hand on Remy's shoulder. *I could sit here forever*, he thought, *rooted in place like these weeds, and I would be happy as long as she keeps her hand on me.* He felt himself falling backward in time, before things went sour between them, to the days of absolute trust and unconditional love, when he used to nestle his small and trusting body into hers, burrowing into her safe harbor.

The high-pitched cry of an overhead bird broke the silence. Remy looked up to the sky, and Shirin's hand fell from his shoulder. Remy leaned to his right to remove a note from his pocket. He picked up a small stone and used it to weigh down the paper against Cyloo's tombstone.

"What does it say?" Shirin said.

"It's a few lines from a poem by Whitman. I wanted to leave it for my brother."

Remy closed his eyes as he recited from memory:

> "*You will hardly know who I am or what I mean,*
> *But I shall be good health to you nevertheless,*
> *And filter and fibre your blood.*
> *Failing to fetch me at first keep encouraged,*
> *Missing me one place search another,*
> *I stop somewhere waiting for you.*"

When he opened his eyes, Shirin was crying. "I'm sorry, Mummy," he said, distressed. "I didn't mean to upset you."

"You didn't. This is how I remember you. Always in your bedroom, reading or scribbling, scribbling away in a book. Remember that brown leather notebook that you used to write in? I bought that for you at Crossword. Even in those days, it was expensive."

Remy had carried that journal with him to America. "I didn't know you bought it for me," he said. "I loved that book. I still have it."

"I had Daddy give it to you for your birthday. That way, you'd treasure it more."

Time after time, she'd removed herself from the love triangle of their family, deliberately assuming a subservient position and nudging him closer to Dad. In order to spare him the anguish of torn loyalties, she had cast herself as the antagonist of their family drama.

Remy exhaled. There was no sense in revisiting a past where every memory was a poison dart. The only way to give his mother's story shape and meaning was to be a good parent himself. He couldn't change even a granule of the past, but he could shape the future.

They had a long drive home and the traffic was unpredictable, and he didn't want to take a chance. He rose to his feet.

"Shall I give you a moment alone, Mama?"

Shirin shook her head no. "No need," she said. "But let's pray two Ashem Vohus before we go."

He waited for her to lead, then joined in. "Ashem vohu, vahistem asti, usta asti," they began, Remy feeling the incongruity of reciting the short Zoroastrian prayer in a dead language, Avestan, while visiting a Catholic cemetery. But why the hell not? He was in Bombay, after all, this wonderful hodgepodge of different religions and creeds.

On the drive home, she turned to him.

"Thank you," she said. "This was the best gift. No matter what happens now, I will always treasure this."

Remy looked out the window, blinking back his tears. *Please don't let anything happen to her,* he prayed. *Now that I finally have her.*

It was a long time before he trusted himself to look at his mother again.

CHAPTER FORTY-ONE

TWO DAYS LATER, the doorbell rang. Remy answered the door and broke into a smile when he saw Monaz.

"Wow, what a great surprise," he said. "When did you get back?"

Monaz walked in wordlessly, but before Remy could shut the door, the elevator opened and a tall man in a short-sleeved shirt got out. Monaz motioned to him.

"This is my dad," she said.

Remy did a double take, then recovered. "Oh, hi," he said, offering his hand. The man's grip was firm. "Please, come in."

Phiroz looked older than Remy had imagined. His silver hair was neatly parted in the middle, and he had a square, handsome face with inquisitive eyes. Those eyes were now scanning Remy, taking his measure. Remy resisted the urge to ask if he'd passed muster.

"Thank you for coming," he said, as if the visit had been his idea. "I didn't know that you were in town."

"We just arrived last evening," Phiroz said. "I insisted on meeting you in person after my daughter gave us the explosive news."

Remy nodded. "Of course. That's understandable. After all, it's a big decision Monaz has made."

"I wanted to shake the hand of the man with such good morals," Phiroz said. "Who was willing to risk losing a child by encouraging my daughter to tell the truth. It is this honesty that makes us Parsis so unique."

Remy looked at Monaz, unsure of how to proceed. He startled as he noticed her red, swollen eyes. His heart sank. Why had Monaz been crying? Had her father mistreated her?

"I'm just disappointed that my daughter didn't have the same virtue, despite her good upbringing," Phiroz continued. "First, to get pregnant before marriage. And second, to be ready to leave India with a virtual stranger without informing her parents."

"I have known your sister Shenaz for years," Remy said testily. "Jango and I are childhood friends. So, with all due respect, I'm hardly a stranger."

Phiroz smiled. "I meant no insult. Quite the contrary. I feel like we have had a narrow escape, thanks to you."

"What do you mean?"

There was a sudden silence, and Remy looked from father to daughter. "Monaz?" he said.

The girl, who had been sitting with her head bowed, looked up. "He wants to keep the baby," she said. She looked at Remy guiltily. There was not a trace of the effervescent teenager he'd come to know and love. "My parents will raise him as their own. I can come back to finish college in Bombay after the delivery."

Remy gasped, felt as if the air had gone out of him. He had not seen this coming. But why hadn't he considered this outcome? Shenaz had told him that her brother was conservative, and he had assumed the man would leap at the chance of an overseas adoption, in order to save face. It had not occurred to him that Phiroz would consider raising the child himself.

He thought about breaking this news to Kathy. Kathy, who had already started clearing out the guest bedroom for Monaz. Kathy, who was counting the days until their arrival. His temper spiked.

"You think your grandchild will be better off raised in small-town India than in America?" he said.

Phiroz's face registered the insult. Even Monaz looked affronted.

"I was raised there, uncle," she said.

"I'm sorry," Remy said hastily. "I was out of line. But, Monaz, you're nineteen. You're an adult. This should be your decision, not your . . . not anyone else's."

Monaz wept softly. Neither man attempted to console her. She brushed her tears away with the back of her hand. "It *is* my decision," she said at last. "If my child is accepted and loved by my parents, if I can see him whenever I wish, then why would I send him thousands of miles away? You can always adopt another baby, Remy Uncle. But this is my flesh and blood."

Remy's face reddened. "So you've made up your mind? Because this time, there's no going back. You understand?"

"I do."

"I see." He bit his lower lip, stunned. What could he say? He didn't yet have a signed contract with Monaz. And even if he had, so what? She was the mother. She was carrying her child. "Does Shenaz know?" he asked.

"No," Phiroz said. "We haven't called her yet."

"I see," Remy repeated. There was an uncomfortable silence, and at last, Remy felt the tears coming to his eyes. "There's nothing I can say or do? To make you change your mind?"

"Remy Uncle, I'm so sorry," Monaz said. "But this is the best thing for us. I will always be grateful to you for encouraging me to talk to my dad. In a million years, I couldn't have imagined this outcome."

"Me neither," Remy said. There was no point in continuing this humiliation. He rose to his feet. "This is it, then. Thanks for coming."

Phiroz extended his hand. "Best of luck to you," he said. "I will pray for you and your wife every single day. I mean that sincerely. And my profound thanks for encouraging my daughter to do the right thing. We will forever be in your debt."

"No problem," Remy said woodenly. All he wanted now was for them to leave so that he could shut the door on this chapter of his life. The museum of failures had claimed its latest victim.

Monaz looked around. "Can I see Granna? To, you know, say goodbye?"

"She's still sleeping," Remy said. "I'll tell her you were here."

Monaz turned to her father. "Can you give me a few minutes, Papa? Just wait for me downstairs."

Remy watched as Phiroz got in the elevator, then turned to Monaz.

"Please don't hate me," Monaz said. "I know I've disappointed you. You have no idea how hard this is for me. I cried all the way from Navsari to here last evening."

"I don't hate you."

"And . . . after I return to Bombay, I'll still stop by to check in on Granna. I promise."

"It's okay," Remy said. "You're about to get really busy. In any case, I wish you well. Please, just put all this behind you. I wish you a happy life."

After Monaz left, Remy went into his bedroom and shut the door. *The truth shall set you free*, they said. But what he felt right now was not freedom. Instead, he felt imprisoned by his own self-righteousness. All he'd had to do was buy a plane ticket for Monaz. But he'd taken the high road. And how it had backfired!

The mere thought of Kathy's disappointment, the thought of breaking the news to Mummy, made him want to punch something. *You stupid fool*, he said to himself. They had both tried to tell him he was making a mistake, but he hadn't listened. Dad used to always say, *Don't ask a question if you are not prepared to hear the answer.*

He called Jango at work and gave him the news. Jango let out a string of expletives, gave voice to the anger that Remy couldn't bring himself to express. "I don't know how I'm ever going to be able to face you again, boss," Jango said. "All we've done is add stress in your life."

"Don't be silly," Remy said. "None of this is your fault. If anyone's to blame, it's me. I should've just kept my mouth shut and taken Monaz with me, as planned."

"I actually agree with you, Remy," Jango said bluntly. "That was a stupid move on your part. I mean, I understand why you did it and all, but still . . ."

"*I* don't," Remy said. "I don't know what possessed me to push her as I did."

"Bullshit. You know exactly why you did it. To prove to yourself that you are not your father."

Remy gasped. He felt as if Jango had sliced through the thicket of his thoughts and delivered him the truth.

AFTER THEY HUNG UP, he replayed the conversation in his head. Jango was right: Daddy had begged him to be a better man than he'd been. This had been his attempt to live up to his father's exhortation.

But it was more than that: this was the first thing Remy had done in his life to prove to himself that he was also Shirin Wadia's son.

CHAPTER FORTY-TWO

SHIRIN WAS EVEN more heartbroken than he was about Monaz's change of heart. "Bring the girl to me," she'd said. "I'll knock sense into her head."

Despite his sadness, Remy smiled. "You sound like a Mafia boss, Mummy," he said.

Shirin didn't smile back. "Who does she think she is, breaking my son's heart like this?"

Earlier this morning, Remy had received a short email from his sister-in-law Karen, expressing her condolences. That was the word she'd used, as if Remy and Kathy had lost a child. Which, in a literal sense, they had. Except that they'd never had the baby in the first place.

"It's all right, Mummy," he said. "Maybe it's all for the best. Kathy and I lead such busy lives. Maybe this wasn't meant to be."

Shirin frowned. "Meaning . . . ?"

"Meaning, I think we're going to hit the PAUSE button. Reevaluate everything after I get back. It's not the end of the world, not having a child. Millions of couples are childless."

"You'll give up that easily?" Shirin turned her head away.

Mummy didn't know about the time and money they'd spent on the IVF treatments, the hope, and the heartache. There was no point in mentioning this to her now. Not when he was flying home soon. Finding a single ticket would be much easier.

"What does Kathy say?"

"We're really not talking about this. She's pretty upset, as you can imagine. For now, she's channeling all her energy into planning my birthday party. She wants a big shindig." His stomach heaved at the thought.

Shirin smiled wistfully. "Your daddy used to take the day off on your birthday. Remember? We celebrated with such pomp."

Remy did. He remembered it all.

A sweet longing opened up in him. He tasted again the creamy richness of the yogurt Shirin used to prepare for lunch, the yellow daal with fried garlic, cumin seeds and curry leaves, the fried pomfret.

"I miss the grand lunches you used to make, Mummy," he said.

"So stay a little longer, na? Celebrate your birthday here."

"I wish I could, Mama. But I've already stayed so long. And Kathy really needs me back."

"Yes, of course. I understand."

They were quiet for a long time. Remy took her hand. "But I'll miss you terribly."

Shirin's lower lip quivered. "If for no other reason, I'll be grateful to that stupid girl for this," she said. "For giving me this extra time with you."

How strange, Remy thought. He had come to India to find a child. Instead, he had regained a mother.

CHAPTER FORTY-THREE

———⤐———

REMY SAT AT the table answering emails. He read one from Eric informing him that they had landed the Wexner Medical Center account, and he let out a jubilant cry. But he also felt a pang of sadness at sitting out the action. *Don't be an idiot*, he scolded himself. *Be grateful that you have a team that can actually get new accounts while you're away.*

He typed a reply to Eric, then leaned back in the chair. A line of poetry was knocking inside his head.

He went into the kitchen to get a drink, then returned to his laptop.

> *I want to grow older here*
> *In this greenless place of grief.*

Here was the truth that he'd been chasing: he wanted to celebrate his birthday in Bombay. Remy remembered his thirtieth birthday party: how his parents had braved the Ohio winter to be there, how Shirin had single-handedly cooked for all the guests. He'd gone into their bedroom that night to thank her, but she'd brushed him off with a self-effacing "Arre, wah. Why thanks? It's the least I could do for my son." How proud and happy Mummy had looked at that party!

He knew he didn't want the big bash that Kat was planning for him. He wanted a quieter pleasure—to wake up on that morning and eat breakfast with his mother. To maybe go to the fire temple with Gulnaz in the early afternoon, while Mummy took a nap. And if Mummy agreed, he could invite a few close friends for dinner, a farewell dinner to thank them for everything they'd done to make this trip more comfortable for him.

Yet Kathy would be crushed if he changed her plans, he told himself. How much more disappointment could he fling at her? This was the only thing she'd asked for—that he get home in time for the party.

Remy glanced again at his laptop, at the words he'd scribbled earlier. He closed the file, then started an email.

Hi, sweetie, he began.

He wrote.

He described to Kathy how his parents had celebrated his birthdays in India, told her about the fried fish and the wooden stool, the paint faded from where he'd stood on it year after year, the little red tili on his forehead, grains of rice pressed into the dot.

He wrote. He told Kathy that despite the distance, he had never felt closer to her. He told her how much he looked forward to coming home and resuming their life—date nights and vacations and walks in the park. But he did want to do this one last thing for his mother before he came home: celebrate his birthday here.

Remy stopped, shaken. He reread the last line, its bald assertion. He wasn't asking Kathy for permission. His hand hovered over the mouse to delete the line or to tame it. He stopped himself, thought: *Fuck it.*

Fuck it.

He would always regret it if he didn't see this through. The truth was that he had changed. He'd seen the way Shirin looked at him these days, the longing on her face, the way she studied him, as if memorizing him for the empty days ahead. He knew that having him here on that day would mean the world to her. There was so little else he could do for her now. But how to explain this to his sensitive, brilliant wife, who had only known one home, one country, who had never known the grief of separation?

They could throw a nice summer garden party later in the year. Kathy had told him, over and over again, to have no regrets when he returned home. A couple more weeks with his mother would help make this possible.

Before he could talk himself out of it, he hit SEND. There. It was done.

CHAPTER FORTY-FOUR

THEY WERE AT Marine Drive at sunset, sitting with their backs to the sea. Remy put his arm around his mother, drawing her close. Despite Shirin's initial refusal to come, she appeared to be enjoying herself.

"You tell me when you're tired, okay?" he said. "Jango's driver has parked the car right around the corner. He can pick us up in five minutes."

"I'm fine," she said. "Don't worry so much."

They sat in peaceful silence, watching the nightly seaside parade unfold before them: old couples, newlyweds, teenagers, parents with children, all savoring the remains of the day. This was the Bombay Remy had known and loved—this melting-pot city, this restless, heaving humanity, moving against the still point of the timeless sea and sky. He noticed several women in black burqas, and even though he felt a slight queasiness at the sight, no one else seemed to notice or care. A middle-aged woman wearing red-top sneakers and a short skirt carried a white poodle as she trotted past them. Two children ran behind her, clamoring to pet the dog. Their parents strolled indolently behind them, making no effort to restrain the kids.

"The dog's going to nip at that kid if the parents don't stop him," Remy said.

Shirin must've heard the judgment in his voice, because she smiled and shook her head. "It's not that easy, watching two children at one time. Believe me. I remember."

He tightened his grip around her. "Was it really hard managing me and Cyloo at the same time? I mean, given the situation?"

"Hard?" Shirin chewed at the question. "It was difficult at times, definitely. I was so afraid of Cyloo hurting you. But it was also the easiest thing in my life. And certainly the happiest."

Remy almost said his inane thought out loud: *I wish I'd been old enough to help you.*

"What news of Monaz?" Shirin asked. "Have you heard from her?"

Monaz had returned home to Navsari with her father. They had found out when Shenaz and Jango came for tea. Before they'd left, Shenaz had also reassured Remy that they would check in on Shirin regularly after he left for America. Remy had felt lighter after that conversation.

"I got an email from her yesterday," Remy said. "I forgot to tell you. She sent her love."

"How is she?"

"Hard to tell. She says she's fine. Says her mother is spoiling her rotten, making her favorite foods and all. But"—he shrugged—"who knows? It's hard to imagine her in that environment."

"Maybe she's where she was destined to be. Maybe it was her naseeb that made you insist she tell her father."

Remy had noticed how frequently Indians spoke of destiny. He had assumed it was the defense of people who didn't feel in control of their own lives, that the gods were a convenient receptacle of blame. But he'd never heard his mother talk in this manner.

"You believe in that stuff?" he asked.

Shirin turned her head toward him. In the glow of the streetlight, her face was pale. "I had a son who was born brain-damaged because of a cord wrapped around his neck for a minute or so. Who was one of four boys out of two hundred and fifty-eight who died in a fire. If I didn't believe in destiny, I would've gone mad for sure."

Remy felt the air go out of his lungs. "Mummy . . ." he said, but Shirin shook her head.

"No," she said. "This is a nice evening. Let's not ruin it with the past. Not when there's so much to look forward to." She took his hand in hers. "Don't give up, Remy. There's a child in your future. You have so much to offer."

"I'm not sure, Mummy. We're getting old. Maybe this debacle with Monaz was a wake-up call."

"Nonsense. It was just a setback."

He couldn't tell her he was now frightened by the prospect of parenthood—the doubt that had crept into his head since he had learned the truth about his family. What if he turned out to be like his father? The thought of ruining a child's life by making one wrong turn, which inevitably would lead to other mistakes, was terrifying.

"Don't worry," Shirin said. "You're not like us. You—you are the best of me and Cyrus. And America is not India. Arre, even India is not India. That was a different time. You and Kathy will make very good parents, believe me."

Once again, he was struck by her ability to read his mind. But unlike in his teenage years, he now was grateful for the fact that she knew the map of his heart as well as she did.

"Thanks," he said.

"It was a different time," Shirin continued, "with so many taboos and secrets. But what doesn't change is this: All children have the same needs, to be fed, sheltered, clothed, and loved. Most of all, to be loved."

Still, he was not convinced.

"You wait until you become a father," his mother added. "Loving a child is the most unremarkable thing. The easiest thing. You'll see."

"Let's see what happens," Remy said evasively. Then: "I'm sorry I was so mean to you all these years. This whole visit has been . . . so important to me." He bit down on his lip.

"Yes. A miracle, I could say." Although Shirin was staring straight ahead, he heard the tears in her voice when she spoke. "And that you're staying in Bombay for your birthday for my sake. I need to thank Kathy. For her sacrifice."

"No, Mummy. I'm doing it for myself. I . . . I want to do this. For me."

Shirin smiled. "We need to finalize the menu. And the guest list."

"Don't worry. I'm going to handle it all, okay? I just want you to get enough rest so that you can have fun that night. But for lunch, it'll just be the two of us, okay?"

"Okay."

They sat in silence a little longer. Remy said, "I dreamed of him last night."

"Who? Cyloo?"

He nodded. Remy had stood alone on a sandy beach, fully dressed in a suit and leather shoes. Someone was swimming in the distance, and as he watched, a man raised a hand in distress. *Holy shit, he's drowning*, Remy had said to himself, panicked. Even from the distance, he knew it was Cyloo. He began to strip, but each movement took impossibly long, his fingers unable to loosen the knot of his tie, his belt buckle refusing to unfasten. And when he was down to his briefs, he stopped, improbably, to remove the sand from his shoes before he ran into the icy waters. But the faster he swam, the farther

away the drowning man got from him. Remy swam even more frenet-
ically, but that simply made the distance grow. Finally, he caught on
and surrendered. *I give up,* he'd thought. He floated on his back, looking up at a blue sky speckled with white clouds. *Cyloo, my brother,
where are you?* he'd thought as he scanned the sky. Just then, a large
dolphin swam under him and lifted him high in the air on its snout.
For a flash, balanced on its nose before the inevitable drop, he saw it
all clearly: the disappointing earth, the illusory sky, his flawed parents,
his betrayed brother, and his cleaved self. Just as he was beginning to
grasp the full, panoramic picture of his life, his heart lightened by this
understanding, he landed on the hard water with a tremendous thud
and woke up, covered in sweat.

Shirin looked at him curiously. "What does it mean?"

"I'm not sure. I think it means I miss him. The brother I barely
remember."

"That's because you're trying to remember with your brain," Shirin
said. "You do remember him where it matters. You carry him here."
She pointed to her heart.

"I hope so, Mummy. It seems impossible to me to think I have so
few memories of the first years of my life."

"Remy, how could you? You were so very young. It's not your fault,
jaan. In any case, your brother will never be far away from you."

"You know what else I don't understand? Why nobody ever mentioned Cyloo to me."

Shirin sighed. "Very few people knew, jaan. No one from Bombay
ever visited us in Jamshedpur, other than my father. None of our new
neighbors had ever met him. And even if someone had heard a rumor,
your father had such authority in those days. They would've never had
the guts to say something to you."

"I guess," he said. "Listen, I wanted to tell you. I spoke to Dr.
Bilimoria."

"To Billy Boy?" She had given the doctor this nickname ever since she'd come home from the hospital. "Why?"

"Because . . . Kathy and I spoke . . . I mean, I hate leaving you alone here, Mummy, in your condition. But I really do have to go home soon. I wanted to ask Bilimoria whether you were fit enough to travel with me. If you could withstand the trip."

"What did he say?" Shirin's voice was a whisper.

"He said it was a risk. That the airlines would have to agree to carry supplemental oxygen on the flight. The pneumonia . . . There's some residual scarring on your lungs, you know?" He turned toward her. "Do you feel strong enough, Mummy? You know how long and tiring that flight is."

Shirin was quiet. "It's not the right time," she said finally. She sounded small, deflated. "I need to get stronger. But after you adopt, I'll come. I'll come help with my grandchild."

"Well, we'll definitely see you before then. Kathy and I are hoping to visit over Christmas. You can go back with us then."

"You don't think you'll adopt before then?"

"Mummy," Remy said with a laugh. "I told you. Honestly, I'm just not sure that we want to. And even if we did, these things can take years to finalize."

Already, he could see ahead to his last day in India—the final hug that would make him feel as if his very soul were being wrung out of him, every step out of the apartment and toward the waiting vehicle a small killing. The hallucinatory loneliness of the airport, his slim body cutting through the crowd as he headed toward the big plane that would take him to another galaxy, to outer space, to the moon. Because eight thousand miles or a billion, what did it matter when you were on the other side of the earth? And that final look out of the airplane window at a city filled with ghosts and ghost stories, this smoggy, idiotic, maddening metropolis, which somehow still retained

its hold on him, whose sweat and grime and noise and chaos had settled on his skin—no, had formed a layer of his skin—whose waters
roared in his bloodstream, its salt commingling with his own.

The sentimental feeling grew, but he didn't want her to see him sad.
He faked a yawn. "Manju must be expecting us home for dinner. Shall
I ask the driver to come pick us up in ten minutes?"

"If you wish. I'm happy to sit here beside you forever."

Behind him, Remy heard the steady lapping of the ocean. What
tales of the city had its waters absorbed? What tragedies had it borne
on its waves? How many rivers of human tears had roiled into its dark
waters? And yet the sea endured, going about its business, one wave at
a time. Which is exactly what he would have to do when he left here.

CHAPTER FORTY-FIVE

ON THE MORNING of his birthday, Remy dialed Kathy's cell. She answered on the third ring. "You beat me to it," she said. "Happy birthday."

"Thanks, love. Although it would be happier if you were here."

"I wish."

He had offered to fly her in for a week, but Kathy had a series of meetings she couldn't get out of. Now, she told him about her meeting with a potential donor. Last November, Kathy had presented her paper on Byler disease at a conference in Denver, and the man, a multimillionaire who had lost his son to the rare condition, had asked for the meeting to find out how he could support her work at her hospital.

Remy listened, thrilling to the sound of her voice; after so many years, it could still give him goose bumps.

"I'm so proud of you, honey," he said.

"Well, he hasn't given us a dime yet. But let's see," Kathy said. "So what're your plans for today?" she added.

"Nothing much. Having some of the gang over for dinner. I'd asked that it be just me and my mom for lunch, but get this. Last night, she tells me she's invited someone else to join us."

"Really? Who?"

"I have no idea. She won't tell me. Says it's a surprise."

"You think it's Roshan and Pervez?"

"God, I hope not. She's not too crazy about them, so I doubt it. Although they've been a lot more caring of late. They're really trying hard."

"That's wonderful," Kathy said. "You know, I'm glad you're there. I'm happy for you."

"Me too. Although I'd give my right arm for you to be here with me."

"It's okay. Tell Shirin I said hi and to keep getting stronger. We'll bring her back with us at Christmas."

"Man, that would be wonderful, Kat."

"I owe her that," Kathy said. "I need to see her. Apologize to her."

Later, he would tell her that his mother didn't need an apology. That she didn't see herself as a hero or a martyr. But for now, the thought of returning in December cheered him up. It would make parting next Tuesday so much easier. "That will give her something to look forward to, honey. As long as you think Rose won't be disappointed if we're not in Columbus for Christmas."

Kathy snorted. "I don't care. She can see us any damn time she wants. But Shirin . . ." Her voice trailed off.

AFTER HE'D HUNG UP, he went into his mother's room and found her sitting up in bed, reading the newspaper. "Happy birthday, my darling boy," she said. "A lifetime of happiness to you. Sukhi reje, always."

"Thanks, Mama." He looked around. "Where's Manju?"

"In the living room," Shirin said.

Manju was standing on a stool, hanging a toran across the front door. Remy breathed in the scent of red roses and white jasmine, the latter reminding him of the honeysuckle that bloomed in his yard in Columbus. The family ses—the silver tray that held the silver rosewater sprinkler and the silver cone—had been dusted off and placed on the dining table. For a moment, he was seven years old again, standing on the red stool, wearing his purple velvet cap while holding the ceremonial ses.

"Let me help," Remy said. He reached for the toran and twisted the other end of the string to the nail on top of the door. He stepped back to take a look. "This is beautiful," he said. "Where did you go to get it?"

"Madam called the fulwalla yesterday and placed the order. He delivered while you were taking your bath."

The doorbell kept ringing all morning. Hema arrived, carrying fresh fish from the market, and immediately headed to the kitchen to start steaming the lentils in the pressure cooker. The man from Parsi Dairy Farm dropped off eight clay pots of yogurt. Shirin had also ordered boxes of ladoos from Tewaris.

"Mummy," Remy said as they sat down to breakfast, "why so much food? It's just the two of us and your secret friend for lunch. This is too much, no?"

"You're home on your birthday for the first time in donkey's years, and it's too much?" Shirin said. "It is not enough. Nothing is enough."

He spooned the sweet vermicelli onto his plate. "I have to hand it to Hema," he said. "She has really mastered Parsi cuisine."

"See?" Shirin said. "I told you to let her cook for your party tonight.

I would've paid her extra. Khali-pili you're insisting on catering. A waste of money."

"It's okay, Mummy," he said. "Let's give the woman a break. Plus, everyone loves the food from Delhi Darbar."

As Manju got ready to leave, Shirin gave her one of the large mithai boxes. "For your family," she said. "And on your way out, drop off this other box on the third floor."

So she'd definitely not invited Roshan or Pervez, Remy thought. "You still won't tell me who's coming to lunch?" he asked.

"You'll see."

"Well, with this level of secrecy, it better be Prince Charles or Beyoncé."

"Who's Beyondsay?"

Remy grinned.

At 1 p.m., the doorbell rang, and Remy leapt to his feet. "Ah. The mystery guest."

It was Dina, carrying a large bouquet of flowers and a wide smile. "Happy birthday," she said. And when he stared at her, slack-jawed, the smile got wider. "May I come in?"

Remy remembered his manners and stood aside to allow her to pass. He watched as Dina went to Shirin, who took Dina's hand in hers.

"Thank you for coming, Dina," she said. "Come, sit next to me."

Remy looked from one woman to the other, caught the exchange of warm, furtive smiles. "Mummy?" he said. "What's going on?"

"How are you, Dina?" Shirin asked, ignoring him.

"Fine, fine. Busy at work. And you? You look so much better than . . . the last time."

There was a short silence before Shirin said, "You'll take something to drink? Juice? Soda?"

"Actually, a cup of tea would be lovely."

Remy's head started to throb. What the heck was Dina doing here? Had Mummy had a stroke? How could she have made such an about-turn in her feelings toward the woman who had been her nemesis for so long?

"Go," Shirin said cheerfully to Remy. "Tell Hema to make us a cup of tea. And then go to your room for a while. Dina and I have some catching up to do."

"What about lunch?"

"We'll let you know when it's time."

A confused Remy did as he was told.

WHEN HE HEARD the doorbell ring again, he ignored it—Gladys would get it. His bewilderment had given way to irritation. Why this coyness? He was happy that Mummy had forgiven Dina, but why plan their grand reconciliation on his day? If this was meant to reassure him, why had he been banished from the living room?

Gladys appeared at the door. "There's someone asking for you, sir," she said.

"Who is it?"

"I don't know, sir."

He rose with an exasperated grunt. Gladys had met most of his friends, so it couldn't be one of them. Maybe the bank manager had sent over a clerk because of a missing signature or something. He had spent the last several days tying up financial loose ends. As Remy approached the living room, he could hear Shirin in an animated conversation with Dina. They fell silent as soon as they heard him.

A middle-aged woman was standing in the hallway. Her hair was tied back into a severe bun, but her eyes were kind. She wore a gray skirt and a thick half-sleeved shirt. The outfit looked like a uniform, and when the silver crucifix around her neck gleamed, Remy realized she was a nun.

"Can I help you?" he asked cautiously, wondering if this was some new and obscure birthday ritual—giving a nun money in exchange for a blessing?

"You are Remy?" the woman asked, a smile on her face.

"Yes?"

"Very nice to meet you. I'm Sister Hillary."

He stiffened, recognizing the name at once. She was gesturing to someone hiding in the hallway just out of his line of vision, and for one irrational, heart-stopping second, he expected to see his brother. But it was a different boy, a small and frightened little boy.

"And this . . . This is . . . This is Anand," Hillary said.

The midday sun fell in a shaft of light into the passageway, illuminating the child. Anand's dark and fearful eyes searched Remy's face.

The world went still and quiet. He knew without turning around that Dina and Shirin were watching him, that all three women were holding their breath, waiting for him to make a move. He turned and met his mother's eyes. They were wet with love and pride. He stood looking at her, trying to process what was happening, what strings she'd pulled to give him this birthday gift. And whether he appreciated or resented her for complicating his life yet again.

The moments ticked by. Remy felt as if he'd forgotten how to breathe.

"Can we get a glass of water?" Sister Hillary said. "The train from Pune was late, so it's been a long day."

"Yes, of course. Forgive me. Come in," he said.

The boy hid behind the nun as Dina rose to greet them. Shirin remained seated but smiled at Hillary and waved to the boy.

"Good afternoon, Anand," Shirin said. "You must be hungry?"

The child didn't answer.

"We have some sweet dahi for you. Sister Hillary says you like yogurt. There's also custard for dessert."

"He doesn't understand much English," Sister Hillary said. "But he's a fast learner." She smiled. "It's nice to see you again, Mrs. Wadia. You haven't changed at all."

Shirin rolled her eyes. "Does the diocese not provide vision care, Sister?" she said.

"Can someone tell me what exactly is going on?" Remy said.

"Well, Remy," Dina said, "we thought, you know, perhaps this would be an auspicious day to introduce you to this young man. If you're interested, of course. He's a very sweet boy. Very intelligent."

"He's four years old," Sister Hillary said in English. "He's an orphan. We've had him for two years, and everyone adores him. If . . . If you and your missus are interested, we can expedite the process."

Remy's head was reeling.

"I would handle all the paperwork," Dina added eagerly. "And I have a contact at the American embassy. We'd work on getting a passport and visa as quickly as we could. Of course, it would still take several months. But hopefully by year's end."

Remy felt dizzy, steadied himself on the back of a chair. "Excuse me. Can I speak to you privately?" he said to Shirin.

"MUMMY?" he said to her when they were in Shirin's room. "I'm . . . I'm speechless. You know I'm leaving in a week. And . . . how? When?"

"As soon as you extended your stay," Shirin said. "I thought, 'That orphanage took away one son. Why should it not give me a grandchild?' You see, I've sent an annual donation to them all these years, even after they shifted to Pune. I always got a personal thank-you note from Hillary, so I knew she was still there. And then, after you invited Dina here, I realized I bore her no animosity. So I thought, 'Who better to help me?' She agreed at once. Turns out, she had served on their board until three years ago."

"But, Mummy, I know you mean well, but this puts me in an awkward position, you know? I mean, I'm really not sure if Kathy and I want to go through this again. I certainly can't take such a step without talking to her. What if she says no? I don't want to hurt this poor child any more than he's probably already been."

Shirin looked deflated. "This may have been a mistake," she muttered. "I'm an old woman, not thinking clearly. I just . . . After all that happened with Monaz, I wanted so much to help. I have been able to do so little for you in your life, Remy. Plus, I had to move quickly so that you could at least meet the child before you leave."

"I appreciate what you've tried to do," Remy said. "It's just that . . . I mean, Anand is a person, not a prop in my story, you know? I really have to be sure, Mama."

"Of course."

"Tell you what," Remy said, noticing how miserable Shirin looked. "Let's go eat. Everyone must be hungry."

"And then?"

He took Shirin's hand. "And then we can decide what to do next."

ANAND LICKED THE last bit of yogurt off his spoon.

"You want more?" Remy asked him in Hindi.

The boy looked at Hillary for permission. When she nodded, he said, "Hah." His voice was squeaky, like a cartoon character, and Remy grinned to himself.

"Here you go," he said.

His reward was a quick smile.

"What do we say?" Hillary prompted the boy.

"Thank you, uncle," Anand said in English. Then he lowered his eyes and focused on polishing off the second helping.

Remy got more information as they ate. The boy had almost been adopted by a couple in Australia, so his case had been vetted. He had

no relatives who were interested in taking him. And Hillary had permission to stay with Anand in Bombay for several more days so that
Remy could get to know the child better. Shirin had earlier offered them
the guest bedroom, but she'd made it clear that it was Remy's decision.
(Remy wondered at his cluelessness—all these plans had been made
right under his nose?) Or Hillary and Anand would stay with Hillary's
sister's family, who were a mere twenty-minute cab ride away. If Remy
and Kathy decided that they were interested in pursuing the adoption,
he would sign some preliminary papers to get the ball rolling.

"Why didn't the Australian couple take him?" Remy asked Hillary
in English.

The nun had a pained expression on her face. She gave Anand a
quick look, but the boy wasn't paying attention to the adults. "They
were going to adopt two boys from us," she said sotto voce. "At the
last minute, they decided they couldn't handle both of them. They took
the younger one."

"Oh wow," Remy said. "That's cold."

Beside him, Shirin sighed. "So they just abandoned him?"

Hillary stared at her plate. When she looked up, her nose was red.
"I'm afraid so, Mrs. Wadia. People are . . . can sometimes be very
selfish."

"Unbelievable," Dina said.

Remy tried to imagine the sting of rejection, the dashed hopes.
Four years old, and the kid had suffered more disappointments than
most adults.

He looked around the table at the three other adults, connected by
the arteries of loss and betrayal, now doing their valiant best to heal
one another by helping him. And this boy . . . What was his role in this
healing? Would he be their best, last hope, or would he add another
sad chapter to their story?

Remy felt his spirits sinking and decided this was not the mood he wanted for his celebratory birthday lunch. He turned to Anand.

"What sports do you like to play?" he asked.

No answer.

Remy tried a different question. "Who is your best friend?"

Hillary smiled at the boy and said something to him in Hindi. Remy imagined how intimidating this lunch must be for Anand, how lavish the multicourse meal must seem, compared to the simple food he was served at the home.

"He's a champion patang flier," Sister Hillary told Remy. "He can beat older boys. Isn't it so, Anand?"

Anand looked suddenly animated. "I beat Gautam the other day," he said. "And he's seven."

"Accha?" Remy said. "But I thought *you* were ten."

The boy giggled. "Nahi. I'm only four." He jumped off the chair and stood on his toes. "I'm just tall."

The adults exchanged amused looks, basking in the child's youth. Remy made up his mind—Anand and Hillary could stay with them. The boy would almost certainly sleep through tonight's party, and Remy could only hope that the presence of a nun wouldn't dampen his friends' spirits too much.

He would call Kathy later tonight and show her pictures of the boy. He himself had no strong feelings toward Anand, had felt no immediate sense of connection. But even if Kathy and he decided against the adoption, at least the little guy would get a short holiday away from the institution. Anand seemed unaware of the reason for this trip, so there would be no sense of rejection. There was no real downside to this, as far as he could tell.

After lunch, he took his guests to their room, carrying the small suitcase that the nun had brought with her. He pointed out the dresser where they could store their clothes, showed them how to operate the bedroom lights, all the time feeling self-conscious under Hillary's penetrating gaze. There was so much he wanted to say to this woman—to make clear that he was unsure about adopting Anand and to please not read too much into his invitation to stay, to ask what she remembered of his brother's life and death, to beg for any insight that would put his father's unconscionable behavior in a better light. It occurred to Remy that the three women in the apartment were the only people who could tell him anything about Cyloo.

He wandered back into the living room, still startled at the sight of Dina and Shirin on the couch, their heads bent close to each other. *Maybe in different circumstances, they would've been friends*, he thought.

"What plans are the two of you hatching now?" he said, forcing a lightness into his voice.

"No plans," Dina said. "Just trying to, you know, have all the paperwork in order before you leave. If you decide to go through with this, of course."

He cleared his throat. "Yeah, see, that's the thing . . . I appreciate what the two of you have done for me. I know it comes from a good place. But I don't want to feel pressured into this. It's too important a decision."

"Remy! Of course! We would never . . ."

We. He heard the *we* and was glad of it. No matter what happened, his mother would have a better support system than before he'd arrived. Shenaz, Gulu, Jango, and now, Dina would help her. He himself might leave here empty-handed—Remy still mourned the loss of Monaz's baby, whom he had come to think of as his and Kathy's baby—but his mother would have a larger network of friends. Funny how things worked; life followed its own script, unspooling as it wished, hardly dependent on its human actors.

"Thanks, Dina," he said quietly. "Thanks, Mummy. I know how much planning went into this."

"You're welcome," they both said in unison.

CHAPTER FORTY-SIX

ANAND HADN'T LOST just his parents in an accident. His mother had been pregnant at the time, Sister Hillary told them.

The boy's father, a truck driver, had taken his family on a two-day vacation in the vehicle. They had been outside the city limits when a cow had darted across the highway and the man swerved hard to avoid hitting the animal. The truck had flipped, killing Anand's parents instantly. Their two-year-old, who had been sitting between them, was, miraculously, unhurt.

"Just a few scratches on his wrist," Hillary said. "We called Anand the Miracle Child. But he was traumatized. He kept telling us that the cow was unhurt. Over and over, he said this. That was how he dealt with it, you know? Because mentioning his dead parents was too painful."

Remy was silent, mute with horror.

"Good that he was between his parents," Shirin said. "They probably protected him with their own bodies." And when neither Hillary nor Remy responded, she added, "Because that's what parents do." She turned to face Remy. "This poor child," she said. "This poor child. He so deserves another chance."

Remy swallowed, knowing what she was thinking: She was imagining her firstborn son, with a different, happier ending. She was rewriting the script for Cyloo. And wondering why, now that Remy finally could do something, he was not rushing in to rescue him.

REMY ASKED HIMSELF the same question. Why was he dragging his feet? Two days had passed since his birthday, and he was no closer to a decision. Kathy had already told him that the decision was entirely up to him. "You understand the whole Indian situation way better than I do. I'm going to trust your judgment on this."

The morning after his birthday party, he had made Kathy FaceTime with Anand, but the boy had stared unsmilingly at Kathy during the entire call.

"What do you think?" he'd asked when he'd called Kathy back.

"He's sweet," Kathy replied. "But . . ." Her voice trailed off.

Remy understood. The fact that Kathy had spoken to Anand in English had made the video chat even more awkward. But the language barrier was the least of their problems. He and Kathy had been so focused on adopting a baby—a new start, a blank slate, an abstraction—that neither one of them could pivot to the reality of a shy four-year-old boy, a child who, surely, was traumatized by not only the accident but also the two years spent among strangers.

Remy was petrified by the responsibility of making the decision. He had spent the last two days trying to draw Anand out of his shell, but every time he asked him a question, the boy looked at him blankly.

Give me something, kiddo, Remy thought. *Give me some sign that you are meant to go home with me.*

He'd be letting down so many people if he left here without starting the paperwork. Every time he interacted with Anand, he was aware of Sister Hillary's eager, expectant gaze. The nun had told him that she'd worked hard to find Remy the most "suitable" boy from all her charges. That most of the orphans never get adopted. The thought of Anand spending his youth at the home filled Remy with despair.

And yet he knew one essential truth: it would be wrong to adopt the child for any reason other than the fact that he was loved and wanted. At the moment, what he felt for Anand was pity. Sympathy. But he was a long way off from love.

Now, he sat on the bed beside Anand while the boy napped. Gazing at the boy's sleeping face, he took in the long eyelashes, the curve of his lips, the black, shiny hair that fell onto his forehead. Remy's hand itched, found its way to smoothing the boy's hair.

He felt a slight tremor, a softening. He remembered the times in his childhood when he'd been the recipient of such parental tenderness; it felt strange to be the one dispensing such care. He leaned over and kissed the boy, then shook his head self-consciously, because he'd caught himself watching himself, monitoring himself for any rush of feeling.

After a few minutes, he tiptoed out of the guest room and phoned Jango.

"How's the boy doing?" Jango asked.

"I dunno. He's a pretty reticent kid."

"I can imagine. Actually, I can't. I can't imagine being an orphan at four."

Was Jango chiding him? Were they all silently judging him, wondering why he was hesitating at giving a young kid the chance of a lifetime? Was he letting his mother down? He understood the symmetry of Shirin's thinking—how adopting a child from the home that had taken away Cyloo would in some way complete the circle, even as it broke it.

"Hey, listen," Jango said. "I know this is a hard decision. And that your back is up against the wall. I'm sorry."

"I leave in four days," Remy said. "*Four days*. How am I supposed to know? How am I supposed to decide?"

"But, boss," Jango said softly, "you'd agreed to take Monaz's baby without even meeting with her."

"That was different," Remy said.

But why? he thought. *Why was it different?*

Because Monaz was a known quantity, given her connection to Shenaz? Because Remy had been naïve when he'd flown here, and the disappointments and revelations of the last six weeks had tempered his enthusiasm and trust?

"So take him somewhere, na?" Jango was saying. "Go to the seaside or somewhere with him alone. You know, get him talking to you?"

"I've tried. He clings to the nun. He won't even hold my hand."

"Shit. That's rough."

"Maybe it's not meant to be. The cultural gap is too great. And this little guy has endured so much I . . . No wonder he's so stoic and stiff."

"What a pity." Jango sighed. "I still blame Monaz for what she did. That would've been a perfect match."

"Too perfect," Remy said, all the while thinking, *When does anything go smoothly in India?*

LATER THAT AFTERNOON, Remy turned off his computer and stretched. He looked out the window. It was an uncharacteristically cool day. He grabbed his house keys.

"I'm going for a walk," he told Gladys. "I won't be gone long."
Everybody else, he knew, was taking a nap.

He walked aimlessly, without a destination in mind. He stopped at a
fruit vendor and purchased six chikoos. The man greeted him by name,
and it made Remy feel as if he were a resident and not a visitor. For the
first time in years, he felt at home in his old neighborhood. He looked
at his watch. Mummy would be up soon. It was time to return to her.

He had almost reached his apartment building when he turned and
walked back to the main street and to the tiny general store. He stood
on the sidewalk and peered into the entrance of the long, narrow shop,
searching for what he wanted. When he caught the attention of the
cashier, he pointed. "I'll take the red one and the blue one."

"Anand," Remy said, shaking the sleeping boy. "Anand, come on.
Wake up."

The boy opened his eyes and looked at Remy fearfully. Instinctively,
he turned to the side of the bed where Hillary was napping.

"It's okay," Remy whispered. "Let her sleep. Look, I've bought you
something. A gift. Come on. Let's go."

Anand's eyes widened. Without saying a word, he rolled out of bed.

They were on the terrace of Remy's apartment building, the only
two people there, the sun warm on their back, their shirts fluttering
in the breeze. Above them, two kites soared in the pale-blue afternoon
sky. Unlike the expensive kites Remy had flown in America, these were
cheap diamond-shaped contraptions, made from paper and bowed
sticks. He had not flown one of these in years, but his hands and fingers knew exactly what to do, and his heart soared along with the kite.
Such a simple pleasure, he thought.

A boy in the adjacent building leaned from his balcony, waving to
them. He was saying something, but the wind carried his words away.

They had been flying the kites for almost a half hour, and Anand hadn't said a word, but his body language had changed—he seemed looser, less wary and stiff. A couple of times a gurgle escaped his lips, and Remy was charmed by how terribly young the boy sounded. But mostly, they held on to their kites in silence, watching them soar against the sky. Remy's arms were beginning to tire, but he was afraid to stop.

Anand's small body leaned into him, and Remy felt an unexpected throb of protectiveness. He imagined taking this boy home with him, the two of them flying kites on vacation in Florida or on the shores of Lake Erie. What would it feel like, to have this shy, quiet boy with him at all times? To provide him with a good home, a good education? He waited for his heart to give him an answer, but it remained silent.

He looked down at Anand, and the motion made his line sag a bit. "Sister Hillary was right," he said. "You really are a champion kite flier. How did you get to be so good?"

Any other kid would've taken the bait, used the compliment as an opportunity to brag. Anand merely squinted his eyes into the sun and frowned. Then he stiffened and tugged frantically on his line as he shifted his weight from one foot to another.

"Cut!" the boy shouted, a fierce look on his face. "Cut!" He looked rapidly from Remy to the sky as he pointed to Remy's swiftly falling kite.

It took Remy a second to realize what had happened. He watched in astonishment as Anand reeled in Remy's broken kite. "Why, you rascal," he roared, laughing. "You cut my line when I wasn't looking?"

Anand shrieked with delight. He tore around the circumference of the terrace in his bare feet, pumping his fist in jubilation, both kites trailing behind him. Remy pretended to give chase. "Stop, you crook," he spluttered, and Anand squealed with laughter.

After a few minutes, Remy stopped, leaning on the ledge of the terrace, pretending to catch his breath. Anand approached him cautiously, still holding tight to his trophy. "Well," Remy said. "You beat me."

The boy looked up at him. Then he grinned—a cheeky, lopsided grin—and a chunk of Remy's exiled, wandering heart fell into place.

"I win," Anand said. "I win." The afternoon sun lit up his hair and eyes.

Remy grinned back. "I'll beat you next time," he said. "Tomorrow, we'll play again."

Anand put his hands on his hips and wiggled them. "You can't beat me," he taunted.

He is a boy transformed, Remy thought in astonishment. Anand had been inhibited in a strange apartment, he realized, with a nun and a woman old enough to be his grandmother. A woman who wanted more than anything to be his grandmother. But here, under the open sky, Anand—free, mischievous, playful Anand—was assuming his true shape.

He could grow to love this boy. He could learn to love each scar and wound that he bore. Because, ultimately, everybody's story was written in scars. Anand's early story had been a tragic one. But Remy was suddenly confident that he and Kathy could ensure that the next chapter in the boy's life would be a happy one. The name Anand meant *joy*. They could help him live up to the promise of his name.

Remy thought back to everything that had happened to him since he'd gotten here: the whirlwind of events, the roller coaster of emotions, the unraveling of family secrets. He thought of Jango, Shenaz and Monaz, Shirin and Dina, Sister Hillary and Gulnaz—all the people who had entered or reentered his life—and how each one of them in their own way had tried to help him. But here on this open-air terrace, the wind blowing in his hair, the sun as warm as a kiss, it was a four-year-old boy who held in his fist the power to define Remy and Kathy's future as much as they could help shape his.

This was how destiny was formed, Remy decided, not by what was written in the stars by some distant god, but by human choice and effort and courage. All he had to do was be brave.

His mother had had the courage to love in spades, even though she'd been forced to measure and dole out that love in the shadows. He, on the other hand, was free to dote on this boy openly. So little was being asked of him, compared to what had been asked of Mummy. Surely, he could set aside his fears of turning out like Daddy and, instead, emulate Mummy's courage?

Surely, at long last, he was capable of being Shirin Wadia's true heir?

Remy yelped.

Anand had smacked his wrist.

"You can't catch me," the boy yelled before taking off.

"You little so-and-so," Remy growled, then laughed as he chased after Anand again. He lunged toward the boy and caught him, smelled the mild scent of soap and sweat. It took Anand only a second to squirm out of his hands. But in that second, Remy felt as if his hands, and heart, were full.

Anand laughed as he ran away from Remy, then stopped and looked back. He raised and lowered his eyebrows several times, in a comic, teasing manner.

Seeing the mischievous expression on Anand's face, Remy Wadia had the strangest realization. *Why*, he thought, *he looks exactly like Kathy.*